THE SUPERHUJINN

THE SUPERHUJINN

A SUPERNATURAL BEING

MAMADOU A DIALLO

ARCHWAY
PUBLISHING

Archway Publishing books may be ordered through booksellers or by contacting:

Archway Publishing
1663 Liberty Drive
Bloomington, IN 47403
www.archwaypublishing.com
844-669-3957

ISBN: 978-1-6657-5408-8 (sc)
ISBN: 978-1-6657-5409-5 (e)

Library of Congress Control Number: 2023923376

Print information available on the last page.

Archway Publishing rev. date: 04/12/2024

THE SUPERHUJINN
FAN CLUB

I would like to dedicate this book to my fellow epic tale lovers. Take a journey inside this imaginary world in which various spirits coexisted: humans, jinns, and hujinns. The jinns and hujinns are supernatural, while the humans are natural.

Enjoy this magnificent legend, which focuses on the life of a chosen supernatural being called the superhujinn. Inside this novel, you will learn about the origins of this legend and the moments when he began to recognize his superpowers. It discusses his revelation and how it influenced his decision to save the world. After the hero acknowledged his gift, he decided to help the less fortunate beings around him before he expanded his horizon. It also explains the physical, mental, spiritual, and financial issues this champion faced before he learned to accept his fate.

After you go through these experiences with this remarkable being, ask yourself these questions: Do you understand the message being perpetuated? Do you agree that time is the most precious gift of life?

Mr. Diallo66three@yahoo.com _MSTACKZD BRAND

CONTENTS

PROLOGUE

James Jordan lived in Ginnia and grappled with the meaning of life until he found purpose in acknowledging the creator, loyalty, and prayer, leading to a stronger connection with God, gratitude, and patience. Moving to Fabrica, he gained adaptability but regretted not completing his college degree, which prompted feelings of disappointment and a heightened appreciation for his own existence.

Following his migration, James Jordan's unique lifestyle attracted the interest of influential federal agents. Ginnia was a spiritual world inhabited by spirits such as humans, jinns, and the advanced hujinn species to which James belonged. He later became aligned with a prominent administration and had familial ties to Mamadou R Diallo, the president of a significant nation.

In Ginnia, the NISA (National Intelligence Spirits Agency) held the highest rank, overseeing supernatural beings worldwide and ensuring safety by monitoring powerful individuals, conducting tests, and collaborating with similar national agencies. NISA assigned agents to oversee special beings, reaching out to recruit them as elite officers if necessary.

Fabrica housed powerful agencies like NISA, BIA (Bureau of Intelligent Agents), and DBI (Department Bureau of Investigation), that oversaw gifted individuals globally and formed alliances with foreign agencies in the world of Ginnia. The NISA and BIA worked as secret services to maintain balance and regulate spirits, seeking individuals like James, a powerful hujinn, for recruitment. These agencies prepared to confront the FARN (Flowropia Association of Rational Nations) leader, one of the most formidable opponent from the of their era.

The story takes place in the early twenty-first century. It marked the start of hujinn spirits, intelligent spirits protecting nations from evil spirits. James, a Drakillian from Freeland, moved to Fabrica in the west of Freeland, consisting of fifty-five states. Although originally from Drakilla, with fifty provinces, James resided in New Amsterdam City, a notable location in Fabrica. In New Amsterdam City, financial success was crucial for earning respect, leading young individuals as young as thirteen to work to support their families. Children from financially stable backgrounds had the freedom to prioritize their education, while those without financial backing had to juggle work and school responsibilities. The availability of financial support significantly influenced academic success among the youth in the community.

CHAPTER ONE

MIGRATION TIME

James Jordan was born on December 28, 1988, in Abattoir, hailed from Freeland where his family had resettled after a period in a neighboring nation. The day of his birth in Abattoir began foggy and cold but cleared up by noon, bringing clear skies and mild winds. Abattoir, where James was born, was a town roughly a five-to-six-hour drive from Connaby, the capital of Freeland. The town was situated on the left side of Drakilla. James was unique as he was of mixed heritage, with a Hujinn father and a human mother. His education and confidence drove his ambition to work for a prestigious agency, where he could educate others about faith and the battle between good and corrupt supernatural forces. With supernatural abilities from a young age, he sought to assist spirits globally, starting with his local community and later expanding his efforts worldwide to combat evil supernatural entities. Hujinns like James were perceived as more intelligent and stronger than jinns, making them highly valued by global organizations. His family's connections to top agencies enabled one of these organizations to later recruit him for his exceptional abilities.

James's father, Alex, had moved from Freeland to Fabrica and resided in New Amsterdam City, recognizing the city's potential. He stayed with a friend who was a WDU (West Drakillian Union) member, a significant agency like the one his father belonged to in Drakilla. Alex then arranged for his wife to join him in Fabrica, while their son James remained under the care of his grandfather, Alhassane Jordan. After eight years in New Amsterdam City, Alex believed it was an ideal place to raise his children despite its challenging reputation. He had applied for a visa for James to join him and his wife, which was later approved. James, unaware of his father's efforts, was thrilled to later learn he could migrate to the renowned city.

James had moved in with his uncle after a terrorist attack by the FARN organization targeted his family due to personal and political vendettas. The attack was in retaliation against James's grandfather, the West Drakillian Director, for his son Alex marrying a human and hindering trade agreements with West Drakilla. Despite the FARN director's personal entanglements with humans, he opposed hujinns in the world of Ginnia unless they benefited him, showcasing both personal complexity and political malice. Luckily, James and his grandfather were unharmed during the attack in Connaby, where they were with James's uncle finalizing travel documents, allowing them to escape the danger.

Alhassane, had noticed suspicious activities between the FARN organization, the countries he represented in western Drakilla, and Flowropia officials, so he grew concerned. He became alarmed when the FARN leader convinced his country's president to engage in business, leading to worries about losing territory to Flowropia. Alhassane was troubled by new diplomats and military camps being set up, indicating a potential threat to West Drakilla's sovereignty. Alhassane, worried about the West Drakillian Union's vulnerability compared to Flowropia and Rancenia, planned to reach out to his friend Mamadou R Diallo, the president of Fabrica. Having met during college when Alhassane studied abroad in Fabrica, Alhassane aimed to inform President Diallo about the WDU's stance against a powerful FARN director and his administration to address the concerning situation.

It was a Wednesday, a cool day near the end of summer with overcast skies, delayed rain showers, and a darkening atmosphere; **the story begins**. Alhassane walked into a convenience store, approached the counter, and gave some money to a man behind it. The man handed Alhassane an international calling card. Upon received the car he immediately scratched it to reveal a number, then dialed President Diallo's office phone number. The phone rang a few times before the secretary answered.

"Hello, you've reached the Fabrican cabinet; Hillary speaking. How can I help you?" Hillary voiced on the other end of the line.

"Hello Hillary, this is Alhassane Jordan, a friend of the president. I wanted to speak to him if he is available," he replied.

"No problem," she said.

"First, I must get confirmation from him. Can you please hold for a moment?" she asked.

"Yes, no problem!" he replied. "By the way, tell him it's Mr. Jordan from Freeland!" he added before she switched the line.

Afterwards, Hillary contacted the president and then transferred the call. Shortly after, Diallo answered the phone and spoke enthusiastically. At first, the president didn't know who the secretary was talking about when she told him that a friend of his named Mr. Jordan was on the line. He knew a few people with the same name, but as soon as he heard Mr. Jordan's voice, he recognized him.

"Hello!" voiced the president.

"PEACE AND BLESSINGS BE UPON YOU!" greeted Mr. Jordan.

"PEACE AND BLESSINGS BE UPON YOU TOO!" responded President Diallo.

"It's Jordan. How have you been, buddy?" remarked Mr. Jordan.

"I'm well, how about you, pal?" replied President Diallo.

Feeling very blissful upon hearing his long-time friend's voice on the other end he was delighted.

"I can't complain, I thank the lord for all his blessings. I've been thinking about you a lot lately," he said.

"That's the way God works, I've been meaning to call you for a few days now. How is the First Lady?" asked Mr. Jordan.

"She's well!" said President. Diallo.

"It's been a long time since I heard from you. What's going on, my brother?" said President. Diallo.

"Well, I believe the leader of the FARN, and some of the Flowropia leaders are planning to take control of my country and a few other western Drakillian countries. I'm telling you, President. Diallo, five of the FARN agents are here setting up as we speak. I heard the Freeland president tell his members that there will be more Flowropian agents coming. They are setting up military bases at our borders. Samuel Shirac and his group are trying to covertly control our country once again. We can't go through this again after gaining our independence from Rancenia in nineteen seventy-four. This is why I'm asking you for help. As you know, we are no match for them," Mr. Jordan stated.

"No problem, my friend. I'll get back to you as soon as possible and I assure you that I'll bring this matter up to my administration," Diallo assured him.

"I almost forgot one more thing, my son needs your assistance. His name's Alex and he's been in New Amsterdam City for a while. He wanted to join one of your agencies, please help him. I would greatly appreciate it if you could put in a good word for him to the BIA. He works part-time as security for the DBI facility," added Mr. Jordan.

"Ok, buddy, I will speak to the directors of DBI, NISA or BIA and see if they would recruit him!" said President Diallo.

"Thank you!" replied Mr. Jordan.

After the president and Mr. Jordan finished their conversation, Diallo called Souleymane Washington, who was the Executive Director of BIA at that point, to inform him about Alex. He also informed Souleymane about Mr. Jordan's recent observation in West Drakilla.

"Hey, pal, it's been a long time since we last spoke. How have you been?" said President Diallo.

"I've been great. How about you and your family?" Souleymane replied.

"We're fine too," said President Diallo.

"Great, how can I be of service, sir?" Souleymane asked.

"Well, my friend, I just spoke to the WDU leader, and he informed me that some Flowropians are trying to invade West Drakilla. They are asking us to help them fight back. I'm worried that if we don't do something soon, they will lose their independence again! We need to step in now and look more into this mess," said the president.

"Ok, I promise I'll have my best agents investigate the matter as soon as possible!" said Mr. Washington.

"Try to deploy the team within three to six months after you look into the matter," advised the president.

"Ok, no problem, I'm going to speak to my wife so she can put together a research team to investigate the situation," replied Mr. Washington.

"I also want you to find his son because he could be useful to your organization. He should fit right in since he has some experience from working as a professional driver for the DBI directors," said President Diallo.

Right after Souleymane hung up the phone, he called his wife, Kadijatou Washington, who was the Chief of Staff of the BIA, and relayed the president's message to her. Immediately after their conversation, Mrs. Washington walked out of her office and went to inform Steve who was the Deputy Director of the agency at that moment. His office was located across the hall from hers.

"I want you to put together a team and prepare them for an upcoming mission ordered by the president. In the meantime, I want you to go to the capital in the morning to help the president find out which of the West Fabrican presidents were associated with the group that is attempting to take over West Drakilla."

"Ok, I'll …" Steve replied before she cut him off.

"Oh yeah, I almost forgot one more thing; my husband said that he wants us to find Alex Jordan. His father was the one who informed us of the Flowropia exploitation of West Drakilla. His father told Diallo that he would rather his son work for us than any other intelligence agency.

Now, since he is just a driver and not a DBI agent yet, I want him on broad. I want you to pick him up before the others do. Observe him for a while, and when you get an opportunity, approach him with a job offer."

A week later, James was peacefully sleeping on a lovely fall morning, feeling the cool breeze. A few hours after he woke up feeling exhilarated after remembering that he would fly to Fabrica on the same day. Soon after, his cousin Alpha, who was the same age as he was, accompanied him to the airport.

Imagining how he would feel if he was in his shoes Alpha asked.

"James, how do you feel?"

"To tell you the truth, I have mixed emotions of excitement and sadness. On one hand, my wish came true, on the other hand, I'm leaving family members and friends behind," James replied with his eyes reddening as if he was going to cry. He took a second to gather himself, then continued.

"I'm telling you, I can't stop thinking about how I'm about to go to a whole different continent. "Can you believe that by tomorrow afternoon I'm going to be in Fabrica?" he said, trying to sound excited even though he was a little melancholy.

"Yeah, right? I can't believe it. Uncle Alex has been living there for close to eight years now, right?" Alpha asked.

"Yeah, we were two when he left," James replied.

After James said goodbye to his cousin and aunt, he walked inside the gate with his uncle, and they waited for their boarding time. A few hours later, they went through security, boarded, and then the flight took off. James sat next to a woman in her late thirties. She looked at him and then told his uncle how cute he was.

"*She keeps looking at me, I wonder if she is trying to use me to get my uncle Vincent's attention,*" he wondered. Halfway into the flight, the provocative lady was drunk, so she couldn't hold herself back anymore and started hitting on James. She didn't mind risking her dignity by going after an underage boy.

"Hey cutie pie!" the lady uttered. "You are a very handsome boy," she added.

James had this effect on most females. They were easily drawn to his attraction. They found him very appealing, even though he was shy. He enjoyed their compliments and their presence, but he didn't know how to entertain them. Therefore, at that point, he isolated himself because of his inexperience. James had been introduced to fashion since he was a baby. As a result, he became an outgoing and outstanding individual who dressed to impress. Everyone who knew James thought that he was a good-looking kid. James carried himself respectfully, therefore most individuals who interacted with him treated him with the same respect.

It had been months since Steve received the call from Kadijatou about recruiting Alex, that same day, Steve decided to follow Alex to the airport and wait by his car in the airport parking lot. It was the morning after they had departed from Connaby. It was forty-five minutes past five a.m. in eastern Fabrica, and the sun shone through the airplane window. James woke up and thought, *"This trip is incredible; I still can't believe I'm going to New Amsterdam City."*

That was his first flight since he was born and his first trip outside of the Freeland. He experienced his first hotel stay and saw a couple of modern developments along the way.

After eleven and a half hours in the air, the Air Rancenia flight landed at MRD (Mamadou R. Diallo) Airport in Weenstone, New Amsterdam City. Vincent and his nephew, James finally got off the plane and walked to the security checking area. After going through security, they proceeded to baggage claim. James is athletic and tall. He was set to turn ten in December of that year, but he is already five feet ten inches tall. He had a rectangular-shaped physique, thin black curly hair, honey skin color, a long nose, radiant rounded classic lips, and a wide set of gray hooded eyes. He also had a firm jaw, a bright smile, and a round head. Vincent was six feet four inches tall and had wavy hair. He had a fabulous smile, a pointed nose, full curvy lips, tan skin color, and a trapezoid body shape. James identified his belongings, a red duffel bag, and a black suitcase wrapped in blue Saran wrap with his signature on them after half an hour. Shortly after, Vincent also found his suitcases. They collected all their luggage and quickly made their way to the exit. After a long walk, Vincent and his nephew walked out of the Air Rancenia arrival terminal gate. As soon as they walked out, James quickly spotted his dad, Alex Jordan, his mother, Holly, and his little brother, Jeremy, waiting for him right up front. Alex had the same features as his son James, so they looked very much alike. He was about six feet five inches tall, about an inch taller than his little brother, Vincent. Alex also had a rectangular body shape, athletic muscles, gray hooded eyes, a long nose, dark curly hair, a strong jaw, full lips, and a dazzling smile. Holly was very charming, adorable, soft-spoken, and she had beautiful curves with an hourglass body shape. She was about five feet eight inches, had honey skin color, a round head, a close set of brown eyes, a bright smile, a small nose, and long black hair. James pushed his luggage cart faster and ran towards them. As soon as James reached the waiting area, he let go of the cart and hugged his mother first. Holly hugged him back and kissed him. The hug was given with such incredible passion that it seemed like she didn't want to let go of him, and he didn't want to let go of her either. However, his brother Jeremy tapped him on the shoulder. Therefore, he turned around and hugged Jeremy, then he looked up and saw his father Alex, whose smile was so bright that it lit up the entire terminal. After their greeting, his little brother took his carry-on suitcase and pushed the cart to the airport parking lot as his parents walked by their side. They all got inside the luxurious SUV, then Alex drove them home. On their way back home, the family discussed the challenges of living in New Amsterdam City and what it took to survive out there.

Shortly after, on their way back from the airport, Alex peeked at his rearview mirror. He saw his wife sitting in the middle row, behind her were his boys. Afterwards, he looked straight ahead and to his right side where his brother was sitting. James was in the back, messing with his little brother Jeremy, who was so excited to have someone to play with. Jeremy was six years old; he had an awesome smile with a solid jaw like his father and brother. He was a couple of inches taller than most boys his age because he was four five inches tall at that point. He had a delicate nose, honey skin color, plump lips, roundish-almond eyes, a rectangular body shape, and medium-length wavy hair. James was a physical kid and Jeremy was very active as well, so they could not stay still. James enjoyed sparring with peers and engaging in playful fights at any opportunity. Alex observed James and his brother, praising their remarkable talent, which led to a conversation.

"Hey James, I see you are fast. Have you been training?" asked Alex.

James looked up and realized that his father was watching them play-fight the entire time. He continued defending himself from Jeremy's quick and lethal blows as he answered his dad, "Yeah, a little bit. Our neighbor Abdullah used to train us on weekends."

When James looked away and still blocked his younger brother's last few swings, he caught everyone's attention, even his brother. Alex could not help but admit that what James just did was fascinating.

"That was impressive. I didn't know you had eyes on the side of your head," Alex announced.

"Thanks pops!" James responded.

"James, how was your flight?" His mother jumped in on the conversation and asked.

"It was amazing! Imagine flying on a plane for the first time?" James replied.

"Oh yeah, that was your first flight," Alex said aloud and reminded himself.

"Plus, you got me first-class tickets. What was there not to like about it?" James added.

Everyone laughed, except for Jeremy, who was distracted by his video game at that point. Jeremy was too young to keep up with the growing folk's business. Jeremy could not be still, so he used his sonic adventure game to keep his mind distracted. He was too young to keep his mind focused on any serious conversation. No more than a few seconds after, it got quiet in the car and everyone had realized that Jeremy was not paying attention. Alex, his brother, and wife looked back at the same time as his brother gave him a nudge. Jeremy looked up and laughed, then he realized that he was a bit late.

"Honey, you are right. I remember my first-class experience too, it was years ago but I still remember. It was extremely amazing. The flight captain and all the flight attendants gave us the best first-class experience, and my favorite part was how spacious the area was," said Holly.

"Well, here in this city, every day is a first-class experience. So, are you ready for New Amsterdam City, James?" Alex asked.

"Of course, as a matter of fact, I was born ready. How can you not, when this is the best city in the world?" James answered.

"You better be, because you are starting school in two days," Holly stated.

"Don't worry, guys. I can't wait," James voiced. Suddenly, Alex noticed a Charger GT trailing his SUV. He whispered to his brother, "I think someone is following us!"

"You think so?" questioned Vincent.

"Yeah, just watch and pay attention to the white Charger."

After a minute of switching lanes and realizing that the car kept switching every time he did, Alex yelled out, "Guys, do you have your seat belts on?"

"Yeah!" answered Holly.

"No, Dad!" Jeremy voiced, as James clicked his seat belt in.

"Put it on, then!" Alex shouted. You can hear the seriousness in his voice because he was loud yet calm. Alex repeated his instruction as he kept glancing at his mirrors. "I don't want to scare my family," he thought before anxiously speaking, "I'm going to drive a little faster so I can catch the game!"

"What game, Dad?" Jeremy naively asked because he was clueless what's happening. Holly and James had caught on and realized that Alex was baffled.

"Jeremy, I said put on your seat belt now!" Alex emphasized once again, then he turned right on the next corner, and stepped on the accelerator. There were three lanes going in the same direction they were heading, with a speed limit of sixty-five. The only issue was that there was a little traffic, so he only drove thirty-five miles per hour as he cut cars off. He continued to swerve through the traffic until he realized that his lane slowed down; he gradually passed a few cars and finally cut off the last car on his left, where the traffic was moving much faster. He made sudden lane changes and took an overpass, unintentionally ending up on the highway going in the opposite direction. He eventually exited the highway and drove for thirty minutes to lose a car following him. After thinking he lost the follower, Alex realized it might have been a regular driver caught in road rage rather than someone targeting him.

"*Wow, this felt like a pursuit of eternity,*" Alex thought as they finally arrived at the residence, One Hundred and Twenty-Sixth Street, on the corner of Martin L King Jr Boulevard. Alex and his wife lived in an area that was very popular worldwide. They stayed in a building next to the Abraham Clinton Junior State Building, which was located between One Hundred and Twenty-Fifth Street and One Hundred and Twenty-Sixth Street, as well as between Sixtieth and Seventieth Avenue. The facility was not only a tourist area, but also a place where most city, state, and federal meetings took place.

After forty-five minutes of driving with a fear of being followed by mercenaries, Alex had finally arrived at his home. He dropped off his family and asked his brother to accompany him to park his car in the parking lot across the building. James, his mother, and his brother each took a suitcase and walked up a few steps to the front of their building. Holly took out her keys, opened the front door, and let them in.

Alex and his brother went back into the car, and the car pulled off. Immediately after pulling off, the same white Dodge Charger with dark blue and yellow stripes came out of nowhere and pulled up behind them. Alex realized that it was the same vehicle that had been trailing them since they exited the airport earlier, and he saw two gentlemen inside. However, he ignored them and still drove into the parking lot. The car stayed outside the lot, while the individuals inside waited for Alex to come out. As Alex and Vincent contemplated whether to go outside or wait for a while, they discussed the unknown intentions of the two men. After about a minute, they decided to go figure it out and walked out. As they got closer to the exit, Alex noticed that the two men were still sitting inside their car outside of the parking lot. They walked all the way up to the vehicle. As Alex approached the car, he thought, "*They must be friendly, if they haven't attacked us yet. If they were mercenaries, they would have ambushed us inside, not here in the open.*"

Right about then, the man on the passenger side rolled down his window and spoke.

"Excuse me! Hello, Alex. My name is Steve Beaumont. This is my brother, Peter," said Steve.

"*How does he know my name?*" Alex wondered as he was shocked that Steve knew his name. Steve was six feet tall, with a cool golden skin color, wide-set eyes, plump lips, a courageous smile, black wavy hair, a Roman nose, and an inverted triangle body shape.

"Hello, as you already know, I'm Alex, and this is my brother Vincent." Alex extended his hand as he responded.

Steve put his hand out too and said, "Nice to meet you. I know you are probably wondering why we've been following you. I wanted to offer you an opportunity to work with us. We work for the federal government."

Steve opened the car door and stepped out, then he continued.

"You see, Alex, we were referred to you by the Fabrican president. We've been watching you for quite a while now."

"You have?" Alex asked.

"Of course, we must be familiar with who we are pursuing. I've seen enough, though, and I'm quite impressed, especially after the way you drove back there. We work for the BIA, the Bureau of Intelligent Agents. We are looking for more talented professionals like yourself." Steve explained.

"Thank you, sir," stated Alex.

"You're welcome, and you can call me Steve," replied Steve.

A couple of minutes later, Steve and Alex had walked back to the car where Peter and Vincent were waiting. Alex shook his hand once again and said, "He looks more like your twin brother, is he?"

"No, he's a few years younger! Peter, meet Alex," replied Steve.

Alex looked at Peter who looked a lot like Steve. He had an amber skin color, an inverted triangle body shape, wide-set eyes, wavy hair, a Roman nose, thick lips, and a conceited smile. He rolled down the window and extended his hand as well. Since Peter always looked down on others, he didn't come out of the car to meet Alex, he greeted him from where he was sitting. "Hello, I'm Peter!" Peter voiced.

"Hello, I'm Alex!" Alex replied.

"Here is my business card. Call me if you are interested. I'll be looking forward to your call!" Steve said as he gave Alex his business card.

"Thank you. I need some time to take all this in, but I'll contact you when I'm ready. I might travel soon also so I'll call you when I return." Alex responded.

"Ok, no rush. Take your time!" said Steve as he got back in the car. A second later, Peter drove off. Alex looked at his brother with a sigh of relief and smiled, then they headed to the entrance of the building where Alex was staying at the time.

When Alex and Vincent walked into the apartment, Holly was waiting for them by the door. As soon as they entered the apartment, she asked, "What took you so long?"

"Can you believe that they were just trying to find out whether I was interested in joining the BIA or not?" Alex responded.

At this point, James, who was in the living room, stood up and walked towards the door to eavesdrop on his parents. He couldn't make out what his parents were saying due to the noise from outside. As the conversation continued, he walked closer to the bathroom and listened.

"Wow, that's awesome. You're always talking about the BIA and how you would love to work for them. There goes your chance!" said Holly.

"Yeah, I know!" said Alex.

"Are they official?" Holly asked. "Yeah, I do. I mean, I think so. They had identification to prove it," Alex responded.

"Great then, give it a try." Afterwards James and Vincent showered, then they gathered to pray for the second prayer of the five normal daily prayers that their family practiced.

Two days later, it was the first day of school. It was a nice day with the perfect fall weather - not too hot and not too cold. James woke up scared and sweaty because he had a bad dream that his father was on his way to Freeland when the plane exploded. Afterwards, he remembered that it was his first day of school, so he was simultaneously excited and nervous. He quickly grabbed his towel and hurried to the bathroom, where he brushed his teeth and jumped in the shower. After showering, he went to his room and put on his blue pants, white shirt, and burgundy blazer. Once James finished getting dressed, he prayed and walked out of the room.

"Mom, I'm ready!" he called out.

"Ok, baby. I'm coming," Holly hollered back.

James appreciated that his school was conveniently located close to his home. Since James didn't speak any English, he was chaperoned everywhere for the first few days. A staff member guided him to all his classes and other school activities. James walked into his first class and sat at the front. He sat in the front in every class, took notes, and listened to the teacher without understanding what he was saying. He was ten years old, and the school was near his home. So, after his first day, James walked to and from school by himself. He was used to going to school and back on his own from his time in Freeland. In Freeland, kids were much more adventurous than in New Amsterdam City, where most kids stayed locked inside their apartments until they were older due to the overcrowdedness and somewhat dangerous nature of the city.

A few weeks later, Alex was in the living room talking to Vincent about James.

"I don't know how he is holding up because when I first came here, it took me almost a year to learn the language," Alex expressed.

"Don't you think you should get him a tutor or transfer him to a school that offers ESL classes since he's not taking any?" Vincent asked.

"Yeah, but I believe he can do without it. James is a clever individual. He is going to be fine."

James had been attending school for over three months, on the last friday at the end of the third month he got into an altercation with another student named Timothy in the cafeteria. They were in the same after-school program, but the confrontation happened during regular school hours. Timothy, a tall, chubby boy with thin almond eyes, earth-colored skin, thin lips, a bashful smile, a big forehead, short freeze hair, and an overbite, was sitting across from James during lunch. He attempted to take a slice of pizza from James's tray however James prevented him from taking a slice by grabbing his forearm and speaking to him in a different accent.

"Hey, what are you doing?" he asked.

Timothy snatched his arm back, not realizing that James had let go at the same time. Thinking he had overpowered James, Timothy stood up and said, "Give me your slice, little man!"

James stood up, leaned in and replied.

"No!" he said.

Everyone laughed, and Timothy, feeling a bit disrespected and embarrassed, sat back down. He acted as if he was going to finish eating his meal, but then he reached into his bag and pulled out a pencil. As soon as James sat back down, Timothy poked him on his right hand with the pencil. In pain, James reacted unconsciously and punched Timothy in the face with his other hand. The punch knocked Timothy out cold, and he was rushed to the emergency room. After the MRI results came back, Timothy and his parents learned that he had fractured his jaw. The next day, Timothy and parents went to the school and filed a complaint against James so the vice principal called his parents. The school had to punish both James and Timothy. James was suspended for three days, but the school community board was still undecided on what to do for his final punishment due to the severity of the injury.

After James got home that evening, he found out from his mother that he had broken his jaw. Later that night, when Alex got home, he also learned that James had severely hurt a kid from his school. Therefore, Alex sat James down and had a talk with him.

"James, I advise you to resolve encounters mentally and don't ever resort to violence even when you are forced to. Son, I went to hell and back for you and your siblings to get a good education, and I'll do it all over again if I must. From now on, I want you to come to me whenever you need to talk. I know you were only trying to defend yourself, but not everyone is going to see it that way. You must be wary of your actions. The mission is to go to school and not get into any trouble until you graduate."

"Ok, dad! I just want you to know that Timothy started it and I didn't mean to hit him so hard," said James.

After James left, Alex remembered that Vincent had given him a good idea earlier that week and thought. *"Vincent was right; I should transfer James to a school that offers ESL. This way, he would be able to relate more to his fellow students."*

The next day, he went to school and spoke to the guidance counselor, Ms. Rosario. She recommended the same advice that Vincent had given him—not only to get him a tutor but also to put him in a school that offered ESL. When Alex got home, he thought about his conversation with Ms. Rosario. He could hear her voice in his head saying, *"James should be around other ESL students to be at ease because he can relate to them more."*

After considering his son's teacher's advice, Alex determined that Ms. Rosario was right. He took his son's suspension as a sign to move James before any more sanctions were taken against him. He used the guidance counselor's advice about James needing to be around other bilingual students to feel comfortable as a reason because he knew he had to justify transferring his child in the middle of the school year.

James didn't know that he was different from most of the beings around him because he was a hujinn. He couldn't relate to most individuals and didn't understand the reason. Even though he was associated with other beings, he still felt different most of the time, so he isolated himself socially. He understood that he was unique, therefore he searched steadily to find someone like himself. After a few days of suspension, James sat in his room and thought of his past. He thought about severe arguments he had with his friend and some of his relatives when he was younger. As he sat there alone, he thought, *"I don't think anyone likes me! …even when I was in Freeland, most of my friends and family members didn't accept me for who I am. I can't help that I'm a maverick; God made me like this."*

A couple of weeks before the end of the semester, James transferred to a new elementary school. Once again, his new school was within walking distance from his home. Not too long after the transfer, the Jordans agreed that they had made the right decision. They were glad that they had sent James to the new school, especially since it was also a private school. The school was perfect because it offered a wider range of curricula than his previous school. Unlike his most private schools, this one didn't discriminate against students with a troubled background, because James would have never been accepted after what he did to Timothy.

A few weeks after James transferred to the new school, Vincent went back home to Connaby, Freeland, and Alex went with him to visit. Alex wanted to go home because he had only been back there once since he had left the first time. He planned to stay for only two to three weeks, but once he got there, he was impressed by the modern developments and the endless business opportunities. He was also fascinated by his brother's business commitment, so he stayed longer to explore his possibilities out there. He contemplated whether he should find work in Freeland next to his brother or go back to his overwhelming job back in Fabrica, but after he was informed that he had lost his DBI driver position, he went with his First Option and stayed. After a couple of months of experimenting with his possibilities in Freeland, he realized that it was tougher than he thought. He discovered that the country had a lot of economic issues and business barriers due to their Flowropia association. He was disappointed, so he went to consult his father, Alhassane. Mr. Jordan advised him to go back to Fabrica and try to work for the BIA and figure out how he can help Freeland with their assistance. He also informed him that he was the one who contacted the president about him in the first place. As a result of his father's advice, he recalled his meeting with Steve and decided to go back to Fabrica and see if the BIA was still interested in him.

It had now been seven months since James migrated to Fabrica, and he was in the middle of the spring semester. He had been at his previous elementary school for close to four months and close to three months at the new school. Many of his classmates and the staff in his school had noticed how fast he learned the English language. James read and wrote better than most of his peers who were born speaking the language that he had just learned. His ESL teacher, Mrs. Houston, invited Mrs. Shirac, the school advisor; Mrs. Dubois, the school principal; and Mrs. Beaumont, the vice principal, to come and make a guest appearance in her class. Mrs. Houston had an average height for a woman, long curly hair, warm tan skin color, a rounded body shape, a delicate nose, thick long eyelashes, hooded eyes, a lovely smile, and heart-shaped lips. Mrs. Dubois had an inverted triangle body shape, warm natural skin color, an average height for a woman, and she was skinny. Her hair was wavy and waist-long—she had a close set of eyes, full lips, a complaisant smile, and a pointed nose. As for Mrs. Shirac, she was tall with a thick triangle body, espresso skin color. She had medium-length hair, deep-set eyes, a beaming smile, a fleshy nose, and plump lips.

It was a stormy day in the beginning of the spring season. It had been raining all morning, and you could still hear the thunder blasts. The wind blew loudly against the windows as Mrs. Houston walked into the classroom, and all her students were already there waiting for her. First, she addressed the class, then she informed them that Mrs. Dubois the principal couldn't make it but she sent the dean, Mrs. Durand in her place. She also told them that Mrs. Shirac, their advisor and Mrs. Beaumont, their vice principal would be coming too. Mrs. Durand had a pear-shaped body, dark skin color, and a medium height for a woman. Her hair was curly and short—she had thin almond eyes, thick lips, an affiliative smile, and a bulbous nose.

As soon as Mrs. Houston finished talking, Mrs. Beaumont, Mrs. Shirac, and Mrs. Durand walked in and they sat next to her. In the reading activity, the first student read, followed by a few more before it was James' turn. Each student had to read a paragraph or two, answer questions related to the reading, and respond to technical questions from the teacher. He read one paragraph out loud, then explained the main idea. As Mrs. Beaumont, Mrs. Shirac, and Mrs. Durand sat there and listened until the end, they were extremely impressed by how much progress he had made since the last time they heard him speak. After James finished reading two paragraphs, Mrs. Beaumont wanted to hear more, therefore she asked, "Can you finish the chapter?"

"His part is done!" said Mrs. Houston.

"I know, I just want to hear him finish up the chapter since there is only one paragraph left," said Mrs. Beaumont.

After James finished reading, they clapped. He was the only one they clapped for thus far.

They quietly talked among themselves so that the students wouldn't hear their conversation.

"If he is reading this well now, imagine how great he'll be when he finishes school?" said Mrs. Shirac.

"Yes, of course, that was excellent!" said Mrs. Durand.

"*Wow, that was impressive. In less than a few months, he is reading at the same level as a sixth grader. If he keeps this up, he might be this year's valedictorian. What an intelligent kid. This is his first year and he never learned English before he came here, yet he was incredible. The BIA needs someone with that intelligence. I'm going to tell my husband about him.*" Mrs. Beaumont thought.

A couple of weeks before the end of spring, Mrs. Houston gave her class a midterm exam. After the evaluation, she decided to call the students' parents to inform them of their grades. Having already spoken to several of her students' parents, it was then time for the teacher to call James' parents. She dialed the number, and right before she hung up, someone picked up, "Hello!" said Holly.

"Hello, good evening, can I speak to Mr. or Mrs. Jordan?" Mrs. Houston asked.

"Speaking, how can I assist you?" Holly responded.

Mrs. Houston replied, "Excuse me, this is Mrs. Houston, James's ESL teacher."

"Hello, Mrs. Houston!" Holly cheerfully greeted her and asked, "How are you?"

"I'm fine, and you?" Mrs. Houston responded.

"I couldn't be better!" Holly answered.

"Well, I just wanted to tell you that James has been fantastic. His improvement has been phenomenal. He has excelled in all his classes, and he is on top of all the activities we do. I also spoke to his other teachers, and they all said the same, whether it was educational or sports. James has been excellent even in his after-school program. Everyone here noticed his brilliance." Mrs. Houston explained.

"Wow, that's awesome! Thank you!" said Holly.

"Even Mrs. Shirac, his advisor, was amazed by how high his intellectual level is." Mrs. Houston elaborated.

"I'm so glad to hear that. I was worried that he might have a hard time since he is bilingual, you know?" said Holly.

"No worries. If James keeps this up, not only will he be the valedictorian, but he'll also get accepted to the best schools in New Amsterdam City!" replied Mrs. Houston.

"Thank you again! My husband is not home yet, but I'll tell him you called," said Holly.

"Bye now!" said Mrs. Houston.

"Bye..." Holly replied and started smiling nonstop.

Holly was exhilarated by Mrs. Houston's kind words about her son. After hanging up the phone, she and her husband walked in and saw her in a state of memorization.

"I can't believe James is fitting in so well! His teachers also see him as a genius. I always knew that my boy is way ahead of his time," she thought.

Suddenly Alex walked in and noticed her radiant smile that was so bright it lit up the entire apartment.

"What is so amusing?" he asked.

"Nothing, I'm excited because I just got off the phone with James's

ESL teacher, Mrs. Houston, and she said that he is doing excellent. She said that he is very special and considered one of the best students in the school," she replied.

Alex had recently returned from his trip to Freeland and was feeling down because he was unemployed. He wasn't sure if the BIA would still be interested in him, so hearing that his son was doing well in school encouraged him. He was thrilled to hear how well James was performing at school. He walked up to her, kissed her, and made a promise to her that he would call Steve the next morning.

After the midterm exams, Mrs. Beaumont was flabbergasted by James because his grades were outstanding. As a result, she asked her husband, Steve, to look further into his identity. She told Steve that she had never met a student with such a high IQ. The next day, Steve did some research and discovered that James was Alex's son. When he got home, he informed his wife about his findings.

"Honey, you wouldn't believe this! Coincidentally, his father is the guy I've been trying to recruit," said Steve with volubility.

"Who?" Mrs. Beaumont asked.

"You know, the boy you told me about yesterday. His family is from Freeland, West Drakilla, to be specific. Our president asked me to pick him up." Steve replied.

"Wow, no wonder he's so brilliant. It runs in his family!" stated Mrs. Beaumont.

"Yeah, definitely, because his grandfather is very close to the president," said Steve.

From that point going forward, Steve and his men watched as the Jordans looked closer into Alex and his family.

It had been close to eight months since Alex was approached by Steve about joining the BIA Organization, and he still had not reached out to him. Not only because he was out of the country when he made up his mind, but after he came back, he was unsure whether Steve's offer still stood or not. On that day, he decided to give it a try anyway. Alex called Steve's office and the phone rang twice, then Steve picked up, voicing himself, "Hello!"

After Steve answered the phone, Alex said, "Hello, can I speak to Steve?"

"It's me, who is this?" Steve asked.

"It's Alex?" He replied, then paused and took a deep breath before continuing, "I know it's been a while, but I was back home in Freeland next to my father, who was seriously ill."

"Oh, okay. Sorry to hear that. Is he doing better?" Steve asked.

"Yes, thanks to God. He was doing much better when I left," Alex answered.

"Okay, great. How can I be of service to you?" Steve demanded.

"I called to see if you are still interested in me?" Alex replied.

"Yes, of course," Steve responded.

"Yes, thank you, I was afraid to call you since it's been so long since you made the offer," Alex declared.

"We are always looking for talented professionals like yourself. You called just in time," Steve responded.

"I cannot thank you enough, sir," Alex voiced before Steve interrupted him by saying, "Alex, I told you to call me Steve."

"Ok, sorry," said Alex. It had been almost eight months since they met, so Alex was surprised that Steve still welcomed him with open arms.

"Listen Alex, I can tell an intelligent jinn when I see one. I know you drove for the DBI so you should know what to expect in this field. We'll train you so you don't have to worry about anything. I have another position more advanced than the one we initially discussed. You'll be working under our Science and Technology Department with the Integrated Missions Team. Trust me, it's an incredible way to begin. That's how I started; my brother also works there," declared Steve.

"No problem, I'm just honored to get a chance to work with you and I thank you from the bottom of my heart. I will not let you down," said Alex.

"That's what I like to hear," Steve expressed.

"Wow, that's cool! so, I'm going to work for the Integrated Missions Center! I can't wait!" said Alex.

"Yeah, and since we are based here in Amsterdam you don't have to travel much. Leaving you more time to spend with loved ones. For the most part, you'll be working around here, occasionally, you might have to go out of state, but that's rare. The best part is that you get to work with my brother, Peter."

Steve said, making it clear for Alex to convince him.

"Thank you, sir. I'm ready to start as soon as possible!" said Alex.

"No problem. Come down to the facility at Madison Park tomorrow, and I'll get you set up," Steve instructed him.

"Great, I'll see you in the morning," Alex affirmed before they said goodbye and hung up.

Next day, Alex went to Steve's office and was hired on the spot. Afterwards, Alex began working for the company.

During the last few weeks of his fifth-grade year, James noticed a beautiful girl outside of his school who caught his attention. It was a sunny day when James walked out of the exit from the back of the school. As he made his way towards the front of the school to go home, he saw a lovely girl walking out the front exit of the school with his teacher, Mrs. Houston. The girl was about five feet tall, with long curly hair, warm tan skin, a rounded body shape, a delicate nose, thick long eyelashes, hooded eyes, a lovely smile, and heart-shaped lips. She looked just like his teacher, Mrs. Houston. James stopped in his tracks, his eyes widening, and wondered, *"How come I've never seen her before? Maybe she's just visiting our school. I've been here the whole semester and never noticed her."*

Feeling shy and not wanting to draw attention to himself, James composed himself and walked away before his teacher realized how fascinated he was by the girl's.

At this point in his life, James was very shy and lacked the confidence to ask any girl out on a date. Although he was infatuated with this girl, he couldn't figure out how to approach her. As a result, he continued to admire her beauty from a distance. He attempted to catch her attention whenever they crossed paths by staring at her or walking next to her, but he failed each time. Despite maintaining good grades in school, James started becoming more concerned about girls and fashion.

A week after, early in the morning, on his way to school, James saw the pretty girl again but this time she was alone. He was walking to school and came across the same pretty girl in the schoolyard, but this time she was walking away from the school. She was wearing her school uniform, and that confirmed that she went to a different school. *"Clearly, she attended a different school. Wow, she's like an angel. Not only is she good-looking, but she's also fashionable and neat,"* he thought. In June of that year, James passed to the next grade and as summer vacation began, he spent his time hanging out with new friends from school.

After two months, it was now September, the summer vacation was over, and school opened back up. On the second day of school, James was confronted by a couple of boys named Rich and Charles at the school's gymnasium. The boys were jinns, and they thought James was a human, so they tried to intimidate him. Rich had a snub nose, curly hair, and was very tall and stocky. Rich's father, Ben Durand, worked for the BIA and owned his own record label company, so he was well off. Charles's father worked for Ben's record label because of their relationship. As a result, their kids started hanging out. Charles and Rich had been friends since first grade, so they knew each other very well. In their community, everyone who dressed in high-end brands were called "Fly," especially if they had a nice style. Rich and Charles were considered the best-dressed students in their school due to their expensive attire. They were flamboyant because they had all the latest gear. Charles had a funny-shaped nose, nappy hair, a wide eye set, and a round-shaped head. Like Rich, Charles was well-built. All their peers believed that they were the most fashionable and popular kids in their neighborhood, so they walked around like they were better than the rest. Their mentality caused them to ridicule anyone who didn't meet their standards.

James was in gym class, practicing his jump shot when Charles and Rich, who were in his grade level, walked up to him. Charles rebounded the ball, but he did not pass it back to James or shoot it; he just held onto it.

"Can you pass me the ball if you are not going to shoot?" James asked.

"No, don't pass him the ball. Only nice people get to play on this court, and from the looks of it, you are trash!" uttered Rich.

"Ha-ha, that's hilarious!" Charles chuckled.

"Kick rocks!" Rich added.

"Excuse me, I don't understand?" James replied.

"You want to play with me?" He added. "What, you aren't no match for me, I'll demolish you!" said Rich.

"If you think you're better than me, then let's play!" responded James.

"No problem, Charles passed me the rock," said Rich.

Charles threw the ball to him and stood back.

They played for about five minutes before it got physical because James did not know how to play at that point, so he was fouling Rich. He was embarrassed and could not handle the loss either. James fouled him over and over until Rich had enough and pushed him, but then he realized that James was tough as iron.

"Stop hacking me. This is basketball, not MMA (Mixed Martial Arts)," Rich shouted out loud.

"Stop crying, I thought you were nice?" replied James.

"Who are you talking to, broke kid...?" James just ignored him and walked away.

Charles and his buddy followed him and continued to make fun of him. The two boys ganged up on James, as Charles talked about his attire, Rich made fun of his accent. They took turns pointing out facts about James.

"Why do they call you Jordan when you can't play basketball for nothing?" asked Rich.

"Yeah, and what are those on your feet? Your gear looks mad, cheap and hideous!" Charles added. A lot of students who were inside the gym gathered around them and started watching. After James finally said something and the spectators heard his foreign accent, they laughed. James recalled the time when he almost got expelled from school after he fractured Timothy's jaw, and he kept calm.

"I promised my parents that I will not fight anymore, especially after my last fight," he thought and left the gym before the situation escalated.

Another short, average rectangular-bodied boy with bronze skin color, a delicate nose, chapped lips, thin almond-brown eyes, a black line-up frizzy hair, and a friendly smile caught up to James. He introduced himself. "What's up, bro? My name is Oumar."

"Hey, what's up, bro? My name is James," James replied.

"Don't mind them, they act like they work for their stuff. At this age, we are all the same. They're just lucky that their parents are rich and they're spoiled brats!" They both laughed, then continued walking and talking.

After getting to know each other, James said, "Thanks, I really appreciate you trying to calm me down back there!"

"You're welcome, and I'm here if you need anything. Don't hesitate to ask," said Oumar.

"Okay, I got you! I'll see you around." Replied James.

Before the situation James had with Rich and Charles at the gym, he didn't know that there was such a thing as being "Fly." He didn't know that there were cool clothes and sneakers to wear or not to wear. He normally put on whatever Holly bought for him and his brother Jeremy from the discount store. After the day they mocked him, he understood that they made fun of him only because of his gear and accent.

At the end of that day, James was leaving school and he saw the girl he admired, and she was hanging out in the front. He also noticed that this time she was wearing the same school uniform as he was. He spotted her standing and chatting with a couple of girls right by the front exit. James felt like the entire area was glowing because of how conspicuous she was. Her energy drew the attention of everyone coming out of the school.

James was deeply captivated by the girl as he found her extremely beautiful. He admired her from a distance and was eager to speak with her. However, he reminded himself that he must not appear desperate, so he restrained himself from approaching her immediately.

He was so infatuated with her dazzling gaze that he became more motivated to go to school thereafter, just to catch a glimpse of her.

After James found out that the girl he had a crush on was attending the same school that he was, every day he looked forward to running into her. He saw her in different areas of the school; sometimes he saw her outside by the school, other times in the hallways or during recreation. He noticed that he saw her more often, therefore he looked forward to their encounters. Since James did not know how to ask a girl out on a date at that point, he acted strange by eavesdropping on her or staring at her to draw her attention. He hung around a lot of girls before but had never made any attempts to get into a relationship with any of them. He had a few girlfriends because of his looks, not because he knew how to mingle.

Weeks later, James was walking side by side with a girl when he heard her shout out.

"Hey, Rose!"

She stopped and looked back and said, "Hey Mary!"

Mary caught up to them and hugged Rose and said, "Was up, girl!"

James had walked a few yards past them, yet he could still hear them, especially since part of his supernatural gifts were intensified senses. His senses had started to improve, so his hearing sense was stronger than the normal human or jinn. He slowed down and listened to their conversation, and that was the moment he discovered that her name was Rose and that she was in the fifth grade, one year behind him.

Since the day Rich and Charles teased James, he promised himself that he would switch up and be more stylish. Due to their mockery, James dressed, walked, and spoke differently so that he would gain the respect of his peers. As for his accent, he tried to sound like a kid who was born and raised in Amsterdam, New Amsterdam city but it wasn't as simple as he thought. He realized that it might not even be possible at that point, especially for an older immigrant like himself. James knew that he would never speak perfectly like an American, yet he tried. Therefore, after some practice, he started to speak a little bit like a kid who was raised in New Amsterdam City. His mother was accustomed to taking him and his sibling to the cheaper stores, but ever since that incident, he went to high-end stores and only bought expensive shoes, clothes, and accessories. He was not into buying expensive clothes or sneakers; as a result, he had to save most of his allowance to buy these materialistic items.

Weeks later, James tried out for his school's basketball team and the soccer team. He didn't make the basketball team, but he made the soccer team. After joining the soccer club, their activities introduced him and his teammates to more places in the city. He began exploring different areas of his neighborhood and became familiar with all four directions of Amsterdam, uptown, downtown, west, and east. In the process, he made a few more friends as well. When he wasn't in school, he explored the city with Sam, one of the friends he met as soon as he arrived in the city. Sam was also from Freeland and migrated to New Amsterdam City around the same time as James. After they met Oumar, another Freeland native who grew up in New Amsterdam City, they stuck together. The three of them were part of the original young immigrant group in Amsterdam who were from Freeland. They kept their circle tight until many more joined them years later. After James became more familiar with the neighborhood, he realized that there were a lot of wealthy individuals in his community. He understood that his family lived in a very popular area and that they were in the center of all the action.

Alex worked closely with Peter for nearly five months, which allowed them to become very familiar with each other. Later they transformed to the BIA Science and Technology department. During their time together, Peter informed Alex about the First Option and mentioned that his brother Steve was a First Option before. Alex found it intriguing that Peter was so obsessed with this position as he constantly talked about it. He was so enthusiastic about the First Option that he convinced Alex to also take an interest in becoming the next First Option, leading to both competing for the position.

After working together for a while, Peter and Alex became very close to the point where they were inseparable. They hung out often before and after work, as well as during their breaks. Occasionally, Steve and some of their comrades from the BIA came along with them, but for the most part, it was just the two of them. One day, Alex and Peter went out to eat. Peter came with his lady and Alex came with his wife. They were introduced to one another, and that was the first time Peter and his sweetheart Mitchell met Holly. During their conversation, Peter suspected that Holly was a human and that Alex could be guilty of violating one of the NISA rules. On the following Friday evening, the two colleagues went out again; nevertheless, this time it was just the two of them. As Peter and Alex were having drinks, Peter brought up the National Intelligence Spirits Agency. Peter educated Alex about the NISA rules and traditions. Since Alex gave him a reason to believe that he was married to a human being, which was not allowed by the NISA, he couldn't stop telling him about their rules regarding that issue.

"Have you ever heard of NISA?" asked Peter.

"No," Alex replied.

"Great, let me tell you about it then. The NISA stands for National Intelligence Spirits Agency. It's a Fabrican agency that monitors the different classes of spirits, intelligent or not. The organization has a machine that detects all kinds of spirits, with or without supernatural abilities, all over the world. Duan Jackson and John Iverson are the top directors, and the organization is classified. Only superb agents, like my brother and only a small number of agents, are aware of their existence.

"Man, that's interesting. Thanks for telling me!" Alex replied.

"They are very strict with their rules and regulations, though, especially when it comes to the mixture of jinns and humans. They are notorious for eliminating anyone who breaks this law. I heard that they have crucified most of the individuals accused of such acts, and no one knows what happened to them and their families afterwards! So, be very careful," said Peter. "Gee, thanks again. I'll keep that in mind," replied Alex.

Peter had suspected that Holly was a human being from the day he met her because of the way she interacted with him. Thus, he planned to get to the bottom of his suspicions. Most jinns were aware of the NISA rule because committing such a crime was lethal. They knew that if they were ever caught in that kind of situation, they needed to keep their identities confidential so that they wouldn't face the consequences of their actions. Anyone who violated the rule not only put themselves in great danger but also their family. It was one of the worst offenses because the NISA actively searched for individuals involved in these cases. Thus, beings who mixed with other kinds of beings hid it from society because any of them who were found would be put to death.

Steve and Peter were Hujinns, but their true identities were unknown, so they searched for others like themselves. Alex felt the burden of violating the rule against jinns mating with humans and risked consequences from the NISA administration. Jinns who had relationships with humans kept their connections hidden. Since Alex had a human wife and hujinn children despite the prohibition against jinns mixing with humans, he kept this secret from others but eventually confided in Peter during a job they were working on together.

It had been a long day, and Alex had just gotten off work. Then he saw Peter ahead of him walking out of the facility, so he ran to catch up with him.

"Hey, buddy. I know we've been partners for a while, and I trust you because you've taught me a lot about our agencies and their rules. Peter, I'm only telling you this because I know you will understand. have children with a human, but I unaware it was prohibited," Alex told him.

"I was young and in love when I found out that it was a misdeed, it was too late; she was already pregnant with my first child. My father advised me to go along with it. He believed it was destined and that the experience would be worth it. My father begged me to stay with her and keep my child because he thought it would be interesting to see what would happen if we mixed with humans. He also believed that the mixture would help us understand each other better because we would have a piece of both in one. Anyone with that gift would be capable of bringing us together and could improve our communication with them," Alex explained.

Peter, upon hearing Alex's explanation, became furious.

"I disagree with your actions; why would you make such poor judgment?" he asked.

At that moment, Alex realized that he was wrong in thinking that Peter would understand. He regretted it immediately because Peter was strongly opposed to his decision.

From the moment Peter found out about Alex and his family, he couldn't stand him. He envied him because he knew that his children were hujinn beings. Peter wanted to expose his private affair to everyone at the BIA agency but decided to take it a step further and report it to the ISA. At that point, Steve had become the director at the agency, but he didn't even tell him because he was afraid that Steve would help Alex. He knew that Steve liked Alex and had no problem with the existence of other hujinns. Steve wanted to discover the superhujinn because he would possess the most dynamic power in the world. Peter vowed to himself that if it was the last thing he did, he would kill Alex and his entire family. He didn't tell Steve because he knew that Steve would try to stop him. At that point Peter decided to notify Mr. Jackson, because expected him to support his plan to kill Alex and his family.

A couple of days after Peter discovered that Alex was in violation of the NISA rules, he called Mr. Jackson and notified him about it. Mr. Jackson was a short man with mid-length curly hair, cool beige skin color, a rectangular body shape, a bulbous nose, down-turned eyes, an enamored smile, and collagen-inflated lips. Mr. Jackson told Peter to give him some time to process this information and that he'd get back to him. After Peter gave the information to Mr. Jackson, he called his partner, Mr. Iverson, immediately and told him the story too. The next day, Mr. Jackson called Peter back, and they came up with a solution: to eliminate Alex first, then his family, and keep their plan confidential.

Suddenly, Alex's secret became a topic of discussion within the agency, leading him to fear for his safety and contemplate leaving his job. He felt betrayed by Peter for exposing his secret and decided he could no longer work with him. Alex suspected Peter of being the one who revealed his secret due to being the only person he confided in about his family. Uncertain about how Steve and the other directors would respond, Alex chose to remain patient in the face of the situation.

A few days later, Mr. Iverson reached out to his partner, Mr. Jackson, and requested a meeting with all the BIA and NISA directors. Mr. Iverson had an average height of five feet eleven inches, had trimmed wavy hair, warm porcelain skin color, an oval body shape, a flat nose, sultry lips, deep-set eyes, and a courteous smile. The next day, they all met at the BIA center.

Mr. Jackson suggested that they discharge Alex from the agency immediately and prosecute him.

"Don't you think that's an egregious punishment for one of our own? It's not like the guy is one of our best," Steve asked.

"No, not at all. He committed the offense and shall pay for it," replied Mr. Jackson.

"That's nonsense. Come on, Mr. Iverson. Tell him! That's not justice. He wouldn't have said that if he was one of his own!" said Steve.

"You're taking it the wrong way and making it personal. You are being biased! You are only defending him because you recruited him!" exclaimed Mr. Jackson.

"Hey, come on, guys! Settle down," Mr. Iverson stepped in. "Mr. Jackson, I think Steve is right. Suspending him should be sufficient," he added.

"How can you side with him when I'm your partner? I will not stop until your guy is terminated. I'm going to report him to the the president, the supreme court, congress and file a complaint to the president against your agency as well," declared Mr. Jackson.

"Be my guest. He's not going anywhere. The best I can do is suspend him. If that's not enough, do as you please," Steve replied and left the room to make a phone call.

"Don't you understand what's going on? His father is very close to our president." Mr. Iverson stated.

"He is? No, I didn't know," responded Mr. Jackson.

"Well, now you know. His father is Mr. Jordan. Don't you remember him? The fellow who went to school with the president?" Mr. Iverson explained.

"Oh, thanks for the details," said Mr. Jackson.

"So good luck trying to get him fired."

After the long debate, the president called and interceded. He called Mr. Jackson before they finished the meeting because Steve had called and informed him about the situation when he walked out. After President Diallo's intervention, Mr. Jackson stopped his threats, and agreed to suspend Alex for three months for violating the law. Right after this meeting, Mr. Jackson called his uncle, Samuel Shirac, who was on a hunt to kill all hujinns, and he informed him about Alex and his entire family.

Alex was really surprised that, after his devotion to Peter since they met, he didn't wish him well. He had finally recognized that the feeling between him and Peter wasn't mutual and was certain that Peter had a lot of animosity towards him. Therefore, from that moment on, he was determined to stay away from him.

At first, only Peter avoided Alex, but when Alex realized Peter's bitterness towards him, he also kept away from him. When Alex was suspended from work, Peter pretended to be genuine again. He made several attempts to reach him. He called Alex every other week throughout his suspension period, even though he didn't get any response from him.

In November, Alex returned to work. On his first day back, Peter walked up to him to welcome him, but Alex walked past him as if he didn't see him at all. It was at that moment that Peter realized Alex knew he was the one who had sold him out. From that moment on, they both recognized that their friendship was over. They avoided communicating with each other, even when they found themselves in the same room. That evening, after work, Alex went to Steve's office and spoke to him about what had transpired between him and Peter.

As Alex walked in, Steve was standing by his office window, looking at the view of New Amsterdam City from the one hundredth floor.

"Good evening, Steve!" said Alex.

"Good evening, Alex. How was your break?" Steve asked.

"It was great. I spent more time with my family since I hardly do when I'm working," Alex replied.

"Great, because I have a lot of work for you," said Steve.

"Cool. I miss working. By the way, did you know that your brother was the only one I talked to about my identity? As soon as I told him, the information leaked," Alex explained.

"Are you sure?" Steve asked.

"I'm one hundred percent sure!" Alex replied.

"So, you're telling me that Peter was responsible for notifying the NISA about your mishap?" Steve asked.

"Yes, Steve, I swear," Alex replied.

"If it's possible, I would like you to transfer me to another department, please. I can't work with him any longer. From the way he treated me, I assume he feels the same?" he added.

"No problem. I'll work on it. Give me some time to find you a place in the intelligence department," Steve replied.

"For now, I suggest you keep doing what you've been doing and stay away from him," added Steve.

"Okay and thank you. I really appreciate everything you've done for me and my family," Alex responded.

There were only a few young Freeland immigrants in their community at that time, so Sam and James stuck together until they also met Oumar. Then it was the three of them. They were inseparable at that point in time, and even though Sam was ahead of the other two in school by one year, they spent a lot of time together. Sam was a very good kid, quiet, and never took part in the street shenanigans, that's why James liked to be around him. They hung out in each other's homes afterschool and studied together. Sam was the reason that James went to most of the schools that he enrolled in. James followed him to the schools that he went to whenever he graduated and had to go to a new school. Though James had closer friends than Sam, they were all in Freeland.

Days before the end of November, it was a public holiday thus school was closed. James and Sam went to hang out with Oumar at his place. It was a snowy Sunday, so they stayed in and played some video games. They played and talked for a while, then James asked, "Have you ever heard of supernatural beings?"

"Yeah, I heard about them, but I don't believe that crap," Oumar answered.

"I do, trust me O, it's true. They have the best supernatural abilities and they are the most intelligent beings around the world," James replied.

"For real, doesn't that scare you guys?" Sam asked.

"Of course, it does; I mean, not really because I heard they are just like us. They are two different types of beings, natural and supernatural! You know what provides me with a sense of comfort and assurance in the universe? Knowing that we are not alone; God and the angels are watching over us," James responded.

Later, on a Saturday evening, the weather was nice, so James and his brother played basketball at the park, a couple of blocks from their residence. An hour later, they came back and Alex was out in front of the building, waiting for them. He wanted to spend time with James since he had a few days off from school.

"I want you to accompany me downtown to the city because I need to grab a few outfits for work," asked Alex.

"Sorry to cut you off, Dad, but what do you do for a living again?" James curiously asked.

"Yeah, Dad, where do you work? You never told us," Jeremy also demanded.

"I'll tell you about work later; right now, I have a few errands to run. Do you want to come with me, James, or not?" Alex asked.

"Yeah, I would love to come. Give me a second, I must use the bathroom," James responded and ran inside.

"Jeremy, go take a shower. I'll tell you where I work when I get back," Alex instructed him.

A few minutes later, James came out and they went to the shopping center down in the city. An hour later the were at the busiest strip in their city. After visiting all the stores that he thought would have what he was looking for, he didn't find anything. All the items that he was looking for were sold out or they didn't have his size. On their way back, they stopped by the stores on one hundred thirty-second street near their home. Luckily, they had the jackets, slacks, and shirts he was looking for there. When they came out of the store, they ran into Antoine and his son.

"Hey, son, I want you to meet my friends, Antoine, and his son Sam. They live a few blocks from our building," Alex stated.

"Yeah, I know Sam, he's my best friend. We're always hanging out, and I've met Mr. Bryant before too," James said.

"Ok then, great… see you tonight?" asked Alex.

"Not tonight, buddy. I was about to call you, we have a family emergency! Let's do it tomorrow," Antoine replied.

"Ok, don't worry about that, take care of your business first. I'll see you tomorrow then."

After they walked to the end of the corner, Sam hollered, "James you want to link up later?"

"Yeah, I'll hit you up!" James hollered back right before he went inside the car. Then his dad walked to the other side and went in the car as well.

James recalled his father's promise before they left and wondered if it would still honor it when they got back. He couldn't wait until they got home, so he reminded his dad in the car. "Dad, you still haven't answered my question from earlier!" he asked. "I worked for a research center in the city." Then he quickly deviated from being further interrogated by flipping the script. Instead of talking more about his profession, he asked, "James, what would you do if you were the leader of an emerging nation and had to protect your country from a larger nation trying to intrude?"

"Well, first, I would notify my allies, if I had any, and prepare for war. If I don't have any help and can't fight them, then I will negotiate with them," James replied.

"*No wonder all your teachers raved about you, you are a genius,*" Alex thought.

He had always thought that James was intelligent, but this insight on that matter assured him that his son was a genius. Alex realized that his son was more special than he had imagined. When Alex returned to work the next day, he relayed the same explanation that his son had told him to his director and colleagues. The issue that they had been discussing was how to prevent an empire from conquering developing nations without becoming an enemy. There were about ten of them sitting at a long, rounded table. When it came to Alex' turn, he stood up, walked to the front of the room, and began his speech.

"Defending smaller countries against larger nations is seen as immensely challenging and almost impossible due to the significant power disparity. Small countries defending themselves against larger nations have a chance with strong allies and united leadership. If all else fails, negotiating with the larger nation becomes essential," Alex explained.

After he concluded, he went and sat down, then Steve stood up and voiced his opinion as well. Steve concurred with Alex and added that they should report their findings to the UNG (United Nations of Ginnia), also. The rest of their comrades agreed with their takes too, so Steve gave them a task. "Now, I want us to figure out how to control these violent protests in the smaller third world countries and in ours. The riots and genocides around the world are worrying me. I want you to find out the causes of these horrific massacres," said Steve.

From the day James questioned Alex about his profession, he had felt guilty for not telling him the truth. Therefore, lately, he had been thinking of telling him. After James told him about the guys who visited his school that day and how they reminded him of his dad. He had had enough. *I believe it's time to tell him about the agency, although I'm not supposed to,* Alex thought. It had been a long day, the weather dropped, so Alex could feel the coolness of the night from inside the apartment. After Alex showered, he went to his son's room. He stood outside of the room for a few seconds contemplating, then finally, he knocked and said, "come to the living room. I want to talk to you."

"Ok," James replied.

"I see you are persistent," said Alex.

"Yeah," James replied. "Don't ever tell anyone about this, though.

Not even your brother. When he gets older, you can tell him too," Alex stated.

"Ok, dad, I promise that I won't," James replied.

"I work for the agency! But I only work on the inside, doing research. I don't go on any missions," said Alex.

"I knew it. So, what have you been working on lately?" James asked.

"In our last meeting, my boss inquired about reducing terrorist attacks and genocides all around the globe. We still can't figure out why so many countries around the world are going through these problems," Alex stated.

"I believe the reason these kinds of issues come about is due to different views. Thus, you should start with better communication. I know it's not as simple as it sounds, but you must start there. The difficulties arise when the leaders and the groups being led are not on the same page or when there is disunity among alliances. If they could understand that with any group, some are leaders and others are followers, and that there will be differences among any coalition, they might accept their places. Now the question becomes, are they fine with that or not? If there is a legitimate reason for the opposition to disagree with the leaders, that's fine. But when the challenge is caused by envy or hatred, then it turns into a difficult situation. I know other reasons for protests could be poverty, hunger, money, and many more like these, which no one is responsible for," James stated.

"That's so true! Controlling the distribution of guns might also help, or even ending their production altogether," said Alex.

"Dad, since we all know that guns are the bread and butter for so many authoritarians, they are not going to allow that to happen. We've tried many solutions except for educating the public about their moral responsibilities. Therefore, I think teaching the oppressors and the oppressed about morality and a higher power might work. If everyone knew that God exists and that He can see everything that's happening with all of us, then they might think before they wrong one another. The only concern is that some individuals don't believe in His existence," he expressed.

"I totally agree with you. It's worth trying. I can't believe it, son! It seems like you have all the answers," said Alex.

A couple of days later, Alex called Steve in the evening after he left the agency. They discussed more ideas on how to better protect the public. Once again, Alex took advantage of his son's suggestion.

"Can you believe how much James has matured? His feedback on our social issues was remarkable. His argument was that the safest way to demonstrate a revolution is to preach about the almighty to the revolutionists and the administration," said Alex.

Steve listened to Alex as he discussed James' hypotheses and then made a comment and then he asked, "James who?"

"Oh yeah, his name is James! That's impressive considering he's very young. How old is he?" Steve replied before he asked.

"He's eleven." Alex replied.

"Wow! You know what, James' proposal could be the solution. I'm going to use that same judgment in our meeting today," said Steve.

Steve shared James' message with his department members during a meeting later that evening.

"Someone very wise suggested that we teach everyone about the Lord and the significance of taking care of lives, including our own. As for the non-believers of these views, we'll attempt to steer them towards understanding in a logical manner," Steve explained.

Afterwards, Steve directed Alex to go to Sékoubaria, G.D. to assist FSSD (Fabrica Secret Service Department) with research on the west Drakillian situation, marking the first time Alex had to leave the state, as it was the end of James's first semester of sixth grade. Since Alex was from Freeland, Steve thought he was informed about the Drakillian government and that FSSD could use his help. Alex was accompanied by two other BIA members, Antoine, and Ben. It took less than two months for Alex and his colleagues to help the Fabrican administration connect the dots. With Alex's aid, FSSD got a lead on which west Drakillian leaders were working with the Samuel's business. Additionally, they discovered that the west Drakillian officials were trading aluminum, gold, and diamonds for weapons of mass destruction and technologies.

During the last week of the year, which coincided with James's birthday, he decided to celebrate by inviting a few friends over. He was having fun, although he was a little upset because his father not only missed the holidays but was also absent for his birthday. They were playing Grand Theft Auto-Vice City when the house phone rang. James ran and picked it up, and it was Alex.

"Hey son, happy birthday," Alex voiced.

"Hey dad, thank you!" James sadly replied, and his father could hear the disappointment in his voice.

"How is the vacation going?" Alex asked.

"Great, how is work?" James responded.

"Work remains work regardless of the occupation one is in. I wish I was with you guys instead. Anyhow, I just wanted to call you and wish you a happy birthday at least since I couldn't be there with you. I know that my work has gotten in the way of our quality time, but I promise I'll make it up to you when I get back. My boss sent us to Sékoubaria G.D. We're trying to finish the project by the end of the year. When I come home, I will make it up to you big time, okay buddy?" said Alex.

"Okay dad, don't worry, I totally understand," James replied with a little more enthusiasm this time.

"Don't forget to pray. I love you, son!" said Alex.

"Okay, love you too, dad," responded James. "Let me speak to Jeremy!" Alex stated.

"Okay," said James. "Jeremy, dad wants to speak to you!" he shouted out, and then he passed the phone to Jeremy.

"What's going on buddy, are you ready for New Year's?" Alex voiced.

"Yeah, are you going to be here?" Jeremy replied and then asked.

"Sorry to disappoint you but no! I'm still working. Hopefully, I'll be back after New Year's," said Alex.

"What a bummer, dad, you miss the whole vacation!" Jeremy stated.

"I know, but like I told you, brother, I'll make it up to you when I get back, okay?" Alex replied.

They talked for a few more minutes then hung up. After their call, they all prayed and then went back to playing the game.

Even though Peter and Alex were no longer in the same department, Peter hated Alex' humanitarianism. Therefore, he still planned to do away with him. He could not get it out of his mind that Alex' children were hujinns, and one of them could be the superhujinn, growing up right in front of his eyes. This fact scared Peter. His hatred for them grew even more, especially after his suspicion about Steve defending

Alex through his NISA trail came true. He realized that Steve and Mr. Iverson were not against Alex. Peter's bitterness caused him to send some of his agent colleagues to take out Alex. Soon after Alex returned from the capital, on his first day back to work, four armed men were waiting in front of the BIA facility. As he walked out, and crossed the street, a car drove by him and two men on the passenger side started firing, while the third one in the back on the driver's side stuck his body all the way out so he could see the other side where Alex was coming from and fired as well. Alex saw their firearms sticking out of the vehicle windows before they started shooting, so he ran and rolled, avoiding all the shots except two. The car kept moving and Alex fell, then crawled behind another car. Another agent came out of the same facility, rushed towards him, called the police, and he was rushed to the hospital where he received treatment. One of the bullets had grazed his left pectoral muscle, and the other one hit him on his left shoulder. The director of his department gave him two months leave of absence to heal from his injuries.

After Alex' recovery, he was picked up by the BIA global access department, which was directed by Aisha Iverson, Mr. Iverson's wife. Aisha put Alex on the same team as the rest of Steve's original recruits, so he was teamed up with members of his previous team, Ben Durand, Antoine Bryant, Christopher Smith, and Gabriel Houston. Aisha called them the top five options. The department was focused solely on discovering and building relationships with foreign administrations. After getting to know Alex, Steve learned from him that Freeland had one of the richest natural resources in the world, yet the country had one of the poorest economies. Steve figured that the country was either terribly managed or suppressed by a much more developed nation. Either way, they needed help. Therefore, he sent Alex and his team members to investigate this matter. Steve already had the president's approval, so he informed the rest of the administration that he was sending a team to Freeland to explore the country further. He wanted to build a relationship with the western Drakillian leaders so that he could assist them against larger nation's aggression. After the mission was confirmed by the administration, Steve called Aisha and asked her if she had a team to go examine the West Drakillia. Aisha was delighted to hear this because she wanted to send the top five options on their first mission and couldn't think of a better place to send them.

Alex and his wife were watching the news in their living room on a quiet Sunday, the first of March. As they sat there, he thought, "*I haven't spent quality time with my family for a long time. Let me take them out to eat.*"

"James, call your brother and come here!" he yelled out.

"Yes, dad!" James responded.

"Hurry up and get ready. I want to take you out to the movies," said Alex.

"Ok, we're coming," said James.

After the boys finished getting dressed, they came out.

"Dad, what are we going to watch?" Jeremy asked.

"We'll decide once we get there but first, we're going to stop at the mall. I'm leaving in the morning and I must grab a few items."

An hour later, they were at the mall, and Alex bought his favorite album so that he could have something to listen to during the flight.

"Dad, I wanted your opinion on this. When I think about it, I believe that all religions are the same; they just have different interpretations of how to worship the lord," James stated.

"I agree with you one hundred percent. If the one worshiping believes in God and does not associate him with any other deity, he or she is on the right path. Your way or someone else's way may not be the best or the only way, but the intentions and character of the individual are what define his or her faith. That's an enlightening insight that could help everyone if they were conscious of it!" Alex replied.

Afterwards they all walked to the movie theater next to the mall and watched a movie.

The next day, Alex and his team went to Freeland for a mission. They were picked up by Mr. Jordan at the airport. Before reaching their destination, Alex separated from his team and went to meet up with Jacoby Barry, the Freeland president who was a friend of his father. He had dinner with Jacoby, then went to a hotel to meet up with his team. After settling down, Alex went to Vincent's place where his father was staying at the time.

Once he arrived and spoke to his father, he also took the time to call Vincent, who had recently migrated to Rancenia. After talking for a while, Alex put the phone on speaker and said, "Hey Vincent, say hi to Dad, he's here!"

"Hey, Pop! How are you?" said Vincent.

"All praise be to the Lord, Vincent. How about you?" Mr. Jordan responded.

"Same here, I thank the lord." Vincent replied.

They talked for a while, then Alex joined the conversation. "I was just telling Pop that a Jinn friend of mine knows about Holly and the children. We were very close, so I thought I could trust him, plus his brother recruited me. I told him that Holly is human!" Alex confessed.

"No, you didn't! I told you not to trust anyone about this matter," said Vincent.

"I know, I made a big mistake," Alex replied.

"So, you're actually telling me that you are in danger?" Mr. Jordan interrupted and questioned.

"Yes, Dad, but it's a bit complicated because his brother is on my side. He defended me against the NISA administration when they tried to discharge me for it. I believe we'll be fine, but I'm just letting you know what happened in case. This dude not only tried to get me fired, but I believe he also sent the agents who tried to kill me. I just wanted you to know, and in case anything happened to me, please make sure to look after my family and tell them about Peter and his malice." Alex stated.

"Look Alex, if you don't feel safe out there, I'm telling you now, quit and move back home or at least here," said Vincent.

In mid-June, a week before the end of James's spring semester, Alex met with Jacoby Barry and the Freeland administration. Alex introduced himself as a visitor, not a Fabrican agent, so that he doesn't blow his cover. During their time there, they attended a few political events and visited multiple places throughout the country and the neighboring countries.

The day before Alex and his team were set to return, his father fell ill. He requested permission from Aisha to stay with his father, while allowing his teammates to go back. He took care of his father for a couple of days, but when he realized that the sickness had worsened, he took him to Rancenia for better healthcare, as their health centers were more advanced. Despite Alex's efforts to find treatment for his father, he unfortunately passed away. Alex and Vincent took his body back to Freeland for the funeral. After burying their father, they stayed with their family to mourn. Alex and his brother then left at the same time, with Alex stopping in Rancenia for a day before finally returning to Fabrica.

A couple of days later, it was the day of James' elementary school graduation. James, who was the valedictorian, gave a remarkable farewell speech during the ceremony. James' exceptional farewell speech during the graduation ceremony left a lasting impression on many of the graduates. Since it was his first time giving a speech in public to such a large audience, he was a little nervous. He was also self-conscious about his accent, which didn't help. Nevertheless, he gave an incredible speech.

"Hello everyone, may God bless you, our parents, our teachers, everyone here, and everyone all around the world. Education is the key to success, and I know we all know this, but I just thought that I should remind you. School is the best way to achieve your goals, but not the only way to succeed. As we all know, it was not easy, and it will not get any easier, but nothing special comes easy. Let's not forget how much our parents sacrificed and paid for our education. Their efforts and expenses are only worth it if we take advantage of the opportunities we have to learn as much as we can."

James went on about life lessons for almost five minutes, then concluded. "I have a few goals in mind, but my top priority is to work for the government, so I can protect and serve this country or any other countries that need our help against tyranny. As a Drakillian immigrant, I know what it feels like to live in an oppressed country. Finally, I believe that immigrants should have equal opportunities as Fabrican citizens. That is why I will work extremely hard to achieve my goals and when the time is right, I will fight for equality for all. Congratulations to you and thank you everyone for your support!" He bowed, then walked off stage, shook a few hands, and stepped down.

A few days after James graduated from elementary school, he was devastated by the thought of moving to a new school for seventh grade because he wouldn't see Rose anymore. Eventually, he accepted the fact that he was leaving and moving on to a new school, even though he still wished to see her again in the future. His best friend, Sam, had graduated the year prior, so James followed him to the junior high school that he was attending. Sam always had the first experience of every school that they enrolled in.

Alex missed the graduation due to the passing of his father and returned the following month. James was not disappointed in him this time for missing his graduation because he understood that he was attending to his grandfather. Once Alex returned to New Amsterdam City, he heard that Mr. Washington had passed away as well. Steve then moved up to become the new lead director of the Agency. Meanwhile, Alex' wife was thirty-four weeks pregnant, so they were expecting the baby anytime soon. He wanted to be present during her delivery and help her with the kids afterward, so he requested time off from work.

Immediately after Alex met with Steve, he congratulated him on his new position and discussed the passing of his father. Then, he told him that he was very interested in the upcoming director of operations position. Even though Alex did not want to be away from his family, he wanted to be the First Option, and if that meant going away again, he was willing to make the sacrifice. Since Steve was the new director of the agency, his support could influence the decision of who would fill the First Option position.

That same week, all the directors of BIA had to vote on who would be the new First Option. Whoever won would be nominated, but if there were any difficulties or ties, then Steve would make the final decision. The day before the deliberations, Alex took his time and called Steve to remind him to put in a good word for him when the voting started. Fortunately for Alex, the members of the deliberation decided not to vote. Instead, they asked Steve to save the trouble and make the choice since he was far more familiar with all the candidates. Steve had promised his brother Peter that he would help him get the spot, but Peter lost Steve's trust after he betrayed Alex. Although even if Peter had not deceived Alex, Steve had more confidence in Alex after getting to know him for the past year. That was the reason he chose him instead of any other nominee.

Only three days into Alex' break, it was a silent night around three AM, Holly complained about her painful cramps. Alex accompanied her to the hospital instead of calling an ambulance; he drove them. Holly was scheduled to report to the hospital in the morning anyway, so they decided to go earlier at that point. Once they arrived, her pain got worse, so they rushed to her section of the delivery area.

It was a hot and humid morning. Alex walked back and forth in the room as he stressed for his wife and their soon-to-be-born child. He went to the window and looked out to enjoy the view. The grass and the trees were starting to change, cooler even though they were still green from the past spring showers. They had been in the delivery room for over five hours when, suddenly, the baby's head was sticking out of her vagina. Holly cried out louder. Then, she slowly pushed and squeezed her husband's hand at the same time. She gripped him so tight that he felt the same pain she was experiencing, especially since he didn't receive any epidural injections.

"Push, baby, push!" Alex said anxiously.

A few moments later, Holly had given birth to an adorable baby girl. There was blood everywhere; on the floor, the bed, the sheets, and the baby so Alex helped the doctor and the nurses clean up. The baby could not stop crying, even after they cleaned her up. When the doctor finally gave her back to Holly and instructed her to put the baby against her breast to calm her down, Holly said, "It's okay, Jolie, mommy is here!"

Alex stood there looking at them both, mesmerized by Holly's strength and exceptional natural beauty. Then he thought, *"Goodness, my wife is so beautiful; drop-dead gorgeous. How can someone look this angelic in this condition!"* When they finally finished cleaning up the mess, his phone rang. Alex looked at the screen and saw that it was Steve calling.

"Waa, waah!" cried Jolie. Alex walked to the window and slid the answer tab to answer the call.

"PEACE AND BLESSINGS BE UPON YOU Steve!" voiced Alex.

"PEACE AND BLESSINGS BE UPON YOU TOO Alex! How are you and your family?" said Steve.

"We are all fine. How about you and yours?" Alex replied.

"Everyone is doing well," said Steve.

"That's great to hear. My wife just gave birth to a girl, right before you called," Alex announced.

"Wow, congratulations. Tell them both I said hello. I suppose you are extremely occupied right now. Should I call you back later?" Steve asked.

"It's fine, we can talk," Alex replied.

"Waa, waah, Waa, waah Waah, waah!" Jolie cried in the background.

"Alex, just call me back when you are free," Steve suggested as the baby cried, "Waa, waah..."

"Sorry, we can talk, sorry, let me step outside. I assure you it's no problem, I'm not doing anything right now. The baby only wants her mother," he added.

"Ok then if you insist. I'll make it quick," Steve assured him as he muted his phone so Steve wouldn't hear him and said, "Excuse me, baby. I'll be right back."

After he walked out, and closed the door behind him, he unmuted the call, and said, "Ok!"

"So, I just wanted you to know that we have reached an agreement for the new First Option! We've determined that you are ready and capable for the position, hence the reason I picked you. If you accept the offer, then you are the First Option," Steve stated.

"Wow, that's awesome. I can't believe I got it! Not to sound ungrateful, but why did you pick me over everyone else, even your own brother?" Alex inquired.

"Don't fret about it, my brother and all the candidates will be fine! I know he really wanted it, but the way Peter has treated you, he doesn't deserve to get promoted. All my colleagues insisted that I make the call, so I went with the best choice even if that means letting the rest of them down," said Steve.

"Thank you, sir! You are an honest man. No wonder you are our leader," Alex replied.

"I'm honored to be a member of your organization. I will not let you down!"

After Alex expressed with gratitude Steve replied by saying, "I know you are grateful. That was one of the many great reasons I chose you. By the way, I know you are on a leave of absence and might need more time, especially since your wife just gave birth too. However, you must leave for your next mission immediately. You must come in on Monday so we can map out a plan. We are sending you out again, only this time you are going to Bellivia instead of Freeland," stated Steve.

"Ok, I'm ready for anything you need me to do," Alex responded.

"Ok, I'll talk to you later. Don't forget to report to my office on Monday," said Steve.

"Understood. I'll be there first thing Monday morning," said Alex.

"You are scheduled to meet with your team on Tuesday morning. If everything goes according to plan, you should be leaving the day after your meeting. If you don't depart on that day, then by Thursday at the latest. There's an economic crisis going on all over Flowropia, so this mission is urgent. They believe there have been mass counterfeiting activities all around Flowropia," concluded Steve.

Alex had just received two incredible pieces of news that same morning. It was a lot for him to take in, so he didn't know how to react. Not only did he get a response from the BIA, but his wife had also just given birth. Although Alex had just heard the best news as far as his career was concerned, he was unintentionally placed in a bad predicament. While it was fantastic that he got promoted, he also had to leave his wife by herself right after she gave birth.

After the conversation with Steve, Alex took a moment to think. Steve is an incredible man; even though I violated the law, he still looked out for me. I will always trust him with my life and my family's, he thought. After reflecting on Steve's character, he walked back to the room. "Hey honey, I've got great news and bad news. The good news is I'm now the First Option of my division, and the bad news is we've been assigned a mission already. My team and I were assigned a mission overseas before we got the positions. He expressed to his wife with a lot of empathy.

"It's okay honey, don't stress yourself. I just called my sister Katherine, and she was planning to come visit me soon since she's on vacation from her job. She was going to come in two weeks, but I'll ask her to come earlier. I'll see if she can fly out and be here as early as Tuesday or Wednesday. I'll ask her to stay a little longer and help me out. In case she can't, then don't forget James and Jeremy will be here to help as well. You just focus on handling your business over there," replied Holly.

"Thank you for understanding, baby," said Alex as he kissed her on the forehead.

After almost two days in the hospital, Holly was finally released on Saturday night. They took Jolie home. "Baby, I must fly to Flowropia in a few days to be there by Friday. This is a stressful time for me because I don't want to leave you in this condition, but I don't have a choice. The mission is already in action."

The next day in the evening, Alex surveyed his house to make sure that he packed everything he needed for his upcoming trip. After he finished checking for his missing items, he called James to have a talk.

"James, come here and call your brother too," he called out.

Immediately after his father called him, James ran out of his room quickly and left Sam playing with his PlayStation, then he knocked on his little brother's room.

"Jeremy, Dad is calling us." James yelled out to his brother. James was almost six feet tall and still growing. Since he grew taller, he looked even more like his dad's twin. Jeremy also looked like his father; the only difference was that he had his mother's appealing smile and brown eyes. James waited for Jeremy to come out of his room, then the two of them walked to the living room together. Holly was holding Jolie and sitting next to Alex. James and his brother came and sat across from them.

"Waa, waah!" cried Jolie.

"I called this meeting to say goodbye and tell you guys that I'm going overseas again. I just got hired to help build a huge power plant out in Bellivia."

The inner corners of his eyebrows raised before responding to Alex, "Dad, are you moving to Bellivia?" asked Jeremy.

"No, it's not permanent; I'm just going to work over there for the next year or two. I will come see you every time I get a break. James, in the meantime, I need you to look after your mother and your siblings. You hear me?"

"Ok, Dad," replied James.

"You too, Jeremy," remarked.

"Ok!" said Jeremy.

"Make sure to take good care of each other!" remarked Alex before the boys went back to their rooms.

The following morning, Alex went to the agency to go over the first task of the mission with Steve. He ran into Peter on his way to Steve's office. Peter tried to stand in front of Alex, but he walked around him. "Congratulations, Alex, on your promotion as the First Option," uttered Peter.

As Alex walked past him, Peter followed behind, continuing to yap away as Alex continued to ignore him.

"Don't think you are special or anything. You were only selected to be the First Option due to your father's ties with our president. I believe it's Alhassane, correct?" said Peter, trying to discredit Alex. He continued babbling, as Alex continued to ignore him.

"Word around here is that he reached out to our president and recommended you for the position. Therefore, Diallo called Steve and suggested that they choose you."

When they got close to Steve's office door, Peter walked away, and Alex walked in.

"Jinnisallam!" greeted Alex. Steve repeated the same greeting back to him and added, "Are you ready?"

"Of course, I was born for this," Alex answered with so much enthusiasm because he felt better about the mission after getting his wife's support.

"I'm a little nervous because I don't know what to expect, but I still can't wait to execute the plan." Alex confessed.

"I know that going to a new country for the first time is going to be an uphill battle, but if anyone can handle it, it's you. I like to assign the most difficult tasks to my best, which is you and your team." Steve stated.

"I like my chances too," replied Alex.

"If I'm not mistaken, you already have a team, but if you prefer to make adjustments, be my guest," Steve suggested.

"Wow, I can choose my own team as well! I love this," stated Alex.

"Well, of course!" Steve replied.

"That's great, but I'll just stick with the same squad I went with on the previous mission, the top five," said Alex.

"I had a feeling you would say that! Great choice, and don't worry, we'll be there every step of the way. Also, you might be there for a long time, so bring everything you might need," Steve added.

"Ok, I will," Alex uttered with a mixture of excitement and concern.

"Is there an issue?" Steve asked.

"No, not at all," he told him with a straight face and a high-pitched voice to sound convincing, since he didn't want to give off any negative energy.

The next day, on Tuesday, all the directors and agents met in the conference hall. The meeting began, and Steve was the first to speak.

"Hello, everyone, and welcome. We need our best agents on this mission, which is the reason you are all here. This mission will be based in Bellivia, where our FRB (Federal Reserve Board) has reported a large discrepancy in the World Trade Organization Banks. Due to the corruption there, the entire world economy is at stake. We need someone who has extensive knowledge in business administration and experience in the banking industry. That's why we assigned this mission to our top five agents from the Missions Center. Alex, you, and your men will be based in Bellivia because it's one of our allies. There you can exist anonymously until you find out which organization is responsible for these matters and where it's located. We've established that Bellivia was the first country affected in Flowropia by these criminals. I've arranged first-class tickets for you and your squad. You are going to be away for a while, so make sure you pack accordingly."

Alex remembered that he made the promise to his family that he'll go back and forth every break he got, so he asked, "Do we get breaks, so we can come back to visit?"

"Yeah, but you get one every six months because we don't want to risk having any of you on the Flowropia watchlist of foreign agents. Traveling too often causes nations to monitor travelers, especially if the individuals have international passports," Steve replied and gave Alex the go to speak next.

"Okay, thank you! First, I would like to thank Steve, all the directors, and every member of our organization. It's my pleasure to accept this mission, and I'll represent us to my best ability. We'll execute as planned. Thank you everyone for your support," stated Alex.

After the meeting, Alex and his team departed from MRD airport around twelve AM on the next day. Ten hours later, their plane landed late on Friday afternoon. As they walked out of the airplane, the sunlight was gentle to the eyes. Alex stood still for a moment and thought about what a beautiful day it was. Planes were landing and taking off, the sunlight was filtered through light clouds, and birds were singing.

Gabriel stood at five feet eleven inches tall, with a light-skinned, earth-colored complexion. He had close-set brown eyes, a chubby oval-shaped body, a gentle smile, and frizzy hair styled lineup. Ben was around six feet two inches tall, with chestnut skin, almond-shaped blue eyes, a big flat nose, swollen lips, and a scary grin. He had long, straight hair and a stocky build. Christopher was five feet nine inches tall, with a slender, triangular body shape. He had ivory skin, straight blond hair, a beaming smile, a delicate snub nose, and droopy, hooded gray eyes.

Bryant stood at about six feet three inches tall, with a pointed nose and a muscular build. He had honey-colored skin, a rectangular body shape, short, wavy black curly hair, deep-set brown eyes, and a fake smile. He also had a square-shaped head. Victor was five feet seven inches tall, with golden skin, a Roman-shaped nose, roundish-almond eyes, collagen-inflated lips, and an envious smile. He had an average inverted triangle body shape.

Victor had been temporarily working as the head of security for BBI (Bellivian Bureau of Investigation) because he wanted to become a special agent for their company based in Bellivia. The director of BBI, Noah DeVos, a great friend of Aisha, sent Victor to meet the BIA agents at the airport and assist them. Victor was their designated driver, so he was waiting for them at the waiting area with a sign. When Ben noticed the sign that read "BIA assistant," he notified his squad and they all walked towards Victor. Victor showed his identification, "Hello guys, my name is Victor," he said.

After everyone had introduced themselves, Victor said, "Great, this way!" as they walked towards the airport exit.

Moments later, they were outside of the airport by the pickup area next to the truck that Victor drove to pick them up. They put their luggage in the trunk and went inside the vehicle. Alex was the last person to hop in the black Cadillac SUV with dark tints and bulletproof windows. Forty-five minutes later, the five options were in a black SUV with bulletproof tinted windows, headed to the administrative center of the Flowropian Union. It was Alex, Gabriel, Christopher, Ben, and Antoine, along with their driver, Victor. Victor drove, Alex sat in the passenger seat, and the rest of them sat in the back. As Victor drove to the destination, they got acquainted with one another. Christopher, who sat right behind Victor, asked, "Victor, where are you from?"

"I'm from Rancenia, but I moved out here a couple of years ago because I was offered a security position. Last year, I was promoted, so now I work with the Bellivian prime minister's security council. I've been driving the minister around for a few months, so I discovered a lot of new places throughout this country. I can take you anywhere, not just Bellivia, but most of Flowropia as well. I know all the public officials, all the night spots, just name the place and I can take you there." Victor named all the areas that they passed before arriving at their destination.

Once the team had settled down, Victor took them for a spin around the community. From time to time, they traveled to Rancenia and the neighboring countries. A few weeks later, they found themselves in the same seven-seater SUV, on their way to the BIA boarding house. Gabriel uttered, "I know my daughter wasn't the only one disturbed by our departure. I left her crying as she had done for the last few days before we left!"

"Not at all, my lady was depressed too," Christopher answered. He wasn't married yet and he didn't have any kids.

"Holly was very sad, but she didn't want to show it. Nevertheless, my boys were dismissive," said Alex.

"Same here, everyone in my house freaked out," said Ben.

"How old are your boys, Alex?" Christopher asked.

"Jeremy just turned eight and James is twelve," Alex replied as he looked around Drusilla, the capital of Bellivia, and compared it to New Amsterdam City.

"What are the odds? My son Rich is also twelve," said Ben.

"Sam is a year older, he's thirteen now." Antoine stated.

"When we get back, we should get them all together, since Sam and James already know each other," Alex suggested.

"Yes, for sure!" Antoine stated before they arrived at the house and the vehicle stopped.

"We are here," Victor announced.

"Okay, most definitely, guys!" Ben answered, then opened the vehicle door.

After Alex and his team's departure, Peter was notified by Aisha that the final decision was left to Steve. Therefore, Peter felt betrayed by his brother and decided to call him on this day.

"Hello brother, it's been a while!" voiced Peter.

"Jinnisallam, my brother. How have you been?" Steve replied.

"You know, taking it easy. Since you disappointed me with your First Option's call," said Peter.

"Not this nonsense again, Peter. When are you going to let it go? This is business, not personal," Steve responded.

"No problem, Steve. If you're going to continue prioritizing Alex over me, then I'm leaving. I can't work for your agency anymore. Why would you choose him over your own flesh and blood?" Peter expressed furiously.

"I don't have to explain myself to you or anyone, and I don't have time for your deviltry. Do as you wish, bye Peter." Steve hung up the phone on him and continued his work on his computer.

Peter sat there for a moment, devastated and embarrassed. From that day forward, he vowed to never trust him again. A week later, Peter declared his resignation.

Steve had only discussed the existence of other hujinn beings and the future arrival of the most powerful one, with his brother Peter and President Diallo, the Fabrican president who was also a hujinn himself. Steve had told Peter about the coming of a superhujinn because he used to trust him with this kind of information. Even though they were aware of the existence of other hujinns besides themselves, they had never met any others before, except for President Diallo. Thus, they had both been scouting for hujinns for years ever since they had heard about the coming of a superhujinn. Peter was certain that the moment Steve discovered that his children were hujinns, he would protect Alex and his family. Peter also knew that Steve's love for his own kind was inexplicable, so he would observe and protect them to see if James or one of his siblings could be the superhujinn. Peter also knew that he would not harm any of them unless they were a menace to society. Unlike his brother, Peter wasn't looking to protect any hujinns, he wanted to kill them all because he was afraid of the thought of other beings like himself being stronger than he was, whether they had matured or not.

After Peter quit his job, he moved to Flowropia as well. However, instead of going to Bellivia, he decided to stay hidden from Alex and his team by going to Rancenia. He had been longing to go to Flowropia from the moment he found out that Alex was there. He called his closest friend, Antoine, who was still active and a member of Alex' squad, to get information on their whereabouts. He perceived Antoine's resentment towards Alex because he spoke about it often. Whenever they talked, Antoine couldn't stop talking about how much he envied Alex, especially after he learned that Alex was the First Option of their unit.

"I'm sick of him, and those hujinn children of his have to go before they finish developing, or we'll have our hands full," said Peter.

"Don't worry, I've got it under control. I understand how you feel. Mark my words, if that is the last thing we do, we're going to annihilate him and his family," Antoine responded.

They conspired against Alex and his family and decided to work together from that point forward. Samuel and his administration were based in Rancenia instead of Bellivia. After Peter arrived in Rancenia, Mr. Jackson introduced him to his uncle Samuel and recommended him for recruitment. Samuel took Mr. Jackson's advice and retained Peter to the FARN. Samuel was thrilled to add someone who was a hujinn and familiar with the BIA to his organization. A few days later, he met with Peter. After getting to know him, he agreed with Mr. Jackson's suggestion. During his time there, Samuel introduced Peter to his only son, Manuel, who was also a hujinn, but no one knew except for Samuel, not even his own mother.

A few weeks later, the fall semester had begun, and James was in the seventh grade. Alex called his wife and told her that he was moving them to a new location. The BIA helped James and his family move to a two-family house in Bronzeville—a town just outside of Amsterdam. After they relocated, James and his brother's schools were fifty-five to sixty minutes away from their house, either by car or one hour and thirty-five minutes on the train and bus. They had to leave very early to make it on time. Jeremy wasn't going to school that day, so James was going to go by himself. He woke up while it was still cold and dark outside. He got ready quickly and left around seven AM. It turned out that he left a little bit late; therefore, after he got off the bus, he ran and jogged the entire way to school. There were steps to go up the hill, at least the equivalent of a ten-story building, but with his strength being greater than the average man or jinn, he made it up the hill in a couple of minutes. Then he sprinted to the entrance before the doors were closed. He ran up the stairs to the third floor and through the hallway to his homeroom. All that running and he didn't even break a sweat.

Five to ten years earlier, Amsterdam was a struggling neighborhood undergoing development. The community offered activities ranging from safe ones like clubbing and movie-going to unsafe ones like gambling and prostitution. Amsterdam was known for a mix of cultural events and illicit behaviors such as homicides, robberies, and prostitution.

James favored his first semester in seventh grade over the previous fifth and sixth grades due to familiarity with school routines. He learned about mature topics through Oumar, who was well-acquainted with street activities and legends in the community. He started skipping school, spending more time out after school, and getting involved in gambling. He encountered sexual activities, gang violence, and prostitution within the community. James had his first girlfriend during this period, but it was not Rose.

During the end of the fall semester, James went on a school trip to the movie theater with his class, organized by his teacher. This was his second visit to the movies since he had moved to Fabrica, as the theater was conveniently located near his school and home. His first time watching a newly released movie was not actually in a real theater; however, he still watched the movie on a big screen, which was the same size as the screens in movie theaters.

It was Tuesday afternoon when Mrs. Houston took her class on the school bus. Once they arrived, they bought tickets for a movie called "The Man on A Mission," a BIA-related film with a lot of action. James had a blast, and since that day, he researched topics about federal agents and agencies, as well as mission executions. That was the time he also discovered that the theater was close to his home, so he began going there often. He even introduced all his fellow immigrant companions to this kind of entertainment. He had such a great time that going to the movies became his favorite hobby because it became a regular part of his life. Providing him with great entertainment and a break from daily routines. At times he went alone and other times he went with his friends every weekend or on special occasions. He also took his girlfriends to the movies on most of his dates.

Alex and his team were still overseas in Bellivia. Victor not only served as their driver but also assisted them in their investigation. He formed close relationships with all the agents, especially Antoine. After collaborating with them, he directed them to a reserve. He had noticed that the financial institution near their location mirrored the system of the FFRB (Flowropian Federal Reserve Board) disguised under the FARN organization but allowed Flowropian banks to conduct business differently. The branch had a false claim act like the legit FFRB, to pretend that they were the same company. Victor was driving Alex and his squad to the administrative center of the Flowropia Union when they passed by the institution which he suspected. He brought it to their attention, stating, "I believe this bank is a cover-up for a trading bamboozlement, and these kinds of operations are what cause depressions. Their sharp practices could be the reason for the economic crisis around here."

Alex took Victor's suspicions about the depository into consideration and decided to investigate the matter right away. A few days later, they began inspecting the Bellivian banks because of Victor's observation. Alex and his team went to visit that financial institution and notice more ambiguous dealings. To their surprise, that bank was not only corrupt, but they were incorporated. The manager told Christopher that they had other institutions if he wanted to open an account with them in many Flowropian countries.

"If we can only find out who is the head of this company, we can tie him to the rest of the branches," Christopher thought. They inspected a few other nearby locations similarly structured and got more insights. During their inspection of the locations in Belgium, they noticed more unusual activities. They learned that those banks were the only investment banks that did not facilitate the flow of funds to their customers and they had their additional trading desk that other Federal Reserve institutions didn't carry. A few days later, they reported the information to their director of their department Aisha.

Shortly after, Alex scheduled a meeting with the bank manager. A few days later, it was the day of the meeting, but as soon as they arrived, before they could meet with the banker, they ran into five guys who were heavily armed. Their interaction resulted in a deadly battle. There were crossfire exchanges between the two groups, and two of the enemies died at the scene. Alex and his entire team survived, but Christopher and Gabriel were severely injured. To maintain their cover, they fled the scene before the Belgian authorities arrived. Then Alex reflected on the circumstances of the attack for a moment.

"I have a feeling that the manager was expecting us. He must have set up the ambush," he thought.

The next day, Alex called Aisha and said, "I need you to do a closer examination of his background and ties."

From that day on, the BIA monitored the bank manager around the clock. They traced his calls and followed his movements on and off duty until he led them to a man who they believed was the head of the organization. Alex and his team noticed that the manager called and met up with a particular individual more than any other. After tracking his calls and listening to a few, they learned that he made calls to someone in Rancenia by the name of Samuel. Then, he called Aisha back to fill her in on their progress thus far.

"Boss, the bank manager led us to a popular individual named Samuel, and we believe he's the main man," Alex explained.

"Through our examination, we confirmed that these businesses are associated with the FARN organization, which is headquartered in Rancenia. These so-called FFRB companies have printed so much money that it's become untraceable. According to our research, these fake FFRB companies have had the highest fraudulent operation in Flowropia in the past five years.

"Roger, Alex, prepare your team to get ready to move to Larycia, the capital of Rancenia," said Aisha.

"Okay, should I notify Steve, or will you?" he asked.

"I'd rather you call him because he might have some more insight for you," responded Aisha.

Later that evening, Alex called Steve to give him an update on their findings. When Steve picked up the phone, they exchanged their usual greetings and Alex recounted their most recent discovery.

"So, after taking a close look at the embezzlement, we believe that all the suspected investment banks are associated with the FARN. The problem is that they are operating with multiple trading desks, different currencies, and trading internationally. As a result of their trafficking system, it's difficult to tie the business to one manager. However, we know that the perpetrator here frequently makes calls to the FARN organization. We believe whoever is behind this operation is based in Rancenia but we can't substantiate our claim until we go there and verify our discovery. Also, we've determined that David Peters, the director of the RBI (Rancenia Bureau of Investigation) is not aware of the FARN organization's double dealings or the extent to which it has expanded. We can't say the same for the First Deputy Prime Minister of Rancenia, Boubacar Boucher, Michael Alexandre, the Ambassador of Rancenia, and Martin Louis, the Minister of International Affairs. We all agree that the head of the institution is not associated with any Bellivian officials at all. Our driver, Victor, who's a Rancenia native agrees with our discoveries so far and confirmed that some Rancenian administrators are aware of the FARN's operations. We must figure out which officeholders a working with FARN." Alex explained.

"Interesting. So how do you think we should proceed from here?" Steve asked.

"We need more time to verify whether the Flowropia officials are aware of the FARN's deceptive actions or not. What do you suggest?" asked Alex.

"I want you to audit all the groups questionable, starting with Samuel's organization, the Minister of International Affairs, the First Deputy Prime Minister, and the Ambassador, so we can connect the dots," Steve replied.

"No problem. What about the DWU?" Alex asked.

"We'll get to them later. Since you're not sure about these administrations' involvement in these distortions yet, let's verify that first. Then we can go after the WDU leader," replied Steve. "Remind me how the WDU got involved in this mess when it was their organization that brought the Flowropian administrations to our attention in the first place?" he added.

"Oh yeah, after my father passed, Ahmed Toure, the runner-up of the WDU organization, began working with Samuel. I know this because my father's secretary informed me that Mr. Touré's campaign was sponsored by them. Therefore, I believe he must be connected to their conspiracy as well," Alex answered.

"Great work, Alex! Keep it up and do what you must. You have my approval to tailor the mission to your advantage. Just be very careful since Samuel is affiliated with all these regimes," Steve replied.

"Understood!" Alex replied. Then they said their goodbyes and hung up.

Alex and his team were very close to confirming the allegation about Samuel's bank manipulations. He knew that if they could prove his association with the Flowropia bank fraud, they could show his dishonesty and connection to the WDU. Nevertheless, Samuel was informed of the BIA mission against him by his Bellivian associates. As a result, he interrupted the investigation by calling his nephew, Mr. Jackson, to relay a message to President Diallo, Mr. Iverson, and Alex. Samuel planned to frame Alex, hoping that it would divert the BIA away from his own mishaps.

Although Samuel knew these declarations were lies, he just wanted to momentarily distract them by accusing the BIA of misconduct. He claimed that the BIA was in violation of the Fabrican administration's rules and regulations by employing a fugitive. Samuel told Mr. Jackson, to inform President Diallo and all Fabrican agencies that his sources had revealed that Alex was a Freeland fugitive who had stolen a significant amount of money. He argued that he should not be working for the BIA due to his falsifications. After Mr. Jackson spoke to Mr. Iverson and President Diallo, he called Steve and said that he should stop highlighting negative situations about members of other agencies and focus on their own, as they had an outlaw like Alex working for them. Mr. Jackson claimed that his sources had informed him that Alex was not only raising hujinns but that he was also a fugitive from Freeland. Mr. Jackson insisted that Alex had been on the run for a decade.

After Samuel's allegations on Alex, Steve advised him and his squad to return until they come up with a better idea on how to stop the FARN. After six months overseas, Alex and his team returned around the end of February. Immediately after Alex, Antoine, and Ben came back from Rancenia, they kept their promise to each other and brought their boys together. Rich, James, and Sam were brought together, but to their surprise, their children were already acquainted with each other.

CHAPTER TWO

INTRODUCTION TO THE STREETS TIME

In James' seventh grade year, most of his peers were participating in merchandise flipping by the second semester. James considered his friends who were involved in this practice to be courageous. Their ambition surprised everyone in their community, especially the citizens, because they were not accustomed to youngsters of that age having such determination to earn money. The young entrepreneurs influenced many workers and small business owners in their neighborhood. However, the young men turned to illegal activities because they were desperate for money and forgot about the morality of working. Their presence in the business industry was overwhelming, causing many of them to drop out of school early or lose interest in education. Their desire for money was driven by their need to wear expensive brands, which was seen as a status symbol in their community. Limited by their circumstances, they thought like typical kids from impoverished neighborhoods. The youngsters were under immense pressure to keep up with the fashion trends of New Amsterdam City, especially for those who lived there. They believed that living in that neighborhood meant representing a particular style. This mentality pushed them to engage in illegal street activities to fit in. They took pride in dressing up and showing off, even if they couldn't afford it. Trying to maintain the image of wealth, many of them unintentionally became victims of quick money schemes on the streets.

The early introduction to the street field taught James and his entourage that hustling was profitable. Another incentive that they learned was that this type of occupation was flexible. However, some of them had legal jobs, while most of them conducted business illegally. Many of them also sold controlled substances or bootleg content because they couldn't resist this toxic business anymore. A few of them discovered that they could simultaneously go to school and conduct business, so they did just that. These young pioneers enjoyed dealing with the rush, and the fast money that came with it was the motivation behind their hard effort. They enjoyed this type of work because it took less time and effort than selling goods legally, which most retailers were doing. The advantage that the street field had over the typical nine-to-five job was not only its flexibility but also its self-employment aspect. Due to these reasons, most of the youth gravitated towards the excitement. These youngsters were very intelligent too because they analyzed their investments to find solutions to their business problems. They were very sharp, so they stocked up on merchandise that was in high demand commercially.

The young bucks stayed in areas that they were familiar with or at least in one that their friends lived in because they were too young to discover the rest of the city or even outside of it. The young hustlers operated mainly in Amsterdam and Bronzeville. Occasionally, they set up shop in Weenstone and Brookstone. They stayed within the four boroughs that made up New Amsterdam City. They sold their merchandise in Bronzeville most of the time because, out of the four, that was the easiest borough to get to. All the locations they traveled to sell were only a few bus or train stops away. The place they chose to set up on any given day depended on which borough hosted the popular event for that specific day.

The young go-getters knew that there was a high risk involved in dealing with their positions, yet they were up for the challenges, even if that meant going to jail. The ones who worked legally were not earning enough money to support their bad habits, so they found other ways to get jobs under the table or create their own businesses. They found distributors of contraband products and dealt with them. They went to different markets out of town and sold their merchandise inconspicuously. They chose the busiest area of New Amsterdam City streets to do their trades. They bought and sold various items, from bootleg content such as music CDs and music DVD videos to DVD movies, cigarettes, clothes, sneakers, weed, or pretty much anything that was profitable. Some of them began their business by selling candy and things of that nature. It was fascinating because these youngsters grew up in an environment that turned them into entrepreneurs early. Many of them had barely hit puberty before they thought outside of the box. Unlike their elders, their generation made some serious money at a very young age. Sadly, choosing their business over their education cost some of them their freedom as well.

James was committed to his education, so he was a straight-A student. From elementary school until he graduated from high school, he had joined the basketball team, the football team, the track team, and the chess club. He excelled in all these areas, and everyone around him began noticing his brilliance. Everyone he dealt with was aware of his ability because he was extremely talented and outmatched all his classmates in every school he had attended. Some of his peers thought that he was an alien, especially since he didn't talk much.

Unlike most of his peers, James realized that immigrants with criminal records often do not successfully go through the citizenship process. He also knew that they would be lucky if immigration enforcement didn't deport them. Nonetheless, he was in the mix but tactful about it. He never actually sold his own inventory; he just hung around his friends who were in the field. He helped them sell their merchandise to get a cut from their profit. He figured out that if he didn't have his own business going and he was just the help, that he would not get in any trouble if they were to run into the police. His mentality of being the help led him to hang around and get involved in his juvenile friends' actions. He stayed mindful so that he does not get in too deep. He realized that he could hang around them and learn how to make the same business moves that they were making just in case he had to help them or if he needed to start his own business in the future. He continued to go out to sell in the streets with his friends on the weekends or whenever he was free. Even though he was around some illegal activities, he stayed calm. He also knew that he was skating between the lines because if he were to get arrested, by the time he could prove his innocence, he would have to go through the jail system first. Which would be pointless by then, so that was the reason why he was not fully active. James did not take those safety measures because he was not as motivated to get money as his peers; he simply just wanted to be cautious. He was one of the children who was fortunate enough to have parents who were financially secure and interested in their children's education. His parents were not rich or wealthy, but their income was moderate enough to help his entire family and close relatives get through their financial issues. Compared to most of the parents in his community, they were doing well because many of his peers in the neighborhood were struggling to make ends meet and depended on public assistance. His parents tried their best to assist him whenever he needed money. They trusted him to focus on his studies, so they always supported him because they did not want him to work until he graduated from college. Therefore, they kept him occupied with after-school curriculums. His parents' support helped him make a lot of right choices; thus, he went further with his education than most of his companions.

It was a nice day around the end of spring break, the sky was clear and serene. James had just returned home to New Amsterdam City two days before because he had traveled to Rancenia during the break.

He had gone to visit his uncle in Rancenia. Late in the evening, James and Sam put on their best outfits and went out. They had double dates with some girls they met the day before at a wedding party. James and his friend Sam entered the express number eight train on one hundred twenty-ninth street, heading downtown. They got off seven stops later, on twenty-fifth street. The four of them hugged and greeted one another, then went to a restaurant in downtown Amsterdam. As they were eating, James started a conversation, "How do you like New Amsterdam City thus far?" he asked.

"Well, from what we've seen so far, it seems like an amazing place to live; but we don't know anywhere. We have been stuck inside since we got here!" his date Ameera expressed.

"We've only been to the movies, the wedding, and the one party," Chloe, who was Sam's date, stated.

"What?" Sam uttered, "I feel your pain, don't worry," he shrugged his shoulders, then he added, "Is this your first time in Amsterdam?"

"Actually, no, but it's only our second time," Chloe replied.

"It's cool, that's where we come in." Sam pointed to James and himself, then added, "James and I will show y'all around!"

"That's what I'm talking about, I can't wait," Chloe uttered. As James got acquainted with Ameera, Sam was getting to know Chloe. They went to a few places and finally, at the end of the night, they went by the river. Their date went well because they got a goodnight kiss before they left. Afterwards, they took the train back to Uptown. As they were on the train, James said, "Bro, I will be a millionaire one day and help make this an even more amusing city for the future."

"I believe in you, bro, because you are one of the smartest people I know; just don't forget me," Sam replied.

"I won't, I promise I'll give you a cut; but only if you don't mess around and become a millionaire too," James replied, and they burst out laughing.

The young women had only planned to stay for a few days in New Amsterdam City, but they changed their minds after they met James and Sam. Therefore, they decided to stay for a few days afterwards. Five days later, the young ladies left and planned to come back to New Amsterdam City to visit James and Sam whenever they got another break. Afterwards, James and Sam missed them a lot. The next day, after the girls departed, it was another incredible day, so they went to the movies to watch a new release they had planned to see with Chloe and Ameera, but they didn't get a chance to watch it before they left.

Following the movie, Rose, James, and Rich met at the shopping center near Rich's house. They then went to Rich's house as his father was out of state with his team and his mother was on vacation, leaving the house empty for them to spend time together. Charles and Oumar, who were typically occupied with their gang, were contacted to join them.

"What's up, gang? What are you up to?" Rich greeted Charles and asked when Charles answered the phone.

"Nothing, just chilling and macking with O and some honeys," Charles replied.

"Copy, why don't you come over? I'm here with Sam and James, and I've got the free crib," said Rich.

"Definitely, we'll be there in a minute!" Charles responded.

"Alright, one!" Rich responded and hung up. Half an hour later, Oumar and Charles came with their female companions and they all spent time together. After playing video games for hours, James grew tired of winning. Therefore, he suggested that they switch to regular television cable and watch a movie. The young ladies, Oumar, Charles, and Rich drank some beers and smoked weed, but James and Sam didn't. They played cards so that everyone could participate. As they were watching, Rich asked James a question, "What do you want to do when you graduate from college?"

"I want to work for the BIA or the DBI," he answered.

"What, you want to be a cop?" Rich asked again.

"No, a federal agent!" James replied.

"Same difference, they all solve crimes," Rich stated.

"Yeah, I guess," James responded.

Then Rich looked at Sam and said, "How about you?"

Sam looked around the living room as he thought and replied, "Man, I'm not sure, but I'm with James. I wouldn't mind working for the agency either."

Suddenly, James observed that his, Rich's, and Sam's parents were always out of town and returned at the same time. He also noticed that they all knew each other. This connection led him to connect the dots. So, interrupted him, asking Rich, "Where does your father work?"

"Well, I don't know. He never told me, and I never asked," Rich replied.

"Cool, no problem! I only asked because I noticed that every time my dad, Mr. Bryant, and Mr. Durand, goes away too. They always leave around the same time and come back around the same time. Don't you get it? I think they might be working for the same company. Not to mention, they brought us together last time they were here," he explained.

"I think you are on to something, you might be right. I will ask him when he gets back this time. He is coming back on Saturday," said Rich.

"You see what I mean? My dad comes back on Saturday too," James responded.

"What are the chances, my dad too. We've got to get to the bottom of this," Sam stated.

"Anyway, I want to do whatever your dad is doing Rich because he's obviously caking. I mean, you all are getting money because you live in houses and Charles and I live in the projects. It's huge and full of expensive decorations," said Oumar.

An hour later Charles, Oumar, and their female companions exited. They walked together until they got close to Oumar's neighborhood, then they separated, and Oumar went away with the young women. The young men did their usual handshakes by hooking their fingers and pound hugging before going separate ways. Soon after, James and Sam left too. Rich, who was a lightweight, was tipsy with just two beers and a couple of pulls of a blunt; thus, he was drowsy on the couch.

Shortly after leaving Rich's home, James and Sam spotted someone getting attacked by three others across the street. James, being the unselfish hujinn he was, ran across and pushed one of them off, causing the others to stop. The three young men had beaten the other youngster badly, as there was blood all over his face. The attackers were stunned by his boldness, so they paused momentarily before rushing at James. He kicked one of them in the stomach, threw another to the floor, and as he turned around, the third one swung a small knife at him. James broke off the swing with his right arm and punched the attacker in the ribs. It only took James the moves to intimidate them. They were all short of breath, so they spent the next few seconds trying to regain control of their breathing. Startled by his strength, they all ran away. James got down on his knees to help the young man on the floor and recognized him.

"Oh my god! It's Charles," he thought.

"Sam, call an ambulance! I've got you, Charles. It's going to be okay," said James.

When James reached home, his mother was feeding Jolie in the living room. She noticed some blood on his clothes and a small cut on his arm and asked, "Are you okay?"

"Yeah mom, I'm fine. I just intervened on some guys jumping my friend Charles, and I got cut. It's nothing though, they were soft," he replied.

"Baby, I hear a lot of that going around lately. The city has gotten a lot more dangerous. I think you should take up martial arts so you can learn how to defend yourself better," Holly suggested.

"Ok mom, if it makes you feel better, I will," he answered.

James chose to join a mixed martial arts class to reassure his mother, even though he already had supernatural abilities. He dedicated himself to training to be prepared to defend himself against stronger opponents. James and his brother Jeremy excelled in karate, mastering all self-defense techniques. His speed and strength were noticed by fellow students and even his Sensei, standing out for his extraordinary skills.

James had become a skilled basketball player and enjoyed playing with his friends, who respected him. Even former bullies like Charles and Rich had become close to him and respected his game now. They often played in teams of two. James teamed up with Sam, Charles teamed up with Rich. Oumar was included only when one of the regular group members was absent, considered the least talented player of the group.

Since James, Oumar, Rich, and Charles were one grade behind Sam, the four of them hung out together more than with Sam. They played dice and cards, not just for fun, but for gambling small amounts of money against each other and others from the community and students from their school. By then, most of their group smoked weed and drank alcohol. Even though James had not started doing either yet, he hung around them when they did. Oumar and Charles had begun hustling since the summer before they started junior high school, but James was still solely focused on his education. Oumar sold everything from candy to drugs while performing excellently in school.

It was April fifteenth, George Washington Day, a Fabrican holiday. James and his family went to the capital, to visit the capitol. His father took them because the agency had given him and his team a three-month break from work. Alex noticed a drastic change in James since the last time he was around. He saw that James had transformed into a grown man because he was very determined and purposeful. He was earnest about his goals and education. James thought his father could help him understand his individuality a little bit more, so he asked him a lot of questions every time they were together. Alex taught him about his heritage and shared his experiences in Flowropia.

A week after Alex took James and his brother Jeremy out to eat. Holly and Jolie stayed home because Holly was not feeling well on that day. On their way to the restaurant, Jeremy said, "Dad, when I get older, I'm going to buy a Lamborghini Murcielago."

"With the highest grace, you will; in the meantime, I want you to focus on your school," Alex replied.

"Dad, how's the economy in Flowropia? Is it as bad as it's getting here?" James asked. "That's all my economics teacher has been talking about," he added.

"Yes, it's the same there. As a matter of fact, that's where it started," replied Alex.

Suddenly his phone rang. "Wait, give me a minute," said Alex.

It had been two and a half months since Charles was attacked by the young thugs in his neighborhood. He had just recovered from his injuries. Even though he was not fully healed, his circumstances compelled him to become active in the streets again. That day was his second day back since he was assaulted, so James, Oumar, Rich, and Charles went to Oumar's place after school. From that point on, James and everyone started calling Oumar, "O."

After meeting up they went to the basketball courts at the park near Oumar's house and played one-on-one. After the game, everyone else left, except Oumar and James. When the two of them shook hands to go their separate ways, Oumar called James over.

"Yoh, James, let me holla at you for a sec! I wanted you to know that you can make money with me. Whenever you're ready, just holla at me. I got weed if you want to smoke or if you want to sell. If you need a front, I got you too!" Oumar stated, took a pull of the blunt then added, "You want to hit this?"

James declined an offer to smoke from Oumar and walked away. His conscience then tempted him with thoughts about the perceived benefits of smoking, such as appearing cool and becoming more mentally advanced like his friend, Oumar. Oumar hollered as James walked through the exit of the fenced court, "Bro, just try it. I'm telling you, it makes you feel great and forget all your stress."

James stopped and looked back but ignored him. Then he turned around again and walked away.

A few weeks later, school was closed, and it was a very hot summer day. The heat had been radiating all day, so they waited until the afternoon to meet up at the courts by Charles's house. After Charles had been jumped by young gangsters, he started carrying a gun whenever he went out. He had never shown it to his friends or mentioned it. While they were playing basketball, a group of hoodlums approached them and tried to rob them. Charles looked around and realized they were outnumbered ten to five, so he ran to the fence where his book bag was and grabbed the gun. As soon as he pulled it out, they all ran, so he quickly put it back in his bag before anyone else saw it. James asked him, "What the hell are you doing with that, bro?"

"Man, I don't want to hear that. This just saved us!" Charles replied.

"Do you have any idea how much time you can get for that?" James asked.

"I'd rather get caught with this than without it. Spare me that bulls***." Charles responded as he walked away.

A few days later, James, Oumar, Charles, and Rich met up at the same park again. After their pickup game, Charles and Oumar were smoking as James continued to shoot around. "Guys, come with me. I got something to show y'all," Oumar stated before he walked to his

corner where his backpack was and picked it up off the ground. They
gathered around Oumar and he showed his firearm.

"Ok cool, my boy got one too?" Charles uttered.

"Hell yeah, you can never be too safe out here," Oumar stated.

"I'm glad you got that because I was about to ask you to do me a
solid. Walking with me; look, guys, I got beef with the lower east side,
and the boys who jumped me not too long ago. Tomorrow night me and
some of the homies from the block are going to retaliate because those
same busters shot at us the other day in front of the barbershop near my
house. You're all down or what?" explained Charles.

"You know, I always got your back, bro," Oumar replied.

"Count me in too!" said Rich.

"No, guys, you're bugging out. You don't need that, you just need
these hands and to have faith in the highest to protect you," James calmly
responded.

"Nah, bro, you're the one bugging out if you think someone or
something is going to protect you other than this gun," Charles replied,
then paused for a second. "Alright, cool, don't even worry about it. I'm
out, I'll see you tomorrow," he added before leaving.

A little while later, they all had left. When James arrived home, he
called Sam right away. "Sam, you won't believe this. You know that
Charles has acquired a gun and he intends to retaliate against the crew
he has been feuding with. He wanted us all to ride along with him and
I told him hell nah but Rich and O agreed to go with him."

"I'm not with that either, they are way in over their heads. Matter of
fact, add them to the line," Sam stated. They added Charles, Oumar, and
Rich to the line. After a long talk which even led to James threatening
to tell their parents. Oumar and Rich backed out as well. Nevertheless,
Charles did not listen.

A couple of weeks later, late in the evening, Charles, and the leader
of his clique each strapped on small handguns and rode their bikes. They
went around the neighborhood, searching for their rivals. The gang
leader, Double R, spotted four young men who had previously fired at
them in front of the barbershop near their building and were also the
same individuals who had attacked Charles. These young men were
sitting on a bench, engaged in conversation and laughter, completely

unaware of Charles and his sidekick slowly approaching them. Double R quietly said, "There they go! Are you ready?"

Charles swiftly pulled out his firearm and aimed directly at his main target; the young man with braids, dressed in a black and white hoodie, blue jeans, and black Jordan ones. Both Charles and Double R fired one or two rounds, causing all the guys to scatter, and run. Out of fear, a couple of them fell, including Charles' intended target. They quickly got back up and started running again as Charles and Double R rode closer, firing two more rounds. This time, the bullets struck the two young men who had fallen. As they reached the entrance of the building they were fleeing to, one young man fell once more after a bullet pierced his thigh, causing him to crawl, while the other was shot in the foot but still managed to limp inside the building. Double R yelled from behind Charles, "Blast that fool."

Charles hesitated, but Double R screamed at him, "I said finish him!"

Double R urged Charles to shoot a young man despite Charles' hesitation. Charles shot the victim in the back because of Double R's coerce, leaving him motionless on the ground. Charles, his gang, and his gang leader quickly fled the scene on their bikes. Police were contacted by someone who witnessed the incident and an ambulance arrived to take the victim to the hospital. The victim was pronounced dead upon arrival at the hospital. Two days later, Charles was arrested at Hilton State, located twenty-two hours away from New Amsterdam.

A month later, Double R went to visit Charles in jail.

"Charles, what happened? You were supposed to show up with the rest of your crew the day we went after the Lions' Den gang," questioned Double R.

I know, King. James talked them out of riding with us," admitted Charles.

"I knew it, that lame! He's a sucker! But I've got something for him," declared Double R.

Double R was furious about this news, so a couple of days later, he paid a visit to James. Even though it was five years ago, Double R wanted to teach James a lesson because he had interfered with his plan. Double R and his mob went to the park where James, Rich, Sam, and Oumar always hung out to beat up James. Little did they know that

James was not a regular person, so they tried to fight him with their bare hands, even though weapons wouldn't have helped them either. Double R approached James as he was sitting down and resting from a game he had just finished.

"Yeah, punk, I heard what you did!" shouted Double R.

"What are you talking about?" replied James.

"Don't play stupid. Charles told me you're the punk who left him hanging the day we went to clap back at those boys from the Lion's Den projects," accused Double R.

"Yeah, I did, and I'm glad I didn't go with you, or else we would've been sitting in jail with him," retorted James.

"Enough! Gang, mess this mother lover up!" commanded Double R.

Oumar stepped in between them and said, "No bro, it's not going to go down like that. You're going to have to go through all of us."

"O, I've got this. Trust me, I've been meaning to beat the hell out of this fake gangster. Not to mention he got Charles into this mess," said James Oumar aside and prepared to engage in a physical confrontation with the Double R by assuming a boxing position.

to the side and put his hands up in a boxing position.

A few seconds, James had easily defeated all five guys by himself. He continued hitting Double R even after he was knocked out. Thankfully, Oumar asked him to stop, and he listened.

FIVE YEARS LATER

Manuel Shirac had taken over the FARN organization after his father, Samuel, passed away the previous year. He stood by his office window, observing the city's landmarks while vowing to identify and seek vengeance on the agents behind his father's death.

A few days later, he met with Mr. Boucher to discuss some business and learn more about his father's past.

"I was inquiring about the business investment we discussed the other day," said Manuel.

"Hello, Mr. Shirac, I'm glad you called and I'll be happy to assist you," replied Mr. Boucher.

"I was telling you that your father and I worked together for a long time before he passed. May his soul rest in peace! We put a lot of money into our off-the-radar FFRB corporations, and it paid off big time because we had over one hundred branches throughout Flowropia before we went into liquidation due to the BIA investigation. So, if you are interested, we can rebuild the business together and open more institutions all over the world," said Mr. Boucher.

"Thank you for sharing information about your past business ventures with my father. I'm sorry to hear about the liquidation of the under the table FFRB corporations. While it's intriguing to think about rebuilding and expanding the business, I would like to know more about the BIA investigation and understand any potential risks involved. Additionally, I would like to explore other business opportunities as well. If you can provide more details about the investigation and the reasons behind the liquidation, I'll consider investing some money and see how that goes, then we can build from there," said Manuel.

Mr. Boucher found pleasure in Manuel's accordance and smile.

"Great, next week, I'll introduce you to the rest of my entourage, Martin, and Michael. We all worked with your father and used these companies to embezzle funds through your central reserve bank," he said.

"Just remember, I want to keep my involvement discreet to avoid any unwanted attention to our FARN business. I can't have the RBI or any of the Flowropian administrations targeting the organization again after working so hard to get it cleared. If all goes well, I'll proceed to open more financial centers all over Flowropia and have my agents manage them for me," said Manuel.

"All right! Before I forget, I've been doing some research, and I may have some information that could help you in your quest for justice regarding your father's passing," said Mr. Boucher.

His heart raced with anticipation. "That's great to hear, Mr. Boucher. Please, tell me everything you know," said Manuel.

Mr. Boucher cleared his throat before continuing. "As I mentioned before, I have contacts within the BIA who shared some confidential information with me. They claim that certain agents were involved in tampering with your father's vehicle, which ultimately led to his accident and explosion."

Manuel felt a mix of anger and grief wash over him. "Do you know who these agents are?"

"I can provide you with some names, but you need to understand that these are sensitive details. Exposing them could have severe consequences," Mr. Boucher cautioned.

Manuel took a deep breath, mustering up his determination.

"I understand the risks, Mr. Boucher. It's time for the truth to come to light. Please share whatever you can," he said.

Mr. Boucher hesitated for a moment then said, "Based on the information I received, three agents within the BIA were involved; Alex Jordan, Ben Durand, and Gabriel Houston."

Manuel's mind raced as he tried to comprehend the names.

"Thank you, Mr. Boucher. This is invaluable information. I will make sure they pay for what they've done," said Manuel.

"Be careful, Manuel, the BIA is not an organization to be taken lightly. It may be wise to approach this situation strategically." Mr. Boucher warned him.

Manuel nodded solemnly. "I will proceed with caution, Mr. Boucher. Your assistance has been immensely valuable. I won't forget it."

As they ended the call, Manuel knew that his quest for justice had taken a significant leap forward. Armed with the names of the agents responsible for murdering his father, he vowed to uncover the truth and make them pay for their actions, ensuring that justice would prevail.

Meanwhile, David Peters called Steve and informed him about

the escalating tension between Rancenia and Bellivia about the FFRB fraud. He revealed that the Bellivian administration was accusing the Rancenian administration for the Bellivian crisis, which was causing unrest throughout Flowropia as well.

Following Steve's conversation with Mr. Peters, he ordered the top five to return to Rancenia and gather information on the new leader of FARN, as well as his association with FFRB. Consequently, Alex and his squad were ordered to go back to Lareseon to complete the mission they had started. They worked tirelessly to gather evidence against the FARN and its ties to the corrupted Flowropian Federal Reserve banks. During their investigation, they uncovered a shocking revelation: Mr. Louis, Mr. Boucher, and Mr. Alexandre were involved in the FARN's operations, making them the real operators behind these activities. Alex immediately stored the evidence on a computer drive and placed it in a secure location. The information they had distinguished the responsibilities of any other Flowropian administrations' involvement.

At that moment, it had been five years since Charles was arrested and he was still locked up. After graduating from junior high school, James, Charles, Oumar, and Rich were accepted into the same high school as Sam. All of them had graduated from high school, except for Oumar, who dropped out when they were in tenth grade. James, a freshman college student, saw significant improvement in his superpowers over three months. He could now hear the thoughts of others from a close distance, alongside his enhanced normal hearing. Initially he was cautious of his newfound ability but he eventually learned to control and selectively listen to mind noise.

Meanwhile, Steve was also informed by Mr. Peters that Manuel was the successor of the FARN organization, so he ordered the top five to prepare to execute an anonymous mission in Rancenia. Alex, Antoine, and Ben were scheduled to go back to Flowropia in a few weeks, so they all gathered at Ben's house to spend time with their boys. During their discussion about the previous mission in Flowropia, Alex observed signs of jealousy from Antoine.

"I can't believe after all this time, you are still the first opinion. If that was me, I would've solved this Flowropia crisis already," said Antoine. "Is that so, and how would the great Bryant do that?" asked

Alex. "Well, for starters, I will not consult with anyone in our agency anymore, and I will not come back until I find the leader of this corrupt organization." Antoine replied. "Ok, good for you! We'll finish this conversation another time, I gotta go. James, time to leave!" Alex hollered with frustration because he had noticed that Antoine was jealous of him for having the First Option position.

"I can't believe Steve chose this maniac as the First Option, he doesn't know how to lead," Antoine thought as Alex and James prepared to leave. James couldn't help but overhear their conversation from earlier. His improved ability to read minds had allowed him to pick up on Antoine's thoughts from the distance he was. Curiosity getting the better of him, he approached Antoine and Alex.

"Hey guys, sorry to interrupt, but I couldn't help but hear your conversation. What is the First Option?" James asked, his curiosity piqued.

Antoine, Ben, and Alex shared a surprised look before Antoine spoke up. "Oh, it's nothing for you to worry about, James. It's just some sensitive matter we're dealing with at work."

"Freaking monsters," he thought as Alex and James opened the door.

A moment later, Alex and James were in the car heading home. James raised an eyebrow, sensing that there was more to the story Antoine had told him earlier. "Come on, dad. You've known me for years. You can trust me. Plus, with my superpowers, maybe I can help," he said.

Alex sighed, realizing that James wasn't going to let it go. "Alright, James. But you must promise not to breathe a word of this to anyone else. It's classified information."

James nodded in agreement, excited to be let in on the secret. "I promise."

Alex explained, "We've been investigating the Flowropia economy situation for a while now. It involves a powerful and corrupt organization called FARN. They have been causing chaos and instability in various parts of the world, and our agency has been trying to track down their leader to bring them down. Antoine is just upset that he is not in charge of our team, I am!"

His eyes widened in surprise. "Wow, that sounds intense. How come I've never heard about this before?" said James.

Alex chuckled. "Well, as I did say, it was classified information. Only a few people within our agency know about it. We've been working on this case for years, but it's proven to be a highly elusive target."

James couldn't help but feel a surge of excitement coursing through him. "Well, if there's anything I can do to help, let me know. My powers have been improving, and perhaps with my ability to read minds, I can assist in finding some crucial information. I overheard Mr. Bryant calling you maniac and call us both monsters right before we walked out."

Lex considered James' proposal and provided a response, "I appreciate your willingness to help, but you are too young to get involved in BIA matters. I'll consider it after you finish college. I'll keep that in mind and discuss it with my director. Just remember, I prioritize your safety. Be careful around Sam since you know how his father feels about us."

James nodded, understanding the gravity of the situation, and said, "Of course, I won't jeopardize my life in federal matters yet. However, let me know if there's anything I can do to help you."

After Antoine and Sam left, Antoine said, "Sam, I advise you to stay away from your friend James, I believe his family are maniacs."

"I know, James is so weird. He's been abnormal. I always thought he was a freak since elementary. I thought I was nuts but, I'm glad someone else noticed it," replied Sam.

The next day, Alex and his team were back in Rancenia. However, that time around they stayed in Stanford, a small country which bordered Rancenia, to stay undercover from FARN associates. After a while, Alex ran out of patience and was bored of commuting to avoid being noticed by a member of the FARN. Therefore, he took his team to Rancenia. He made this decision on his own without consulting his crew or his directors. Upon their arrival, they studied the activities around the FARN headquarters and followed the members of the organization for a few days.

As Manuel and his troupe were making plans about how to go after Alex is his team. Alex and his group were making significant progress in their investigation. They were determined to expose the corrupt activities of the FARN and its ties to the Flowropian Federal Reserve Board. With the evidence securely stored, they were ready to confront their targets.

Not too long after Alex and his squad went to Flowropia, Manuel assembled a team of five agents and traveled to New Amsterdam City, intending to take down the BIA agents responsible for his father's death. However, he soon received a concerning message from Mr. Boucher. He informed him that Alex and his squad were back in Larycia, investigating their administrations and the FFRB. Realizing that his other illegal operations could be exposed, he flew back to Rancenia the following day. Having done some research on the last time the BIA was in Rancenia and finding out that Victor was a huge lift for them, he reached out to him. Manuel hoped to sway him to his side of the battle. He convinced Victor to join him and his organization and destroy any evidence that implicated him in the corruption and offered him a significant stake in the FFRB, along with promises of power and control. After some initial skepticism, Victor was convinced by Manuel's guarantees of bureaucracy and agreed to join forces.

With Victor now on their side, Manuel saw the advantage this partnership would provide, especially since Peter, the only guy affiliated to his organization, had returned to Fabrica after Samuel's passing. This new alliance would give them an advantage over Alex and his group or the other Flowropian administrations that might come after them. Samuel was aware of the scrutiny from the BIA, RBI, and BBI, but he also wanted to be wary of any other unknown top agencies that might pose a threat to him.

As the tension escalated, both sides were gearing up for a showdown. Alex and his team were determined to bring down the FARN, uncover the extent of their corruption, and their accountability for the Flowropia crisis, while Manuel, Victor, and their associates were prepared to protect their illegal empire at any cost. The stage was set for a high-stakes battle that would test the alliances, strategies, and loyalties of everyone involved.

James had attended college for close to three months by then. Though that was the first time he decided to enroll in a different school than the one Sam was attending, it was the disagreement between Alex and Antoine that caused the friendship between James and Sam to completely fall apart. James was thankful for his cousin's migration because he was his partner in crime since they were toddlers. They had a close bond and enjoyed chasing after girls.

A few weeks later, the fall semester ended, so James was on break from school. It was freezing cold, with the howling wind blowing heavily. Everyone outside was bundled up with multiple layers. Before leaving the house, James looked at Alpha and said, "It's freezing out there. That's not going to be enough, here you can wear my NORTHFACE Jacket!"

"Ok, thanks!" replied Alpha. James and Alpha walked out of their house, wrapped up, and headed to the shopping strip next to his cousin's job, looking for a girl. Moments later, James said, "You feel that?"

"Yeah, it's super cold," Alpha replied.

They stopped by a store to warm up and looked at some outfits. Then James said, "Cousin, here in the city, if you want to get respect and get laid, you must dress to impress. Get stuff like this!"

"Bro, how am I going to afford these kinds of clothes?" Alpha questioned James.

"Don't worry, you can use my clothes and sneakers," replied James.

It had only been close to five months since Alpha moved to New Amsterdam, so he didn't speak much English at that point and James wanted to help him overcome his language barrier and improve his communication skills with girls. After browsing for twenty minutes, they saw a girl walk into the store they were passing, and James noticed Alpha's excitement towards her. He assumed that Alpha found her attractive, so he pushed him and said, "Go after her!" Alpha followed her in the store even though it only carried female products. He tried to communicate his feelings but struggled to express himself, so she walked away. James noticed that he was having a hard time, so after his second attempt, he tried to teach him how to talk to girls. The next girl they ran into, James said, "Watch this!" to his cousin. He approached the girl, spoke smoothly, and got her number, then walked back. "Listen, bro, in this country, first you have to get the money, then you get the power, then the girls will come," he said, a funny inside joke they had about the movie Scarface. They both burst out laughing.

A few days later, it was a very cold day. There had been a blizzard the night before, resulting in two to three inches of snow, and it was still snowing. Despite the cold and snowy conditions, Alpha, Rich, and James decided to venture out to Amsterdam Park to celebrate his birthday. As they explored the area, they happened to pass by the BIA building where their parents were employed, triggering memories of a previous conversation they had shared. While making their way back, the trio passed the federal building adjacent to the BIA center once more when James noticed flames engulfing a building across the street. Without hesitation, he sprinted towards the scene to rescue those trapped inside. Little did they know that the fire had been deliberately started by Manuel's men as a distraction, allowing them to set up surveillance in the nearby buildings surrounding the BIA center.

Alpha had started working for Benjamin, his older cousin who was Vincent's first kid. Benjamin had his own clothing store so Alpha and James hung out there often. Even though James didn't work there, he could not stay out of the store. He learned a lot about business management, investing, advertising, and fashion from being around the establishment. It was the day of New Year's Eve, and Benjamin invited a famous boxer to help promote his business. The store was packed, and the line went around the corner as the undefeated fighter signed autographs, took pictures, and spoke to the customers and bystanders.

Immediately after the promotional event, James, Alpha, Benjamin, and another employee were cleaning up the place when two armed robbers entered the store. One was wearing a black mask, while the other was wearing a blue mask. They pulled out pocket pistols and said, "Everyone get on the floor and empty out your pockets." The robber with the black mask stopped and looked at his partner, then said, "Killer, collect the money." He paused, then continued, "Wait, which one of you has the keys to the safe and the register? I want all the money in here!"

As Benjamin started to rise his hand, James raised his hand before him and said, "I do!"

With a look of confusion and concern, Benjamin laid back on the floor, and the robber instructed James to get up.

"Ok, where is it?" the man with the gun asked.

James pointed to his right and said, "It's in the back."

Cool, let's go get it, hurry up!" he said, pushing James with the gun. "Killer, watch them!" The robber said and followed James to the back.

As soon as the gunman saw the safe, he tried to hit James with his gun. James quickly sensed the threat and applied one of his self-defense techniques to disarm the robber and take his gun. The sound of the attacker falling caught the attention of everyone else in the store, causing the other thief who was watching the hostages from a distance to become distracted. Seizing the opportunity, Alpha and Benjamin swiftly stood up. Benjamin grabbed a baseball bat from behind the counter, while Alpha picked up a piece of wood that they used to hold the doors together during closing hours. They threw the objects at the distracted burglar, but he managed to dodge them and fled towards the back to check on his partner. However, he ran straight into James, who swiftly slammed the door into him, knocking him unconscious. James then stashed away both pistols and proceeded to drag both intruders out of the storage room.

Weeks later, Alex and his crew were confronted by security for trespassing. After the clash they killed ten FARN agents who were on duty and Alex inspected the facility and found some signed documents in Manuel's office. These documents tied Mr. Boucher, Mr. Louis, Manuel, and Mr. Alexandre to each other and the FFRB fraud. Later, he contacted Aisha and disclosed their discovery to her. Aisha was surprised yet proud of his decisive command, especially the fact that he relocated to Rancenia without permission.

Following his request, Aisha turned over the official papers that she got from Alex to Steve and contacted Steve. Aisha expressed her concerns about the economic crisis impacting Flowropia and emphasized the need for prompt action and warned against retaliatory attacks without solid evidence. Aisha informed Steve that Bellivia was targeting Rancenia and stressed that it was crucial to not blame the entire country, but rather focus on the FARN organization and its associates. She also suggested that Steve notify the Fabrican president so he can assist by informing Noah DeVos about their new developments.

After Steve reviewed the documents that exposed Manuel and his associates' corruption, he called Aisha back the next day and confirmed that he believed that their analysis was accurate. As soon as Aisha finished talking to Steve, she called Alex right away and congratulated him and his team and told him that he will order a meeting with his cabinet and all the leaders of the Fabrican agencies.

"Great job, guys. I spoke to Steve, and we agreed that you have enough evidence to convict Manuel and his associates," said Mrs. Aisha.

"Terrific! Where do we go from here, should I pursue the mission or look for more evidence?" asked Alex.

"Stand by until Steve shares the findings with our president or the UNG and see what they decide," replied Aisha.

"Very well, just give me a buzz," said Alex.

Due to Victor's betrayal, Alex and his squad had to change their approach to the mission, even though they retrieve crucial information about Manuel's operations. Thus, after only a couple of months in Rancenia, they left again before completing the mission. Wanting to prevent any unnecessary conflict, Alex delivered the records he found at Manuel's establishment to Aisha himself. "Manuel and Mr. Boucher are the main cause of the Rancenian and Bellivian dispute. The FARN is manipulating the Rancenian Federal Reserve banks so I suggest you inform Steve so he can notify the president, Mr. Peters, and Mr. DeVos about the situation," Alex shared his perspective with her.

Alex recommended to Aisha that she ask Steve to request the president's intervention, advising the Bellivian president to postpone attacking Rancenia or other countries until their investigation was completed.

Weeks after, it was the time of rebirth; most trees had blossomed and the flowers had finished pushing through. Steve was staying at the Fabrican capital for a few weeks because he was helping Diallo make a choice for the next head of FSSD. Alex walked side by side with Aisha as he looked at the vibrant greenery and took a deep breath to enjoy the fresh scent of the rain. Alex had accompanied Aisha to Sékoubaria, G.D. for the BIA meeting. It was the day of the meeting ordered by the Fabrican president. An hour later, Alex and his partners waited outside the room as Aisha, Steve, and the rest of the directors were inside the BIA headquarters Assembly Hall. Steve addressed the congregation first.

"Good afternoon, everyone! Thank you all for being here. As some of you know, I called for this conference today to inform you all that we have a serious problem in Flowropia. If you don't do something right away, it might backfire on us. As you all know, Manuel and his entourage have run one of the world's largest bank frauds, and before him, it was his father, Samuel. He can't be trusted at all. Given their prior experience, I want the top five options to continue leading this investigation. Steve, when the time comes, I trust you to send your best team over to Rancenia. For the time being, just have some of your agents monitor Manuel's movements. Once I coordinate with the UNG, I'll inform you. Then your agents can move in with a more strategic approach to capture him and his entire association," Steve explained.

Two hours later, Aisha, Alex, and his colleagues were on a plane flying back to New Amsterdam and discussing what transpired at the capitol. "The president plans to take swift action to address the situation, so for now, just hang tight," said Steve.

"Thank you for sharing this information, Aisha. I really appreciate your trust and support," replied Alex.

Meanwhile Manuel had recently noticed that the documents that linked him to his double-dealings were missing, he became worried so he called Mr. Jackson. "I want you to retrieve Peter's contact information. Having worked for the BIA, I believed that he could be very useful, so I need to speak to him," said Manuel.

"Give me a minute," said Mr. Jackson. He put the call on hold and reached out to some of his colleagues and acquired Peter's phone number then reconnected with Manuel, "Ok, I found it!" said Mr. Jackson.

"Ok Duan, thank you. I'm going to call him now, I'll call you later!" said Manuel.

"Ok," replied Mr. Jackson.

A few minutes after Manuel and Peter were on the phone.

"Some BIA agents attacked my men and stole some very important documents of mine. Do you have any idea who it might be?" said Manuel.

"I think it's the same guy I told your father about before his passing, Alex. He's the reason for this ongoing investigation because he is the most intelligent individual I have ever come across. Plus, he's the BIA First Option. I know it's him," said Peter.

"Alex and anyone traceable back to us must be destroyed as soon as possible. I'm going to send Victor out there to do the job for me. Assist him as you know he's not familiar with your country. Peter, I already have an insider and he doesn't work for the BIA, his name is Mr. Jackson. He's one of the directors of ISA," he said.

"Oh yeah, that's right. Your cousin, I know him! Did you know that he was the one who introduced me to your father?" replied Peter.

"No, I didn't have any idea. That's fantastic! So, the next thing we need is someone who still works for the BIA that we can trust to help us," said Manuel.

At that point, Peter remembered that Antoine was not fond of Alex either because he was jealous of him for being the First Option. "I know the perfect man; his name is Antoine. Not only does he still work for the BIA, but he's also part of Alex's squad. I'll introduce you guys later."

A few days later Manuel called Mr. Jackson to inform him about his plan. "I'm going to send some of my guys after Alex until I'm free to go. It's only a matter of time before they come for me, so I must retrieve my documents and destroy them before they end up in the hands of the UNG. I must eliminate Alex and all his associates also because this ongoing investigation will not stop until he's dead. Since I'm occupied finishing up some settlements with Mr. Boucher, I sent Victor and some agents instead." Manuel explained.

"Ok, I'm here if they need assistance and my men are also on standby," replied Mr. Boucher.

Right after Manuel's conversation with Mr. Jackson, he sent his representatives to Fabrica. A few hours later, since Manuel knew Victor would be in the air and wouldn't not have any connection, he called Mr. Jackson back and asked him to relay a message to Victor.

"I'm going to fly out there in a couple of weeks. Tell Victor and all my men out there to go after Alex with all that they have. Also, don't forget to pay a visit to his home and the homes of the members of his squad as well," said Manuel.

A few weeks later, Manuel, along with some more of his men, also landed at MRD airport. Manuel and his men were picked up by Peter, Victor, and Antoine. Peter introduced Antoine to Manuel, together they all discussed the task. "With your help, since you still work inside the BIA, we will get Alex in no time," said Manuel.

"Since we are in Fabrica, I would like to take the lead, plus I know everything about the BIA and the director is my brother," Peter proposed.

"Is that so? That's great to know. Tell me more about the BIA and why they chose him over all the other agents to be the First Option?" said Manuel.

"For starters, I used to work with Alex before I found out he was a sellout because his wife is human and they have hujinn children," Peter added.

Manuel and Victor both frowned when Peter mentioned that his wife was human, so Manuel questioned him before he continued. "Wait, you mean to tell me that his children are hujinns?" Manuel questioned.

"Yes, he told me himself," Peter replied.

"I tried to take him out, but the BIA was on his side, so I gave them a proposition: to either keep him or me. As you can see, they chose him and made him the First Option," said Peter.

"Please don't remind me of how they picked that prick over the rest of us," said Antoine.

"The entire agency is led by my brother Steve, and Alex is just an agent. If kept alive until they mature, his kids could be very dangerous," Peter stated before Antoine cut him off and spoke.

"Yeah, but the main individual we need to be concerned about for now is Alex because he is onto us. Alex is very intelligent, as are the rest of his team and family members. We'll deal with them after he's gone," said Antoine.

"Look, Manuel, we wouldn't be vindicated even if we kill Alex unless we kill the leader, Steve, all his team members and their entire families as well! Believe me, we must take out all of them. Even his children because they are more of a threat to us than he is," said Peter.

"No problem, we'll get them all, but meticulously because I don't want this to trace back to us. Understood?" asked Manuel.

"Yes, understood," Manuel replied. "We'll proceed with caution and ensure that we eliminate the entire threat without any trace leading back to us."

Manuel then turned to his men and gave them specific instructions. "Listen up, everyone. For now, our target is Alex and his family. We need to approach this carefully and methodically. Gather all the necessary information about their daily routines, habits, and vulnerabilities. We'll strike when the time is right, making sure to leave no room for mistakes."

Afterwards he looked at Peter and Antoine and said, "Since you have insider knowledge about the BIA and Alex, I want you to actively participate in planning the operation. Use your knowledge to our advantage. Victor, I want you to coordinate the logistics and ensure that we have all the necessary resources in place."

Manuel paused for a moment, his gaze focused and determined then he continued.

"This operation needs to be executed flawlessly. We can't afford any slip-ups or for anything to lead back to us. Remember, our main goal is to eliminate the threat completely. Once we take care of Alex and his family, we can then deal with the rest of the BIA and his crew if necessary."

The men nodded in understanding, their determination matching Manuel's. They knew the risks involved, but they were willing to do whatever it took to protect their organization and ensure their own safety.

Later that day Manuel called his cousin Mr. Jackson.

"I just discovered that Alex's children are hujinns," said Manuel.

"Yeah, that's the rumor that's been going around for a while now," Mr. Jackson confirmed.

"Well, if this is true, they all must be destroyed as soon as possible. I can't risk having a hujinn come after me. I might as well kill them while they are young," Manuel added before ending the call and dialing Mr. Boucher to fill him in on his plan.

"If you must know, Alex also fathered hujinns.

"I don't think I heard you correctly. He what?" Mr. Boucher exclaimed.

"You heard me correctly; he's married to a human, and they have two or more hujinn children," said Mauel.

Mr. Boucher was surprised by this revelation so he made a menacing remark.

"Now, we must murder Alex and his entire family; your father told me about hujinns before he passed away," he said.

A couple of weeks later, Alex met with Steve to get an update about Aisha's plan on Manuel. As soon as Alex went inside the building, Antoine called Manuel and informed him about Alex's position, mentioning that Alex had just gone inside the BIA facility to meet with one of their directors. Half an hour later, Manuel and his group parked their car, a Two Thousand and Five Cadillac Escalade with pitch-black tints, a mile away from the meeting location and waited for Alex to come out. Alex and Aisha were inside the United Nations building having a meeting when Manuel noticed the high security around the facility. Manuel was determined to ambush Alex, regardless of the protection.

"We must attack him today. I'm tired of all this camouflage, and I want to get back to business," Manuel proclaimed.

"We can't attack him here; let's wait until next time he goes to Sékoubaria, G.D. where he'll be isolated." Peter suggested.

"How would you know the next time he goes there?" Manuel questioned him.

"Trust me, I know him. Antoine told me that Steve takes him there every other week to meet with the president and Mrs. Washington, who is from there," replied Peter confidently.

"I think Peter is right. Let's hold off for a while!" Victor chimed in.

Having Antoine as his mole, Manuel believed he had an advantage over Alex. He asked Antoine to provide him with Alex's direct cell phone number. Afterwards he called him, "This is Samuel's son!" said Manuel.

"Come again?" Alex double-checked the name and number, as he asked. "I said the man you killed in Rancenia about two years ago was my father. You probably thought you were going to get away with it, but I'm going to make you pay for that!" said Manuel before he hung up.

At that point, Alex was extremely bothered, and concerned about his family, so he called Steve. "Hey buddy, can you put Gabriel on the line as well? I have something very important to share with you two," Alex said.

"Hang on," Steve replied and added Mr. Iverson to the line. Thus, they were on a three-way call. "Hello, Gabriel, Alex is on the line, and he asked me to add you," said Steve.

"Okay, no problem. Hey Alex, how are you and your family?" Gabriel uttered on the other end.

"Hello, Mr. Iverson, they are fine. It was like you read my mind. That's the reason why I wanted to speak to you. Lately, the FARN officials have been calling me and threatening me, my men, and our families. I just wanted to inform you," revealed Alex.

"I understand that you're concerned about the safety of your family,

Alex. It's important to have a support system in place in case of any unfortunate circumstances," stated Gabriel.

"If something happens to me, can you please look after my family?" Alex asked.

"Well, of course! I understand how vital it is to have trusted individuals who can assist and support your family during difficult times. That's why I enforced that rule in the department for all our agents," replied Steve.

"I understand that you're concerned about the safety of your family, but planning for the worst-case scenario can be counterproductive. Instead of focusing on what might happen, it would be more beneficial to focus on ensuring your safety and taking precautionary measures to protect yourself and your family," responded Gabriel.

While Steve, Christopher, Gabriel, Aisha, and Alex were at the capital, Antoine sneaked into the BIA Security Council and stole Manuel's original documents. Then Antoine met with Victor and gave the executive order documents to him. These papers contained agreements and weapons distributions between him and his associates and went back to Flowropia. Once Manuel got a hold of the documents, he decided to prioritize them over Alex's life, so he left, leaving Victor and Peter in charge of dealing with Alex and his crew.

A few days later, Steve called Aisha and asked her to deliver Manuel's records to the Secretary-General, Jim Adams. Steve also informed her of Manuel's latest violation of stealing the files and returning to Rancenia with them. "I want you to map out a plan on how to go about retrieving the files and keep it confidential until we are cleared to return to Rancenia. I don't want the NISA or any of his inside associates to warn him. In the meantime, I suggest that Alex and Gabriel go and apologize to Mr. Adams on our behalf for not having the necessary documents and explain their discovery verbally. Tell them to explain the situation and provide a brief overview of their findings. Additionally, they should tell Mr. Adams that we'll provide the documents as soon as possible to assure him that we'll make alternative arrangements to retrieve them. This will demonstrate our professionalism and commitment to providing concrete evidence despite the setback," stated Steve.

"Ok I'm on top of it," replied Aisha.

The next day, Aisha sent Alex and Gabriel to handle a task that Steve demanded. Shortly thereafter, Alex and Gabriel found themselves in Mr. Adams's office seated in front of his desk. Alex proceeded to deliver his director's message, "Mr. Adams, we learned that Manuel and Mr. Boucher were responsible for the conflict between Bellivia and Rancenia. Mr. Boucher, along with Manuel's late father, Samuel, designed the structure of the operation. Since Samuel was the chairman of the official RFRB (Rancenia Federal Reserve Bank), Mr. Boucher joined forces with him, and they started the generation of hush money. At first, they only operated in Rancenia to gain the trust of FFRBG (Flowropian Federal Reserve Board of Governors). Then, after gaining credibility, they expanded throughout Flowropia. Starting with Bellivia, as a result, the Bellivian economy crashed faster than any other country in Flowropia."

"I need some time to discuss this matter with our Security Council, Antonio Rodriguez. Afterwards I'll notify you," said Mr. Adams.

"Okay, Mr. Adams, when should we follow up with you?" Alex demanded. "Give us a few days, and we'll have an answer for you," replied Mr. Adams.

Directly after Alex and Gabriel left the UNG building, Mr. Adams made his way to Mr. Rodriguez's office and began explaining Manuel's situation to him. "I just received some news about Flowropia from the BIA. The agents informed me that the Flowropian economy is going through a depression, and that Bellivia has been the most impacted. Therefore, the Bellivian administration plans to retaliate against Rancenia, the country that they believe was responsible for the crisis. They believe they have enough evidence to attribute the cause of the inflation to the Rancenian administration," said Mr. Adams.

"Very well then, we should schedule a meeting in two weeks' time to give everyone enough time to prepare. We're going to invite representatives from each nation that is involved to present their evidence and concerns," replied Mr. Rodriguez.

"Great idea sounds like a plan, this way we can negotiate a fair-trade agreement," said Mr. Adams.

As the preparations were underway, Mr. Adams and Mr. Rodriguez also reached out to some more top international organizations to garner support for the fair-trade agreement they are planning to establish. They knew that to negotiate a favorable deal, they needed a strong alliance behind them.

Two weeks later, all the representatives were gathered in the General Assembly Hall. After everyone was seated properly Mr. Adams addressed them first, "I want to highlight the urgency of this situation and emphasized the need for open and honest dialogue. Remember the goal is not to assign blame but to find a solution that would benefit all nations involved," he commented.

Mr. Rodriguez elaborated on the issue then Noah, who was the Bellivian representative communicated his administration's concerns. "These records clearly show the impact of the fraudulent activities on our economy," said Noah.

After Noah addressed the congregation, Mr. Louis spoke on behalf of Rancenia. He was accompanied by Mr. Alexandre but Mr. Louis spoke for them. Following Mr. Louis's speech, the next representative went and so on until all representatives presented. Everyone listened carefully, until the end of the first day, then Mr. Rodriguez acknowledged the seriousness of the situation by responding before the next representative started talking. "Mr. Adams and I assure you that your concerns would be considered during the negotiations," he said.

Over the course of the meeting, various trade proposals were put on the table. Mr. Adams and Mr. Rodriguez facilitated the discussions by ensuring that all nations had the opportunity to voice their opinions and concerns. At the end of the meeting, Mr. Adams closed the discussion by saying, "We encourage you to compromise so we can find a mutually beneficial agreement. Later we'll come up with reforms that include measures to stabilize inflation, encourage investment, and promote sustainable economic development. For now, just bear with us."

A couple of days after Alex and Gabriel returned to the UNG to get an update from Mr. Adams. "After days of intense negotiations between all parties, a fair-trade agreement was finally reached. The agreement addressed the concerns raised by all the nations while also safeguarding their interests. It also included measures to prevent future fraudulent activities and fostered a more transparent and accountable trade system in Flowropia." Mr. Adams communicated.

Following his conversation with Mr. Adams, Alex relayed the message he received from the UNG to Aisha. Later, she called Steve and informed him about the signed agreement among the Flowropian nations. Both BIA directors were pleased with the outcome. "I'm pleased to hear that, because this fair-trade agreement would not only repair the damaged relationship between Bellivia and Rancenian but also set a precedent for fair and ethical trade practices in Flowropia." Steve replied.

As soon as Mr. Alexandre and Mr. Louis returned from the UNG meeting, they reported to Manuel and Mr. Louis explained what transpired with Mr. Adams.

"The UNG has negotiated a fair-trade agreement, which prevents us from doing business with other nations until further notice. They plan to bring in economic experts to analyze the situation and propose a solution that would benefit all Flowropian countries."

"I must fabricate a testimony against the BIA and have Mr. Boucher, Mr. Alexandre, and Mr. Louis sign it then give it to Raphael Laurent. He might support us with all our signatures," Manuel thought.

Later, Manuel arranged a meeting with Mr. Boucher, Mr. Alexandre, and Mr. Louis.

"I want you to help me get rid of the BIA investigation. First, I'm going to write a proposal and have you sign it and deliver it to Laurent and see if he can assist us. Then, once we get the UNG to lift the new policy, we can move some of our institutions out of Flowropia," said Manuel.

"Okay, I'll speak to our president tomorrow and request him to petition Fabrican intelligence for sending spies to their country," replied Mr. Boucher.

A few days later, Laurent, who was the Racenian president at the time, called Mr. Adams and passed along the message that Mr. Boucher had brought to his attention. "The Fabrican government has been blacklisting Manuel, I want you to request their president to demand them to stop spying on my administration because their declaration was based on false allegations." Laurent stated.

"My team and I will examine the situation, then give you a response," replied Mr. Adams.

"All, right. When you confirm our petition, I don't want any foreign intelligence services investigating the Rancenian administration anymore." Laurent proposed.

"If you are correct, you shouldn't worry. I'll see to that," replied Mr. Adams.

Mr. Adams traveled to Sékoubaria, G.D. to discuss Laurent's recommendation with Fabrican agencies and vote on it. Steve asked Alex to meet him there to provide detailed insights on the Rancenian government. Alex, worried about security due to threatening calls, agreed to bring at least one team member, despite his partners being on break. As a result of his panic, he sent a group text. Antoine had schemed to get closer to Alex to be aware of his exact position, so he seized the opportunity and volunteered to accompany him.

Before Alex and Antoine left to go to Sékoubaria, G.D. Manuel called Victor and gave them instructions on how to approach the trapping of Alex and his crew. "First, I want you to keep Antoine's family under surveillance and make sure that he doesn't lead you into an entrapment," ordered Manuel. "Don't you think that'll make him become disassociated?" asked Victor.

"He wouldn't have a choice but to comply with us. Wait until they depart, then go to his home and hold his family hostage. If he doesn't keep his promise, kill them all," he added.

Immediately after Manuel hung up, Victor did as he was commanded and called Peter to go over the plan. The next day after James and Antoine got to the capital Victor called Antoine and discussed how he should tackle the master plan. "Manuel and I wanted security because we doubt that you'll sell out your partner just like that. That's why I paid your family a visit and I am here with them," said Victor.

"Please don't hurt them, I promise I won't betray you!" Antoine pleaded.

"Don't worry, I won't hurt your wife and kids if you deliver on your promise," replied Victor.

"I would have done it either way but since you have my family, I will kill him myself," answered Antoine.

"No, don't even try to attack him by yourself. We just need you to keep an eye on him and act like you are watching his back. When the time is right, call me and give me your location, and we'll take it from there," replied Victor.

"Okay, consider it done!" Antoine replied. "Don't worry, I will not hurt your family if you comply. This is just for security," Victor added.

Antoine accompanied Alex to the capital and stayed with him for the most part. After Anticipating the hours left before their flight during the previous gathering that morning, Antoine came up with an excuse to separate. There were five hours left before check-in, so they went back to their hotel. The moment they walked into the building, while they were still in the lobby, Antoine said, "I just remembered I have not seen my mother in a while. She lives nearby so I'm going to go visit her quickly."

"I would come with you, but I am exhausted from all the running around we've been doing lately. I'll take a nap while you take care of that," Alex replied.

"Okay, I'll be right back. Call my phone in case of any change of plans," replied Antoine.

Antoine notified Victor instantly after walking out of the building. "We just got back to the location that I initially sent you. Hurry up, the coast is clear right now because the security is getting ready to change shifts. He's in room Ten B, that's the tenth floor, second door to the right when you come out of the elevator!"

"Great work, Antoine! My men should be there in no time," replied Victor.

"By the way, he should be napping when you get here! I told him that I must make a quick run, so I'm leaving now!" added Antoine.

"No problem, they'll be there shortly!" said Victor.

Victor had his army on standby a few minutes from the location, so five minutes later, they surrounded the area. After storming into the building and tying up the staff and security on the ground floor, the head officer instructed ten men to go up with the elevator, ten more to take the staircase, ten to post up in the lobby, and the rest to stay outside. "If you can capture him alive, that'll be awesome. However, we're not only interested in keeping him alive; so, if he gives you a hard time, kill him by any means necessary!" yelled out the army leader.

Alex had just laid down so he was still half asleep, half awake. The noise from the intruders picking the lock woke him up. Consequently, he jumped up right away and grabbed his revolver, and stood against the wall by the door. He held the firearm tight and waited for the first few to come in. After the first two walked in blindly, he shot them both in the back of the head. Then two more walked in, aimed, and shot at him, so he dove onto the bed and rolled over to the floor as they fired. They missed, so he fired back from the prone position and hit their legs and feet. After they fell, he shot at their bodies and heads to finish them. At that point, the others hesitated for a moment, so he picked up two guns from the dead fighters and tucked them. He began to walk out when six more men came out from the elevator firing. To avoid the bullets, he flipped back into the room and shut the door. Then he took advantage and grabbed the bed sheets, tying them together, then to the bed leg. Right away, the gunmen kicked the door open and stood in front of the room firing aimlessly as he hid behind the nightstand. When they ceased fire to reload, he picked up a machine gun that one of the dead armed men had dropped. He fired and simultaneously walked out of the room, killing five more men. The last agent from the first ten batch that went up on the elevator pulled back to warn the others who arrived as the elevator doors closed.

"Guys, he easily took out the others. He's not going to let us take him alive," voiced the agent through the walkie-talkie. The men stormed out from the staircase doors, so Alex shot more until the gun was empty, then he ran back into the room. He picked up the sheets he had tied on the bed leg and jumped into an apartment below to escape the agents. Soon after, Alex regathered himself after the jump. He peeked out of the door of an apartment he ended up in, did not spot any agents on the floor, and ran down the hallway. Alex accidentally ran into an older lady who had come out of her room to investigate the noise. After bumping into the lady, he pushed her back inside and quietly instructed her to stay indoors and call the police. Once he got to the end of the hallway, he cautiously approached the staircase door and listened. Hearing more men running up the stairs, he swiftly moved to the other side to avoid confrontation. The commander was informed by retreating mercenaries about Alex's exceptional agility and skills, so he decided to abandon the capture plan and instead chose to have Alex killed.

Moments after, Alex had made it to the third floor. He aimed two guns and walked slowly. He looked out through the window again and noticed that he was surrounded. Men were climbing up the building from the outside. Realizing he needed backup, he called Antoine, but didn't receive any response. He picked up the call again and saw gunmen coming out of every direction before he could hit the end button. Taking cover, he shot the ones in his sight as he ran through them one by one until he ran out of ammunition. Running close to the windows, he jumped through the glass once more, landing on one of the men on a rope and using it to strangle him. He took the man's gun and used the rope to descend to the ground floor. It was then that he realized there were over twenty more men waiting downstairs. He exchanged fire with them, killing some, before the remaining men who were upstairs looking for him came down and began firing as well. Finally, Alex was hit in the stomach and severely injured. Crawling to a nearby pillar, he used it as cover. The men kept shooting nonstop and, when they finally stopped, Alex was gone. The entire ground floor was destroyed, causing the building to collapse on top of him. The remaining men set up bombs and ignited them after they left, to destroy all evidence of surveillance.

While Alex was under attack in Sékoubaria, G.D, Peter sent some assassins to his home. They arrived right after sunset. Fortunately, James sensed them pulling up to the front of the house so intensified his hearing. Therefore, he heard them discuss their plan before they came out of their vehicles. "Manuel wants you to kill them all, he doesn't take any hostages, just kill them," directed the head of the squad.

At that moment, James looked out the window and saw five individuals with all kinds of weapons. He ran and grabbed his brother, taking him to his mother and said, "Mom, take Jolie, Jeremy, and go down to the basement. There are armed men outside, and they are here to kill us. I heard them with my own ears. Hurry, Mom!"

"What about you?" demanded Holly.

"Mom, don't worry about me, just take my brother and sister and hide at our secret hiding place, I'll be fine!" he replied with a sense of urgency.

After James walked away, he ran quickly to his father's office and took his backup handgun, then he turned off the electricity in the house. The assassins were surprised when they walked in and the lights went out, so they turned on their flashlights. James could see even in the dark, so he slowly crept up on them and took them out cold one by one with his bare hands. He didn't even use the gun, instead he tied them up and called the police.

Victor also sent some assassins to the rest of the top five crew members. Luckily, Rich was with Oumar at his house when they showed up at his residence. Mrs. Durand was the only one there, or they would have decapitated him and his mother altogether. Christopher had left town with some of his associates before the multiple attacks took place. Mrs. Houston and Rose were out and about as well. Ben and Gabriel were at the agency waiting to welcome back Alex, Antoine, and Steve. However, only Steve had shown up. He had returned from the capital a few hours prior to that, so they decided to postpone the meeting until Alex and Antoine returned. As soon as they left and got in their vehicles, they were also attacked in the parking lot of the BIA facility. Fortunately, only five men were sent after them, so they managed to escape with injuries. Both men were hurt, but Gabriel's injuries were minor. On the other hand, Ben was critically injured. He suffered from a gunshot wound which prevented him from engaging in most physical activities. After Ben was released from the hospital late that night, he learned that he had lost his wife and that she was tortured before her death. The next day, Ben and Gabriel were informed by Antoine that Alex was ambushed in the capital at his hotel room and that he was killed.

Due to the vicious attacks by Manuel's men on the agents and their families, many all of them reconsidered working with the agency. Ben quit the force right after he lost his partner Alex and his wife. He figured that he was wealthy and did not need the agency anymore, because he owned a motor vehicle production company. Ben moved away and didn't tell anyone where they went, and Rich moved away with him. Gabriel and Christopher asked Steve to switch their roles from going on missions to working from inside the organization. They were terrified, so they didn't want to go back to Flowropia or any other missions pertaining to that maniac Manuel. After a while, Christopher and Gabriel worked as part-time agents only.

Later, Steve recognized that Antoine was the only top five member not traumatized from the recent disaster. What was more alarming was that none of his family members were disturbed by Manuel's attacks as well. Consequently, Steve called him in for questioning about what happened at the capital. "Where were you during the ambush of Alex?" demanded Steve.

"I went to visit my mother," Antoine nervously answered.

"How did you find your family when you returned?" Steve asked him another question. "My wife and son were at peace!" replied Antoine.

"You mean to tell me there were no intrusions at all to come after your family when all your entire team's families were attacked?" he asked suspiciously.

"Nope, I guess they might not be aware of my activeness," replied Antoine.

"Why do you think I had something to do with it?" he added.

"No, not at all, I was just curious because all of your team members or their families were attacked," Steve responded.

"That's sad to hear, I still can't believe it myself!" said Antoine.

The Flowropian and West Drakillian economies had taken a downturn, so the Fabrican president Diallo invited leaders from all over the world of Ginnia to discuss why it was time to go after Manuel, who was the biggest threat to their economy, and why the UNG needed to change the initial agreement. FSSD, ISA, BIA, DBI, BBI, RBI, FFRB, DWI, and many more organizations were present at this meeting. After everyone settled down, Diallo addressed the congregation.

Steve had a private conversation with the president after the meeting, but it did not unfold as he had anticipated.

"It's important to consider other potential factors that may have contributed to the economic downturn rather than solely blaming Manuel. Perhaps discussing broader economic policies, global market trends, and internal issues within the countries involved could provide a more comprehensive understanding of the situation. Additionally, instead of focusing solely on targeting Manuel, exploring diplomatic solutions and collaborative efforts with all parties involved could lead to a more sustainable and effective resolution," Diallo proposed.

Steve was impressed by the president's proposal, despite losing the lead agent on the FARN mission and failing to secure Fabrican administration's votes due to insufficient evidence. As a result, Steve decided that he needed some time off from the business so he called Diallo to discuss his foresight.

"Although I still plan on completing the task, after this setback I needed to regroup and determine how to retrieve and present the official documents that reveal the Rancenian administrators' fraudulent dealings. Then I can present them to you, the UN, and FSSD to get your support to send another team of agents to Rancenia," Steve suggested.

"That sounds like a great idea, Steve! I'm with you on this, let me know when you resume," said Diallo.

"It's gotten to the point where only you could override the UNG's decision. I don't want your intervention without their approval because that could wage a war between the nations. Nonetheless, I'll keep in mind that from this point going forward, Laurent is an accomplice of the FARN corruption. I promise that I would continue to put the mission on hold until the law is amended," Steve expressed.

"Thank you, my friend. We'll talk again soon," said Diallo.

CHAPTER THREE

FIRST TIME AWAY
FROM HOME

James considered leaving for school after the recent tragedy but stayed to support his mother. He took on additional responsibilities and delayed seeking justice for his father's death. Holly received a phone call as she was heading to the garage, days after Alex's passing and just weeks before school began.

His phone rang three times before she answered.

"Hello!" she said.

"Hey Holly, how are you doing?" said Vincent.

"Hey Vincent, I'm fine. How about you?" she replied.

"I'm hanging in there. How about the children?" he replied

"They are all doing okay as well!" she replied.

"Great, how about Benjamin?" he added.

"He has been here since Alex passed, and he has been a great deal of support. He just left to go to work," she said.

"Okay, I just wanted to give you a heads up. I am leaving tomorrow early in the morning, so I should be there around eight at night!" he said.

"Okay, I hope you have a great flight. I'll have James pick you up from the airport. We'll be here waiting for you," Holly stated.

"Okay, God willing, I'll see you tomorrow. Thank you!" he said.

"You're welcome, bye!" she said then hung up.

The next day, Vincent arrived at night. As planned, he was picked up by James, who had obtained his driver's license during the last few weeks prior to his high school graduation. Vincent stayed for a few weeks after the funeral.

Since Alex died, James had constantly experienced anxiety attacks. As a result, the entire time has been a blur for him. He was having a hard time adjusting, so Benjamin became a close mentor. It was the end of the summer, and the weather was beautiful at sixty-five degrees Fahrenheit. It was also a little bit windy, so James, Vincent, Benjamin, and Alpha were hanging out in front of Benjamin's shop. As they were associating with each other, Vincent pulled James to the side and said, "I want to talk to you privately!"

"Ok, let's go inside so we can sit down," said James.

"Your mother told me what you did that night when the bandits stormed into your home, so I want to let you know that I'm proud of you, and Alex would be too. Protecting your family, the way you did when you were attacked by the executioners was magical. That's why I wanted to let you know that your father came to me a while back and warned me about a few agents in the agency who may have wanted him dead because of his interracial marriage. He told me to look after you if anything happened to him. He said that he mistakenly told one of his coworkers, by the name of Peter, about his secret marriage to your mother. You do know that you and your siblings are mixed beings, right?" said Vincent before he paused and questioned James.

James listened intently to Vincent's words, feeling a mix of amazement and confusion.

"Yeah, Dad told me that we are mixed," replied James.

"Good. Like I was saying, he believed that this Peter guy didn't like the fact that you would have overwhelming supernatural abilities. In fact, Peter resigned after he found out about your family because he didn't want to work with your father anymore," explained Vincent.

James took a deep breath and placed his hand on his chin then said, "Huh, that's a very interesting uncle. Thanks for that information, I'll keep that in mind!"

"When Alex and I were young, I was around your age and he was Benjamin's age; your grandfather told us a tale. It was about the coming of a mixed being with God-given abilities who would change the world by equalizing the forces. After you were born, I remember we were astonished because you never cried as a baby, therefore we believed that you were the one dad told us about. You were special from the day you were born." added Vincent.

"My dad used to tell me the same thing. At first, I undermined it but ever since I started changing and gaining extraordinary powers, I'm starting to believe it!" James said.

"James, you are! Trust me, that's why you have paranormal powers. Just make sure to follow in your father's footsteps and use it to fight evil," advised Vincent.

"I do and assure you that I would follow in my father's footsteps. I want to honor his legacy and use my ability to make a positive impact around this world," said James with determination in his voice.

Afterwards they returned outside to where Benjamin and Alpha were standing. James found comfort in his family members, his cousin Benjamin, Alpha, and his uncle Vincent, who have always supported him. Then he recalled his father mentioning a prophecy that is now beginning to come true, shedding light on why they were being targeted by agents. Little did James know that his journey towards self-discovery and protection was just beginning. The prospect of discovering his hidden powers and exploring his spiritual heritage filled him with anticipation. There was some uncertainty in his heart, but he was ready to face it head-on. Little did he know that his journey towards self-discovery and finding out his purpose was just beginning. The thought of being the most advanced superbeing had once frightened him, now it ignited a determination that would shape his life in unimaginable ways.

Holly resumed working to supplement the income from the monthly survivor benefits she received, which covered household bills and James' tuition. James took on the responsibility of looking after his younger sister while his mother was at work. Recognizing his mother's financial strain, James proactively sought job opportunities during summer vacation to assist financially. He had volunteered at a few institutions before and after he graduated from high school; however, he had never worked. Right after he began his sophomore year of college, he landed his first job because he had built a network of contacts.

It was the national holiday in the fall semester so school was closed for ten days. James called Rich, who had moved to New Paris, a four-hour drive from New Amsterdam. During their conversation, they agreed to meet up the next day at a park near Rich's new home. It was a nice winter day when James got in the car that his father previously owned and drove off. Once James arrived at the intended location, he saw Rich and walked up to him. They sat at the park for a while and then drove around the town. This was the first time they had spent so much time together since the disaster that happened to their parents, so James tried to observe Rich thoroughly. James empathized with Rich, even though he was acting strange. James assumed that Rich needed help, so he intentionally tried to read his mind. Upon hearing Rich's thoughts, James heard him saying, "I have to find the men responsible for my mother's death, so I can avenge her."

"I know, bro, I hear you. I can't wait to find the men who killed my father too so I can kill them," James unconsciously responded to his friend's thoughts. Therefore, Rich was baffled and scared. As a result, he said, "What! How did you know that's what I was thinking about? I didn't say anything; I just thought it."

James laughed it off and said, "Lucky guess, I just figured we were thinking about the same thing. You know what they say, great minds think alike."

"Yeah, that's a fact. I can't stop thinking about it; I guess that's all you think about too!" Rich asked rhetorically.

"Yeah, what else am I going to think about? They took them away from us, but it's okay because I'm not going to rest until I find the people who were responsible for it," said James.

"Me too, even though that's not going to bring them back!" said Rich as his tears started to flow.

At that instant James put his hand on his shoulder, hugged him and said, "Don't worry, I'm here for you Rich!"

Upon realizing that Rich was really hurt yet optimistic about finding the silent assassins who killed his mother, he asked, "I know it's not going to be easy, but you have to be strong."

"I know I'm going to be fine, it's just that I can't believe they killed my mother!" said Rich.

"Yeah, I'm sorry, bro but you know if anyone can relate, it's me because I lost my dad too!" James responded he pulled out a bag of marijuana and a cigar, then began splitting up the cigar in the middle.

"Oh, hell nah! You smoke now?" exclaimed Rich.

"Yeah, bro, ever since my father passed, this is the only thing that's been helping me get through the harsh reality of his absence," James replied.

"Me too, you know I used to smoke here and there, but now I'm a heavy smoker. I mean, four to five blunts a day!" said Rich.

"How's school?" James asked.

"Man, I didn't even go to school this year. I need at least a year off for myself and to look after my pops because lately he's not the same. He hasn't left the house for over five months now. He even quit his job at the agency," replied Rich.

"WORD?" asked James, his eyes opening wide in surprise.

"Yeah, bro. Plus, I can't focus right now, so I don't want to waste my time stacking up school loans," added Rich.

James finished rolling the weed, so he sparked the blunt as Rich asked, "How about you?"

"Yeah, but just like you, I'm struggling with my motivation for school because my mind is not there. So, I'm planning to move to College Town next year so I just applied to Spirits University, School of the Gifted!" replied James.

"Good luck, man. I'm going to start next year and I want to major in

Political Science and later along the lines, I want to intern for DBI also. I'm looking forward to that so I investigate the cause of the casualty." said Rich.

"Cool. I'm going to switch my major to Criminal Justice or something along the lines of law enforcement too, so I can pursue a career with the BIA or the DBI."

Afterwards they had a moment of silence before James added, "Trust me, that's my word. If it's the last thing I do, I'll find them and make them pay for our losses."

"Me too, bro. I'll be right there with you whenever you're ready!" Rich assured him. Then, they shook hands and went their separate ways.

It was the day after New Year's, and James was sleeping in the afternoon due to exhaustion from a party the night before. There were still a couple of inches of snow on the ground from the night before so it was freezing outside. He had thought about his father prior to falling asleep, so he dreamed about him. He saw himself running down the steps to the kitchen enthusiastically. When he reached there, his father was making some tea as he stood next to his mother. Holly was fixing herself a plate, as she had already made one for the entire family.

"Good morning, everyone," said James.

"Good morning, James," they all responded together.

"Dad, I had a weird dream last night. Two men with black and white suits and dark shades, accompanied by one of my professors, came up to me. They asked me what I wanted to be when I graduate from college; guess what I said?" said James.

"What, James?" Alex responded.

First, James smirked with a delightful expression, and then said, "I told them that I wanted to be a BIA agent."

Alex had a smirk on his face as well, showing the same joyful expression as his son, then replied, "What do you know about the BIA?"

James swallowed the piece of pancake in his mouth and licked the syrup off his lips. Then he poured some orange juice into a cup and looked up at his father and said, "You'll be surprised, Dad. I do a lot of research on the BIA. I find their system fascinating, and I love how they execute missions overseas. The first line of defense missions is my favorite. I would love to become a First Option one day. According to my research, they only recruit people with special skills in that department."

"Okay, okay, I guess you did. So, what does the BIA stand for and what are the responsibilities of their agents?" Alex followed up with more questions.

"The BIA stands for the Bureau of Intelligent Agents, and their agents work for the government by searching for information and collecting it to help defend their country. They are assigned to national security and international missions, where they are sent to different countries to spy on their citizens and governmental operations. They observe these countries to find out whether they are a threat or not. If the agents figure out the enemy's plans, they stop them," James said with confidence.

"Wow, son, impressive. Enough said," Alex stopped chewing his food and said proudly.

"You couldn't have explained it any better than that. I have a few friends in the force; I'll try to introduce you. I'll tell you about other types of missions you can be assigned to and the important subjects you need to take and excel in to have an advantage on your quest to becoming a BIA service agent. If I remember correctly, all my friends said it takes necessary steps to become an agent. I'll tell you all about it another time," Alex replied, then looked at his other son and added, "What about you, Jeremy?"

Then Jeremy swallowed his food quickly and said, "I don't know yet. I'm still contemplating between being a professional basketball player and a business CEO. I just might do both."

"I'm proud of you boys. It seems like you've got it all figured out," said Alex.

"Jolie, tell them what you want to do when you get older too!" Holly asked, joining the conversation, and including the baby as well.

"I want to be a nurse like you, Mommy," replied Jolie.

She was adorable because she had just learned how to talk properly, and this was the reason everyone adored her. They all smiled and looked impressed as they glanced at one another.

Suddenly, everyone else vanished, and James found himself transported back in time before his dad revealed his identity as an agent.

They materialized in a car, with James joining him on the way to the airport. Alex, driving with his left hand, turned his head slightly, looked at James, and said, "I love you son!"

"I love you too dad!" James replied.

James felt that his dad worked for the bureau, which was why he tried to persuade his father into confessing.

"Where are you going?" he added.

"Just going to a business meeting," replied Alex, avoiding the question because he knew a smart young man like his son would figure out that he was going on a mission. James remained silent for a while and looked upset. His behavior caused Alex to feel bad for not entertaining his son.

"Remember when I told you that I had friends in the BIA and that I'll introduce you?"

"Yeah Dad," James replied enthusiastically.

At that moment, Alex turned to the left to look at James, and then he said, "I am sorry, son! Look, I understand that you are passionate about the agency, so I am going to tell you the truth about my line of work. I see that you've already figured it out. You're correct, I work for the BIA. I am going to tell you the cheat code. Listen to me carefully."

James became excited when his father admitted that he worked for the BIA, so he was extremely engaged in his father's advice. "Yeah dad, trust me I am. Please continue," he said with curiosity.

"I thought, what a coincidence that my son wants to join the agency. When you time comes it will be simple for you because your bloodline is mixed with jinn. This makes you overqualified for the company. I am a jinn, and your mother is a human, which means you are a hujinn," said Alex.

"A what?" asked James.

"A hujinn, from the mixture of me and your mother. I'm jinn and your mother's human. Jinns are known as intelligent and powerful spirits that are much higher in rank than humans. However, hujinns are spirits higher in rank than even the jinns and they are right under the angels, who are the highest after God. There are others out there looking to destroy your kind so never disclose this to anyone unless you are one hundred percent sure you can trust them. All you need to do is keep a strong faith, and you'll be able to contribute to the safety of the world," replied Alex.

"Wow, wait, what you're saying is that I'm ah...?" James blurted out before Alex sharply interrupted him, saying, "Yeah, James, you are. But listen here, son. There are many evil spirits out there trying to find you to kill you before you reach your maximum power level because they will be no match for you when you do. You must be very discreet. What I am trying to say is that you should never share your spirituality with anyone but your own kind, and even then, be careful which ones you confide in."

James nodded his head and said, "Okay, dad, I won't. But dad, where are you going? You still haven't responded to my question!"

Alex blinked his eyes twice and said, "Oh yeah, I almost forgot." Before he finished speaking, the car blew up and James woke up due to his fear. At that point, James opened his eyes and realized that it was just a dream. James was sweating bullets, not because of the weather, but because the dream was very alarming.

James sat up in bed, trying to calm his racing heartbeat. "It was just a dream," he said to himself repeatedly, taking deep breaths to steady his heart. He couldn't shake off the disturbing feeling. The vividness of reliving his father's demise lingered in his mind. Wanting to distract himself, he decided to get out of bed and focus on something else. Thus, he decided to visit Benjamin. He got dressed, walked out, and made his way to the store.

Later after James arrived, he stood in front of the boutique for a moment, then he walked in and saw his cousin behind the register.

"Hey Benjamin, can I talk to you for a minute?" James asked.

"Of course, James. I'm always here whenever you want to talk," Benjamin replied.

"I was just wondering why dad and uncle Vincent left Freeland?" asked James.

"Great question! They were forced out by the government because they took a stand against collaborating with Samuel Shirac, a Flowropian official who wanted to collaborate with Freeland's administration. You see, Grandpa was the leader of the WDU, and our parents were ministers of Freeland before they fled the country due to the FARN takeover."

Benjamin replied, providing further explanation about their political background and the reasons for their migration.

Eight months later James completed his freshman year at a New Amsterdam City college, however before the end of the year he was accepted to one of the top ten universities in the country. An institute that was located outside of New Amsterdam State and was called Spirits University, School of the Gifted. The school was in College Town, a small city in Hamdallah State. The university had a total of twenty colleges all over the state. Compared to Spirits University School of Hamdallah, Spirits University, School of the Gifted, was much bigger and served as the main campus. Although the campus had regular students, it comprised over fifty percent of individuals with extraordinary abilities.

In the fall James moved to College Town and began attending Spirits University. He was enrolled in five classes and one of them was political science. For their first project assignment, they were tasked with researching the top five BIA missions in the past decade. During the research, James hacked into the NISA database and discovered insightful information about his father's work history. He learned that his father initially started in the Science and Technology department and eventually became the BIA top agent. James also uncovered that Alex's last mission involved confronting well-connected and powerful leaders from a large organization who were still at large. He also discovered that Manuel and Victor were responsible for the disastrous attack on his family and that they had insiders working in the Fabrican agencies. They were on the BIA most wanted list and were also connected to all the powerful leaders and organizations around the world. At that point, he knew all the information that the BIA had on the case of his father's passing. James took note of the names and locations of everyone in the organization responsible for his father's death. He made a promise to himself that he would find them and make them pay for it. Until that point, he had been on top of his classes and helped others as well. He had not gotten involved in any type of illegal activity, even when most of his circle did. Keeping his promise to not involve himself in any mess, primarily because he was afraid of disappointing his mother, and more importantly, as an immigrant, he did not want to tarnish his name. He had turned out to be a great example for the average youth in the slums. James desired to maintain a good reputation and understood the importance of building a positive image and not tarnishing his family's name. He had not only benefited himself but also inspired many of his companions to pursue their goals and stay away from illegal activities. His commitment to his education and personal integrity had made him a role model for his community.

A week after his discovery, James fell into depression. He slowly began detaching himself from school and increasingly relied on partying, drugs, and alcohol to help alleviate his depression. Since his family was very far away from him, he didn't feel apologetic. During that time, he started smoking more frequently. James even tried other drugs that were stronger than the potent marijuana he was already used to, and these new drugs made him lose track of his studies. James fooled around and wasted the entire school year. By the end of the semester, James's grades had dropped tremendously, and he traveled a lot, visiting three different states besides New Amsterdam.

Feeling older without a job and struggling with expensive habits, such as smoking weed and drinking, became too much for him to handle. He felt bad because he wasn't working, which meant he was spending his mother's hard-earned money in vain. He didn't want to waste his mother's money anymore. He realized that the amount of money he used to live the rockstar lifestyle demanded much more than that of the average college student. He decided to use the same money he had spent on drugs, parties, and alcohol to help cope with the stress of feeling broke during his time in school.

Weeks later, James was on his way to class when he spaced out. He stood by the Residence Hall's exit deep in his thoughts, still feeling overwhelmed by the recent discoveries about his father's mission involvements. Finding out that Manuel and Victor had some representatives on the inside providing them with the BIA business tasks weighed heavily on James, to the point where he was incensed. James contemplated the guidance from his father Alex that he received in a recent dream. In the dream, Alex highlighted the importance of James's unique nature, saying that superhujinns are chosen individuals who are selected for their strong faith, separated from ordinary people, and destined for special positions in the world. Hujinns are depicted as beings superior to humans and jinns, possessing supreme intelligence, power, and strength. His father mentioned that angels oversee all creatures, and the highest power governs everything, including advanced organizations like federal agencies. Alex emphasized that maintaining commitment to learning, doing what is right, showing gratitude, and maximizing one's abilities through faith are crucial.

After daydreaming about his most recent dream of his late father, James snapped back to reality and walked toward a park that was located between the student union building and the dining hall. He walked past the student union building and stopped again, staring at his fellow students while reasoning the message of the dream. He observed students riding on bikes, walking by, and sitting on the grass either studying or eating. James continued walking across the park when he was met and blocked by a fellow named Rob and his entourage. Rob was a nineteen-year-old junior, while James was a seventeen-year-old sophomore at the time. Rob was very tall and had an athletic, rectangular body shape. He had a captivating smile, golden skin, a flat nose, split lips, down-turned eyes, and long brown braids. He liked to show off to his fraternity brothers and the sororities as he was the president of his fraternity, which was the reason nobody wanted to get into any altercation with him.

"Hey dude," Rob said, his voice carrying an air of confidence. "Where are you rushing to?" he asked.

James was aware of his reputation and didn't want to provoke any trouble. "Uh, just trying to make it to class on time," he replied, keeping a casual yet brave tone.

Rob interjected, a hint of fearlessness in his voice. "Just wondering what made you think you can walk through here like you own the place. We've got seniority, you know!" he said.

James took a deep breath, trying to calm his racing heart. He had worked hard to leave his past behind, to find peace within himself. "I didn't mean any harm," James replied earnestly. "I'm just a student like you, trying to get to class in time," he added.

Rob smirked and leaned against a nearby tree, his friends mirroring his position. "Well, well, you're just another newbie enjoying our territory, huh?" he said.

Feeling a hint of Rob trying to intimidate him, James tried to remain calm. "I'm sorry, I didn't realize the park was exclusively yours," he said, hoping to defuse the tension.

Rob chuckled and glanced at his friends. "You are trying to be smart huh, it's not about who owns the park. It's about respect, you know?"

Taking another step back, James rallied his determination, trying to resist the temptation and maintain control over his next actions.

"I understand the unspoken rules of the college hierarchy so I apologize if I've unknowingly disrespected anyone. I'll be on my way then," he said.

As he started to leave, one of Rob's friends stepped forward and stood before him, a smug expression on his face. "Hold on a minute, newbie, we're not done talking to you. Where are you from?" the friend said dismissively.

Feeling a mix of curiosity and apprehension, James took a few steps back. Knowing that he could be stronger than most, if not all, of the beings living in his era, James had promised himself that he was not going to fight anymore. However, Rob was making it difficult for him to fulfill that promise because he seemed determined to drag him back into the world of conflict.

As he struggled with his emotions, James reminded himself of the promises he made to himself. He wanted to be a different person, to choose a path of peace and understanding. Confronting Rob would only lead to more pain and destruction.

Looking at his watch and feeling a sense of urgency, James replied quickly.

"I'm from Freeland. Look, man, I really must be in class by four-thirty. Can we talk later or walk and talk?"

Not getting the reaction he expected from James, the friend turned to Rob for a hint on how to proceed. Rob gave him a head nod, as to say go ahead. At that moment he added, "I like your hat."

"I got this from New Amsterdam City," said James modestly.

"You're in College Town now so you better recognize," said the friend as Rob chimed in again.

"He didn't ask you where you got it from. He means you should give up your hat before we take it from you!" said Rob.

"Don't even try that with me; I'm warning you," and finally said.

Rob was even more angry after James said that to him. "I was just messing with you but now if you don't give me the hat, I'm going to f*** you up," Rob snapped.

*"This new kid thinks he's all that. I'm about to show him who's the man around here. I'm going to F*** him up and embarrass him,"* Rob thought as he stared at James dead in his eyes.

Little did Rob know that James could hear thoughts, especially when he felt threatened or needed to activate his mind-reading ability. James hesitated, unsure of how to respond after hearing Rob's thoughts of him. *"Heard enough of your bulls***, you're really going to make me break my promise to my parents,"* he thought. Ready to discipline Rob, James felt his heartbeat race, but he maintained his composure. "Excuse me, am I done talking?"

"I've never been soft. I will never be, not for you or any army, and you better recognize. No one can take my stuff from me, not even you, tough guy," Rob stood dead silent for a moment, looked around, and then said stiffly as he stuck his chest out, "You think you are tuff, but you are out of your mind. At first, I was just messing with you but now I'm going to f*** you up for talking s***. Even if you give me your hat, I'm going to spank you." Rob rapidly tried to make James jump, but he did not move or even blink, and he gave him the stare down. Then Rob's friend jumped in the middle again and said, "Rob, let me smack this punk for you."

James took a step forward and said, "I don't know how things run around here, but I am not the one to play with. So, I am only going to ask you again nicely, get out of my way before it's too late." Rob was surprised by how stubborn and confident James was, so he responded with ferocity, "What do you mean, too late? You must be smoking rocks." Finding the last bit of patience left inside him, James replied, "Look, be smart guys, stop trying to show off."

Meanwhile, Gabriel, the student advisor, was sitting in his office, which was in the student union building. He was on the phone with his best friend, Christopher, who was running a BIA recruitment center in New Amsterdam City at that time. Despite the tragic loss of their colleague, Gabriel, Christopher, and Steve continued to work together outside of their specialties.

"I'm telling you Chris, I've been thinking about new ways to start recruiting agents here," said Gabriel. "I want to hear your take before I proceed," he added.

"Sounds like a great idea. You should start an after-school program and have a meeting with potential scholars to test them," Christopher advised him.

Before Christopher could finish expressing his thoughts, Gabriel heard students yelling, "Fight! Fight! Fight!"

Gabriel served as the students' advisor and was responsible for both advising them and overseeing the security agency that protected the college James attended. He was still affiliated with the BIA as well. After hearing the students yelling outside, Gabriel interrupted Christopher.

"Excuse me, I have to take a look at what's going on out here." A few seconds later, he added, "I believe that's Rob getting into it with another student. I must go check this out, so I'll call you back in a while." Then Gabriel hung up the phone and walked outside to figure out what was happening between the students. Gabriel peeked out and saw Rob push James with all his strength. However, James didn't budge.

"Everyone here knows you asked for it. You pushed me first," said James as he walked around him. As soon as he passed him, Rob threw a punch and simultaneously said, "Boy, you talk too damn much!" Since James had the ability to sense threats from behind, he instantly ducked and turned, avoiding the punch, and tackling his feet. Before Rob hit the ground, James had thrown an uppercut, connecting with his stomach. Then, one of his friends squared up and threw a kick, but James flashed before his eyes and passed him, lightly hitting him on his neck. Meanwhile, another friend had stepped forward and attempted to grab him, but James tackled him to the ground as well. James hit them just enough to put them down without causing any permanent internal damage. At the same time, a fourth friend tried to strike James and was met with a lower block from James. Finally, the rest of their friends joined the brawl. James was too skilled and powerful for them, so he calmly avoided all their strikes while striking back and putting them all down one by one, either with a block, a punch, a kick, or a tackle.

Afterwards, James stopped, looked around, and saw that there was no one else left trying to attack him. Rattled, Rob and his fraternity brothers couldn't believe how proficient James was. "Oh s*** my arm is twisted!" called out Rob. "I think my leg is broken," one of his friends cried out. "I can't feel my stomach," said another. "He's not human!" said a third bully as James stood over them for a moment before saying, "I tried to warn you, but none of you would listen. I am surprised, though, because you had a lot of mouth yet you couldn't back it up. Perhaps there was a way to defuse the situation without resorting to violence, but you were too busy trying to bully me to see that."

As soon as James started to walk away, Gabriel caught up to him and said aloud, "Excuse me, young buck, what happened here?" James stopped abruptly, then turned around and looked at Rob and his crew. They all backed off and looked intimidated. "They started with me. I warned them all to leave me alone multiple times, and they would not listen. They tried to jump me, so I defended myself," said James.

Gabriel nodded his head in agreement and said, "I understand that, but around here, it doesn't matter who started the fight. Retaliation is not the answer, and avoiding confrontation is. You should have told the staff."

James expressed his remorse and said, "Please don't tell my parents about this because I promised them that I won't be involved in any more altercations. Please, sir, I really tried my best not to resort to violence. I even tried to walk away when they attacked me from behind, all because I didn't give up my hat. At that point, I didn't have a choice but to defend myself."

"I believe you because Rob and his friends have that reputation around here. Don't worry, if you promise to stay out of trouble from now on, I'm not going to contact your parents."

He paused for a moment and dadding, "A youngster with your skills needs to join my after-school program. It's called the Special Scholars Program. So tomorrow, you should stop by. It's in GD Hall, the building next to the Student Union."

James felt like a burden was lifted off his shoulders so he replied cheerfully, "I will."

"I can imagine, it's not easy when others try to provoke and harass you. Nonetheless it's important to remember that violence is never the answer, even when defending oneself. However, I believe you because Rob and his friends have a bad reputation around here. Don't worry if you promise to stay out of trouble from now on; I won't contact your parents." He paused for a moment and added, "A youngster with your skills needs to join my after-school program. It is called the Special Scholars. Tomorrow, you should stop by. It's in GD Hall, the building next to the Student Union."

Feeling like a weight of the world was lifted off his shoulders, James replied, "Yes, I will."

"All right, make sure you show up tomorrow as agreed. This program provides students with new opportunities and support. Remember to continue making the right choices and staying out of trouble. If you need any further assistance, now you know where you can find me." Afterwards, Gabriel turned towards Rob and his crew, finally managing to stand up. "Get over here, Rob!" said Gabriel as he knew Rob was the ringleader, he dismissed the others. "The rest of you, get going!" said Gabriel.

As soon as Gabriel called him, Rob started pleading, "Mr. Houston, please! You know what my dad said last time that he would send me away if I got into any more fights. I am begging you, sir, please! I don't want to go away. I promise I'll do anything, sir."

Gabriel contemplated for a moment and said, "I don't know, Rob. You always disappoint me. I'll keep this between us under one condition; next time, I don't even want to hear about it. I want all of you to join our special after-school scholars' program."

"Okay, I'll do anything you want," replied Rob. "Okay, join the program and we have a deal. The program prepares gifted students for their future careers. Come to my office tomorrow after school to check it out, and if you decide not to join us, I'll understand. Now, go home!"

The next day after his Political Science class, James went to meet with Gabriel. As James sat across from him, Gabriel explained the program's objectives. "This program is for special scholars who are interested in working for our federal government. Our goal is to guide talented individuals like yourself to get exposure and eventually get recruited by the Fabrican administrations." Gabriel looked around then took a few moments before looking back at him and continued, "I got a glimpse of what you can do yesterday when you were defending yourself, and you were spectacular. What's your major?" asked Gabriel.

"I'm studying International Relations, because I want to work for the BIA after I graduate!" replied James.

"That's exceptional of you. Where are you from, James?" asked Gabriel.

"I was born in Freeland, Drakilla," replied James.

"'Boy-oh-boy you are a long way from home!" stated Gabriel.

"Hey, I migrated to New Amsterdam City when I was ten. So technically, that's my new home. I have been there since but after I finished high school and attended college for a year, I transferred here in August," replied James.

After James described his journey, it reminded Gabriel of Alex, the first person he knew who was also from Freeland. Therefore, he asked, "Wait, what's your last name James?"

"Jordan!" replied James.

Right then, Gabriel noticed the resemblance between James and his father so he smiled. "Don't tell me Alex is your father?" said Gabriel.

Astounded to learn that Gabriel was familiar with his father James replied, "Yeah, how did you know?"

"We used to work together. My name is Gabriel Houston!" Gabriel stated.

Fascinated, he looked at James with admiration. "*That explains your skill set; you are a hujinn. I've never seen anyone your age with that kind speed and strength,*" he thought.

"I see talent runs in your family; your father was the First Option for our squad," he said.

"Thank you, it's an honor to hear that come from someone who was very close to him!" James replied humbly.

"If you were in the BIA with him, you must've recently moved out here too?" implied James.

"Yeah, you know; after that disaster, I couldn't stay there anymore. A I thought let me move next to Ben, another one of my team members," replied Gabriel.

"What a coincidence, I know Mr. Durand too. I moved out here to be next to Rich as well. Since they moved here, I decided to come to this school," said James.

"Well, you made the right decision because you are on the right path. Spirits University is one of the top ten schools from which BIA, DBI, ISA, and FSSD recruit their agents," said Gabriel.

Afterwards, James was ecstatic about the opportunity, especially after discovering that the program was associated with the Fabrican agencies, which he wanted to follow in his father's footsteps. "Sounds like the perfect training for me. Please sign me up right away," stated James.

Before James walked out, another student knocked on the door. "Coming on in," said Gabriel.

"Hey, meet Kevin. He is a brilliant individual like yourself. You two need to get to know each other," added Gabriel. Kevin had red hair, gray eyes, a pointed nose, delicate lips, closely set blue eyes, and a round head.

James greeted Kevin with a smile and a handshake after being introduced by Gabriel and said, "Nice to meet you, Kevin!"

"Nice to meet you too, James!" responded Kevin.

Later, after Kevin left, Gabriel took a moment to consider the potential impact of James joining the Special Scholars program.

"It's great to have someone of his caliber. I believe with his skills, passion, and expertise, James would greatly benefit this program," he thought. Eager to share his finding about James with Christopher, he called him right away.

Gabriel started raving about James immediately after Christopher picked up. "Christopher," Gabriel said, excitement evident in his voice.

"A new student just joined my program, who happened to be a brilliant individual. His expertise and enthusiasm are truly remarkable. Rob, who was the most accomplished in the school, liked to challenge new students. Well, yesterday he tried the wrong one. I also believe my wish just came true. You know I have been looking for a skilled individual with elite skills to show me the way to becoming a BIA agent, and I think I found one. The best part is that he has supernatural skills," said Gabriel.

"Wow, Gabriel, that sounds exciting!" Christopher replied.

"Finding someone with those qualities is no small feat. Can you tell me more about this supernatural young man?" asked Christopher.

"Remember the gossip about Alex having a human wife?" asked Gabriel.

"Yeah," replied Christopher.

"Evidently, it's true," said Gabriel.

"That's impressive," replied Christopher, intrigued by Gabriel's revelation.

"So, what exactly does this mean for James? Will being a hujinn affect his standing in the supernatural community?"

Gabriel shrugged, contemplating the potential implications.

"It's hard to say for certain. The supernatural community can be quite traditional, you know. Some might see it as a breach in the supernatural world, but others might view it as a unique opportunity to discover elite supernatural beings."

Christopher nodded, understanding the complexities of the situation.

"What James, mother, and siblings? Are they aware of the supernatural world?"

Gabriel took a sip of his drink before responding.

"From what I gathered, they have no knowledge of it. Alex had been keeping his wife and children's existence a secret from the supernatural community, at least before he died. He wanted to protect them from any potential threats or ramifications that could arise."

Christopher leaned in closer, his curiosity piqued. "Do you think Alex's son could be a superhujinn?"

Gabriel's eyes sparkled with excitement.

"It's possible! Given that Alex himself possesses extraordinary skills and his son's remarkable talent in combat, it wouldn't be surprising if the boy turns out to be a superhujinn. Only time will tell, my friend."

As their conversation continued, Christopher and Gabriel contemplated the implications of this newfound knowledge. It was clear that the existence of a superhujinn had the potential to spark both controversy and fascination within the supernatural community.

"What makes you so sure?" asked Christopher.

"Well, he easily took down Rob and his crew in a matter of seconds. Ten well trained young men attacked him, and he defeated them all using a single blow to each and they were done. I say that to say, it was like he had eyes in the back of his head. He saw all their moves before attacking. He knew when and where to block or strike. Seriously man, they were no match for him," said Gabriel.

"Holy cow you are kidding?" asked Christopher before pausing, then continuing.

"No, I'm not!"

"I must meet this youngster. What's his name?" Christopher asked cheerfully.

"James... James Jordan!" replied Gabriel.

"I guess that settles it then," said Christopher. "If this young man is more skilled than Alex, then it's very likely he's a hujinn. It's fascinating how genetics can play such a significant role in determining one's abilities. What's his name?" he added.

"His name is James. Apparently, this fellow is not your average Joe; he has potential to be the best we've ever come across," replied Gabriel.

Christopher was stunned, "So, you think he's that special?" he asked.

"Exactly. Imagine beating up a gang of trained jinns effortlessly. Rob was the most skilled in the school but James took him out along with his crew in the blink of an eye," Gabriel responded.

Christopher looked up, took a deep breath, and let it out, "Yeah, you're right. I guess it's hereditary because Alex was a specialist himself. Steve used to say that he was one of the best agents he'd ever encountered!" he said.

"I believe that with a little guidance, his son will join him on that list. I mean, the kid took out all of them simultaneously with a single attack. What impressed me the most, though, was how calm he was while doing it! He has the 'it' factor. Even when I showed up, he kept his composure," Gabriel continued, praising James.

"Now you just need to confirm whether his mother is human because his father was jinn. If she's human, then we've got ourselves a hujinn," he replied.

As Gabriel went on to describe his qualifications, Christopher couldn't help but feel excited about the thought of James being the one.

"His talent makes me interested in returning to the BIA!" said Gabriel.

"It's clear that James would be an invaluable addition to the BIA, bringing new insights and a fresh perspective. Don't forget to tell him about our internship program," said Christopher.

With their conversation coming to an end, Gabriel and Christopher had a renewed sense of anticipation and enthusiasm for what James would bring to the developments. They knew that his presence would elevate and enrich their work, and they eagerly anticipated the day when James would officially join the BIA.

A couple of months later, the BIA learned that a student from Spirits University, School of the Gifted had hacked their database. Even Steve was surprised by what had transpired. As a result, he asked Gabriel to find out which student was able to access their database without permission.

After uncovering the truth about his father's role in the BIA and the ongoing mission against powerful leaders, still James couldn't shake the feeling of unease. Questions swirled in his mind so he sat in his dorm room wondering, "*Why did my father become involved in such dangerous missions? What is this organization and why were they still on the loose?*"

James knew he couldn't let this information go unnoticed. He decided that the next day he would speak to his advisor, Gabriel, who had expertise in government affairs.

The next day after class, James lingered behind and approached Gabriel "Mr. Houston, may I have a word with you?" James asked, trying to sound calm despite the turmoil inside him.

"Of course, James. Is everything alright?" Gabriel replied, concern evident in his voice.

"I was doing research for my International Relations' class and I stumbled upon some information about my father's involvement in the BIA and the ongoing mission against powerful leaders in Flowropia."

Gabriel listened intently, nodding along as James spoke. Once James finished, Mr. Houston leaned back in his chair, deep in thought.

"You've uncovered something quite significant, James," Gabriel said finally.

"Your father's involvement in the BIA and the mission against powerful leaders might be more intertwined than you think. The BIA is known for its secrecy, especially when it comes to matters involving First Options. However, I'm going to tell you more. When we arrived in

Flowropia we stumbled upon a threat that needed our attention. Despite the risks involved, we decided to complete the mission."

James absorbed the information, realizing that his father's role in the BIA might have been as noble as it was dangerous. However, after Gabriel told him that the organization had continued its business troubled him deeply.

"What should I do, Mr. Houston?" James asked, his voice filled with determination.

"I can't just let this go. I want to find out more. I want to make sure my father's work was not in vain."

Gabriel smiled approvingly, "I admire your spirit, James. But diving headfirst into this dangerous territory is not advisable. However, I have some contacts within the government who might be able to shed more light on the matter without putting you in harm's way yet. Let me make some inquiries and see what I can do for you!" he said.

Grateful for Gabriel's assistance, James nodded.

"I trust your insight and hope you could provide some more details about the BIA and its business practices. I'll be ready to follow whatever path unfolds. Thank you, Mr. Houston. I appreciate your help and guidance," he said.

With their plan in motion, James felt a renewed sense of purpose. He knew that uncovering the truth about his father's mission and the organization they were up against wouldn't be easy, but he was determined to see it through. In the meantime, he focused on his political science project, using the information he found in the NISA database to delve deeper into the top five missions of the past decade.

Little did James know, his journey would lead him down an unexpected path, entangling him in a world far beyond what he could have imagined. However, with the support of Gabriel and the skills he honed at Spirits University, James was prepared to face whatever challenges lay ahead.

A week later Gabriel provided James with more information regarding his father's passing. After James learned that Alex was ambushed at his hotel room and killed in Sékoubaria, G.D., he was fuming.

"Someone must have given up my dad's location. I think the FARN had someone working for them on the inside!" he said.

"There's a chance because we also suspected a mole or two within our organization. Although we're not sure yet who the agents were!" replied Gabriel. Even though Gabriel was shocked to find out that the student who tapped into the NISA databases was James, he kept it to himself.

Meanwhile, Mr. Jackson had received word of a college student cracking the government's database, so he assigned agents to look for and monitor the student. After a period of observation, Mr. Jackson and his team discovered that James was the one who breached the agency database. Therefore, he informed Mr. Iverson about the breach. However, instead of disciplining James for violating school law by hacking the federal database, Mr. Iverson found him and tried to enlist him to ultimately work for him.

A couple of months later, near the end of the semester, James was on his way to visit Rich. After getting off the bus that took him there, he walked a few blocks and turned into an alleyway. There, he spotted four men following a young woman, and he decided to follow them to assess the situation. As the criminals got closer to her, they split up and approached her from two different directions. Two of the men ran in front of her, while the other two stayed behind her, causing her to stop and look around. James realized that the young lady was in danger, so he ran towards them. As he got closer, he recognized her. "*That can't be Rose*," he thought, starstruck by her once again. "*That's her!*" he thought as he froze for a second, staring at her in shock as if he had seen a ghost.

Then James snapped back to reality as he remembered that she needed his help, so he crept up on the assailants. One of the men, who appeared to be the leader, had a muscular, inverted triangle body shape, warm natural skin color, a bulbous nose, chapped lips, thin almond eyes, a gap-toothed smile, and long ponytail hair. He had a lustful expression, akin to a hungry lion spotting its prey. As he prepared to assault the young lady, he unbuttoned his pants, licked his lips, and callously said, "I want first dibs on that."

"Hold her tightly, P and make sure she doesn't move," the man commanded the other guy. Pat, who Sean called P was short and stocky with a big Roman nose, a long beard, braided hair, fat, dry lips, Asian eyes, a goofy smile, and no neck. The other two guys were in the back of the alleyway keeping watch. She tried to fight back, but Pat was too strong. He grabbed her and pinned her arms together. However, as soon as Sean began unbuttoning his pants and started pulling up her dress, she managed to headbutt him and kick Pat in the groin, causing him to release her and scream, "F***! Give me a second!"

Pat finally stood up straight after bending over for a moment due to the excruciating pain in his groin. Then, he slapped her, causing her to fall to the ground. "Pat, are you trying to tell me that this woman is stronger than you?" Sean asked.

James popped out just as Pat tried to grab her arms again, only to find Sean with his pants halfway down. "Leave her alone!" James shouted. Sean turned around and looked at James, up and down. Confused and incredulous, Sean checked for the other assaulters. He noticed they weren't paying attention and were smoking a blunt instead, so he yelled out to them, "Mike, Billy, what in the world are you doing? Weren't you supposed to be on the lookout for me?"

Raging, he yelled out to them, "Mike, Billy, what are you doing? Weren't you supposed to be on the lookout?"

Sean turned his attention back to James and said, "Now, what were you saying, brave guy?"

James stood there, feeling disgusted, staring at Sean who was talking with his pants halfway down. "I said, leave her alone!" repeated James.

"Why don't you make us, Captain-save a h**?"

"Don't worry, I will," he replied. At this point, Sean was very frustrated and angry because he was looking forward to the pleasure of being intimate with the young lady.

With his emotions running high, Sean thought, *"This dude has the audacity to confront us unarmed."* Then he burst out laughing and said, "You must be asking for a death wish or trying to save your little girlfriend. Either way, we're about to f*** you up. Yoh, guys, let's teach this sucker a lesson!".

Suddenly, they surrounded him and pulled out their knives, positioning James in the middle, just like they had done to her. They all squared up, as James calmly stood there. Before they could raise their hands, James had already jumped over one of them and shielded the young lady with his body. Then he reached for her hand and helped her stand up before turning back to the bandits.

James put his hands in a self-defense position then started ducking and weaving, leaning back and forth to avoid the swings of the knives from the rapists. James backflipped as they advanced towards him. Then he dropped into a squat position, tackled the first guy to the ground and back kicked the second guy on the head. Pat tried to stab him from behind, but James sidestepped and kneed him in the gut, twisted and broke his hand. At that point, Sean realized that James was far more skilled than he had expected, so he went for his gun. Before he could grab his gun, James spun around and hit him in the head with his own gun, causing him to be knocked out as well as the others.

James turned and saw Rose standing with her arms folded, shivering. Rose stood at a height of about five feet eight inches, exuding a seductive aura. She had honey-colored skin, a firm Grecian nose, long wavy brown hair, roundish-almond deep-set gray eyes, full hips, an hourglass body shape, wide hips, thick thighs, a small stomach, and a fascinating smile that could light up a room. Rose was of mixed heritage, with a Rancenian father and a Drakillian Fabrican mother. "Are you okay?" he asked.

Rose whimpered and replied, "Yeah, I'm fine, thanks to you."

"Don't mention it, it was my pleasure!" James replied.

"I don't know how to thank you. Wait, you look familiar! If I'm not mistaken, we went to the same middle school, right?" asked Rose.

Feeling exhilarated that she recognized him, James smiled and replied, "That's right, we did go to the same elementary school."

"What are you doing out here?" she asked.

"I just started attending Spirits University!" he replied. "My name is James, how about you?" he added.

"My name is Rose," she responded.

Curiosity got the best of him, so he asked, "Don't tell me we're attending the same school again?"

"No, I go to another branch, thirty minutes away from your school, called Spirits University, School of Art. However, I'm always at your school because my dad works there," she replied.

"That's awesome. It must be convenient for you to have your dad working at the best school in the State!" said James.

"Yeah!" she replied, realizing that her shirt was ripped because her sweater had been stripped off and her jacket thrown on the ground by the attackers.

James picked up her dirty and ripped clothes from the ground and passed them to her. Rose looked up into his bright gray eyes and said, "Now I'm terrified to walk by myself. I hope it isn't too much to ask, but can you please walk me home?"

"Well, of course, I'd love to take you home. Let me make sure these guys stay put," James replied and walked over to where the predators were lying. He pulled off their clothes and used them to tie up their feet and hands. He called the police and then left.

They weren't too far from her house, so they arrived within fifteen minutes. As they got closer to the house, Rose remembered that her father was home. She had to explain the situation to him, so she said, "I'm nervous to face my father after what happened today because I don't know how to tell him."

"It's completely normal to feel nervous about discussing difficult situations with our parents, especially if it's something you think they might not react well to. Remember that open and honest communication is key in any relationship, and it's important to express your feelings and concerns to your loved ones." He stopped and looked her in the eyes, and added, "Remember, if you ever need assistance in communicating with your father, I'm here to help."

Gabriel arrived a few seconds before Rose and James. He parked the car and got out, spotting his daughter walking with another young man, he waited for them to arrive. He recognized his daughter, but he didn't recognize her friend. So, he waited for them to arrive. As they got close, he realized that the young man was James. When Rose was face to face with her father, she cried out, "Daddy!" as she ran and hugged him tightly.

Gabriel noticed that his daughter was frightened, so he hugged her back and asked, "What happened, baby?"

Feeling ashamed, she continued to cry. "It's okay, baby, you're home now!" he added before noticing James standing there calmly so he directed his question to James instead. "Hey, Mr. Jordan, what are you doing here with my daughter?"

Gabriel's voice was filled with concern as he waited for James to provide an explanation. James sensed that Gabriel was disturbed by his daughter's reaction and felt responsible for her bafflement. Thus, he quickly clarified, "Mr. Houston, it's not what you think. She was in trouble, and I helped."

"Trouble? What kind of trouble?" asked Gabriel.

James took a deep breath and replied, "I was on our way to meet Rich when we noticed a group of people chasing after her. They seemed aggressive and she looked really scared, so I stepped in to help her."

Gabriel's worry intensified as he listened to James's words. He looked at his daughter, still clinging onto him, seeking comfort and reassurance. "Why were they chasing after her, James?" Gabriel questioned, his protective instincts kicking in.

James hesitated for a moment before responding, choosing his words carefully. "I think they were trying to sexually assault her."

Gabriel's brow furrowed with concern as he processed the information. He gently stroked his daughter's back, trying to calm her down. "Rose, sweetheart, are you hurt? Did they do anything to you?"

Rose shook her head, tears still flowing down her face. Rose looked up at her dad in tears and tried to express herself. "No, Daddy, James... James saved me! He found me near the alley, in danger of being raped and rescued me. These two guys were beating me up and trying to take off my clothes when James came out of nowhere and fought them. They had weapons, but he handled them, then made sure I was safe by bringing me home. He is my hero!"

Gabriel looked at James with gratitude and said, "Wow, James, way to go! From the moment we met, I knew you were special. I couldn't have been prouder of you man. Come here, thank you, James. Thank you." Gabriel opened his arms and hugged them both. "Thank you for protecting my daughter, James. Why didn't you call me right away and call the police?" he added afterwards.

James sighed, understanding the concerns Gabriel had. "We did call the police after. As for not calling you, I think Rose was too frightened and didn't want to worry you until she saw you in person."

Gabriel's expression softened as he considered Rose's fears and intentions. He hugged her tighter, whispering reassuring words in her ear. Then, Gabriel turned back to James. "Alright, James. I appreciate your help, truly."

James nodded, relieved that Gabriel seemed more understanding now. "Of course, Mr. Houston!" he said.

Gabriel turned his attention back to Rose and said, "We'll get through this together."

Shortly after talking to his wife about what had happened to Rose earlier that day, he called Holly. After a few rings, she answered, "Hello!"

"Hello, may I speak to Mrs. Jordan, please?" said Gabriel.

"Speaking, how may I help you?" she answered.

"This is Gabriel Houston, James' advisor at Spirits University. I used to work with your late husband at the BIA," he said and then inquired about her well-being.

"Pretty good, how about you and your family?" she replied and asked.

"Can't complain myself!" he replied, paused for a moment to gather his thoughts, then continued, "Alright, I wanted to thank you for allowing James to come this far for school!"

"You're welcome; you know James needed a fresh start after his father's passing," she replied.

"I wanted to let you know that I've noticed how incredibly talented your son is. In less than a semester of advising him, I believe he'll meet all the requirements needed to get into his major. Not only is he performing excellently in school, but he is also serving the community."

"That's incredible. That's what I expect from him. I was a little concerned that the recent tragedy would affect his focus, but I never doubted his intellect for a minute," Holly remarked.

If you haven't heard yet, your son is a hero out here! Hence, the reason we would like to assist him further. If he keeps this up, he'll have the chance to get a full scholarship and a paid internship at our BIA center in New Amsterdam City for the upcoming summer," said Gabriel.

"Wow, thank you very much, Mr. Houston!" said Rose.

"It is my pleasure. Your husband told me that if anything ever happened to him, to look after you all. God willing, I will do exactly that," said Gabriel.

With their conversation coming to an end, Holly expressed her belief in his counseling.

"It's great to know that! You've been doing a fantastic job advising James, so please continue supporting him throughout his education. With your guidance, he should have no trouble graduating and following in his father's footsteps."

During that spring semester, James built a strong relationship with his roommate and some outgoing and supportive students. Having a close group of friends made the semester even more meaningful and enjoyable to James. His circle felt like family; they told each other pretty much everything.

A few weeks into the semester, James was in his dorm room napping when LV, his roommate, unlocked the door and pushed it inward. LV was born in a different country called Maryland and migrated to Fabrica when he was a toddler. He has a slightly chubby build and an average height of about six feet. LV has fair porcelain skin, nice soft curly hair, a pair of close-set brown eyes, a flat nose, split lips, an engaging smile, and a round body shape. The sound of the door opening woke him up. James had a dream that his father was still alive and tied up in a burning house. He sat up and talked to LV for a while, expressing his feelings about the nightmare he had about his father. Afterwards, James walked out and called his mother, Holly.

"Mom, I'm telling you, I keep dreaming about Dad. The other day, I dreamed about accompanying him to the airport. Today, I dreamed that he was held hostage in Freeland. What do you think this means?" James voiced.

"James, your father is dead. Nothing bad can happen to him anymore," his mother said as she grabbed her purse and signaled Jolie to hurry up.

James walked back and forth in front of his dorm, then he broke down and cried, asking, "Why did he have to die?"

His mother realized he was weeping, so she said, "James, he'll always be a part of us. Remember what he always used to say?"

"Yeah, I know, Mom," he replied before adding, "Nothing is as bad as it seems!"

"I know you, James. What's really bothering you, baby?" Holly asked, trying to understand the root cause of James' distress.

Not wanting his mother to discover that he was investigating his father's death, he tried to avoid answering.

"It's just these dreams!" he said.

Holly noticed that James was holding something back so she said "It seems like you are struggling with the unresolved mystery surrounding your father's death."

"Yeah mom, you're right." James confessed then explained. "I recently learned that they still have not found Dad's killer because everyone in his squad was afraid to go back to Flowropia. Therefore, the mission is postponed for now. I discovered that Dad is after the deadliest terrorist in the world. He's in charge of one of the most powerful organizations globally. Even the Fabrican government hesitates to apprehend him after their unsuccessful attempts over the past five years. His name is Manuel, a Rancenian citizen. His company has businesses all around the world and affiliates even here. Their organization has been manufacturing and distributing weapons and hacking bank systems in Rancenia, Bellivia and West Drakilla for decades before expanding to the rest of the world. I just completed a project on this case, which is how I learned about all of this!"

"Wow, that sounds like quite a dangerous and complex situation. I can understand why the agency hasn't been successful in dealing with this lunatic. It's important to prioritize your safety and the safety of others before getting yourself involved. If you have just completed a project in this case, it might be helpful to share your findings and information with a trustworthy individual, such as Mr. Houston or Steve, the BIA director. They may already be aware of the situation but your insights could provide additional details that could assist in their efforts. It would be wise to maintain a cautious approach and not put yourself in any direct danger. I know it must be difficult for you to process all this information right now, but I want you to take it one day at a time. Remember, safety should always be the top priority. Don't get yourself into any trouble by looking too far into the agency's secured files. I'll call you later so we can finish this conversation. I must leave now," Holly advised James before she hung up her cellphone."

Afterwards James walked back into the room, LV asked him, "What's good, bro? Is everything okay? Your eyes are super red, it seems like you were crying."

"I'm good!" replied James.

Sensing that he didn't want to talk about it, LV said, "OK," and tossed the NBA 2K game to James. "If you say so, look at what I just got!" he added.

James caught the disc, placed it inside the system, and handed LV the other controller. After James and LV played for a while, B Money and Slim knocked on the door. B Money was a Fabrican, but his parents were from Freeland, the same birthplace as James. He was five feet seven inches tall, with cocoa skin color, short black hair, droopy hooded brown eyes, a big, pointed nose, an overbite with an engaging smile, and a husky rectangular body shape. After opening the door, James saw that his partners were with their girlfriends Mary and Emily. Mary was with B Money and Emily was with Slim. Mary was from Zendiana, a country which was in south Fabrica. She was five feet seven inches tall, with blue eyes, a heart-shaped head, a delicate nose, and plump swollen lips. Emily was from Fabrica. She was five feet six inches tall, she had a Roman nose, a warm tan skin color, flat lips, long straight hair, a Coca-Cola body shape, brown Asian eyes, a faded smile, and a diamond-shaped head.

A few minutes later, Smokey also showed up, so it was getting crowded in the dorm. To feel more comfortable, they all went down to the lobby and continued playing the "TWO K EIGHT" video game. Smokey was from Portisia, a country located in Flowropia. Unlike most people with that name, Smokey, who usually had a very dark complexion, had a natural skin color. He had gray eyes, a delicate nose, collagen-inflated lips, a cheeky smile, and stood at about five feet eight inches tall. He also had short, wavy hair. They played together a little more before heading to the cafeteria for dinner.

As the group made their way to the cafeteria, they chatted about their day. Slim shared about his classes and the exciting project he was working on in the communication's department. The others listened intently, impressed by his knowledge and dedication.

Once they reached the cafeteria, they grabbed their trays and went on the line. The wonderful scent of freshly cooked food wafted through the air, making them anticipate what meal they were going to choose. They loaded their plates with their favorite dishes, then found a table to sit together.

As they enjoyed their meal, they engaged in lively conversations, discussing the upcoming events on campus. Smokey's funny remarks and infectious humor kept everyone entertained, making the dinner an enjoyable affair.

After finishing their meals, everyone except for Smokey, who lived off campus, decided to head back to the dorm to relax for the evening. As they walked back, Mary and Emily suggested they watch a movie together in their room. The idea was met by the fellows with a lot of energy and they quickly agreed on a film to watch.

Back in the dorm, they settled down in the comfortable beds, pillows, and blankets next to the television. They all got cozy, ready to enjoy the movie night. LV had a knack for finding the best songs to play and movies to watch, thus everyone looked forward to his choice.

As the movie played on the small flat screen, they laughed, gasped, and got completely engaged in the storyline. Time flew by, and before they knew it, the movie had ended, leaving them all wanting more. It was getting late, so they bid each other goodnight, thanked each other for the wonderful evening, and retreated to their own rooms. The dorm slowly quieted down as everyone settled in for the night, their bonds of friendship strengthened by the shared experiences of the day.

It was the next morning, and James shared his feelings with LV.

"I can't keep spending my mom's money like this. I want to make a change and use her money more responsibly," he expressed.

LV listened attentively until James finished pouring out his feelings and gave his perspective.

"It's understandable, James! You feel overwhelmed and conflicted about your father's past, and that's impacting your academic performance. I suggest you manage your stress and make better choices. Prioritize your studies, seek guidance and support. You should reach out to a counselor or academic advisor."

"Ok, I will. Thank you a million!" said James.

After school that day, James was at Mr. Houston's office getting advice from him. "I want you to find a part-time job, which would not only provide you with a source of income but also help you build a sense of responsibility and independence. Surround yourself with positive influences, consider spending time with friends who prioritize their studies, and have a positive impact on your life!" said Gabriel.

"Remember, change takes time and effort, so it's important for you to be patient and kind to yourself throughout this process." He added as James was walking out.

"Ok Mr. Houston, I appreciate your help!" replied James.

After school closed, James went home for summer vacation. He had been offered a summer internship by Christopher. Two weeks after arriving in New Amsterdam City, James started the internship. He worked at a company that offered transportation to national and international political leaders, as well as federal agents, around the city. The day was cloudy, windy, and humid, so the shade from the clouds was much appreciated. As James cruised through traffic on GW Dr. Southbound, which led to the facility where he was interning, he weaved in and out of traffic in his mother's silver Jeep. His destination was Long Bay City, Weenstone. Upon arrival, James was welcomed by Christopher and his colleagues with open arms, as he had been referred to them by Gabriel.

After settling in at the company, James was assigned the task of transporting the BIA agents. As he was already familiar with the city, he started the job on the third day after learning about the company's procedures and protocols for ensuring the safety and security of their high-profile clients.

The next few weeks, James had the opportunity to observe firsthand how the company coordinated with law enforcement agencies and government officials to handle the logistics of transporting important individuals. He saw how critical it was to maintain utmost professionalism and discretion in their operations. He met many former BIA members and their families. Halfway through the internship, Christopher hosted a party at the facility for his top five team members in honor of Alex. Everyone showed up with their families. Christopher was there with his wife and stepson, Noah, who was studying abroad in Rancenia but was in New Amsterdam City for summer vacation. Gabriel was there with

Mrs. Houston and their daughter, Rose. Antoine came to the event with Sam. Even Ben showed up with Rich.

During his time there, James gained valuable experience and knowledge in the field of transportation and security. He developed a deep understanding of the importance of attention to detail and effective communication in this line of work.

James also had the chance to network with Christopher and other active BIA agents, who shared their industry insights and provided guidance for his future career aspirations. He even got a chance to meet Steve. He made sure to learn from their experiences and ask questions whenever possible.

A few weeks later, James was on his way to the center, and it was a rainy evening. Puddles began to form as the rain got heavier. Meanwhile, after stopping to chat with Christopher about politics, Mr. Iverson was stuck at the office due to the bad weather. He had a flight to catch but it was canceled due to the heavy storm, so he was still at the office. Mr. Iverson wanted to stay at a hotel until the airport resumed its schedule but he couldn't leave yet because he couldn't find transportation. That was when Christopher remembered that James usually came to the office at that time, so he called James to double-check. Christopher doubted that James would be so determined for the job that he would come in under those conditions.

As James drove slowly and watched everyone outside running for cover as the strong, gusty wind blew harder. Moments later when he looked out the window, he didn't see anyone anymore—only a few cars were on the road. James was driving the bulletproof truck that Christopher had given him to use for work. He drove past the smaller cars that were stuck along the way due to the rain. Suddenly, his phone rang, "Ring! Ring!"

"Hello," answered James.

"Hello, Mr. Jordan, I hope I'm not interrupting anything!" came the voice from the other end.

"Not at all, Mr. Smith. Just on my way to work." James replied.

"Are you coming to the office today?" asked Christopher.

"Yes, sir. I'm on my way to the office. Is there something you need?" replied James.

"Well, actually, it's about Mr. Iverson," Christopher explained. "He's stuck here due to the bad weather and is looking for transportation to a hotel until the airport resumes its schedule. I remembered that you usually come to the office around this time, so I thought you might be able to help him out."

James glanced at the pouring rain outside and thought for a moment.

"Sure, I'll give him a ride when I get there. I'll be there soon!" said James.

"I really appreciate this, James. I hope it's not too much trouble for you," said Christopher.

"No problem at all, Mr. Smith. I'll be there shortly," James assured him.

After hanging up, Christopher and Mr. Iverson patiently waited for James. James drove to the office, maneuvering carefully through the rain-soaked streets. When he arrived, Mr. Iverson was waiting under the sheltered entrance.

Moments later, James arrived and jumped out of the truck with a huge umbrella that was big enough to shield all three of them. Mr. Iverson and Christopher were standing under the big custom glass and metal awning with Mr. Iverson's suitcases.

Mr. Iverson sounded relieved. "Oh, James, you are fantastic. I've been trying to figure out transportation for ages. Thank you so much!" he said.

"No problem, Mr. Iverson," replied James. He then picked up the suitcases and placed them inside the vehicle.

Christopher remembered that his car was very low, so he followed them and got inside the car as well.

"You're coming too?" asked James.

"Yeah, I need you to drop me off too. You know my car is too low for this rain," said Christopher as he walked to the car.

James opened the back door of the Jeep and they jumped in. Mr. Iverson and Christopher quickly hopped into the truck, grateful for the dry and secure transportation it offered. "Thanks again, James. I really appreciate you doing this for me!" said Mr. Iverson.

"It's not a problem at all," James replied with a smile. "I'm glad I could assist. Let's get you to that hotel safe and sound."

As they drove through the stormy weather, James and Mr. Iverson engaged in friendly conversation, providing some distraction from the dreary conditions outside. James demonstrated reliable driving skills during a challenging weather condition. The sturdy bulletproof truck contributed to a smooth and safe journey. James drove them both to their destinations; he dropped off Mr. Iverson first at the hotel, since it was next to the company.

Upon reaching the hotel, Mr. Iverson thanked James once more for his assistance.

"I don't know what I would have done without your help," he added.

James waved off Mr. Iverson's gratitude and said, "I'm just doing my job, sir."

With that, Mr. Iverson entered the hotel, leaving James with a feeling of satisfaction in knowing that he had been able to assist his boss and his colleague. Then James headed to Christopher's house. Along the way, Christopher asked him to go home for the day. Therefore, after dropping off Christopher, he turned the truck around and headed back into the rain, thankful for the opportunity to lend a helping hand when it mattered most.

A month later, James went to the facility. Normally, whenever James visited Christopher's office, the routine was the same. He would hand his identification card to the secretary, and she would give him a check. After that, he would start his shift. On that day, he completed the routine more efficiently because it was his last day with the company.

James walked in and greeted, "Hello there." He handed his card to Katherine, and she handed him a check. He turned and walked out. However, as soon as he stepped out the door, she called out his name loudly.

Katherine, who was Morovian, had dark skin, a Coca-Cola-shaped body, and long natural hair. "James," she exclaimed, catching her breath before continuing as she ran after him. "Excuse me, James. Mr. Smith would like to speak with you for a moment!" she said.

James turned and replied, "Okay." He walked back, entered the office, and sat across from Mr. Smith. They had a conversation.

"How are you doing, Mr. Jordan?" Mr. Smith asked. "I'm fine, sir. How about you?" James replied.

Christopher continued, "If you have a minute, I have something very important I would like to discuss with you."

"Of course, I do!" James replied,

"Well, Mr. Jordan, I wanted to tell you that you are exceptional. I think you should apply for a position with our organization as one of our agents after you graduate. When the time comes, make sure you reach out!" Christopher suggested.

"Definitely! Thank you, Mr. Smith!" James assured him and then shook his hand.

As the summer internship came to an end, James felt grateful for the opportunity and the skills he had acquired. He knew that the experience he gained during his time at the company would greatly benefit him in his future endeavors. With a sense of accomplishment, James returned home ready to apply what he had learned in his academic and professional pursuits.

There were a couple of weeks left before he returned to school. A few days after completing his internship, James was arrested for smoking marijuana in public. When James got caught, he was with Oumar, their girlfriends, and his cousin Alpha. As a result of these arrests, James went through the criminal justice system for the first time in his life.

A week later, he was arrested again on the scene after buying a small amount of marijuana but that time he was only with Oumar and their girlfriends. He left them in the car and went and bought two grams worth of weed. When he returned, undercover police surrounded his car and pointed all types of guns at them. The officers took James to jail because the substance was in his vehicle and no one took responsibility for it, while the police let go of his girlfriend, his cousin, and his cousin's girlfriend. He was detained at the precinct for a few hours before being taken to the bookings to see the judge. Since it was the weekend, he had to wait close to forty-eight hours to see the judge. He didn't need a lawyer to defend him; the judges released him immediately after he saw them.

CHAPTER FOUR

THE COME-UP TIME

After that summer, James started his junior year and transitioned to off-campus housing. Due to the loss of his father, he had matured into an individual, who possessed leadership skills and an entrepreneurial spirit. Thus, he believed living off campus will provide him a sense of independence. He had grown his circle significantly since the previous year, however he was not as well-known in the community as he would like to be. Moving out of the school's dormitory and into off-campus housing to share the unit with B Money, LV, and Slim would give him more freedom and become more social. Smokey, who already lived off campus since the prior year, was still in the same complex with three other gentlemen. Together these five individuals formed a tight-knit group and had exciting and memorable experiences. From living arrangements to meals, games, and parties, they did everything together. The bond between them was so strong that they rarely spent any time apart, except during school breaks when they returned to their respective hometowns. However, even during these breaks, they tried to meet up and stay connected. Living off-campus provided James a sense of independence and freedom. It allowed him to create a space where he could grow and thrive, surrounded by friends who shared similar ambitions and interests. The unity and camaraderie among them fostered an environment of support and encouragement, enabling James to further develop his leadership and entrepreneurial skills.

After making some money during the summer from his internship, James had become accustomed to earning his own money and not relying on his mother or taking out school loans for personal expenses. Accumulating unnecessary responsibilities like spending money on clothes, parties, alcohol, weed, and traveling, he began breaking down his expenses. He started thinking about ways to make money during or after school hours,

A few weeks into the semester, on a crisp and bright day at the end of the summer, James had come out of his only class on Fridays and went to hang with Smokey at his place. Upon arrival, they went to the balcony and rolled some blunts. Sitting there as a gentle breeze blew by them, James took a pull from a blunt of Blueberry Haze before passing it to Smokey, who grabbed the blunt from him and kissed the tip with such passion that one would think he was just taking his first pull of the day, as if he hadn't already smoked his second blunt, and it was only noon. The two companions debated about who had the best weed in that town. At that moment James had entered a state of being high, and ideas started popping up in his brain. Therefore, he examined the marijuana consumption in his community and wondered, "*The demand for weed around here is very high, and I am well acquainted with the best marijuana distributors. Imagine if I were one of the distributors in this community. I would've been making a killing! If I sell a small amount of weed on the downlow, I could at least use my profit to smoke instead of spending my hard-earned money from my parents."* Afterwards, James stood up, gave his comrade a handshake, and walked out of the house to his old, yet still in good condition car parked in the parking lot. He hopped into the nineteen ninety-eight Nissan Maxima and drove back to the student living complex where he resided, which was only a few minutes away.

A week later, on a Friday evening, after James got to his apartment complex from school, he quickly packed his bag. Around two p.m. he hopped back into his car and pulled off. He was on his way home to New Amsterdam City. However, this time, he went to New Amsterdam just for just the weekend and not for any school breaks. The drive was long, as it took approximately four to five hours, depending on the flow of traffic. Along the way, he called Oumar, who was well connected in the business field he wanted to start. The phone rang for a while before Oumar picked up; then it took him a moment before he made a sound. James heard a lot of noise in the background so he said, "O, can you hear me, hello?" Most of his friends called him, O so James called him that.

"Hello, yeah Stackz, sorry I'm a little busy," Oumar finally answered James, as most of his friends had started calling him Stackz, because that was his nickname.

"O, what's good with you? Just giving you a heads up, I'm on my way to New York. When I touch down, I'm coming straight to you!" he said and paused due to the loud music and chatter in the background.

"Hello, O, can you hear me?" he voiced on the other end.

"Yeah Stackz. No problem. Perfect timing, everyone is here bro. We are out here chilling and maxing, drive safe!" Oumar finally replied.

James was in the middle lane, controlling the steering wheel with his left hand while simultaneously holding his phone with his right hand. Oumar was five feet eleven inches. He is mixed, Drakillian and Bellivian, and was built like Mike Tyson. He had short, nice dark curly hair, brown roundish-almond eyes, an average body shape, an artificial smile, almond skin color, and a droopy nose.

"Copy!" James replied as he heard a young woman saying, "Hurry up my love!"

Oumar turned and hollered, "Coming boo!"

The call was fast. After Oumar answered, James hung up and drove faster because he only wanted to get his message across.

James arrived at his mother's house around seven p.m. that evening. It took him five hours because there was a lot of traffic along the way. He talked to Holly for a while.

"Mom, do you know why dad wanted me to go to Spirits University?" he asked her.

"I believe it was because his friends Gabriel and Christopher are alumni, and they highly recommended the school for you. He also said that the school offers the best intelligence program and has the highest BIA recruitment," responded Holly.

"Sounds like dad really values the recommendations of his friends and believes that the school they recommended would be a good fit for me. They were right! It's great to attend a school that offers a strong intelligence program and has a high recruitment rate for the BIA, even though I've been struggling lately!" he remarked.

"You were doing excellent last year. What changed?" she asked.

"Well, I'm getting homesick, but I'm trying to get back on track," he replied.

"It's completely normal to miss your family, friends, and home, especially when you're attending a new school. It's great that you're trying to get back on track despite feeling homesick. Try and stay connected with your family and friends through phone calls, video chats, or messages. Get involved in activities or clubs at your school to meet and make new friends. Establish a routine that includes time for study, relaxation, and social activities to help you feel more settled. Remember, it's okay to feel that way, but with time and effort, you can adjust to your new environment and excel in your studies!" she explained.

Since James had gone away to college, whenever he came home, he was a little uncomfortable staying with his family considering his smoking habit. He never smoked as much before he went away, and his mother still didn't know he smoked.

"James, please stay for the night?" Holly asked with a soft, anxious voice.

"Mom, I already told Alpha that I'm on my way. He's been waiting for me since I got here!" he said just as he opened the front door.

She said nothing so he turned just as the door opened and glanced at her. She looked defeated so he walked back and gave her a hug.

"I love you more baby. Tell him I said hello!" she finally managed to say as she got up and walked towards him.

"Ok mom," he replied as she kissed him on the cheek.

As James cruised through the busy streets of Amsterdam, he saw kids playing tag, biking, walking, some in the park playing basketball, while others were watching. The older moms and pops were talking, barbecuing, and the elderly ladies and men were in their wheelchairs watching the action.

"I know she missed me, I can tell the way she was looking at me but I can't be myself around here. I want to smoke, drink, and party with some fine ladies," he thought.

He felt free when he was with his peers, knowing that he could smoke, drink, and party with his buddies all night. He always had options because all his friends invited him every time he returned to school. Though he was welcomed with open arms by all his friends, he often stayed with Alpha. When he got close to his destination, he called Alpha. "Cous, this time around I'm going to stay with Oumar since I'm trying to get in business with him!" said James.

"Ok, that's cool," Alpha responded.

"You want to go out tonight?" asked James. "Nah, bro, I'm staying in with my shortie," Alpha replied.

Moments later, James arrived and parked a few blocks away from the residence because he couldn't find parking next to it. It was a few minutes past nine p.m. when he knocked the door of the apartment softly. No one answered, perhaps due to the loud noise inside or the music. He knocked again with more assurance. Someone opened the door. After walking in and seeing that it was too messy and overcrowded, he thought, "There are too many guests in this place; I should've crashed with Alpha." Then he walked out instantly and stood outside the apartment to call Alpha again. He dialed Alpha's number and waited for him to pick up anxiously. "Yoh cous, you better wait up for me. I'm not spending the night here anymore, it's too crowded. As soon as I'm done handling business with O, I'm coming over," James whispered so Oumar nor anyone in the apartment could hear him. "No problem, Stackz, just hit me up. I'll be here," replied Alpha.

"Copy!" said James.

Oumar was a very wise individual. He had a few older brothers who schooled him about the ins and outs of hustling since they were in high school. By his sophomore year in high school, Oumar was a veteran in the streets. He had become a big-timer. At that point, his business was booming better than ever.

After James shook hands with a few familiar faces, he walked to the back of the hallway with Oumar as they talked. "Bro, I thought I saw you walk in. Where did you go? You know you're good here!" Oumar questioned James.

"Nah, bro, it was not even like that. It was too loud in here, and I had to talk to my cousin quickly," James replied and added, "What's up with you, though? How's business?"

After James settled in, he walked back into the huge apartment, socializing with different individuals. It was one of those old-school places with high ceilings, long hallways, and big rooms. There was enough space for everyone to chill, but not enough to sleep comfortably.

After having a few shots of rum, James cut straight to the chase, "Yoh O, I need your help! I want to get into business with you, but I don't have any money right now. Can you look out for your brother and front me an ounce or two?" he expressed himself with desperation.

He took a moment to comprehend what he had just heard from James, as excitement flooded him. Oumar stopped dead in his tracks, placed his hands on James's shoulders, and looked James straight in the eyes.

"Of course, bro! I got you, say no more," said Oumar. He was thrilled to hear that a well-educated college student like James wanted to join his kind of business. "Walk with me!" he added.

They walked back to the living room while they continued their conversation. Oumar then stopped in the middle of the hallway, the only place where there was no one. Even though no one could hear them due to the music, he just wanted assurance. "Look Stackz, I don't usually do this, but since you're my brother from another mother, I made an exception. I'll give you two ounces of some Reggie to begin with. That's worth three hundred dollars!" he said.

"Word?" James uttered in excitement.

"Yeah, that means you bring me three hundred dollars next time I see you," Oumar said with a slightly more serious tone and a look of determination in his eyes.

At that time, James stared back at him right in the eyes and said, "Trust me, I got you."

Then Oumar loosened up and smiled broadly then asked, "So what's up, you are spending the night?"

He paused and winked before adding, "You know I got some bad broads for you!" he added.

"Nah Brody! I promised Alpha I would pull up on him too, but I will stay for a while so I can Make with some of these ladies you got for me," James replied regretfully as realized that he might be letting the opportunity of getting laid for the night slip away.

Oumar nodded his head, signaling James to follow. "Alright, come on then, follow me. I'm going to take care of you first, so we can party after!" he said.

They walked in the bedroom, Oumar went to his stockpile and pulled out a big bag of marijuana from it. He took two bags and gave them to James then put the rest in his backpack and stashed it in his closet.

"Keep it in your room for me until I'm ready to leave," whispered James.

"Ok," answered Oumar. He grabbed his bookbag and hid it next to his stash before they walked out of the bedroom.

Itching to flirt with some ladies, right after they came out of the room, James asked, "Bro, where are the joints you were talking about?"

"I got you!" said Oumar as they walked back to the living room. "Tatiana, Ashley, pull up!" he yelled and simultaneously gave the young ladies a hand gesture to walk toward him.

"Ladies, this is my brother; make sure you show him a good time! He's a college student, so give him the special treatment," said Oumar.

James, who had become a ladies' man, showed interest in Ashley by approaching her and ignoring Tatiana. His indirect actions made it clear to Tatiana that he was not interested in her. James and Ashley then left excitedly to go to the bedroom together. After entering the room and locking the door behind them, they made out for a moment before engaging in sexual activity. James pulled down his pants, while Ashley unbuttoned hers. They touched each other's genitals. After some strokes, they became intimate, and a moment later he ejaculated.

"Gorgeous, you're the bomb! I would love to kick it with you all night, but I got to dip soon. I have some business to handle early in the morning," he expressed as he rinsed his private part.

"It's ok, you already gave me some, so I'm going to let you slide! You better call me though," Ashley responded as she wiped her private area with some wipes that she had inside her purse.

After cleaning up and fixing their clothes, they walked out, taking the walk of shame as they went through the crowded hallway to the living room. Most of their acquaintances were paired up and cuddling with their partners. The living room was filled with couples hanging out together, which helped James and Ashley blend in more than when they first left the bedroom.

A half an hour later, James had lost track of time. It wasn't until around eleven p.m. that he started to excuse himself from Ashley. However, he stuck around for a while longer until he convinced her to come with him. He approached her in the kitchen where she was smoking hookah with her girlfriends.

"I'm about to head out. Are you ready?" he asked with a look of urgency in his eyes.

Sensing exhaustion from James and feeling tired herself she murmured, "Yeah let's get out of here' I'm tired."

"Alright, wait here. I'm about to holler at O quick," said James. He got up and went to see Oumar, who was already in the room waiting for him. James quickly grabbed his backpack, shook his hand, and left the room. Then he took Ashley's hand, walked across the room, and exited the apartment.

Once James and Ashley arrived at his cousin's place James rang the bell. After opening the door they walked in. Alpha pulled him to the side and quietly said, "S***, you didn't tell me that you were bringing a guest!"

They both smirked as James saw Aisha, his cousin's partner, sitting on the modern red and black leather loveseat. He walked to her, bent down, and gave her a kiss on the side of her right cheek, saying, "Hey Aisha."

"Hey Stackz," she replied.

Afterwards he sat on the single couch next to the big couch that Aisha was sitting on and gestured for Ashley to come sit on his lap. Alpha sat back down next to Aisha. "So, what's good bro? I miss you man, how is school?" he asked.

"It's cool, how about you?" James replied.

"I'm good too, just trying to get this money," uttered Alpha.

"That's what I'm trying to do, be on your type of time," replied James as he pulled out the bags of marijuana then continued.

"I figured since I always keep this around me, I might as well sell it."

Alpha laughed and said, "You were serious, huh?"

"Of course!" replied James. They lounged around for another hour before Alpha excused himself and went to his room with Aisha, leaving James and Ashley in the living room all to themselves. They got intimate again before going to sleep.

Next day, James was back at school with a small amount of marijuana, ready to launch his business. Meanwhile, Peter was trying to track down James for months. He had been scouting for James in colleges all over New Amsterdam and had not found him yet.

A month and a couple of weeks later, it was halfway into the fall semester. It was a cold and breezy day; he was at his off campus housing complex, hanging out with one of his girlfriends when his cell phone rang. James answered, and it was LV.

"James!" exclaimed LV.

Sounding out of breath as if he had been running, but the reality was that he was just eager to share some good news. "Vicky offered to treat the whole crew to dinner. Let's meet up at the school's cafeteria in half an hour," he added.

"Copy!" replied James.

An hour later, they were all gathered in the cafeteria, seated around a table, enjoying dinner and having a conversation. LV only wore high-end name brands; his parents were wealthy.

"Guys, check out LV, always flaunting his style - a new Burberry belt and matching LV glasses," Smokey pointed out.

"Are you kidding me? These were all gifts. I just happen to have friends in high places!" LV retorted.

"Yeah right, and I'm the richest man on the planet!" Smokey said jokingly.

Smokey winked and tapped B Money lightly on his foot. "Man, I'm serious. Some of us need you to let me hold something. I mean look at Slim, for example, his kicks are cooked!" he said.

Everyone burst out laughing except for Emily who gazed at Slim.

"Stop Smokey, you almost made me choke on my food!" said Mary.

Slim surged and exclaimed, "You better mind your business, man. If you stopped being obsessed with things you can't afford, you wouldn't be so thirsty for these expensive name brands. Unlike you, I'm good with the cooked kicks. I don't need material things to make me confident."

LV, and Smokey chuckled before Slim continued.

"LV just knows how and what to spend his money on. You also like to splurge a lot. I bet if you traded in that Gucci bag you bought Tiff for her birthday, you might be able to afford some Burberry items!" he added.

"Guy, you need to cut it out. We're here to enjoy dinner, not to evaluate who dresses best or who has the most money. That's childish; we're grown!" B Money weighed in.

"Man, if you don't shut you Smurf look A** up… I was just kidding!" said Smokey disdainfully.

LV gave a halfhearted laugh, leaned in, and kissed his girlfriend Rebecca, ignoring their back-and-forth banter.

It got quiet for a moment until James broke the silence and took the time to advertise his merchandise.

"Speaking of economizing, don't forget to tell everyone you know who got that piff."

Everyone at the table stopped eating and laughed except for B Money after James promoted his product. He just sat there and gazed at them. Mary noticed a change in his facial expression and spoke.

"What happened, babe?" she asked, with googly eyes and pursed lips as she tried to console him. "You've got to admit that was funny," she added.

B Money never liked the fact that James was selling weed; he always felt like it was a distraction for a smart student as intelligent as he was. He said nothing for a moment then gave a gentle nod as to say she was right. "Man, if you don't take your fake Stacks no Bundles a** back home and studying for the exam, I'm going to call Mrs. Jordan and tell her that you are out here throwing your life away." He finally managed to say.

James ignored B Money and his remark.

Rebecca decided to chime in, "Stop hating man, the man is just out here trying to make a couple of dollars."

Smokey readied himself and spoke. "She's right, we're grown now. I'm just saying, I'm with James on this one; sometimes you must hustle."

Shortly afterwards, when they were done eating and relaxed a little bit more, everyone scattered quickly because they all had a midterm exam the next morning. Nobody wanted to hang out, not even the couples of the crew - Rebecca and James, LV and Emily, or Mary and B Money.

Back at his student living complex, James sat in his room at the desk and opened his Linguistics book to chapter one to read. He read for at least forty-five minutes, but he didn't understand much because his mind was not engaged. He was distracted by his dealing aspirations, thinking more about how he could take over the marijuana distribution around town. He decided he had had enough, so he looked for his weed stash and rolled a blunt. He smoked, ate some cornflakes, and about an hour later he went to sleep.

It was the day of the exam—James walked into the classroom and sat next to a lady named Britney. She was a classmate of James who was very quiet and reserved. James and his entourage respected her. She had an elegant attitude, and many of them had a crush on her because of her demeanor. Britney was also so good-looking that she scared the fellas away. However, James liked to take on challenges, so here and there, he tried his luck to see if he could get with her. Britney was about five feet eight inches, mixed with Britalinizian and Rancenian. She isolated herself often. She was the only girl who James seemed not to figure out because he couldn't break through her guards. James tried so many ways to get with Britney, but he hardly succeeded; it was tough to speak to someone who did not want to be spoken to. "Hey, beautiful, hope you studied because I didn't. I was hoping to cheat off you," he said flirtatiously.

She said nothing and just stared with no emotion. He looked back at her and realized that she felt uncomfortable by his remark. Her sharp gaze told him that his comment made her nervous.

"I, I was," he stammered. "I was just trying to make you laugh; I have a photographic memory. If anything, you might need my assistance. In case you do, give me a signal, and I would be glad to show you my answers," he assured her.

"Do I look like I'm in a laughing mood?" she asked.

"No, I mean yeah!" he replied softly.

"Well, I'm not!" she replied gruffly. She shocked him, so he just stayed quiet. There was a brief silence before the professor walked in, and the exam began.

It was at the end of that semester when Peter found out that James had gone away to school and was no longer in New Amsterdam. He promised to find out which school James was attending and disrupt his education. After a long search, Peter started speculating that, as a hujinn, James must be enrolled at Spirits University. Therefore, he contacted Mr. Jackson and informed him of James and stressed the importance of identifying him before he fully developed his powers, asking him to help confirm his speculations.

Peter held a meeting with his associates, Mr. Jackson, and Mr. Johnson, where they discussed their plan against Alex's family. They acknowledged that James's connection with the BIA and his genius level made it difficult to directly harm him. Mr. Jackson suggested establishing probable cause to prosecute James rather than resorting to simple methods like expulsion or financial harm. Mr. Johnson proposed a plan to isolate James, gather incriminating information, and, if necessary, set him up for prosecution, gaining approval from all present at the meeting.

After some time, Mr. Jackson called Jeffrey Johnson, the secretary of DE (Department of Education), and told him more about James and how crucial it would be to surveil him. He hacked the federal database to discover information on his father's death. At this rate, he could implicate me and my associates, so I must get rid of him before it's too late. Due to the brief breakdown, Mr. Johnson called Gabriel. However, the conversation wasn't going well, as Gabriel was stunned that the Secretary of the Department of Education was asking about James.

"Just tell him, maybe he's asking because Rob told him about how James easily dismantled him and his crew!" Gabriel thought.

"Give me a second," he said as he looked around the room, wondering, *"What could possibly be the reason that Mr. Johnson is asking about James."*

He gasped then finally said, "Ok, I guess I'll tell you what a brilliant individual he is. Most faculty members know him as an excellent student, but to my family and me, he's a hero. Once, he saved my daughter from some rapists and protected his family from some mercenaries."

"Yeah, I heard; that's why I called you. I wanted to find out if the stories are true and his school curriculums so I can send him my regards. I need a gifted man like him on my team," explained Mr. Johnson.

"Ok, just know, as his mentor and advisor, he's off-limits for now. His mother and I agree he must graduate before he signs any deals," Gabriel remarked.

"He's a student at Spirits University. Rob didn't tell you how easily he conquered him and his fraternity brothers?" asked Gabriel.

"No, I guess he must've been too embarrassed to mention it!" replied Mr. Johnson.

Sensing that there was more to his concern, Gabriel wanted to ask Mr. Johnson what he really wanted with James, but he didn't want it to sound disdainful.

"Just double check," he told himself.

"What do you want with him?" he finally managed to ask.

"I don't know about you, but I find it impressive for a college kid to be so skilled that he can compromise digital networks to access federal database accounts without authorization. I assure you, I'm not searching for him to eliminate my son's competition but rather to ensure his safety and appreciate his exceptional individuality!" said Mr. Johnson.

After learning more about James, he didn't take the information well. Finding out that James was more talented than his own son Rob automatically made him despise the boy but kept it to himself.

As soon as Mr. Johnson finished speaking to Gabriel, he called Mr. Jackson and informed him that he had discovered that James was attending Spirits University. He also confirmed that Peter was correct about James being paranormal. Mr. Jackson shared his passion for going against James after confirming that he could be a hujinn. Consequently, due to their disdain for James, a week later, Mr. Johnson, Mr. Jackson, and Peter conspired to set him up or murder him. They then assigned some agents to monitor his activities at Spirits University.

At that point, due to his popularity, many people were seriously interested in getting in touch with James. He knew everyone; he was close to the teachers, the ladies, the nerds, the drug dealers, and the users. He had a nice hooptie to take him back and forth from Amsterdam to College Town. He traveled every other week to buy more weed. He sold out fast whenever he went back to school, yet he still bought small amounts because he was still on the come-up. He sold out fast because he was organized and dedicated; he had some colleagues working with him. He had two females and a young man who was one grade behind him distributing as well. Sometimes his clients picked him up from class even before his classes ended. His phone was ringing off the hook, from customers, friends, to family. He got calls from all angles to the point he bought another phone. He used one for his personal use and the other for his business. He was overwhelmed because he was going to school, working hard, and serving the distributors and users. All the chicks were trying to get to know James because they had seen or heard that he was the man on campus.

While James was having the time of his life in college, Mr. Johnson, Peter, Mr. Jackson, were planning to scrutinize him. "You should've heard Gabriel raving about him the other day," said Mr. Johnson.

"I know, that's how my brother felt about his father!" remarked Peter.

"I'm telling you right now, if he's as brilliant as they said, I want him working with us. If he denies the offer, then we can discontinue his enrollment here and find an alternative solution to get rid of him!" said Mr. Johnson.

"I say let's waste him now, if we don't, soon he'll be our biggest threat by far. If we are not careful, he will take down all of us," suggested Mr. Jackson.

"Mr. Johnson, Mr. Jackson is right. I've been trying to eliminate his entire family since his father was alive. Back when he told me about his human wife!" said Peter.

"Samuel told me about the danger of hujinns too, right before he passed. He said they'd been expecting a superhujinn for centuries. All this time, who would have thought that one could be emerging right before our eyes!" admitted Mr. Jackson.

"Maybe Antoine could help; he did assist in setting up his father," said Peter.

"Ok, contact him and see what he has to say," said Mr. Johnson.

Afterwards, Peter placed the call.

"Yeah, of course. Since James is attending Spirits University, why not have my son Sam who's already familiar with him transfer to the same school. From there, we'll have him spy on James and see what he can dig up so we can use that to set him up?" proposed Antoine.

"That's an incredible idea. In the meantime, I'll ask the secretary of the Department of Education to speed up and facilitate your son's transfer. With his command, Sam could be at Spirits University as soon as tomorrow," Peter assured him.

During that short period of selling weed in College Town, James made a lot of money and became more popular. He became even more distracted because he was more concerned about making money, doing drugs, partying, and chasing women than he was with his studies. He was addicted to the lifestyle of dressing up with his boys and attending parties all over the country. He was well-known in his school because he was outgoing, so he was invited to most parties. His connections to the New Amsterdam City streets gave him a high status among his circle; therefore, he had high status in the community. When he realized that he was well-connected, he cared about gaining fame, power, and the respect of his peers instead of sticking to the script of graduating from college. He became so popular that he stood out to everyone in the area, even the police. He forgot to consider the law and the consequences of his actions.

The previous semester, James had learned that he was on academic probation but he'd overlooked it. In fact, he'd only been concerned about making money and growing his social life. It was a Thursday night at the end of November and finally occurred to him that he neglected his education. However, it was his friend's twentieth birthday, so he didn't want to go out with his boys. Yet, he also couldn't spoil his friend's birthday just because he was feeling down. Consequently, that evening he sat in his room and reflected on his college journey up to that time. Soon after, he called Alpha.

After a few rings, his cousin picked up.

"Was sup, cousin?" Alpha uttered excitedly,

"Could be better, but I'll be alright. How about you?" replied James. Alpha sensed that James desperately wanted someone to talk to, so he asked, "What's going on with you?"

"Well, I'm a little down because it's LV's B Day!" said James then he paused and took a deep breath, shook his head, and continued expressing himself. "My entire time in college has been a blast, but nothing compares to the time I'm having now since I'm the man in this community. Everyone comes to me for bud, life is incredible. I'm freaking stressed out though because all the girls and the parties are interfering with my education. Last semester I failed two of my required classes, so I lost my scholarship."

"Sorry to hear that but If I were you, I'll worry about that tomorrow. If I was you, tonight, I'll just go and party with the boys!" replied Alpha.

"You know what, you're right. I should enjoy myself. I'm in college living my best life, no financial responsibility, no family responsibilities, or any serious responsibilities, except to go to school!" said James.

"Tell LV I said happy birthday. Don't let anything ruin your day, bro!" said Alpha.

"I'm about to get lit, I'll call you later!" said James.

"That's the spirit!" remarked Alpha.

After disregarding the fact that he was a probationary student, it had finally dawned on James, yet he kept thinking that he would eventually prove himself and continue to study at Spirits University. Thus, he continued to lead a fleet lifestyle. Before he had started hustling, his social life was ok, but afterwards, he realized that it was immaculate. He was selling the best product in his community and he started to become idolized. He felt powerful and famous wherever he went. He was determined to get bigger by continuing to distribute marijuana. He thought less about his education and more on expanding his business.

After contemplating whether to go out or not he finally decided to go out so called B Money, "Yoh, bro, where are you at?" he asked.

"On our way to pick up LV, then go out to campus to turn up, party!" said B Money.

"Copy, on my way. I'll meet you at LV's," said James.

It was the first week after the winter break, and James was getting ready to celebrate his friend's birthday. James got dressed up nice and went out to meet the rest of their friends at one of their apartments. After they all got together, they went to a few clubs downtown and stopped at a fast-food restaurant before they returned to their off-campus housing for the afterparty. By the end of the night, James was intoxicated because he smoked a lot of marijuana and drank a lot of different alcohol. He mixed rum, whisky, brandy, tequila, vodka and gin. James started hearing the thoughts of everyone around him. He was overwhelmed by the voices in his head, so he screamed, "Shut up!"

Everyone stopped dead, looked at him in surprise; all his friends were stunned and some of the females were even scared. "I can't listen to all of you guys at the same time!" said James, then paused and said again, "I can't listen to all of you guys at the same time!"

They were confused because he had never done that prior to that night, so they thought he went mad. James couldn't tell if they were speaking to him or just thinking out loud because he had never experienced multiple voices at the same time. Usually, when he heard thoughts, it was from one individual and only when he provoked his mind-reading ability. That time his nervous system malfunctioned, largely because of the liquors.

Next day, LV, B Money, and Slim knocked on his door, but James was still deep in his sleep. First, LV knocked softly, but after a couple of knocks, he banged on the door with more assurance.

James jumped out of his sleep and staggered to the door. After two more loud bangs, he opened it. They went inside and started talking about the incident that happened the previous night.

"Bro, are you good?" LV asked.

"Yeah, I was just knocked out," replied James.

"Nah, Stackz! That's not what he was talking about," said B Money.

"What do you mean?" asked James with a stunned facial expression.

"Wait, guy, he really doesn't remember?" said LV.

James was starting to lose his patience, so he exclaimed, "Stop playing, guys! Remember what?"

"You really don't remember!" LV repeated.

"How you were bugging last night, talking to yourself and all!" said Slim. James lost his consciousness so he held the door for support and closed his eyes for a moment to regain consciousness, then opened them again and said, "You play too many games, guys. I'm hungover and tired, so check me later."

"Alright, guys, obviously the man is exhausted, let's give him time to rest. Let's go; we're going to check back on you later, Stackz!" said B Money.

LV and Slim said nothing, just gave simple nods as to say, "Ok."

They walked out the room and B Money turned back just as the door was about to close. "Get some rest, and see if you can remember last night," he said and closed the door behind him.

James sat alone in the room, and thoughts started swirling in his mind. "I need to quit smoking weed and drinking alcohol altogether so I can focus more on school," he thought.

Later that evening, after he was sober, James made a call to B Money so he can recap to him about the night in question.

"Are you serious? I did what?" asked James.

"Yeah, man, you were yelling and screaming at everyone there." B Money replied.

"Was LV upset at me, because I ruined his birthday!" said James.

"No, he's cool. You just scared off all the girls. I know you're fine, but taking care of your mental and physical health is crucial Stackz. If you've feeling overwhelmed or struggling with addiction, seeking help from a counselor or support group could also be beneficial." B Money advised him.

"I got you bro, thanks again!" replied James.

After not hearing from James for a while, Gabriel contemplated whether he should give him a call or not.

"*Why would Mr. Johnson be interested in his safety or want to appreciate a young man like him? I don't trust him a bit; he could be working with Manuel or his circle. I need to warn him as soon as possible!"* he thought. Sitting down in his office chair, Gabriel thought about Mr. Johnson and how he was checking on James. He felt that it was time to inform James that Mr. Johnson had been asking about him. Right after his consideration, Gabriel searched his name and placed a call.

The phone rang a few times, and no one answered, so he left him a message.

"Hey James, this is Mr. Houston. I haven't seen or heard from you for quite some time now, so I'm checking up on you. I also wanted to tell you that the man who was responsible for murdering your dad has unlimited ties. He probably has eyes on you, so I want you to be careful because he will not stop searching for you until he kills you and your entire family."

Gabriel waited for a few days, but still received no response from James. He grew concerned, so he called Christopher and notified him.

"Hello, buddy. How are you doing?" said Christopher.

"I'm fine; how is the business doing?" Gabriel asked.

"Actually, better than I expected!" he replied.

"Good, I'm calling you because Mr. Johnson asked me about James. I wasn't sure if it was for his benefit. However, when he convinced me that it was to congratulate him for his divinity, I loosened up," said Gabriel.

"No, what would he want with him?" said Christopher.

"Yeah, I was thinking the same thing but still gave him the position!" Gabriel responded.

He paused, dreading the moment, and wishing he could bring it back to change his decision, then continued.

"So, I've been calling to warn him about it, but he hasn't picked up. I've noticed some changes in him lately; he is not communicating with me anymore."

"I doubt a brilliant individual like James would allow himself to get distracted; it might be deeper than that," Christopher remarked.

"He was distracted due to his discovery about his father's passing. I thought he had regained control of himself, but we spoke and he interned for you. He must have lost interest in becoming an agent because he doesn't reach out, and when we do, he doesn't respond," Gabriel elaborated.

"Ok, keep trying so you can give him a heads up before it's too late!" suggested Christopher before they ended the call.

A few days later, Mr. Jonson paid his son a visit, and they discussed James and a strategy on how to jeopardize his future.

"My colleagues and I need your help, son. Mr. Jackson, an NISA director, called me last night and he wanted me to get rid of James as soon as possible. I believe you could help us out since you attend the same school as he does." Mr. Johnson explained.

He paused for a moment and stared at Rob as if he was trying to read his mind, then finally said, "Well, can you?"

"Of course, dad. That's a great idea, I can't stand that dude!" replied Rob.

Immediately after Rob replied, Mr. Johnson smiled so bright that it could light a fire.

"Good, so, I thought we could kill him!" he said, then paused.

"That will bring a lot of unwanted attention to our situation, especially since I'm positive that the BIA is watching his back," continued Mr. Johnson.

"Do you have any ideas?" he asked.

"*Hum, he's been taking all my clients since he started selling weed. This is a perfect opportunity to take him out.*" Rob thought before responding.

"I think we should have me or another student spy on him for a while. When the time is right, my partner will reach out to him and find a way to get close to him. Then find dirt on him that could damage his reputation," he said.

"Ha-ha-hah, ha-ha," laughed Mr. Johnson.

"Like father, like son, I told my colleagues the same thing, digging up dirt on him would be better. That's why I came to you; I knew you could help," he said.

"Yeah, I heard rumors about him dealing drugs in town. All we need is an undercover student to gather some evidence," expressed Rob.

"Plus, we just initiated a transfer Sam, the son of a friend who could help you do just that. They are not fond of James either. So, we're going to have you two work together to bring him down."

"Mr. Johnson assured his son.

"No worries dad, we're up for the job!" said Rob.

"I knew I could count on you. Ok, speak to you later, buddy!" said Mr. Johnson

"Oh Rob, I almost forgot. Mr. Jackson also promised that upon completing the task, he will give whoever assists us a letter of recommendation for the ISA, BIA, or any agency they would like to become a part of in the future!" he added.

"Ok! Thanks dad, I keep that in mind and relay it to my partners!" Rob said cheerfully.

Right after his father left, Rob reflected on their conversation then thought.

"I got it! I'm going to have Louis spy on him since he already buys weed from him from time to time."

Shortly thereafter, he called Louis.

"I know this is going to sound crazy, but I need you to go after James," said Rob.

"You sure that's a good idea, he's our supply right now. Setting him up leaves us dry." Louis reminded him.

Rob was furious after Louis reminded him that James was his secret contact. He exclaimed, "I don't care. We were doing fine before we started buying weed from him, so we'll be fine. In fact, that's exactly the reason I want him gone; he took all our clients. The worst part is that we can't even scare him off. To make matters worse, I heard he's a hujinn. I came up with a plan on how to do away with James. If you follow my lead, you will get recruited by NISA or any of our top agencies. I just need you to do some undercover work."

After explaining the situation to Louis, he simply accepted the job and promised to follow through. Therefore, Rob explained to him how to execute the task and then hung up.

It was the middle of October, close to two months since James had started marijuana in College Town and he had realized that he was making money not just to survive but enough to spoil himself as well. He jumped out of bed after feeling the afternoon sunlight up his apartment complex with its warmth. James got dressed and went out to shop at an electronics store near his residence. When he arrived at the parking lot, he spotted Louis and an old friend named Sam, whom he had known since his elementary days in Amsterdam. They were standing in front of the establishment he was heading to. James and Sam recognized each other, so James walked toward them. After they greeted one another, there was an awkward moment of silence.

Sam cleared his throat then spoke, "It's been a long time, James." After we moved out of Amsterdam, I lost contact with you, and since I didn't hear from you, I assumed you didn't want to hear from me…"

"I see, it's all good Sam. How's Mr. Bryant?" asked James.

"He's fine, I heard about your dad too, I'm sorry!" replied Sam.

"Nice to see you again, bro. I'll hit you up later," said Sam.

They caught up and exchanged contact.

"By the way, this is my brother from another mother, Louis. His dad is Mr. Jackson, one of the NISA directors," he added.

"We already know each other; we linked up a few times," replied James.

"Yeah, that's the guy I was telling you about. He got the best weed in town," said Louis.

Afterwards James spoke to Sam and his friend Louis a little longer, then he went inside the store. He bought a big flat-screen television, a system, and a game. When James left the department store, he stopped at the nearest money transfer station and sent some money to his mother and siblings. When James got home, he prayed first, then ate, rested, and decided to go out to the bar since it was Thursday night. James and his entourage went out every night except for Mondays and sometimes Tuesdays.

On that same day, James ran into Sam and Louis again at the club, only this time they were with Rob. They all hung out with a few of their comrades almost the entire night. They were trying to show off by competing on who could out drink the others. They drank to the point that they were all drunk. Because James could not control his actions, he began to run his mouth.

"S*** I am making a killing. I am thinking about expanding my business but I need more money to get a few pounds instead of ounces!" said James.

"I wish I can help you but times are hard right now. Let me know next time you re-up, so I can get some more bud." Louis responded after James finished rambling.

James took another shot of Captain Morgan as Louis was talking.

"Wait, hold that thought! Let me call my cousin and see if he can help me out with something," he said before he slipped out of the bar.

By that time, they were all drunk except for Louis, who'd been recording James for the past few minutes.

James was so drunk that he barely made it outside without bumping into everyone he encountered. Standing outside in the freezing cold without any sense of it, he placed a call.

"Couso, I need a favor from you. I want to buy distribution, so I need you to front me some money to make it happen!" said James.

Alpha took a deep breath, laughed and thought. *"Darn it man, I just started saving some money. Just tell him you don't have it because if he can't pay you back, you can't do anything. On the other hand, if he was in my shoes though, he would've done it. Plus, he's a man of his word."*

"Ok, I got you," he finally managed to say.

"Alright, thanks. I knew I could count on you," replied James.

"Trust me, Alpha, I'm not going to let you down!" he added.

"I already know! That's why I'm giving all my savings thus far!" Alpha replied.

"I appreciate you, bro," James stated before he hung up the phone.

When he went back inside the bar, he realized that Sam and Rob were more drunk than he was because they had passed out at the bar by the time he returned.

A few days later, it was just another regular day at Spirits Town, and James came out of his political science class. Sam and Louis popped up on him again, but this time Sam got more personal. "I heard you got the best weed in town, I'm trying to get some, can you hook me up bro?" he said.

"No problem I got you when I get back, I'm running low right now!" replied James.

"Alright cool, hit my jack when you're back on deck," said Sam.

At that point James was hungry for money and naive to the notion of the reproduction of his dealing, plus he knew Sam since he was in elementary school so he figured he can trust him. They told James that they wanted a large amount, he was more interested in serving them. They met up again a few days later when James came back from New Amsterdam City.

The week after, one of the most expensive cars at that time pulled up at his school to pick him up. This was the day he realized that he had become conspicuous and renowned. Sam and Louis pulled up in the new custom-made yellow and maroon Lamborghini, and a third car, a white Aston Martin, driven by one of the most attractive women he had ever encountered. The stunning female stuck her head out the window and said, "Hop in!"

James, stunned, exclaimed, "That's an Aston Martin!" he pointed out, his face beaming.

He felt his heartbeat racing faster than the car he was looking at going at max speed. He readied himself like a kid with a new toy as the passenger door elegantly opened.

Sam and Louis continued to monitor him for a while so they could tie him to more crimes if possible. Louis had recorded an exchange between him and James when he told him about his association with selling marijuana, so he brought the audio recording to his father, Rob. Rob relayed it to his father, who passed it on to Mr. Jackson, and so on until their entire circle heard it. Sam also notified his father, Antoine, about James and his drug dealings.

"I knew it was only a matter of time before he slipped up and gave them a reason to arrest him!" said Antoine.

"Cheers!" he added.

"Cheers, he thought he was invincible, moving around here like he owned the town. That's good for him!" replied Sam.

"I can't wait until they put him away. This will also get him disqualified from working for the government," said Antoine.

Around that time, James traveled often to New Amsterdam to restock his merchandise with one of his friends named Ray, who helped him distribute his weed around the community. Ray didn't attend the same school; he was in one of the Spirits University branches which was two hours away from the main campus. However, he was always there to buy weed from James to redistribute in his own school. They drove together to re-up on many occasions. They had grown very close after working with each other. Ray drove most of the time, and James took over when he got tired. Ray was from Seneciario, a country in the Maritime, a place that was between North Fabrica and South Fabrica with a few islands next to each other. He was short, about five feet five inches, with long black hair, brown eyes, a husky build, big droopy nose, dark skin, and he was very quiet. Ray was both a soldier and a brother figure to James. He would do whatever James requested, and the same applied vice versa.

On that Friday evening, James was accompanied by Ray. As they were on their way to New Amsterdam City, the sun was shining softly on them. During the drive, James had a conversation with Ray about his master plan.

"Yoh bro, this time I'm getting mad weight, we are about to take over the game!" he said. Ray looked at him and smiled broadly as if he was going to give him everything he buys from the dealer.

"That's what I'm talking about, let's get it, Brody. There is no competition out there. We are already killing them with a QP; imagine when we expand our distribution," James answered rhetorically.

"Word!" he replied.

Once James and Ray arrived at their destination, they discussed some personal issues for a few minutes with their connection, Jose. Jose was the main drug lord James bought weed from; occasionally, he bought from other small-timers, but for the most part, he dealt with him. He was very short and skinny, yet he ran the organization like he was taller and bigger than his entire crew. He had a Grecian nose, down-turned eyes, and a mysterious smile. He never rushed any transactions; he made it seem like a family meeting instead of a business meeting. After a long talk, James told him that he wanted to buy more weight this time.

"Yoh, little homie, I'm proud of you. How do you go from an ounce to a couple of Ps (pounds)? You must have that town on lock," said Jose.

"Yeah, of course, now I'm the man out there, so the demand is crazy high. My boy, Ray, got his own hustle going on in a different town too!" replied James, then glanced and pointed at Ray.

"Not to mention, we don't want to make too many trips anymore. You know it's risky going up and down that Interstate eighty-eight!" he added.

"Yeah, you are a genius; that's why I mess with you, young buck. Just remember one thing though, homie; getting money feels good but don't forget you are doing something illegal. I'm telling you Stackz, if you don't move a certain way, you are going to get jammed up. It's all good if you make sure you don't stand out. Don't ever be the man, even if you are the man; let someone else be the man in your place." Jose expressed as he encouraged James on his decision.

James nodded and said, "Alright, OG, I heard you. Thanks again. I'm going to fall back and work smarter. I'll see you in a few weeks."

Despite operating more discreetly from that point moving forward, he was too late. He had been dealing with confidential informants sent by the Secretary of the Department of Education, Peter, and Mr. Jackson prior to his new way of operating.

Hours later, James was back at College Town in his room, bagging up his weed. After Ray left that night, he thought about the conversation he had with his drug supplier, Jose, regarding working smarter. He went in and out of his residence a lot, getting picked up in fancy cars, different ones each time. He was very busy and felt that he drew a lot of law enforcement's attention. The way James moved, even if it wasn't for his marijuana business, made it hard for him to be discreet. Additionally, James and his friend were very popular. He told himself to try anyway and then planned to operate differently. James employed more people to be in disguise so he didn't have to serve himself. He decided to sell or give it to them on consignment so they pay him after they sell the merchandise. Even though he sold a little, he let his workers sell the majority. He inspected new people in his life before he got close. He changed the way he dressed from the hip-hop style to the business style, with shoes, suits, and ties. James stopped telling people he had merchandise and said he knew who got it. He also stopped partying as much and focused more on his business and education.

At that point, James could not stay away from the bars so hence a week later, on another cold night, he was out with his friends. The strip was busy, and the club was jammed with a long line in front. On his way in, another group pushed roughly past him and his friends, and one of them bumped into one of his friends. That incident nearly caused an altercation between the two squads, but LV calmed everyone. Less than a minute after walking inside, James went straight to the bar and started drinking. An hour before the nightclub was set to close, James saw a man and a few women emerge from the entrance to the nightclub. He was tipsy by then, so the four exquisite ladies easily got him excited. He couldn't keep his composure, so he walked up to them.

"Hey ladies, I was about to leave, but you just turned me up even more!" he said.

They removed their coats and held them in their hands. At that instant, James noticed that one of the young women had a see-through dress, a Chanel bag, and Christian Dior heels. He stared into her blinking eyes until she got the hint of his lust for her. Even though he hung out with all of them, he showed more interest in the young lady with the see-through dress.

James started to walk back and suddenly froze for a second as she winked at him.

"Can I buy you drinks?" he asked.

"Of course, handsome!" The beautiful young woman nodded and she smiled.

After a couple more drinks, he sat with the ladies and the gentleman who came with them. As they prepared to leave, he extended his hand to the one he was lusting for.

"Come here, beautiful!" he said deductively.

After sticking her hand out and the breathtaking woman walked to James, nearly gasped. He felt his heart jump from excitement.

"The night is still young, you should come hang with me at my place." he continued.

They murmured a few words as her friends patiently waited for her. Then she walked back to her friends and told them and said, "I'm leaving with him."

"But girl, you don't even know him!" one of the ladies took a step forward and whispered to her.

"He's cool, that's enough for me. I'll see you in the morning!" she replied and walked away.

By that moment James had walked to her so he gestured toward the exit and said, "After you lovely!"

Back to his apartment with the erotic woman. She took off her clothes as James admired her every curve, taunting to touch her. He walked over to her, taking in the fresh scent of spring showers from her body. He stopped and gazed at her for a moment and said, "God, you are gorgeous!"

He shook off the chills he got from her good looks and smiled broadly. She smiled back and he noticed how full her lips were and how straight her teeth were, then he leaned in and kissed her. They got intimate straight away and had sex a few times before falling asleep.

In the morning, he was hungover again. After waking up for a moment, they took a nap before he took her home just before noon that day. He remembered that it was the day he planned to go borrow some money from his cousin to buy a large amount of weed. After James dropped off his female companion, he left around one in the afternoon for his drive to New Amsterdam City. He left early so that he could come back the same day. There was no traffic on the way, so he got there fast. James was very close to Alpha, and he was financially stable. Therefore, James thought it was best to ask him for a loan to expand his business. Alpha was simultaneously running his business and going to school at an early age. He was about five feet eleven inches tall, with a bulbous-shaped nose, swollen lips, and round eyes. He was a people person just like James; they both loved and respected each other and confided in one another. James called and spoke to his cousin about the same subject he had discussed the prior night.

"What's up Alpha, I just wanted to give you a heads up, I'm on my way to see you," he said cheerfully.

"Ok, see you in a while," said Alpha before then clicked off the phone.

Three hours later, James arrived at his cousin's clothing boutique. Around five-thirty, half an hour later, he got the money from him and went to his connection and bought five pounds of exotic marijuana. He then drove back to school before ten-thirty PM. The entire trip took him about nine hours because he only spent about an hour in New Amsterdam City.

In less than four months, word around town was that James had the best weed that the community had ever come across. Therefore, most of the drug dealers in town were in competition with him. The weed he was bringing was so pure that his competitors were envious of him. Nonetheless, even they couldn't resist the marijuana he was selling. Since his marijuana was much more potent, some of them began buying weed from him for their own personal use or to mix with their own weed and distribute.

At that point, James and his circle were addicted to living life in the fast lane because they partied every day without a care. They either threw their own parties, attended others, or went out to the bar. They also went to a bunch of big-time concerts because many rappers were hosting shows at their school. They got to see performers such as Lil Wayne, Drake, Jay Z, and T.I. in live performances. Each time at one of those gatherings, he tried to hook up with a different woman. That day was just another one of those times when he succeeded in his aspirations. The night was young, and he stood at the bar with a full glass of whisky, surrounded by glittering lights illuminating the room. He was drinking with some of his friends when two women accompanied by a man who appeared drunk made their way across the room to him. He assumed that the male was the significant other of one of the females. Even so, he was going to try his luck with both until one of them took the bait. The woman he lusted for had bow-shaped lips, hooded eyes, and she appeared promiscuous.

After spending a few minutes flirting with her, they started dancing.

"Hey sexy, what are you doing afterwards?" he whispered in her ear provocatively.

"Nothing!" replied the female. Her male companion tapped her on the shoulder, "What's up, we're about to leave."

She ignored him; he tapped her again and said, "Britney, are you coming or not?"

Sensing the jealousy in his face, James said, "I guess not. Do you mind, can't you see us vibing?"

He stared at him with a savage expression. Feeling embarrassed, the man walked away to his other girlfriend.

In less than an hour, James and Britney were back at his off-campus apartment. Once they arrived at his place, everything happened so fast. He had intercourse with her then they laid on the bed and talked.

"I heard about you, Stackz," she said with a giggle.

James ignored her at first and stood up. He walked over to his stash and pulled out a pound of marijuana.

She glanced at the large amount of weed on his hand and spoke.

"I guess it's true, you are the man!"

"Where did you hear that, sweetie?" he asked as he sat down, pulled out a Dutch master and started breaking it up.

"From Rob, the Alpha Phi Omega president. The other night he was talking about his competition to his buddy Louis and they said you were the only competition that they feared."

"*I'm finally getting to the completion!*" he thought then laughed and nodded as if to say yeah, he was.

"The man is an understatement for what I'm about to do around here. I'm about to take over this whole city."

"So, can you put me on? I want to make some money too if you know what I mean?" she replied.

He gave a half-hearted laugh, stunned by her expression. "*She's serious,*" he thought.

He sparked the blunt.

"In fact, I was looking to expand soon. Now that I got someone who's down, I'm going to make it happen," he stated then paused, allowing her to process his words.

Her eyes sparkled and her heart raced. "That's wonderful! You are fabulous, no wonder the ladies love you around here."

He passed her the blunt, she sat up, covered her body with the sheet, then reached out to grab it.

"Actually, they don't but they love my hustle and I love them," he said.

"*Wow, this is the best weed I've ever smoked. This is going to work; anyone who gets a whiff of this is going to want more!*" she thought.

James heard her thoughts, then looked at her and smiled. She didn't have to say thank you; her beaming expression said it all.

He continued, "Like Bonnie and Clyde we're going to make a great team!" They cried out laughing.

"*With a strong lady like her on my side, I'm going to be invincible!*" he thought. Immediately after they finished smoking, they had intercourse again.

CHAPTER FIVE

ANXIOUS TIMES

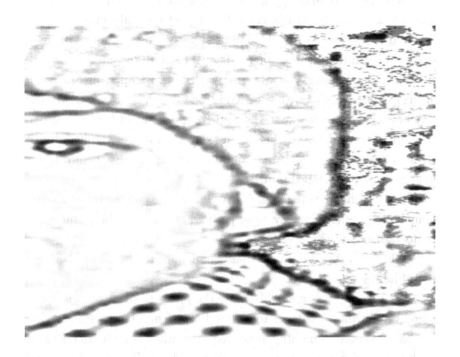

After hustling for almost the entire fall semester and gaining popularity, James started to question his association with the distribution of narcotics a week before the break. He felt that he was becoming a real drug dealer, so he called his cousin Benjamin.

"Bro, when I started selling, I told myself that it was just for fun. I have a feeling that if I don't stop dealing soon, something bad is going to happen to me. I always told myself and all my friends that I was going to stop sooner than later and I'm still doing it," he said.

"Yeah bro, you told me the same thing; that you were selling weed in the meantime to help pay some bills. The addiction to the lifestyle of making money is making you lose your direction; you need to stop soon!" replied Benjamin.

After the call he was laid on his bed and looked up at the ceiling.

"I'm skating on thin ice, and I should stop hustling. I'm getting a lot of money though; this is my chance to succeed, and I'm not going to let fear of getting arrested mess that up!" he thought.

He continued thinking as he considered whether to stop selling marijuana or not. Suddenly, the other side of his brain kicked in and diverted him from his initial thought about trying to control his own destiny by eliminating any potential conflicts with the law.

The following week, on a Thursday evening, after playing basketball at the gym on campus with his friends for a couple of hours, James and Smokey were on their way to their off-campus student housing. When they got close to the unit where James stayed, Smokey, who had driven them, noticed the police cars around the complex. Just before James exited the car, he warned him.

"Bro, where are you going? Can't you see the police cars all around your house?" asked Smokey as he pointed at cars with blue and white lights flashing nearby.

"Oh s***, I didn't even see that! Thanks for the heads up. Let's get out of here!" James replied.

The warning was crucial because the police were still in his house searching for more evidence to charge him. When James realized that Smokey was onto something, he stayed calm and asked him to take him back to the school gym to lay low. An hour later, Slim called him and told him how the College Town police had stormed into their apartment.

Slim, who happened to be in the apartment when the raid took place, explained to James how their apartment was raided and that the police were looking to speak to him as soon as possible. He said the police had left him a notice and that they had flipped the house upside down in search of more evidence for the case they were building against him. Even though he got raided right before winter break, he still planned to go to South Beach, Carami for winter break with his friends.

The raid happened the day before the winter break began. Fortunately for James, he wasn't there at the time of the raid, so he was still not in custody. Even though they didn't find anything except for his stash, they already had all the evidence they needed, and they were just looking to arrest James at that point and gather extra charges or evidence along the way.

The next day, James and eight of his friends rented two vehicles and headed to South Beach, Carami. There were four individuals in each car. After an eighteen-hour drive, taking turns, they finally reached their destination. They had already booked a hotel online, so immediately upon arrival and checking in, the party started. None of them wanted to rest after that long drive. Even though they were tired, no one showed any sign of fatigue, only an urge to visit the city and meet some females. Wasting no time, they got right to it, hopping from bar to bar, store to store, and at night they went to the club. They ran into a few colleagues who had attended the same school as they did. They kept up the same energy and schedule for the entire time there.

In the evening, James and his friends were sitting at the beach and hanging out when he slipped away from the group. He went and sat alone, watching the sun set.

"No wonder South Beach is one of the best places on the planet; this is the only place that can help me escape from all problems!" he thought.

A few minutes later, he returned and rejoined his colleagues where they were gathered. They stayed by the beachside for another hour, playing cards, board games, and discussing life experiences.

A few days into the break, Gabriel was informed by Kevin that James was under investigation. Upon hearing this news, thoughts of Mr. Johnson sparked in Gabriel's mind. He regretted providing him with information about James. He feared that he had put James in this predicament by revealing his location to Mr. Johnson, so he wanted to speak to him desperately. Therefore, Gabriel called James incessantly for several days and finally left him a message.

"Hey man, this is Gabriel! James, I need to talk to you, and it's very important, so please get back to me as soon as possible!" said the message.

Little did Gabriel know that James had recently changed his number, which was why he didn't receive the voicemail Gabriel left him. James had changed his number due to feeling anxious, especially after hearing about several arrests in his neighborhood.

A few nights later, they were so drunk, and James fought LV. Despite their altercation, they didn't let it ruin their friendship or enjoyment, so they continued partying every day and every night until the last day. On the way back to College Town from Carami, they stopped multiple times for gas, food, and drinks. After making it halfway and stopping for the second time, when James got back in the car, it was his turn to drive. He readied himself, stretched his legs, stepped into the vehicle, grabbed the steering wheel, and fastened his seat belt. Later, after an hour of driving, reality hit James as if he had been hit by a car traveling three hundred miles per hour.

After one week and James had still not returned his call, Gabriel was in his office, pacing back and forth, nervous.

"*Let me call his mother,*" he thought.

It was the day James was scheduled to return from Carami. Around noon that day Gabriel called Holly. When she picked up the phone and they greeted each other, he explained the reason for the call.

"Mrs. Jordan, you might not be aware that your family has gone through a lot due to your husband's BIA association. I believe there is a pending investigation on James."

"What! For what?" she exclaimed.

"At the moment I'm not sure that's why I want to get in touch with him so I can get more insight," he replied.

"Last, I checked he was in Carami with his friends for the break. Let me call him and make sure he's fine!" she said.

"I'm sure he's not in custody yet," he assured her.

"Ok, I'll get back to you when I get in contact with him!" she said.

"Ok. In the meantime, it might be a good idea to consider possibly increasing your security measures."

After the call, Holly contacted James right away.

"Hey baby, I just got off the phone with Mr. Houston and he wanted to speak to you. Are you okay?" she asked.

Sensing the trauma in her voice, he assumed she found out that the police were looking for him.

"Yeah, mom, I'm fine. We are on our way back. Is everything okay?" he demanded.

Concerned about embarrassing him in front of his friends, she pretended not to know about the investigation.

"Yeah, I just want to know if you are okay because he said he's been trying to reach you for over a week now. Call him back as soon as you get back and call me back too when you settle down," she said.

"Okay, mom, he doesn't have my new number, that's why!" he replied.

"How could you not update him with your contact? You know he has been your best mentor. He is worried sick about you, so he wanted me to deliver a message to you. Make sure you call him back!" said Holly.

"Okay, mom, I'm going to call him back as soon as I get home," James replied and hung up.

As he sat in the back seat with his hand under his chin, he thought, *"He must have heard about my warrant. After all, he did work for the BIA."*

Considering that half of the day had passed and he had a few errands to run, he asked his friends to drop him off before they went anywhere else. "I have to go speak to the head officer in my case!" he remarked.

When James got home, Britney was already there waiting for him. After almost two years of pursuing her, he had finally succeeded. He trusted her, so he confided in her about a lot of serious issues he was dealing with. She was an enticing girl standing about five feet ten inches tall. She had a welcoming smile, deep-set eyes, an athletic Coca-Cola bottle body shape, a pointed nose, and long curly hair. They had a friends-with-benefits arrangement, meaning they were together but with no strings attached, allowing them to see other people. James shared with Britney about the raid on him before the winter break vacation to Carami and how stressed he was, wondering what the detective had on him. She calmed him down and advised him to find out why he was raided before panicking. After prayer and careful consideration, he decided to listen to Britney and pursue the matter further.

He felt a bit more relaxed. "You know what, you're right. I should find out what they are charging me with and if they have any evidence against me first before I overreact!" he said.

At that moment, he remembered that he had to call Gabriel, so he dialed his number.

"Hey, Mr. Houston, it's James!" he said nervously.

"Hello James! I haven't heard from you in a while!" replied Gabriel with a sound of disappointment echoing in his tone.

After catching up for a few minutes, Gabriel informed James that he had heard about the police raid.

At that point, James felt embarrassed and had no choice but to confess about what transpired before he went to vacation in Carami.

"I don't know why they raided my apartment or why they wanted to speak to me because I was at the gym when they arrived. I decided to go to Carami anyway since I had planned the trip before the raid. Therefore, I was in Carami for the past ten days, which is why I still haven't had the chance to find out yet. However, I'm planning to go to their police station to speak to the head officer of the case later after we finish!" he explained.

As James explained his circumstance, Gabriel was puzzled.

"Goodness gracious! It sounds like you are in a dilemma," he said.

"Anyway, it's good that you are planning to go speak with him to get more information. Update me on what you discuss and make sure you don't keep in the dark this time!" he added.

"Yeah, I know. I'm sorry I'd been meaning to call you but I was in Carami for the last ten days and that's why I didn't seek you for your advice."

It was around five p.m. that evening when James went to see the leading detective of his investigation, Franklin Bryant. Upon meeting the investigator, he thought, *"He looks so much like Mr. Bryant. He might be his brother."*

Once inside the interrogation room, the detective questioned him for almost an hour, trying to figure out whether he could find more evidence that might further incriminate James in the case. Franklin offered him a deal—either closing the case entirely or charging him with a lighter offense in exchange for helping the prosecution make more arrests, especially in relation to the person or organization from whom he was obtaining the narcotics. He even presented James with a more detailed written statement about his criminal activities with the confidential informant to persuade him to testify against his main source.

After trying every approach to get him to give up his connection and failing, the detective gave up.

"It will be in your best interest for you to cooperate with the authorities. But since you think otherwise, I suggest you seek legal advice. You are under arrest for intent to deliver narcotics!" said Franklin.

His face darkened, and James was stunned because he didn't expect to get arrested. He thought that Franklin was just going to clarify the investigation against him and let him go home.

"Stand up. Do you have anything in your pockets?" he asked.

"No," replied James.

The detective nodded as he began searching James.

"Spread your legs."

Franklin ordered as he continued feeling on James, looking for drugs or weapons.

He finally put the cuffs on James and said, "If he needs any further assistance or guidance, you can reach out to a trusted adult or legal professional when you get to the jail."

By the end of the night, he was in the county jail. Fortunately, James was granted an unsecured bail worth ten thousand dollars that same night. James was given unsecured bail released shortly after he appeared before the judge via a video call. Consequently, he was able to contest the case while remaining outside, enabling him to complete the current semester and the subsequent one.

After hours of thinking about who could have been the CI, James had finally narrowed down his suspects. "*The most recent transactions I recall are with Sam and Louis. Plus, they suddenly bought large amounts from me. They are the only customers I've been working with frequently, and my other customers didn't buy as much as the affidavit says,*" he examined thoroughly.

Next day, Franklin Fox called Antoine and told him that it was done, referring to the arrest of James. Antoine then informed Mr. Johnson about James being charged with intent and delivery of marijuana, which was illegal.

"We got him, sir, on multiple counts! Don't worry, he is going to be done after this!" Antoine bragged about the arrest.

"Ah, um, wait, you mean to tell me the plan actually worked and James is behind bars?"

"Yes, sir, my brother arrested him last night after he went to the precinct to speak to him," Antoine answered.

"Incredible," he said as he took a moment to think about how Rob will react to this news.

"Thank you. Let me call Mr. Jackson and inform him. I'll speak to you later," he added.

Mr. Johnson was delighted and couldn't wait to inform Mr. Jackson and spread the word. Eventually, the rest of their circle heard about the arrest. Mr. Jackson made it clear that he didn't want anyone in their secret circle involving Mr. Iverson in this matter. Since the time Mr. Iverson defended Alex when he was accused of having hujinn children, Mr. Jackson knew that he was a heavy supporter of the Jordan family so he didn't trust him with these kinds of matters.

A week after school opened for the spring semester, James went to the courthouse to talk to his lawyer. This was going to be the second time he would speak to his public defender since he was assigned to him. That same day, he learned that the district attorneys had more evidence on him when he overheard them talking. As James waited for his lawyer to arrive, the district attorneys were having a conversation about his case.

"This case is personal because he was targeted by a director of ISA, a former BIA agent, and the secretary of the Department of Education. They all want him incarcerated, so we must make sure of that!" said one attorney.

"That's not going to be difficult given that we have audio recordings, pictures, and confidential informants," replied the other.

After his public defender who was representing James arrived, he basically explained the same details to him.

"Listen to me, James, you had to make the decision on whether to plead or take the case to trial. I can't make that decision for you; however, I assure you that this is not going to be as simple as you think. It's very complicated due to the evidence they have against you. From the looks of it, you are going down either way," said the lawyer.

"I want to fight because I don't want to do any jail time," replied James.

"If you don't take the plea, your life will be ruined because you'll lose, and they'll give you the maximum punishment. Don't forget you are going against the grimmest judge in the county," said the lawyer.

"Ok, I need some time to think about it, and I'll get back to you," James responded.

Close to the end of June that year, James returned to the courthouse for his third meeting with his attorney. That day when he got home, he was overloaded, therefore, he contacted his cousin, Alpha.

"The lawyer said that I would be sentenced three to six months at least for each count. For now, I have two counts. Which means that I'm going to get ordered to serve the time conservatively by the judge," explained James.

"Dam!" exclaimed Alpha then he leaned back on the wall as he took a moment to consider the justification of the punishment options on the table for his cousin.

"That's not right, that's way too much for possession. If that were here, it would be a slap on the hand!" he added.

"I know, at least that's what I thought. That's what I get for moving out to a commonwealth state for school," James expressed.

They weighed his options together and realized that the plea deal was his best option as far as the right solution to the problem. Afterwards, the next concerning issue was what lie James was going to tell his mother and his friends about his upcoming incarceration.

"Why not just tell them the truth?" asked Alpha.

"As for my mom, I'll think about it but the others I'll just tell them I'm studying abroad. I mean, my lawyer said I will serve more than six months."

A week later, James called his mother and informed her about his arrest and his attorney's consultations. However, he only shared part of the truth - that he was going to jail - and altered the reason why he was raided in the first place. He decided to disclose his case to his mother as his sentencing neared. He didn't know how to convey the news to his mother, the woman who had sacrificed everything for him to receive a quality education. It was a hot and quiet day in the fall, and Holly was on vacation overseas, returning to her home in Freeland. James called his mother using a calling card. The phone rang, and his mother picked up.

"Hello, sweetie," uttered Holly with a sweet soft voice.

"Hi, Mom. I have something I want to discuss with you," murmured James.

"I'm all ears," said Holly.

He took a deep breath, readied himself, and spoke.

"Sorry, Mom, but I got myself involved in a serious matter. Now I'm in a dilemma..."

"James, you've already said that. Can you just tell me what's going on?" she said with more force in her voice.

Holly interrupted him, as she had become impatient. He stood up and took another deep breath. "One of my friends gave me a bag to pass on to another friend, and it happened to contain some controlled substances. I was stopped by the police, and after the investigation, I have been charged with committing counts of felonies."

"Oh, my Lord. Tell me you are kidding James," snapped Holly.

"Honey, honey!" she called out as James remained silent.

"Tell me I'm dreaming and wake me up, please...," cried Holly softly as she trembled.

James remained silent for a moment, feeling embarrassed but after realizing that his mother was still crying and couldn't speak anymore, he cleared his throat and continued.

"Mom, it's okay, don't worry. The good news is that my lawyer said he can negotiate and bring my charges down to misdemeanors instead of felonies."

She said nothing and continued to weep quietly.

"Please don't cry, Mom. I can handle it. I mean, it's only six months, and I will be out soon enough to return to school and earn my degree," he added as he paced back and forth in his bedroom.

Holly finally managed to pass the phone to Vincent as she sniffed constantly. He had been there for a week after hearing about the arrest and the charges against James from his mother.

Vincent took the phone and spoke as he paced back and forth.

"Hello, James. What happened, and why is Holly crying?"

James told him what he had just recounted to his mother – that he was going to jail soon.

"I can't believe you, James. You threw away your future over nonsense... I'm disappointed in you. However, you are a man now, and I'm going to say as your father would have said, "you do the crime, you do the time!" said Vincent, as James tried to justify his actions but couldn't get a word in.

Suddenly, Vincent abruptly hung up, leaving James with the sound of the click on the other end.

Later that day, James thought about how he had just made his mother cry, therefore he cried too. James was so disturbed by his mother's reaction that he could still hear her voice saying, *You made me cry, you are going to cry the worst tears.*

Afterwards he went and prayed before leaving to go spend time with his friend, B Money. As a result of all the stress, James found it a lot harder to concentrate on anything but his legal issues.

"I'm tired of this case; let me smoke some weed so I can forget about it," he thought.

He pulled out an entourage from the gold pack, rolled some weed, and smoked.

After Holly regained control, she called Gabriel. She was so upset that she didn't even say hi before crying to him.

"Gabriel, I need your help. James is going to jail."

Gabriel felt his brain tighten, so he was lost for words. He took a deep breath and let it out as he analyzed the situation then gave his take.

"I did a little digging myself and found out why he was targeted and charged for the crime. Even though we can't exclude him from the blame, the men who have been after your family for years may have something to do with his audit. They had been watching you long before he went away to college, even before we went on the Bellivian mission. I believe it all began when an agent at the BIA found out that he was married to you and that you had children who were presumed to be hujinns. The envious agent leaked your husband's personal information within and outside the agency because he felt threatened by your family. He formed a circle with other agents who despised hujinns, and they plotted to murder him. After his death, Manuel, our target for the

Flowropian missions, wanted to get rid of all of you, but he got distracted by his trades with the West Drakillian Union. They offered him their natural resources in exchange for weapons and technologies, so he is focused on those deals."

"Yeah, as sad as it is, that's our reality. Why do you think they murdered my husband and tried to kill us?"

She responded and continued weeping. He paused for a moment to allow her to process all the information he had just uncovered, then continued.

"If James is facing the risk of going to jail, it's crucial for him to seek proper legal counsel. In the meantime, establishing open and honest communication with your son about the consequences of his actions is crucial in helping him understand the gravity of the situation. Supporting him through this difficult time and guiding him towards making the right decision can make a significant impact on his future."

"I've tried that, but apparently, he's not listening. You know James, always keeps bad company. His father and I told him a million times before to stay away from those good-for-nothing so-called friends of his. They are nothing but gangsters," Holly stated.

Feeling a little responsible for what had happened, Gabriel emphasized the importance of supporting James.

"James is going through a tough time. Above all, showing him some empathy and understanding during this difficult time can go a long way in helping them navigate through these challenges."

"Don't worry, let me investigate it and get back to you. I'll make sure that no matter what happens, he comes out of this fine and better," Gabriel said, trying to sound confident even though he was worried too.

After the call Gabriel sat back on his chair and thought.

"This is all my fault, I exposed him to these vultures!"

After Gabriel explored further into the case and found out that James was guilty as charged, he was very disappointed in him, so he called Christopher.

A few rings after, Christopher answered his phone.

"Hello!"

"Hey Chris!" Gabriel replied.

"Hey buddy!" Christopher responded.

"Let me add Steve on the line as well," said Gabriel.

When all three of them were connected, Gabriel addressed them first, since he orchestrated the call.

"I just got off the phone with Holly, and she told me that James has been in serious trouble with the law. I don't know if he was set up or if he really did it," Gabriel stated.

After Gabriel and Christopher went back and forth on how to approach the investigation on James, Steve chimed in.

"Christopher is right; we should allow him to go through the trials and tribulations to learn a lesson or two about ethics and morality. He should have known better than to involve himself in such an offense," expressed Steve.

"Why don't we get him out of this situation so we can handle the deal with him ourselves?" Gabriel proposed.

"You worry too much, brother. He'll be just fine!" said Christopher.

"If indeed he ends up serving time, it will be the perfect opportunity to guide him further," said Steve.

Gabriel hesitated then cleared his throat and said, "It's just, I hate to be the one to question you, sir, but what good is all the training if he ends up dead? Keep in mind that the same way we plan to guide him from the inside is the same way they might be scheming to take him out from inside."

"You are forgetting who we are talking about here. He's not your average individual; he is not only a hujinn but could be a superhujinn. Plus, he made a poor decision, for him to grow, we must let him take responsibility for his actions. We can't support his unlawful act or bail him out of it. Allowing him to deal with adversity will only strengthen his faith."

Feeling outnumbered on the correct decision for how to handle the situation, he finally admitted that his colleagues were right.

"Ok, sounds good to me!" replied Gabriel.

"I just feel a little guilty because Mr. Johnson called me some time back and mentioned James and how he wanted to give him his regards, so I gave him his location. It just dawned on me that this might be the reason for the investigation," confessed Gabriel.

"No problem, in the meantime, I'll dig up some information and find out who's involved so we can have a better understanding of what we are about to face," Christopher said.

"Gabriel, I know Alex asked us to keep an eye on his family, but it's impossible to be on top of college students unless they allow you to. Look at it on the bright side; ultimately, James is going to come out of this a better man!" said Steve.

The summer vacation had begun the week prior to that, James stayed in College Town and worked a banquet serving food. He was embarrassed to face his friends and family that's why he found a job in College Town instead of New Amsterdam. For him, that summer went by quickly because of the criminal charges he was dealing with. Even though everyone else's life was still going on, he felt his had stopped. Getting locked up was all he could think about since the first time he spoke to his attorney. He didn't know how to cope with the pressure; all his attention was on figuring out what to do with his case. He only confided in Alpha and Benjamin after his arrest, so he only spoke to those two about the charges against him until it was time for him to make the deal. At last, James consulted with his cousins Alpha and Benjamin. They both told him that they could not help him decide between taking the case to trial or taking one of the plea deals because they had never been in that predicament. They advised him to do what he believed was best for him and that they believed he would make the right decision. His mother was still not speaking to him so he didn't know who else to turn to. He had not interned with Christopher, he didn't get in touch with Gabriel or anyone at the BIA. He had blocked out everyone he knew including the members of the BIA.

In the middle of the summer, James decided to go to New Amsterdam City for the weekend to visit his mother and siblings. On his way there, three cars caught up to him on the highway and tried to cause him to get into an accident. These individuals were masked, so he could not tell who they were. The random hoodlums fired at his vehicle from multiple directions as he avoided a few bullets with incredible driving skills, he sped up and continued his own way as if nothing had happened. Half an hour later, he arrived home. Once there, everyone gathered in the living room for dinner. Shortly after, James and Jeremy walked out to the front of the house to get some fresh air. James shared with his little brother a few stories from school and discussed what it felt like to be away from home.

"Don't ever go away to school, Jeremy. I'm telling you, it's the worst. You'll either get yourself into debt before you even start working or come back home feeling like a stranger," James advised his brother.

"Bro, my dream is to live on campus and be far away from Mom so I can experiment!" replied Jeremy.

"Well, unless you are going to stay focused and not mix with the wrong crowd, don't go. I'm only telling you this so that you can avoid making the same mistake I did," said James.

"I understand what you are saying, James, but I'm still going away for school," said Jeremy with a lower tone, emphasizing his determination.

Later that night he went to visit Alpha.

"This case is ruining my life. I should have been graduating within a year and a half or two. As a result of this crime, I'm going to miss some critical time, and moving forward, I'm going to have a criminal record, which will disqualify me from working for the government," he shared.

He paused, allowing Alpha to process all the information he was bombarding him with, then shook his head and continued.

"If found guilty, I'm looking at least six months. They are claiming that I sold drugs in school, which turned out to be a higher charge, and they upgraded it to two counts. The charges were considered felonies; one was intent to deliver, and the other was Delivery. I'm charged with the intent and delivery of a controlled substance."

The next day he was back at College Town working at his low-income job as he tried managing his stress. One night, a couple of days before the school opened for the fall semester, he was in his room experiencing some inner turmoil. He had been constantly considering his options regarding his criminal charges throughout the summer and still could not come up with a solution. However, at that point he perceived the evidence they had against him was very strong, even though he believed they exaggerated the severity of the offense. Though he knew taking the plea meant he had to serve six months in jail, he was fine with that just to avoid the felony charges.

"Take the plea because if you take it to trial and are found guilty, you are risking a two-year jail sentence and still having the felonies on your

record, especially since your chances were slim to none with the confidential informant's testimony!" he told himself as he went over the charges.

"*Don't be scared to take it to trial. It's their word against your word. Maybe some jurors or the judge would believe you!*" he continued talking to himself.

After hearing one of his roommates in the kitchen, he took a break from deliberating and went out to the living room. He found B Money there fixing himself a frozen Chicken Fettuccine. Upon seeing James and reading his expression, B Money placed the meal in the microwave and spoke.

"What's going on, Stackz?" he asked.

"Thinking about my case is burning me out!" James murmured as he walked around the kitchen counter, opened the fridge door, took some juice, and poured himself a drink.

"I know you're tired of hearing me talk about this, but I was thinking about my charges!" he continued.

B Money stopped dead in his tracks and said, "And?"

He paused, looked up, and met B Money's gaze.

"I still don't know whether to take the plea or go to trial. The plea means I must serve six months in jail but I'm fine with that just to avoid the felony charges!" he said desperately.

Feeling a bit irritated, B Money disregarded James, by walking past him, sitting down, and watching the Spirits football game. A few minutes later he got up, opened the microwave, took out the meal from the microwave, sat next to James on the couch, and started eating. Halfway into the meal, he paused, drank some water, leaned back, and spoke.

"I'm going to tell you, like I told you before, get a lawyer."

"I have one!" replied James softly.

B Money shook his head as to say that's not what he meant.

"Not a public defender, a real lawyer!" he said.

"I can't afford one," said James.

"Well, I can't help you man. I don't want to steer you the wrong direction," he said calmly.

"I just want to know if you were in my shoes, what would you've done?" he asked desperately.

"I wouldn't know because I'll never do something that stupid. I mean, I tried to warn you, but you wouldn't listen," he said heavily, indicating that he had heard enough about the matter.

James said nothing afterwards, he simply nodded, as B Money continued grubbing on his warm fettuccine pasta. There was a brief silence as they sat on the couch and they watched their school's football team play on television.

Feeling the tension rising in the room, James got up.

"Thanks for nothing bro," he mumbled and walked away.

Back in his room, he broadened his focus and thought deeply about his plea bargain.

"Don't be scared, it's their word against your word, maybe some juries or judges would believe you. On the other hand, if I fight and end up being found guilty, the felony on my record will follow me forever, so I'm not doing that," he thought. *"I'm going to plead guilty to the two counts of misdemeanors and avoid these felonies. This way, I could finish my education and be able to find work!"* he thought.

Half of the semester had gone by, and James had kept more and more to himself. He was more focused on his education because of the issue he had with the law. One day during this period, James ran into his friends, and they asked him to go along with them to hang out at a fraternity event. He denied the invitation and said he had to go to the library and study.

"Yoh, what's up with you, Stackz? Lately, you've been MIA (missing in action). Every time we're about to spend time together or go out, you have something important to handle," said Smokey.

"I know, bro. I'm just trying to be more focused and prove to myself that I learned from my mistakes," James replied.

"I feel you. Do your thing," said Smokey.

"You know, I have a lot of ground to make up since soon I'm going to miss some more time! Even though I feel like it's too late now because I must do some jail time soon," said James.

It was the middle of December, a week before the end of the semester. James had been involved in after-school extracurriculars and in his overall education more than he had ever done. He attended all his classes, paying more attention, partying less, and working very hard at his low-paying job. That day, he had his final meeting with his lawyer; that was the day he had to make a choice as well.

While waiting to be called, James had considered all available options. He finally decided to go with the arduous choice.

"I swear to God, I'm going to man up and do the six-month sentence and get two misdemeanors, instead of taking the probation and getting two felonies or taking it to trial," he murmured to himself.

A few minutes later, a middle-aged woman appeared, wearing a grandma dress with a blazer and thick glasses.

"James Jordan!" she called out.

"Yes, yes, I'm here!" he answered as he jumped up and then pushed through the crowded room.

"Don't take the easy way out; it would hurt you in the long term," he said to himself as he walked across the room.

A moment later, sitting across the desk from his lawyer, he sat up straight and spoke.

"I decided to go with the plea, even if that meant I must go to jail. In the long run, I believe this would be the right choice," he said.

The lawyer scribbled some notes and looked up, nodded, then smiled.

"I must admit, I thought you would go with the probation and take the two felonies. But I commend you for your bravery. Not many individuals would choose to serve time if they had the option not to," he said.

James grinned and replied.

"I know what's at stake, my future. I would rather avoid the felonies than be free and have them on my record."

The two men continued discussing the case for a while, and the public defender finally told James that he would start serving his jail sentence on the tenth of the following month before he left.

Immediately after getting home that afternoon, James felt dizzy. His mind was filled with conflicting thoughts, so he grabbed his head to maintain his balance as he battled his brain.

"Don't take a plea; they're just bulls******you. They don't have anything on you," he thought from one side of his brain.

"Stay grounded and rely on your own inner judgment rather than giving in to negative influences," he said to himself.

"At least take the two years of probation, so you don't have to go to jail," he thought from the other side of his brain.

For a moment, he couldn't think, then he remembered to call Gabriel and seek advice.

"Hello, Mr. Houston, I just called to check up on you and inform you that I decided to take a plea deal."

After talking for a minute or two, Gabriel told James that he had been fired from Spirits University and that he believed Mr. Johnson had something to do with his dismissal. He also shared his intuition about the secretary with James, urging him to stay away from the secretary, his son Rob, and anyone associated with them. Afterwards, James told Gabriel that he had accepted the plea and didn't want to take the case to trial or settle for the felonies. Gabriel was very pleased, so he commended him for it. Given that Gabriel was in New Amsterdam at the time, shortly after their conversation, he met with Steve to reveal the news about James.

"Even though we could've gotten him out of these charges, I hope you see why letting him go through the experience will develop him into a wiser and stronger individual," said Steve.

"Now I see what you meant. It would be easier to shape him while he's incarcerated because he's too distracted out here," Gabriel admitted and laughed.

"Listen, Gabriel, a wise man once told me that if you want to teach a man how to swim, you must throw him into deep waters. I say that to say if you want to help James, we can't fix his problems. We must allow him to deal with the consequences. He was destined for this or someone as intelligent as James would never put himself in this type of position," Steve pointed out.

It was the winter break, and the fall semester had gone by quickly for James. At that point, it was getting very close to the sentencing day. A week prior to that, James had taken his important belongings back to Bronzeville, where his cousin Alpha stayed. He wanted to let Alpha hold the items until he came out of jail because he didn't want to lose or waste his property. While he was in Amsterdam, he had also contacted some family members and friends and told them that he was going to study abroad for the next semester, among them were Oumar and Benjamin, informing everyone except his mother and Alpha, that he was going to Flowropia.

During the break, James went to the property management office and scheduled to terminate his lease the day before he had to turn himself in for sentencing, which would be a week after the school opened for the spring semester. There was approximately a week left before school opened. He vowed to celebrate and enjoy the remaining time by excessively drinking, smoking, and partying until the last minute, especially on the night before when he was planning to throw a party.

In the following days, James and his entourage lived up to his promise and attended almost all the events around campus. Meanwhile, Rose had come up to visit the university because she was interested in attending the school in the upcoming fall term. On that Wednesday night at a school party, James bumped into Rose for the first time since he rescued her and took her home. After that encounter, he believed it was destined for them to develop a relationship. Excitement fueled him; as he fixed his gaze on her, he got flashbacks of their elementary days.

"If not now, then when?" he thought.

Suddenly, he walked confidently towards her intending to make it clear that he harbored romantic intentions. As he got closer, she met his gaze with her beautiful roundish-almond deep-set gray eyes. She recognized him and headed towards him. They met in the middle and hugged. She was as blissful as he was, so they talked for a while. They had a brief chat, then he expressed his admiration for her. Before parting ways, they exchanged phone numbers. After exchanging contacts, they agreed to go out the next day.

As soon as she turned to walk back to where her girlfriends were standing, they all chuckled.

"You go, girl!" Mary cheered.

"Yeah, yeah, yes, sir…we see you, Stackz!" hollered Slim and LV at the same time as James walked back with a poker face, trying not to show his exhilaration.

From that day moving forward, Rose and James kept in touch with one another. James couldn't get her out of his mind, so he wanted to spend every minute with her. Despite being infatuated with her and feeling that he loved her, he understood that they were still in the process of getting to know each other. And since he really liked her, he took his time.

Later, James and his partners found out that Mary was Rose's cousin, and she was the reason Rose had been visiting their school frequently. Mary, originally from New Amsterdam, had brown eyes, a small nose, a pretty round face, a slim yet curvy body, and short hair. Since they first met at the party, James and Rose spoke on the phone every day. They only went out once to a restaurant, and then they went to the movies together.

James and Rose also went out on Friday and Saturday evening before James and his close friends began their club touring. Ultimately, James told Rose how he really felt about her and that he would be pursuing his studies overseas the next semester. During their date on Saturday, he told her about the party he was hosting the following day and invited her. She gladly accepted the invitation.

"I'll be there early," she said as she smiled gently.

"I'll be looking forward to one last time before I leave!" he said as he smiled smugly.

"I promise I'll be there," she assured him and blushed.

It was Sunday afternoon, and James and his friends had been partying since Wednesday night. When James woke up, he took a moment to reflect as it dawned on him that it was the last day before he turned himself in to serve the six months sentence. However, he quickly forgot about the hearing as he remembered Rose. Despite feeling exhausted, he was thinking that the party was far from over, as it was his last day to celebrate freedom before he had to turn himself in for sentencing the following morning. Afterward he hopped in the shower, cleaned himself, and then stood in front of his closet to pick out the outfit he had prepared for the day.

"*Tonight, I'm getting messed up!*" he thought as he grabbed his G-Star navy blue and white T-shirt and blue jeans. Then he placed his blue Yankee fitted cap on his head to match his blue, red, and white Prada shoes. After finishing getting dressed, he prayed, as he had started praying more often. Fifteen minutes later, he walked out of the room, sat in the living room, and waited for LV, who was always the last to get ready whenever they were going out. A couple of minutes later, they walked out and drove to downtown where the school, all the restaurants, shops, and bars were located. They were out there until the evening and ate dinner and hung around for a while, then went to their off-campus community apartments for a pregame party. By the end of the pre-game party, there were already so many gentlemen and beautiful women in front of the recreation area of the complex.

"I'm going to drink, smoke, and enjoy the hell out of this party," James thought as he walked past the guests.

"I'm drinking until I pass out; I need to walk into the courtroom drunk and high as a mother f*****. Need to get some buns tonight too since I can't get any for a while," he continued thinking.

Shortly after the party was getting started, the music was loud, everyone was drinking, dancing, and having a good time, except for James.

"The clock is ticking!" he thought as he was still stuck on the fact that the next day he'd be locked up. Every time James started to forget court, reality hit him again, and he remembered doomsday. He couldn't help his mind from drifting on and off from the party to the upcoming sentencing. Later, B Money had recently returned from picking up his girlfriend Mary and her friends. Immediately after his arrival, he spotted James standing by himself at the end of the pool.

"Excuse me babe, I'll be right back," said B Money as he let go of Mary's hand and headed towards the other end of the pool.

"What's up with you, Stackz?"

"I'm chilling," replied James.

"You look down," B Money said.

"You're right, I am. It's not like I'm afraid of what I'm going to experience in jail," James looked up and admitted. He paused, then dropped his head again as he took a moment to let his friend observe what he had expressed then continued.

"I'm just thinking about the fact that I'm going to miss doing this. I mean seriously, I'm going to miss everything, our school activities, our party routines, and just being in school. I know it's going to be challenging surviving behind bars for months without this kind of comfort, but I'm not worried about being taken advantage of because I can defend myself."

"My fault, I totally forgot about that. I hear what you are saying, Stackz."

B Money expressed sympathetically as he recalled the hearing. Instantly, he remembered that he had left Mary waiting, so he glanced back.

"Look here, man," he continued.

"It's your last night, come on, Stackz, we need to turn up. Let's worry about that tomorrow because right now there are a lot of beautiful women here trying to have a good time," he said as he glanced back at Mary and her friends one more time.

Wondering what the reason was why B Money kept looking back, James took a glimpse and saw Mary and Rose.

"Oh s***Rose is here!" he thought.

"Alright bro, f… it, come on, let's do it!" said James as he quickly stood up and stormed off towards Rose.

Puzzled by James and his sudden mood change, B Money shouted as he followed him.

"Wait for me, bro."

B Money ran quickly and caught up to James. They walked side by side to the other end of the pool where the grill was. James embraced Rose softly, giving her a kiss on the side of her right cheek, then stood around her. After noticing his friend's face light up as James interacted with Rose, B Money finally understood the reason for his unanticipated contentment.

A few hours later that evening, due to the lateness of the hour and everyone's fatigue, the party had transitioned from outside the complex to inside their apartment. James was sitting next to Rose with his arm around her shoulders. Mary was sitting to the left of Rose, and Amanda, another one of their girlfriends, was sitting on the edge of the couch beside them. Suddenly, B Money appeared with three Standard Red Wine glasses of tequila.

"Hey ladies, here's some tequila," he said.

After serving the young ladies the drinks which they gladly accepted, B Money looked at Mary and continued.

"Having fun, babe?"

"Of course," she replied with spirit.

B Money laughed and said, "I'm glad my baby's enjoying the party!"

A moment later, he looked at Rose and questioned, "It's Rose, right?"

"Yeah," she replied with a smile.

"Can I steal my boy for a minute?" he asked.

"Of course," she said freely, then paused and took a sip from the glass and continued.

"He's all yours, but make sure you bring him back soon. James, when you finish fooling around, I'll be here!"

James stood up, and together he and B Money walked across the room to the kitchen table where the rest of their friends were standing impatiently waiting for them to return so they could drink their shots of Hennessy.

Upon arriving, LV raised his shot of Patron in the air and yelled, "To Stackz!"

Everyone else followed suit, shouting, "To Stackz!" in unison.

James, B Money, Slim, and Ray, raised their shot glasses also and they took their shots together.

Only Smokey, who didn't drink at all, was around them without a shot glass.

LV, who was tall, dark-skinned, athletic, with brown eyes, and known for being very stylish, shouted, "Hey, guys, one more! This is to us, the Fly Guys!"

Thirty seconds later, they took two more shots, totaling four shots of liquor.

Smokey had tried alcohol before but didn't like it, therefore he had walked out as soon as they had their first shot. Ray, who drank occasionally because he only drank on special occasions like New Year's, also followed Smokey outside, where they began rolling some weed. Smokey knew James enjoyed smoking too so he wanted to share a blunt with him on that special night.

After smoking the first blunt, Smokey opened the door and signaled James to come out to the porch. A few seconds later, he opened the door again and called out, "Yo, Stackz, hurry up! We are having a cipher, and it's your turn!"

"Alright, bro, I'm coming!" James replied and quickly ran out to join them. James, Smokey, and Ray smoked the second blunt together. As they sparked another one, James felt sentimental and nostalgic with each puff. He began to value every moment spent with his friends more, reminiscing about the good times they had shared in the past. James and his friends' bond was strong, especially when they come together to share special moments like smoking blunts or taking shots. James, B Money, LV, Slim, Ray, and Smokey were all very close, and these kinds of moments were a testament to their camaraderie.

Suddenly LV appeared and interrupted the cipher.

After they finished smoking, LV came out to the porch and asked James, "Stackz, you good?"

"Hell yeah! Why does everyone keep saying that?" replied James with base in his voice trying to sound enthusiastic.

"It's just, I've been watching you with a shortie, and I couldn't help but to notice for some reason, you're very quiet. What's up with you? Usually, you're the life of the party, especially with a bad joint like that!"

"Yeah, I know, it's because I keep remembering tomorrow," James responded.

"I hear you, let's go back inside before these guys finish all the alcohol," said LV.

James got up and headed inside with LV, leaving Smokey and Ray outside as Smokey was finishing up rolling another blunt. As they were walking back, LV stopped midway and said, "Listen to me, Stackz."

He paused and looked around to make sure no one else could hear him, then continued.

"Right now, you have this beautiful woman in front of you. She is basically begging you to hit it, and I'm not going to let tomorrow or anything mess that up. Wake your A** up, bro. If you play your cards right, she could be the one to keep you company while you are there. She might even wait for you until you come home."

"I hear you, thanks for the reminder!" said James.

LV had taught James a lot about women and relationships, thus he took his advice seriously. He listened to LV also because he was living proof of a healthy relationship. James felt that he was someone who practiced what he preached since he had been with his girlfriend since their freshman year of college.

Britney, another one of his girlfriends, was there as well, so she walked up to James and said, "I'm going to miss you, boo."

"I'm going to miss you too, baby!" James replied to her, and they hugged. After Rose saw James and Britney hugging, she was jealous, so she got up and went after him. As soon as B Money started to pour more alcohol, James heard this soft-spoken voice whispering to him.

"Hey James, are you going to be chilling and drinking here with your bros all night, or do you want to come with me?" she asked as she grabbed his hand.

He looked back and smiled then said, "Nah, give me a second!"

"Excuse me," said James as he looked at Britney, then he walked away with Rose. He held her hand, and they walked towards his bedroom. At this point, the liquor had kicked in, and he was no longer thinking logically or being hesitant. After all those drinks and blunts, he was much looser; he forgot all about the reality of the next day. All he wanted now was to get laid by the sexy lady standing in front of him, a long-time crush of his. He was so attracted to Rose, especially after the fact that she was the only one who didn't give in on their first date. Even though he respected her classiness, as soon as they walked into the room, he thought, "*No holding back this time!*"

James went for the kiss, and she didn't resist him.

"*Her lips tasted like fresh strawberries and watermelon,*" he thought as her tongue twirled against his like a French kiss. James felt his heart explode with joy; he was satisfied even if the kiss was all he got. He stopped kissing her for a moment and looked into her lovely eyes and spoke.

"I told you I'm leaving in the morning, right?"

"Yeah, I hate that you have to go away as soon as I start falling for you," she answered then expressed.

"I promise, I'll try to keep in touch as much as I can," he said, and paused as it dawned on him that jail could be different than what he would expect.

"If for any reason you don't hear from me, I'll be back in six months for sure," he continued, trying to indicate to her that he might not be in control of his freedom, thus preparing her for the worst-case scenario.

"You should be able to contact your friends and family from anywhere around the world. I mean, it's not like you're going to jail or anything," she suggested, then burst out laughing. He gave a halfhearted laugh because he felt guilty for not telling her the truth.

"Yeah, right. I don't know, I'm just saying, in case I don't, please trust me on this. It wouldn't be in my control," he responded quickly before she could detect his insincerity.

"I hope that it doesn't take six months or more before I see you again or speak to you again. But if it does, don't worry I'll wait, I promise!" she assured him.

"Is there anything wrong? Why do you insist?" she asked.

"No, everything is good. I'll contact you as soon as I touch down," he said with an expressionless face.

Afterward, he went and locked the room, dimmed the light, and turned on a few strawberry candles. Then they went right back to kissing.

"Baby, you smell like the sweetest roses I've ever smelled," said James and thought, *"Her skin is so soft, tender, and warm."*

Afterwards the two love birds ended up on the bed. James helped her take off her jeans and her shirt slowly, leaving only her bra and panties on because he enjoyed having intercourse with a little clothes on the woman. Then he rubbed her breast, kissed her again, placed his penis on the side of her buttock, and slowly entered her vagina. She calmly lay there, looking into his eyes as he penetrated gently. He stopped for a moment, gazing back into her eyes, and said, "I love you, girl. I really, really love you, Rose."

She grabbed his waist, pulled him closer, and said, "I love you too, James."

An hour later, Amanda knocked on the door and yelled, "Rose, if you're in there, we are leaving!"

"Yeah, Amanda, give me a second," Rose answered as she got up and walked towards the door.

"I'm coming," she added after cracking open the door. Then she gave James a long kiss as he was putting on his clothes.

"I can't wait to see you again James, make sure you call me," she said.

"I will, sweetheart, trust me, I will." He said before walking her out. When they walked out of the room, they noticed that most of the guests had already departed, except for a few who were close to his roommates and their partners.

James walked Rose out to the car with her girlfriends, then returned to the room around thirty minutes to five a.m. He knew he had to wake up in two and a half hours to make it on time for the hearing. He fell asleep not long after lying down. At fifteen minutes past seven a.m., the alarm went off, "Ring! Ring! Ring!" James opened his eyes, stumbled out of the room, and walked through the living room and the kitchen, seeing all the bodies asleep. Some guests hadn't even made it out of the apartment and had passed out due to being drunk and hungover. He knocked loudly on all the doors of the other rooms to wake up his roommates. Money, Slim, LV, and James all woke up feeling dizzy and drowsy from the previous night's partying. Ray and Smokey had spent the night on the living room couch, so they were there to accompany James.

They all rushed to the bathrooms one by one, cleaned up, got dressed, and drove to the courthouse. They were worn out and dispirited not only because James was facing time away but also because they were sleepy and hungover from the excessive partying.

James already had an idea of what was going to happen when he entered the courtroom. He had been preparing for this moment for over nine months. As he made his way into the courtroom, he saw Mr. Johnson, Mr. Jackson, and Anthony Palmer, the director of DMCE (Department of Migration and Customs Enforcement). Mr. Palmer was invited by the other two so they could show him who James was, as they had planned to detain him under the DMCE agency after he finished serving his initial sentence. James recognized Peter, Mr. Johnson, and Mr. Jackson, but didn't recognize the other individual they were with.

As it was a plea deal, immediately after the hearing started, she asked if all parties were ready, and she proceeded without delay.

After asking James a few questions, she finalized her inquiry with, "Do you understand that you are pleading guilty to two counts of marijuana possession, Mr. Jordan?"

"Yes, your honor," he replied.

Afterwards she sentenced him to three months for each count, totaling six months with good behavior. He had to serve this time consecutively and would have probation and parole afterward.

James confirmed his understanding, and after signing the necessary paperwork, he bid goodbye to his friends. He then gave himself over to the officers, who handcuffed him and led him away. Looking back, James saw his friends still standing there with long faces as they watched him get taken away.

A couple of hours later as James got close to the county jail where he would serve his time, he saw the barbed wire on the fences and thought, "*Holy s*** I'm going to be here for at least six months. I better man up, well, I don't have a choice anyway!*"

During the classification and assignment process, he saw a familiar face; Louis, was also being processed.

"*I guess they swept up everyone I worked with,*" he thought.

A few minutes later, an officer called out, "James Jordan!"

"Yes, ma'am," he replied. The officer opened the gate to the holding cell, and James changed into an orange jumpsuit before being sent to his holding block.

CHAPTER SIX

INCARCERATION TIME

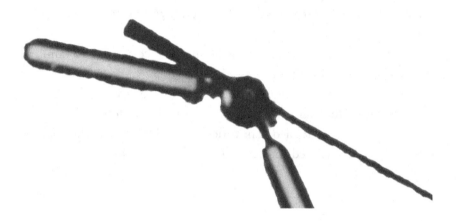

Following James' sentencing, Peter and his group were discontent and assembled to further strategize against James.

"It was a successful day. James is finally behind bars, time to celebrate and he's been sentenced to six months. However, the job is not done yet. This is the perfect opportunity to do away with him," said Peter.

"In order to follow through with our plan, I sent Bill and George after him. I also notified DICE about him just in case our agents are unable to do away with him by the end of his sentence, we'll have them pick him up," Mr. Jackson announced.

"Great, I guess we're all on the same page!" said Mr. Johnson.

Meanwhile James was still in the holding cell where inmates stay until they find them a cellblock. The decision of which holding block an inmate got assigned to was made based on the inmate's crime and necessary security level. All the inmates wore either a solid orange or black-and-white striped top and bottom. A few hours after sitting in a holding cell waiting to be processed, James was served food through a pie hole. When he first walked inside the cell, he was calm. However, when one of the Corrections Officers gave him a meal on a worn-out tray, he realized that he was in for a long and terrible experience, so he became very concerned. After the officer passed the food to him, he looked and thought, "*This is the worst food I've ever seen in my life. I would rather starve to death than eat this.*"

He didn't want to eat the food because the tray that it was served in was also used up and appeared disgusting. Since he was used to fasting, going a few hours without food didn't bother him, so he left the food as it was. Later that evening, he realized that he didn't have any other choice and began eating little by little, starting with the fruits and drinks. He was so concerned about how to adapt to the environment that he forgot how long his sentence was. Reality kicked in once he remembered that he would be in the same place for the next six months. After a few days, it started to register with him that he wasn't going anywhere. He didn't have a choice of what to eat, what to wear, what to watch, and so on. Therefore, he freaked out momentarily.

Later when he understood that to make his life easier there, he needed to get comfortable and adapt to his environment, he did. Before he knew it, he got used to the food. To his surprise, the food was not so bad once you got settled in. He realized that it was cleaned to the best of its ability. After all, he also realized that the food tasted incredible. His favorite meal was when they served rice and chicken or pizza. He started to trade his commissary food for the jail food on days that he wasn't too fond of the food.

Other things that bothered James were showering in front of other inmates because the showers were in the dayroom and the early curfews, which meant they got locked in early, even if they didn't want to sleep. They went no further than downstairs to the dayroom and the recreation room, which were all only a few feet from each other. They woke up very early for count and for breakfast. During inmate counting, if one of them wasn't up and ready, he got written up and sent to the hole. They were counted three times a day, around breakfast, lunch, and dinner.

A few weeks later, Gabriel called Steve to share a recent discovery related to James' case.

"I have recently uncovered a complex and intriguing situation in the case of James v. College Town Police. Did you know that Mr. Johnson and his son, Rob, orchestrated the conspiracy against him."

"Is that right, and what makes you say that?" asked Steve.

"They had Sam and Louis supply the police with the information about his criminal activities for a few months," said Gabriel before pausing and flipping through some documents then continuing.

"Sam's involvement in James' case is perplexing as he was not originally part of the school but was revealed to be one of their secret sources. The rapid and smooth transfer of Sam during the semester adds to the mystery surrounding his role in James' case. Sam being one of the undercover students also brings me to his father, Antoine, and his intended presence with Alex during the ambush by Manuel's mercenaries. It's crucial to gather more evidence and further investigate all parties involved."

"You are right, something doesn't add up. I always question his sincerity since the day Alex was killed and all your family members were attacked except for his. He's our lead to discovering the rest of their association. We should investigate all of them further, especially Antoine."

"In the meantime, find an agent to send after James so he can assist him and communicate this message to him," said Steve.

"We should send Mike instead, since he is already familiar with these kinds of missions," suggested Gabriel.

"If you believe a college student can do the job, then by all means do it."

"I have the utmost faith in Mike; plus, you're forgetting James doesn't need protection. He's too skilled; he just needs company, and we need someone to give him our message."

"That's right, he's hujinn," replied Steve before they wrapped up their conversation and ended the call.

James could only contact his mother, brother Jeremy, and cousin Alpha in the initial weeks as those were only phone numbers he had memorized before being locked up. He had written down all the contacts of his family and friends whom he wanted to get in touch with, but he lost the paper during processing. However, after reconnecting with Alpha, he got the contacts of some of his partners from Spirits University. It was his second day inside, and James didn't have any money in his account, so one of his fellow inmates generously allowed him to use their credit to make a call to request commissary funds. His first call was to Alpha. After dialing Alpha's number, he waited as the call connected.

"You are receiving a call from an inmate at the county jail. Press one to accept the call," the automated machine for the county jail announced. Alpha already knew it was James, so he accepted the charges.

A couple of seconds later, James heard many voices in the background.

"Hello," Alpha voiced from the other end.

"What's up, cousin? Sorry it took me a while to call you. I didn't have any money in my account," James explained.

"I didn't know you needed money to make calls. I would have sent you some," Alpha responded.

"Yeah, me too. But it's all good. I miss you, cousin," James expressed.

"I miss you too, cousin. How are you holding up there? Are you okay?" Alpha inquired.

"Yeah, I'm fine, how about you and the family?"

They conversed for about ten minutes, though to James, it felt like a fleeting moment. When the time was about to run out, they quickly said their goodbyes and ended the call just before the time was up.

After talking to his cousin, James began imagining what it was like out there because it reminded him of the outside world more than ever. He was homesick, so he walked back to the round table where his fellow inmates were sitting, playing card games. That time, they were playing poker, but they also played spades or blackjack at times. James stood at the back as he often did and watched them play unless they were playing for fun, which no one liked to do because it was not as interesting as betting with their commissaries or daily meals on the games.

The following month, James had just finished serving his first month. It was the afternoon when he was hanging out with his closest fellow inmates—Mike, Cam, and Miles, all of whom were being held in cellblock B. One of his closest colleagues there was Mike because of his leadership and intelligence. He was from Wishkeon, a country that was in Flowropia, and he was fearless, powerful, and well-built. No one in that jailhouse wanted to get on his bad side. He was determined and imposing, which intimidated almost everyone there, even the guards. However, James was not afraid of him as he saw similarities between himself and Mike. They had mutual respect which led to a strong friendship between them. Little did James know, Mike was sent by Gabriel from the BIA to help protect him and provide training. Cam was another inmate James enjoyed spending time with. Cam was an incredible basketball player, known for his sharpshooting skills and rich swagger, much like Rich, his friend from elementary. Their shared love for basketball kept them engaged in friendly competition. Like Mike, Cam was also cool and smart, which solidified their bond. They were often joined by Mike, who had his own established presence, and Miles, who was strange and intimidating but very self-assured. These inmates filled his time and made it worth. They were not only his friends but also his allies, ready to support him in case any other inmate or group tried to challenge him. This dynamic created a clear class division and motivation within the incarcerated community. James and his friends considered themselves at the top of the food chain, deterring any potential drama from arising with their group. As he was locked up with all kinds of criminals from one who committed level three misdemeanors to class A felonies. Dealing with these individuals and coming from a life of bliss before his incarceration, James learned the value of time and its importance.

James was a curious guy, so when he had the time, he asked a lot of questions to his elders and to his peers. Since he had all the time in the world, he planned to grow his hair and try braids for the first time. Braiding his hair was always something he wanted to do since he was a kid, but his parents didn't allow it. Since he was far away from his mother or anyone who could potentially see him and tell her what he had decided to do, he was going to take advantage and braid his hair.

Later that day, Mike placed a call to Gabriel and they discussed James.

"Tell James to be much more careful. Also, let him know that if all goes well, there's a possibility that he could get out earlier because of a potential conspiracy. However, we can't guarantee anything," Gabriel ordered Mike.

A month later James had been in jail for a couple of months, and still no one had visited him yet. He was getting used to the day-to-day life in jail and losing hope of receiving any visits from his family or friends. He understood the reason why his family hadn't visited up to that point; they lived in a different state, which was over six hours away by car. However, his schoolmates were only a couple of hours away, so he felt that they let him down.

After making the most of his time during his bid by focusing on self-improvement and pursuing his passions, he started receiving a great deal of support from friends and family during the last two months of his six-month bid. They visited him and corresponded with him more frequently, providing him with financial assistance for additional phone calls.

The next month, James was surprised to receive his first visit from his crew. The visit took place around quarter to five in the afternoon, with the corrections officer opening the steel door to allow him access to the visitation room. As he walked energetically down the hall to the visit area, feeling a little bit more special that day. After the door on the other side of the thick and heavy glass opened, B Money, LV, Smokey, and Ray appeared; basically, all his close friends came to visit him except for Slim. Ray was a year younger than the rest of them, so he was treated as such, always the subject of laughter or the last to partake in any activities that they partook in. However, Ray and James had become very close before he was sentenced, due to their business partnership. Because of their close friendship, Ray assisted James more than anyone else in their circle throughout his incarceration.

"Slim didn't make it this time around since he had a family emergency to attend to," B Money explained.

Ray stuck his head out to speak on the phone so James could hear him and said loudly, "His father was admitted to the hospital and diagnosed with brain damage."

Sensing that Ray and James had much to discuss, B Money handed the phone over to Ray.

"Sorry, bro, to hear that. Tell him I said what's up, and my prayers go out to his dad," James expressed with sincerity.

"I will! Mary was asking around about you too. She asked me to tell you that Rose said that she was still waiting for your call. What she wanted to tell you is very important, but she only wanted to tell you," Ray told him.

Then he asked Ray if he got her number, but he said no and that she figured he had it. James said, "No, I don't. I lost all my contacts, Ray, please, you must get her number for me." They said their goodbyes and went their separate ways.

After the visit from his friends, James returned to his normal daily activities. His fellow inmates were playing poker as usual. As James watched them play, he thought about the times when he used to play similar games with his friends. Even though most of the time he didn't play because he didn't like to gamble, he passed time spectating and mentally comparing his moves to the players' moves. He enjoyed watching his fellow inmates use their tactics on one another. He was standing next to Troy, another inmate who also liked to watch but only because he didn't have the means to gamble with. They talked quietly in the background as they watched.

"You must remember that here, everyone is trying to occupy themselves with activities that help them pass the time. Outside, you are trying to save time, but in jail, you are trying to kill time," said Troy.

"Yeah, right?" James acknowledged, then he got distracted for a moment from the commotion between some of the inmates, then he continued.

"I'm going to try to get better at every game and I'm going to practice my reading, writing, and card game skills. I didn't know how to play poker, spades, chess, or blackjack, but I'm going to learn them and try to perfect my skills, especially in chess. So far, chess has been my favorite because it passes time quickly, and I enjoy one-on-one battles. As for recreation activities, I plan to play handball, basketball, volleyball, and soccer, and work out often. I'm going to take advantage of this time to perfect my skills because I will be too busy with responsibilities outside."

Later that evening, Ray asked B Money to talk to Mary for him and try to get Rose's contact. When B Money spoke to Mary and told her that James wanted him to get Rose's. Mary said she'd relay the message to Rose and get back to him.

Understanding how much Rose had cried over James, Mary thought that she would be intrigued to hear that he wanted to get in touch with her, so she called her right away. Despite how much Rose had missed James, she had given up on him. So, when Mary called and conveyed the message, she burst into tears.

"You see what I mean, Mary? He is full of s***. I don't know what to believe anymore. One minute he can't communicate with me because he is overseas, and the next minute, he lost my number. Forget him; I'll see him when I see him. Don't give him or any of his friends my number; I'm tired of being lied to," she said.

"I understand, don't worry I won't," replied Mary.

A week later, Ray went back to see James and told him what had occurred, that Rose believed he was running games on her.

"Wow, this means it's been over three months since you last heard from one another?" said Ray.

"Yeah, bro, that's why I'm asking you to help me."

Afterwards James asked him to go to Rose in person and tell her the truth about his incarceration and see if she might change her mind and speak to him again.

A few days later when Ray saw Rose, he went and tried to speak to her. She walked right past him, didn't make any eye contact, headphones on, music blasting. Ray tried to talk to Rose, but she ignored him. Afterwards, he felt sorry for James as it seemed he was chasing someone who didn't care. Therefore, he chose to write a letter to James detailing the encounter with Rose instead of visiting him.

A week later, James received a letter informing him that Rose no longer trusted anything he or his friends had to say. When Ray tried to speak to Rose, she quickly shut down the conversation, refused further contact, and even threatened involvement of authorities if approached. Rose ignored any attempts to assure her of the truthfulness of the message James intended for her. After reading the letter, he was heartbroken as the woman he truly cared about misunderstood his intentions. He considered reaching out to her again to have an open and honest conversation about the situation but remembered that she had.

He went through a tough time processing it. It took some time for him to accept and heal.

"She must have been upset with me for not calling after I had promised to call her. She probably thought I was playing games with her and that I'm not incarcerated. If seeing her again in the future is meant to be, I trust that things will unfold naturally," he thought.

Close to completing four months, James was reflecting on his father's advice to focus on his education at Spirits University School of The Gifted, James internalized the need to address his choices upon his release, acknowledging his priorities. James began suspecting a conspiracy involving Mr. Johnson, Mr. Jackson, and Mr. Palmer, a man he couldn't identify at that time. Despite knowing they were all connected, James pondered the identity of Mr. Palmer, the third man present during his hearing. The demeanor of the three mentioned individuals suggested they were not on his side, leading James to plan future investigations post-release.

As he sat in the cell and was making sense of the familiar and unfamiliar faces he saw at his sentencing hearing, heard the main door to the jailhouse open and in walked Louis. He had a wide set of gray eyes, a flat nose, thin lips, and a squared head.

He had a bad instinct from the moment he saw Louis because he was one of the individuals whom he suspected had told on him. He didn't want to read too much into the coincidence that he ran into a fellow student, but they were sentenced the same day, sent to different holding blocks, and now they were in the same house. James felt unsure and uncomfortable around Louis, considering he could have been the one who told on him in the first place. After seeing him during processing and encountering him again in the same holding cell block after a few months, he became extremely aware of his surroundings just in case Louis or any other inmate attacked him. His intuition had also been telling him to be careful around two other inmates, Bill, and George. Those two individuals had been around him since processing, and unlike Louis, they were assigned to the same cellblock right away. James likely felt even more suspicious about them since later, when Louis came into the holding block B, Bill and George took him in and formed their own circle. After receiving hostile glances from this group of three, James understandably became more cautious and alert in their presence.

A few weeks after, Mike approached James during recreation and told him a message that he got from Gabriel.

"I work for the BIA; no one else here knows about this, so keep it classified. I've been watching your back since you walked in here. Gabriel told me that you are very important to the world, so we need you to make it out alive. James, some men in here are undercovers and they are after you; they were sent by a secret organization associated with the remembers of ISA."

"I think I know who they might be," said James. Then he paused for a moment, surveyed the room, and spotted Louis, then continued.

"One of them could be the guy talking to the corrections officer, who was transferred here a few days ago."

"Could be but, the guys I'm referring to either came in before you or at the same time you did. Anyway, their boss also wanted to recruit you, so he ordered them to check with you to see if you would agree to join them, and if you don't accept their offer, to kill you!" Mike explained.

"Thanks, I'll be on the lookout!" said James.

"Based on historical trends, guys like that usually attack their target around the end of his bid, so be on alert because they could come after any time now," Mike warned him.

Knowing how important it was for him to prioritize his safety and well-being while in that environment, he informed Mike about the other two inmates he suspected as well. Together he and Mike began to become more observant of Bill, Louis, and George.

Days later during recreation, James was standing next to Mike in the tight room that they used to exercise or play sports in. James had not used his mind-reading power in years, but due to his fear of being attracted, it automatically reactivated. As they stood there and waited for the next basketball game, Mike thought, "I love recreation!"

After hearing Mike's thoughts, he initiated a conversation in relation to it.

"Don't you love the day room? It's one of the best times I have had here," he asked.

"Yeah, you can exercise, play poker, chess, basketball, volleyball, different types of card games, and more. You could interact with others, watch television, and hear stories about the outside," replied Mike.

"You know what else I enjoy in here, the Chea-chea," said James. (Chea-chea is the name James and his fellow inmates used to describe food that they make by using ramen noodle as a base and adding other items from their commissary.)

"You know what my favorite part about being locked up is?" asked Mike.

"Let me guess, working out!" replied James.

"You got it, I love to train, so if you are down, we can work out together from now on," Mike suggested.

"I knew it because I always see working out ever since I've been here," said James.

From that day on, Mike trained him five days out of the week.

A week later, Bill and George approached James in the dayroom. After discussing the reason for their arrest for a while, Bill, who had recently been assigned to the same cell as him, asked him to teach him how to play chess. Word had gotten around that James had become a formidable chess player. James was reluctant to trust Bill, especially given the warnings he had received from Mike. He felt unsure about getting involved with them, so with caution, he politely denied the request and maintained his distance.

James had gone through some challenging times in the previous months. He thought lockdowns were toughest on him, especially when they lasted for long periods so he disciplined himself through prayer, which also aided his personal growth. He used his time in confinement to explore new hobbies, improve his skills, and reflect on the value of freedom and patience. He found solace in exercising and playing sports, particularly basketball. He kept himself occupied and used the time to maintain his physical health. He dedicated himself to engaging in physical activities like lifting weights and playing various sports since he didn't have any responsibilities or anywhere to go. He wrote many journals, enhanced his reading and speaking skills through the new vocabulary he acquired from reading numerous novels. He crafted his own stories, songs, and films, which he grew to love. He learned to be more patient and humbler, realizing the weight of losing his freedom.

James kept a countdown calendar in which he crossed out a day every morning upon waking up. After looking at it earlier that day and crossing out the day, he noticed that it was the first day of the last month of his bid. It was just another day in jail since every day seemed like the others, but to him, it was special. He was excited about completing five months, so he reflected on his time in jail up to that moment with his cousin by speaking about it.

Around that time, Slim also went to visit James for the first time, and they discussed his father's passing. James gave Slim some valuable advice by recommending a book that he had recently read, which helped him finally cope with the reality of the tragedies of his father's passing. The book had such a positive impact on him.

"Bro, you must read The All-Mighty Message. It's amazing how a book can trigger a love for reading and help improve your skills. Writing can be a great way to express yourself and share your experiences with others as well. That's how I turned my stressful experiences into a creative outlet and a way to document my journey," said James.

"That's a fact Jail does inspire a lot of great individuals to discover their hidden talent or work on their wishes or skills," Slim responded.

"Men, I remembered the first time I began writing; I was under so much stress from being institutionalized I wanted to share my experiences with the world. When something passes, we quickly forget whether it's good or bad. I realized living organisms tend to forget due to our entrapment of the moment. This was a moment I wanted to document, so I started to write a story relating to my experiences. I also wanted to save my pain so that I won't ever forget," James explained.

"It was difficult for me to deal with being locked down for all those hours or in some cases, days, especially when I was stuck with someone I didn't get along with. One time we were on lockdown, and that was the first time I ever smelled another grown man's poop. We were in a tiny room with no air coming in or out. I tried to hold my breath, but after a while, I couldn't breathe. That is when I took a deep breath and the smell hit me and I was in total distress." He explained as Slim sat on the other side observing and imagining the scenarios.

"S***, I can imagine. Knowing me, I would've probably fainted," Slim remarked, then they simultaneously laughed.

"I'm telling you, bro, if I could, I would've disappeared. Unfortunately, a few days after that lockdown, I went through another terrible experience. I was sent to the hole without a reason. However, I prefer solitary confinement over the general population lockdown if I must endure another man taking a dump again," said James.

After the visit, James went back to the day room and placed a call to Oumar, and they were discussing the same topic.

"I'm telling you O, the only other situation that was more terrifying than a lockdown moment was when I was in the hole. It was worse because during the general population lockdown, we were still able to speak to our cellmates or someone next door, whereas in the hole, it was just you and the four walls," said James.

"Oh no, I can't imagine living in that type of condition. I would've probably taken my life," Oumar replied.

"You won't be the first, because one of the times that I was there, someone hung himself with the bedsheet," said James.

"Say word?" exclaimed Oumar on the other end of the call.

"I swear, bro! Anyway, I miss having a fine woman next to me. Here we only have magazines, and I'm tired of flipping through the pages and drooling over sexy models in bikinis; yet I can't get laid. Looking at models in magazines is how we satisfy our lust. I just finished drawing this fine * model and a film star. She was very appealing, and I am very attracted to her; this made me feel super horny," said James.

Oumar laughed and said, "I understand your pain, bro. Just hang in there; I'm going to have a nice joint waiting for you when you get home."

"I miss everything, man, like listening to my favorite songs. All I hear on the radio is popular music or the same songs over and over. I missed listening to my favorite rappers so much that I requested one of their lyrics. I rapped the lyrics out loud in my head just to satisfy my desire. Most of all, I missed being outside, especially the weather. Thank you, God. It's going to be all over soon because I can't take any more of this," said James before the time ran out, and the call was cut off.

James felt the need to tell everyone he talked to about the lockdowns, so a couple of weeks later, when he called Ray, he told him the same story about his cellmate dropping a deuce while he was in the cell.

"I'd rather die than smell that again; other than that, everything is everything. I've learned a lot, especially the importance of time and freedom. I've learned to appreciate the better things in life, not just the material things in the world, like health, freedom, food, family – the things that all of us are blessed with unless you are dead or going through a momentary challenge," said James.

"Preach, my boy, that's why it's called a correctional facility; sounds like you've been corrected all the way!" said Ray.

As time passed, the support from outside started to dwindle as even his family and friends gradually began to forget about James. He had funds in his account, but few of his loved ones wrote to him or visited him. On that day, he felt profoundly lonely.

"No one cares about me!" he thought.

James struggled to accept that life was continuing outside and that just because he was incarcerated and had ample time on his hands did not mean everyone else out there shared the same leisure time. He mused to himself, *"You are imprisoned and have limited activities, while on the other hand, they have a multitude of tasks to complete on a daily basis."*

Louis approached James a couple of weeks before his release date and informed him that NISA was interested in recruiting him once he completed his sentence. He communicated his preferences clearly to Louis by expressing interest in joining the BIA instead of ISA. A few hours later, Louis told Bill and George what transpired between him and James and asked them to try to take him out before he gets released. At that point, James and Bill were still cellmates. The next day during recreation, Bill premeditated to kill him and discussed the plan with Louis and George. Little did Bill know that James overheard their conversation. Having been dubious towards Bill and his posse, James stayed vigilant and informed Mike about the planned attack to ensure his safety.

A few days later, Bill stole a plastic spoon from the tray and hid it. When an inmate took plastic spoons or forks from the food tray, it triggered an automatic three-day lockdown or more, depending on how the COs felt. The entire block was thoroughly stripped and searched naked. After the lockdown ended a few days later, Bill managed to retrieve the plastic spoon he had stolen from the tray because he had hidden it by the recreation area. Later that night, around 3 a.m., James heard movement from the top bunk as Bill went for the plastic knife that he had made from the spoon stolen from the food tray. However, James continued to pretend to be asleep. As Bill hung half of his body from the top bunk, holding on with his left hand and attempting to strike James on the neck with his right hand, James acted swiftly. Just as the knife was about to reach his throat, James blocked Bill's hand, pulled him down, and they exchanged blows for almost three minutes because Bill was also a very skilled fighter. Ultimately, James was able to drop him to the floor and place his knee on his throat until he passed out. James was able to defend himself without causing further harm to Bill, as he did not wish to face new charges. He then simply knocked Bill out and placed him back on his bunk until morning when he requested a cell change due to feeling threatened by his cellmate. The next morning, there was a shakedown and the correction officers found Bill's knife, resulting in him being sent to the hole.

A week after Bill's return from solitary confinement, it was a typical day in the jail, occurring one week before James' scheduled departure. Bill linked up with Louis, and George teamed up with a few of their inmate companions. They had planned to attack James one more time before he left. The following day, James and Mike were in the gymnasium training when Bill, George, and three other inmate friends of theirs stormed in with clothes covering their faces so that they wouldn't be recognized. They surrounded them and approached them from different directions in the room. They all had small objects in their hands. James and Mike were on the floor doing sit-ups when they quickly stood up to defend themselves and threw a few blows of their own. James grabbed Bill's hand and flipped him, but then two more attackers struck him from behind. The fight slowly made its way out to the day room, resulting in a huge battle between all the inmates in that cell block - everyone either fighting or hiding. Then, the COs threw out a couple of smoke bombs to render them unconscious. The fight continued for a few more seconds before the guards activated the alarm, signaling an emergency lockdown. After reviewing the video, they were able to identify the faces of Bill, George, and some of their partners, leading to their transfer to the hole. Bill yelled as the COs dragged him and his partners across the room, "James, you haven't seen the last of us yet."

A few days later, after the failed attempts to kill James, Louis called Mr. Johnson to inform him that James was not interested in joining them. He also mentioned that they had made several unsuccessful attempts to kill James.

It had been close to a few months since Mr. Jackson, Mr. Johnson, Peter, and Antoine had met, so after receiving the update on James from Louis, they arranged a meeting and invited Victor, Manuel, and Mr. Palmer. As soon as Mr. Palmer walked in, he overheard Mr. Johnson saying, "Our courier Louis informed me yesterday that James has chosen to pursue the opportunity to join the BIA instead of accepting your offer, Mr. Jackson. He also told me that the agents couldn't dispose of him, so we must come up with another solution before his release."

"Time is running out, and if we don't apprehend him soon, we must devise a new plan or proceed with our original one," Mr. Jackson proposed. Mr. Palmer deduced from Mr. Jackson's remark that the meeting was intended to determine the next steps in framing James, so he put in his two cents.

"That's where I come in and have DMCE detain him briefly so your agents can finish the job," he recommended.

"Yeah, worst-case scenario, he gets released before your agents slay him. Either way, they'll have some time to try and destroy him," replied Mr. Jackson, pausing for a moment to allow everyone in the room to acknowledge Mr. Palmer's recommendation.

"I agree that having him in custody while we arrange something will assure us that he's not out of reach," he continued.

"I agree; we should extend James' detention and repatriate him. Don't forget he's hujinn, an exceptionally bright one with formidable powers. We have witnessed his exceptional abilities!" Peter advised.

"I say if your agents haven't destroyed him by now, why not allow him to get released, so we can finish the job on the outside," Victor proposed.

"Very well then! If your operatives do not eliminate him by the time of his release date, we'll proceed with Mr. Palmer's suggestion," said Manuel.

It was the last day of James's sentence, thus in less than twenty-four hours, he expected to be free. Early the next morning, he packed up his belongings, said goodbye to Mike and his other fellow inmates, then went to the front. As he sat there waiting impatiently to get released, he could feel the outside air, see himself taking a fresh shower, celebrating with his friends, eating good food again, only to find himself an hour later facing another legal situation. After serving his time, he had hoped to go home, but now it seemed like he was back to square one. He was detained by DMCE, and he had no idea for what or how long he would be held. DMCE was a federal organization in Fabrica that prosecuted immigrants after they had been convicted of a crime. Having two misdemeanors meant he could be facing serious consequences, including deportation.

An hour later, two DMCE officers picked him up, and suddenly, he remembered the moment when two other DMCE officers interrogated him about his immigration status during the first week of his incarceration. He didn't consider the DMCE questioning to be a serious matter as it pertained to himself, since he was a green card holder, not an illegal immigrant. Therefore, he was very surprised by the detention. Only after these officers picked him up did James realize that he had misunderstood his rights and privileges as a permanent resident. He learned the hard way that green card holders have certain rights in Fabrica and that there are also responsibilities and limitations that come with that status. This was a challenging and confusing situation for James because he was unsure of his rights and options. He had little knowledge about immigration matters, but he knew that dealing with these issues was even more stressful than facing criminal charges because he had not anticipated it.

CHAPTER SEVEN

SET BACK TIME

After the unsuccessful attempts to turn and kill James in the county jail, Manuel and his secret Fabrican circle decided that the DMCE prison was another opportunity to do away with him. Therefore, they had sent Jason to the DMCE facility to ensure James's fate. Consequently, when James arrived, Jason was already present at the same location.

Being that James gave away all his money and belongings at the previous jail, he was not able to contact anyone a couple of days after he was transferred to the new prison. On the third day, just before that evening, one of the detainees allowed him to use his funds to place a call

215

to his mother and update her on his whereabouts. Holly picked up the phone with so much empathy in her voice, and she didn't want to show it, but she could not control her emotions. Even though she was still disappointed with him, she confessed how much she had missed him.

"Hey, how is my baby? I missed you so much; words can't describe it," voiced Holly.

"I'm fine, Mom. How about you and everyone else?" replied James.

"I miss you so much honey," she said.

"I miss you more mom," he replied.

"Anyone tried taking advantage of you?" she asked.

James sensed she was very concerned about his well-being; he answered calmly yet added some bass to his voice to make it seem like he had the situation under control, as if being detained by DMCE was no big deal to him.

"No, Mom, you know I can defend myself. I'm only here because I wanted to be. I could have broken out of here a long time ago, but I'm trying to get my papers in order. Don't worry about me; I have elite God-given ability, but I just try to fit in."

"Your dad always said the same thing. Now look, he's gone," Holly said and paused for a moment. He heard her pause on the other end as she sniffled, before continuing, "Remember, James, he also used to say the worst happened before the best comes so hang tight."

With his ears glued to the phone, James listened closely and thought, "She must be crying a little, but she doesn't want to let him know. I must reassure her that I'm doing well."

He hesitated as he didn't know the best way to comfort her, but finally stammered as he spoke up, "Mo-mom, I'm doing great. Please stop worrying about me. Is Jeremy home?"

"Yeah, he's upstairs!"

"Can I talk to him?"

"Ok, give me a second," she said and rushed upstairs to Jeremy's room and yelled out, "Jeremy! James wants to talk to you."

A few seconds after Jeremy opened the door, she passed him the phone.

"Hey, big bro, how are you doing?" he voiced.

"I'm cool. I missed you, bro," replied James.

"I missed you too James, how are you holding up?" said Jeremy.

James had only spoken to his little brother once since his incarceration, so he was thrilled to finally hear from him again, and he babbled on, "My first day here was not as bad as my first day in the county jail because I was familiar with the jail system. I knew the process and what kind of people or food to expect. The only thing that's bothering me is the fact that I don't know when I'm going to get released or why I'm being detained in the first place. At least when I was at the previous jail, I was just in there momentarily because I knew my release date. I was already sentenced, but at this moment, I'm just being detained without a clue about my future. I'm confused because I thought my green card was good enough to keep me away from immigration enforcements. But they are saying I could be deported unless the judge gives me asylum."

Jeremy sat there observing as James explained to him, and after he finished, he replied, "Don't worry, James. Remember how you always say that everything is always going to be fine?"

"Yeah," replied James.

"Well, you'll get through this soon," Jeremy reminded him before returning the phone back to their mother.

It had finally dawned on James that he was involved in a very serious matter. Before they finished their conversation, he asked his mother to get in touch with Gabriel and instructed her to ask Gabriel to find him a capable lawyer; otherwise, he might face deportation.

Afterwards, she called Gabriel, who referred her to Steve and gave her his cellphone number. Immediately after she finished speaking to Gabriel, she placed another call, but this time to Steve.

"It's important for James to have strong legal representation to defend his rights and navigate through the DMCE system effectively. Hopefully, with your help, he can find the best attorney to represent him when the time comes," she said on the other end of the call.

They talked for a while before Steve wrapped up the conversation by saying, "I assure you, Mrs. Jordan, I will find the best attorney out there to defend your son. I will make sure James receives the representation he deserves. If you have any questions or need further assistance, don't hesitate to ask; feel free to call me at any time."

After Steve talked to Holly, he called Gabriel and Christopher.

"I'm not surprised that James is still in custody, as they will try any and every tactic to destroy him!" Gabriel admitted.

"If he had reached out to any of us throughout his incarceration, do you think we could have done something earlier?" Gabriel asked.

"Excellent question, but I don't believe so," said Steve.

"Well, I speculate that DMCE targeted him because he was an immigrant with a green card," said Gabriel.

"I believe that the same adversaries likely seized on his immigration status to prolong their hold on him with potentially harmful intentions," said Steve.

"Either way this is becoming a very tragic situation. I'm concerned that he may have informed us too late about his situation due to trying to solve problems on his own," Gabriel expressed.

"I'm perfectly fine. However, find out the DMCE prison James is in, arrange for someone to protect him, and hire a skilled lawyer to help with his case. Having a skilled legal ally familiar with the laws and processes will be crucial for his case," Steve suggested.

"Ok, I understand the urgency of the situation so I will immediately investigate which DMCE prison he is being held in and arrange for someone to watch his back to ensure his safety," replied Gabriel.

"Prior to coming here, Gabriel and I did some digging and found that Hussain Muhammad has been detained by DMCE for quite a while now. He is being kept in the same cell block as James so I asked him to keep an eye on James for us," said Christopher.

"Okay, sounds like a plan, keep me posted!" Steve acknowledged Christopher's suggestion before hanging up.

After one month of exploring James's situation further, Gabriel and Christopher discovered that Manuel was leading the scheme, which included Mr. Johnson, Mr. Jackson, and Peter. They also found that this group was collaborating with Mr. Palmer to exploit the DMCE detainees, so they shared this information with Steve.

"We discovered a manipulative scheme led by Manuel and his Fabrican associates using DMCE as a front. Detention, coercion, memory erasure, and brain implants were methods used to exploit detainees with supernatural abilities. DMCE facilities housed individuals convicted of minor crimes, detaining those who opposed their executives' decisions."

After Gabriel finished revealing some of their discoveries, Christopher continued.

"Detainees were offered immunity if they agreed to work for DMCE but faced prolonged detention, isolation, and torture if they refused. Brain chips were implanted in detainees to control them even after release. Many high-ranking officials globally were involved in the project. You should arrange a meeting so we can clearly present these findings."

A few days later after Steve walked into the conference room to join his colleagues Christopher, Gabriel, Aisha, and the Chief Staff in the conference room, Christopher announced a significant discovery made by Gabriel and himself.

"Manuel has influenced many Fabrican and international officials to work with him. They are using DMCE as a front to manipulate and involve supernatural agents who are not cooperating.

After Christopher finished explaining, Gabriel elaborated further, emphasizing the importance of documenting proof of the actions of Manuel and his associates to effectively address the situation. Then Aisha expressed her view that the DMCE issues presented a complex and serious situation requiring careful handling by the team. Afterwards, the team agreed that it is crucial to take appropriate action and address this situation promptly.

After forty-five minutes of discussion, Steve concluded the meeting by recommending actions.

"In the meantime, let's continue to gather more evidence, engage with allies, enhance communication, and ensure the protection of ourselves and our agents.

A couple of months later Steve had just been informed by Gabriel that James's lawyer said he needed to serve an additional six months in prison to qualify for asylum. James remained in custody despite legal efforts and was now expected to spend at least nine months at the DMCE detention center. James had been in jail for a year, split between DMCE prison and county jail. Steve felt guilty about the situation, so he reached out to Gabriel to discuss James's situation further as he intended to delve deeper into James's circumstances.

"Enough is enough, I'm going to reach out to Anthony myself," declared Steve.

"You have a point," Gabriel started to speak, then Steve interrupted and continued.

"I changed my mind about leaving James incarcerated, especially under those circumstances. It was a big mistake," admitted Steve.

"I think you should try to clearly communicate the urgency of the matter to Mr. Palmer by explaining why it is crucial for James to be released promptly," Gabriel suggested.

"Request regular updates from the lawyer on James' case progress and follow up if necessary to ensure that efforts are being made to expedite his release. In the meantime, I plan to contact Anthony to discuss the situation further," Steve instructed.

Steve called Mr. Palmer later that day, but the conversation did not go well when Steve tried to convey the urgency of the matter to him.

Steve spoke after Mr. Palmer answered the phone.

"Hello! Can I speak to Anthony?"

"Speaking!" Mr. Palmer responded.

"Okay, I'll make this short. My sources believe that your organization has detained numerous immigrants without reasonable cause to aid outside infractions in the country," said Steve.

"Your sources have misled you; we are merely conducting experiments to prevent threats to democracy before we release or deport detainees," replied Anthony.

Steve said frantically, "Anyway, you have an individual by the name of James Jordan if you don't give him asylum, I'm putting your entire department under federal review. I will use my power and influence to shut down the entire organization if we find any truth to these accusations!"

Since they were in the same cell block, Hussain had been indirectly training and teaching James since he arrived at that jailhouse. At that point, James had just completed the fifth month of training and learning, so Hussain contacted Gabriel and Christopher because he believed that James was ready for the BIA. However, by the end of the following month, Mr. Palmer had arranged for James to be transferred to the same holding block as Jason, who was tasked with killing James. After six months of not interacting with Jason, James finally ended up in the same block as him. Therefore, James no longer had Hussain by his side.

Since they were on lockdown for five days when James arrived, they had not interacted with each other yet.

James had a strong religious upbringing by his father, leading to a deep connection with religious texts. Being incarcerated had sparked his love for reading and provided an escape from his confinement. He found solace in various genres of books such as fantasy, biographies, science fiction, and adventure stories, recognizing that reading satisfied his soul and offered a way to cope with his isolation. Throughout his time in prison, he made sure to have the holy book with him and read it daily, along with other genres of literature. He had read close to fifty books or more while incarcerated, exceeding the number of books he had read before being imprisoned.

It was post-lockdown when Jason approached James, offering him the opportunity to earn freedom by working for one of the organizations he worked with. As Jason had an important topic to address, he took over a chess game James was playing. However, the conversation between them during the game did not progress satisfactorily.

"Excuse," said James with a puzzled face. He was confused and looked at Jason to see if he was joking.

"I work for ISA, and we are affiliated with DMCE, FARN, and many others off the radar. If you don't cooperate, you are going to face severe consequences," Jason's tone softened as a few other detainees approached.

Afterwards Jason informed James that their leaders wanted him to assist Sam and his father in stealing classified information from the Executive Office database. At that moment James became wary of Jason's motives, also realizing Sam and his father's involvement in the plot. James was shocked, he vowed to seek vengeance on those involved in his father's death. He felt intense pain in his heart as if he were embarking on a war and had just been struck with a sharp dagger. He looked down for a long period and finally looked up and responded to Jason.

"I'd rather die than work for your piece of **** boss," he said, then walked away, leaving Jason at the table alone all confused.

A month later, James fought with Jason over a TV channel choice, and they were both sent to solitary confinement. Meanwhile, after speaking with Steve, Mr. Palmer had come to understand that with the ongoing investigation, it was only a matter of time before his double dealings were exposed. Therefore, he instructed guards to drug detainees' food, including James, to knock them out for brain surgery to erase their memories and implant a chip.

After James ate his first meal in solitary confinement, he lost consciousness. Shortly after, a DMCE surgeon entered his cell to perform brain surgery, erasing some of his memories. After undergoing brain surgery, he awoke early in the morning on the following day, experiencing a severe headache. Struggling to recall why he was incarcerated, the duration of his imprisonment, or his release date, he felt overwhelmed with boredom and despair. He even contemplated suicide at that point. However, he noticed a book on the floor in his cell, later revealed to be left by an angel. After much contemplation, he decided to read the book and gradually absorbed its contents. After he read the entire book, it became a beacon of hope for him, transforming his outlook on life and inspiring him to leave a meaningful impact on the world. It not only altered his perception of life but also provided clarity and purpose. This newfound perspective empowered him, offering insights into life after death and incorporating narratives encompassing diverse cultures and historical events, leading to a sense of hope and the possibility of redemption through divine mercy. On the third day in the cell, following his reading of the book left by an anonymous being, he reflected on his belief in God's will and acknowledged the impact of being introduced to religious texts from birth. While experiencing extreme loneliness and grappling with dark thoughts, he stumbled into another book in his cell which he read. He finished reading the second book late at night the following day, making it five days since his arrival in solitary confinement with only the two books. Suddenly, an individual resembling Hussain appeared before him and began speaking to him.

"Brother James, Peace, and blessing to you. I'm Angle G, I was sent here to give you a message that was given from the Lord of the universe. I'm here to give you a message from the lord of the universe," said Angle G before pausing and looking out through a thick small glass window in the cell to see the outside, then continued.

"Your lord has given you wisdom and superpowers to help you with the rest of your journey in this world. You have been chosen for a specific purpose that you may not fully understand yet. There's a battle between good and bad supernatural beings, with many of the corrupted beings in power taking advantage of the weaker supernatural beings and natural ones. With the good side led by figures like the Fabrican presidential administration, Steve, and other world leaders. The bad side is led by Manuel and his associates. Your main task is to defeat Manuel, a powerful leader who, like you, is a hujinn. By strengthening your faith and seeking the lord's blessing, you have the potential to surpass his power. You must work with Steve, the director of the BIA, to bring down Manuel and his followers. It is essential not to rush into this mission when you get released but to wait for the right time to fulfill your divine calling."

James had only accessed fifty percent of his power before meeting Angel G, but now he had reached full power. By the end of the day, James's powers had vastly increased. He discovered he could control objects with his mind, making him even more special and gifted. Angel G had unlocked James's full powers, granting him the ability to fly, teleport instantly and more. That night they explored various locations worldwide and even ventured into space.

After their return and Angle G had left, James sat in his cell, feeling mesmerized, making him ponder. "No wonder organizations like WDU, BIA, ISA, DBI, FARN, and DMCE found me so intriguing," he thought.

At that moment, James came to realize that his struggles were not only due to disobeying the law but also stemmed from his disobedience towards his father's advice about believing in God. He believed that his setbacks were God's way of showing him the right path, as he had doubts about God's existence before his recent experience. From that point moving forward, he decided to prioritize his actions based on his own moral compass and God's perspective rather than being swayed by societal norms or fear of the law.

A month later, Mr. Palmer sought cooperation with Steve to avoid being exposed for his manipulation and association with the FARN. He contacted the Judge to request asylum for James, emphasizing the risk to their jobs if it was not granted. The Judge agreed not to deport James, who had one month before his final court date. James was moved to a jail for his hearing, and upon his departure, Jason was released.

A couple of weeks before the final judgment, James called Gabriel to share his newfound knowledge and epiphany about his beliefs in the Creator's role in his experiences.

"Hey, Mr. Houston, how have you been? How's Rose and Mrs. Houston?" asked James.

"They are all doing fine. How about you?" replied Gabriel.

"I'm feeling good," replied James.

"Are you ready for your final upcoming hearing?" Gabriel asked.

"Of course, I've been looking forward to this. You know, Mr. Houston, I must admit—I've always believed in God but had questions about Him. After this challenging experience, I now have no doubts and believe it was willed by God to prepare and educate me. This experience has strengthened my faith, and I believe everything will be fine," James explained.

"This is what I love most about you; you can remain positive in difficult situations. Maintain this mentality; you will be home soon!" said Gabriel.

"Sir, do you think I would still be able to work for the agency despite having a criminal record?" James asked.

"Yes, you could still work for the agency as long as they don't put you on probation or parole; in that case, you would need to wait until you complete that time," Gabriel replied and paused to look through some documents before he continued.

"I want you to ask your family, friends, and any others you had professional relationships with to write to the judge and tell him how great of an individual you are. Also, write to the judge and include your father's patriotic service as a BIA agent, and ask the judge to allow you to follow in his father's footsteps."

"Ok, thank you sir, I really appreciate your help and support!" said James before the call ended abruptly.

After exchanging greetings, during which Gabriel mentioned James and his upcoming final hearing, they discussed strategies further.

"If it's not an inconvenience to you, we should be there to support James and provide references to help avoid deportation," said Gabriel.

"It's no trouble at all, I'll be there," Steve assured him.

A few days later it was his final day in prison, James is anxious but hopeful as he prepares to address the courtroom, expressing his growth in knowledge and understanding during his incarceration. The night before his final hearing, James couldn't sleep from anxiety.

After waiting months, James enters the courtroom to find out about potential deportation. Mr. Palmer orchestrated James' release to prevent exposure of his dishonest actions. The judge allows James to speak before deciding.

"Good morning, Your Honor, and thank you for this opportunity. I have learned much during my time here, focusing on education and stimulating my mind through reading and writing. I have grown in knowledge and understanding of human concerns," said James. He continued expressing himself for a couple of minutes. The judge and the audience listened, as they couldn't help but feel sympathy for him.

An hour later, James was granted asylum and released from prison. He changed into new clothes and reunited with his family. He was picked up by his mother and cousins. On their way back to New Amsterdam, he sat in the front of the vehicle to prevent his usual motion sickness. During the journey, they caught up on each other's experiences. James shared his time in prison, and his family filled him in on what he missed. He also discussed his encounter with the holy books and vowed to improve from that moment onward.

CHAPTER EIGHT

FIRST TIME BACK HOME

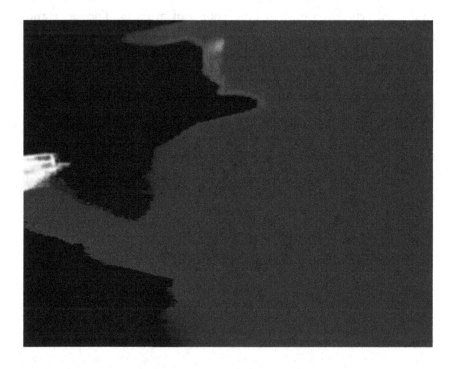

James had finally been released and picked up by his family, preventing federal scrutiny of DMCE because Steve shifted focus to pursuing Manuel and Victor, with Manuel's strong Fabrican political alliances making him increasingly frightening. James, after his release, couldn't work with BIA due to probation and parole. The agency placed him on a probationary period as well. Steve instructed everyone to stay away, while selected agents were to monitor him discreetly.

James prioritized staying out of trouble and isolation to maintain his probationary status. He aimed to catch up intellectually with his peers, dedicating himself to studying despite previous efforts to educate himself in prison.

When James arrived Jeremy and Jolie were there to welcome him home with excitement. As soon as James opened the door, they embraced him tightly. They held onto him for a moment, then Jeremy let go and said, "Welcome back, James, I've missed you so much."

James briefly expressed his longing for his siblings before he remembered the distinct odor associated with someone who has recently been released from prison. He excused himself and headed to shower where he reflected on his time in institutions and the distinct smell associated with it. Before coming out of the shower Oumar and Rich had arrived so he got dressed quickly and they spent some time together before leaving.

Afterwards, James retreated to his room to reflect on his life. Feeling like a failure, he pondered, "*This police incident has derailed my education. I dropped out of college and lost my BIA internship, and now I'm back home when I thought I had left for good. I should be ashamed. How did I transition from being an aspiring college graduate with a promising future to a grown man back home living with his mother, intruding on his siblings' space?*"

While his peers had successful careers, James recognized that he had to start fresh after his release from prison. He lost confidence and became isolated from family and friends. News about his incarceration had spread, leading to strained relationships with some loved ones who thought he was away for school instead of jail. After four weeks of sitting idly at home, his mother asked her brother Abraham to hire James. Abraham was a stout man with a big gray beard, bulbous nose, hooded eyes, full lips, and a round face. He was a successful business owner and was knowledgeable about both street smarts and business acumen. Consequently, at his mother's request, James began working for his uncle, who owned a couple of small businesses and paid him low wages. He didn't mind, as he wanted to utilize the opportunity to learn how to conduct business. Over the next couple of months, James didn't have many associates; he didn't even have a girlfriend or anyone to talk to about his situation except for his cousin, Alpha. He had become depressed and questioned the purpose of his existence, doubting his faith again. He contemplated between going back to school or continuing to work, opting for the latter due to age and responsibilities. Despite feeling embarrassed and depressed about working for low-paying jobs, he reminded himself it was to avoid the risk of violating his probation and parole and losing his freedom again. Due to his despondency, he turned to illegal activities for the next three months. After recognizing he was repeating past mistakes, he shifted his focus towards self-improvement.

Abraham's business involved the sale of both legal and illegal products, with illegal items disguised by the legal merchandise. While working there, James reconnected with illegal wholesale products. Abraham found joy in working with James due to his loyalty, trendsetting traits, and popularity. James brought attention and style to Abraham's business, expanding the client base. His popularity in New Amsterdam reignited old relationships from College Town, surprising many who were unaware of his freedom.

At the time, Abraham's store was a hotspot known for keeping up with the latest fashion trends and setting new styles. The store's popularity led to unplanned encounters with many individuals, including guest stars making occasional appearances. The business attracted a lot of traffic, helping James reconnect with family, friends from his former school and around the world.

While working for his uncle, James began to establish himself once more, relishing a stress-free and prosperous life. However, challenges arose as he faced temptation to smoke again, encouraged by coworkers Chris and Rahim, who were affiliated with a dangerous gang and persistently tried to involve him in smoking during their lunch breaks.

The coworkers became close and hung out often after work. A few days later it was a very hot and humid day and they walked to a quiet block away from traffic. One of them asked James why he didn't want to smoke with them.

"Stackz why don't you smoke anymore?" Rahim questioned.

"I'm on probation and parole, and I want to avoid violating any rules right now," James answered.

"There's a new type of weed called Wicked that is not real marijuana, so it does not show up in drug tests," said Rahim.

Upon hearing about the new type of weed that doesn't show up in drug tests, James expressed interest in smoking it because he had been wanting to smoke but was concerned about violating his probation. James started smoking a very strong weed called the Wicked, which significantly dulls his senses. The weed caused him to slack off at work, lose focus and power, and forget his promises. His behavior changed, leading to disrespect towards his family and others. James became arrogant and lost the respect of many of his associates.

During the summer, around the first week of June, James felt a nostalgia for his college days and started attending parties like he used to prior to his incarceration. He reminisced about the old times in school, leading him to contact B Money and their other friends. They decided to reunite during the school festival in July, a time when many former students would visit the school. The next day, the person thought about his conversation with a schoolmate from Spirits University the day before.

James had been released from prison three months earlier. In July, Rich visited James at his workplace and they had a conversation. During their conversation, James learned that Rich and his father had returned to New Amsterdam around the time of James's imprisonment. He also discovered that Rich was interning at Christopher's transportation company, the same place James had interned at previously. Rich mentioned his goal of joining the BIA, and Ben's intentions of talking to Steve about helping him get recruited. Before Rich left James told Rick about his plan to meet his college friends at their old school and invited Rich to join him if he decides to go.

James had been indecisive about attending the reunion for over one month. It was now Wednesday night, so he had to make up his mind because if he decided to attend, he would have to leave the following day. He continued contemplating as he sat on the chair in his room facing the laptop.

"*I should go; it might be fun,*" he thought.

He browsed the social media profiles of his college friends for a few hours as he continued contemplating about attending the event. Then stood up and paced back and forth in his room, biting his nails as he continued thinking, "*Considering I dropped out and have this low-paying job, I shouldn't go, or else they'll look down on me.*"

He sat back down and called Oumar. After calling Oumar and having a conversation, Oumar tried to persuade James to attend the school event by offering to go along with him. However, James insisted on explaining his reasons for feeling hesitant about attending.

"I'm going to be feeling out of place as I work on rebuilding my situation while they are already well-established," he explained.

Oumar acknowledged James with a nod, indicating his understanding before speaking.

"Stackz, trust me, I know where you are coming from. When I was down, I stayed isolated too unless it was for money. I hung out with a few homies here and there, but I was on my grind!" he said.

"When I was younger, I anticipated graduating from college and starting my career by now, only to realize that the future is unpredictable," said James.

Oumar agreed and said, "Don't worry; dropping out of school does not make someone inferior to those who have graduated."

"I have to admit you're right. Plus, I really miss my former school," said James before falling silent briefly and added, "I'll think about it since I already promised my schoolmates that I'll go and I invited Rich."

"You've been thinking about it. Just make up your mind already," said Oumar.

"Okay, okay, you've convinced me, but you, Rich, and my cousin have to come with me," said James.

Oumar exclaimed, "That's the spirit! Let's add them to the line."

A moment later Rich and Alpha were included, and they all decided to join James for his old school's festival in College Town. James decided to return to his old school to reconnect with his old friends and possibly run into Rose during a special event. He had not visited his college town since being released from prison due to feeling hesitant and harboring resentment towards Hamdallah State, where he had been arrested and mistreated. James had lost contact with most of his classmates and distanced himself from them, except for the friend he was very close to. He kept in touch with LV, Ray, Slim, Smoky, and B Money mainly through phone calls as they no longer lived near each other and were caught up in their respective businesses.

The next day, James, Rich, his cousin Alpha, and Oumar met up at twenty minutes past noon to go to James' college town for the school festival. He rented a Chrysler Two hundred and drove to his old school with Oumar, his cousin Alpha, and Rich. Four hours later, they arrived, and James was surprised to find many former classmates and some current students in attendance. As James expected, he found that most of his peers had graduated and moved away. Some peers were still living in the area where he had known them. Upon arrival, many of them gathered at Ray's off-campus housing complex. Some visited their girlfriends' places to spend time together. After the pregame, the group drove to the campus to attend a step show and a few parties.

The next day was a joyful Friday for James. He unexpectedly met his long-lost love, Rose, at a party at night. It seemed like they arranged to meet for the school festival, although they had not been in touch since the evening of James' sentencing. James was overjoyed to see Rose, feeling happier than ever before, but he was unsure how to approach her until B Money intervened to make it easier. B Money approached the women by running towards them and calling out loudly, "Mary, hey Mary, wait!"

James and B Money approached Mary, Rose, and their friends together. Upon reaching the group, James made eye contact with Rose, suddenly stopped, and smiled widely before speaking. "Hey, beautiful, I feel like I just found my soul!" he told her.

Initially, she was a little hesitant. As she began to turn away from him, he insisted, saying, "Please, Rose, I know I have a lot of explaining to do. Let's catch up since we're both here."

Despite the initial reaction, he insisted they catch up as it seemed like fate had brought them together. He pleaded for Rose's company, expressing his desperation by putting his hands together and saying, "Please, pretty please."

Rose rolled her eyes and expressed skepticism towards his promises.

"Oh, please, you and your promises. Give me a minute to chat with my friends."

She turned and faced her girlfriends; they all encouraged her to give him a chance to explain. Afterwards, they spent time together, watched a comedy show, went to a club, and ended up at an off-campus after-party. At the after-party, everyone was paired up with someone. As they spend time together James explained to Rose why he had been away for so long without communication. He was excited to see Rose and partied more than usual. As the night progressed, the alcohol took its toll on him, and he became highly intoxicated because he had become a lightweight in drinking. Consequently, he discreetly left with her to her off-campus housing where he spent the night.

The next morning, Rose made breakfast and had a long conversation with James, during which she revealed details about her life. She disclosed that she had a son whom she believed was James's and that she had returned to school the previous year. Their son was staying with her parents while she finished her bachelor's degree. James discovered that she had been isolating herself since becoming pregnant, just as he had been keeping a low profile since his release. He learned that she had been struggling to balance motherhood and studies, leading her to leave their child with her parents while she visited regularly. She also mentioned taking time off during the Technical Skills Fest weekend to socialize and party with friends, as it fell during the summer vacation.

As they discussed their past, leading to understanding the true reason behind their fallout, James mainly listened as Rose had a lot to share.

"The reason I lost interest was because I felt like you were playing me. You made false promises and did not contact me after the night we made love," she said then paused and looked down before continuing.

"You told me that you were going overseas to study abroad for one semester. I waited for a few days, then I called you, but I didn't get a response. At first, I thought you were busy or unable to talk, but after one month of calling your phone every day, multiple times a day, and it kept going to voicemail, I thought you blocked me. I expected you to return after six months as you promised when we got intimate, but you never did. I tried calling you multiple times over a year with no response. Eventually, I lost hope of your return because you told me that no matter what, you would be back in six months. That's why I didn't even want to hear from you anymore," Rose explained.

James felt guilty after listening to her side of the story and then proceeded to explain his own perspective.

"I apologized for disappearing the way I did. I didn't want to reveal my jail sentence immediately and wanted you to get to know me first. However, I faced communication challenges in jail because I was unaware of the process for making calls. These issues were why it took me a while before I tried contacting you. I promised to be back in six months because I thought I would be released after my original sentence ended, nevertheless, I was detained for nine more months. I ended up being away longer than expected due to unforeseen issues with the DMCE," James explained.

James's explanation about his jail situation led to her better understanding; therefore, she loosened up and started feeling remorse for not being there for James during his incarceration. She then began discussing his child with him.

"I can't wait until you meet your son!" said Rose as she tearfully expressed her excitement before adding, "One of these days, I will bring him so you can meet him."

"Me too. What's his name?" he said.

"His name's Joseph," she replied.

"It's my fault for not being upfront with you from the get-go. I'm sorry, Rose," said James.

"From now on, I'll always be honest with you!" he added after they shared a kiss.

"I feel extremely happy. It feels like the time when we first met. The only difference is that we are now parents," she expressed as she hugged him tightly.

Rose and James continued talking and seeing each other after a weekend together. A few weeks after their reunion at College Town on a hot and humid day around noon, Rose dressed up and got into her white Lexus car as she planned to surprise James by introducing their son, Joseph, to him for the first time. She arranged to pick up Joseph from her parents' home in New Amsterdam. She called her mother to inform her about the plan and asked her to get Joseph ready. Mrs. Houston expressed uncertainty about her decision to let James back into

Joseph's life. However, Rose reassured her mother about her decision to give Joseph's father a chance to be in his life.

James called Rose a few hours later to check if she had left. He also wanted to know if she needed him to prepare anything for her. She did not need anything from James when he called and said she would be there in less than two hours. An hour and forty-five minutes later, James was surprised to see his son Joseph with Rose, noticing their resemblance. He was speechless, embraced Joseph, then kissed and hugged both Joseph and Rose. Over the course of their time spent together, they went out to eat, visited the park, and eventually returned to James's home. At the end of August, Rose began attending school, leading to less frequent visits to see James. James was still working for Abraham, so he struggled to visit due to work commitments.

A few months later, Charles, who had recently been released from jail, visited James's workplace to reconnect with him after over a decade of being apart. James had been incarcerated before and understood the challenges of re-entering society. As they met and shook hands, James reminisced about the struggle of readjusting to the outside world after his release. Charles updated James about his current experiences and struggles during their conversation.

"Stackz, I've been facing mad challenges since I got home, I feel like I'm being tested by the Devil. With all the financial difficulties I'm going through right now, consider taking the easy route to address my situation," said Charles.

"Bro, when I first got home, I was in a tight spot too. I found strength in remembering the promise I made to the Lord, which helped me resist the negative temptations," said James.

"What was your promise to God?" Charles asked.

"I promised to prioritize and humble myself before the Lord. After realizing the importance of putting the creator above oneself, I feel guided and blessed by him, so I continue to be grateful and by recognizing his role in my life. It's very important to acknowledge God's grace, purpose, and blessings, which will lead us to the habit of praising and thanking him. We should also encourage others to do the same," James shared, and Charles nodded his head as he spoke.

"You know what? I think you're right. I found God while I was in prison too, so I intend to heed the advice you gave me and practice it with patience," Charles responded affirmatively.

They hung out for a while longer before James reminded Charles that he was working.

"Ok, I'll let you go. Thanks, James," he responded before leaving.

After James met his son, he became more motivated to succeed. He reformed his life by investing money wisely and giving up smoking, painkillers, and heavy drinking. He started praying more and giving back to the community. After new year's, he noticed that Abraham was considering closing one of his businesses. He had saved money by staying with his cousin, Alpha. James proposed starting his own small business to Abraham, using his savings and parental donations to do so.

James had resumed school at Queenstown College in New Amsterdam State while simultaneously managing his own business. He employed exotic females to attract customers and sold items like jewelry, mixtapes, and belts. Despite being more educated than his uncle, Abraham, James struggled with managing employees who lacked responsibility. After just one year of attending Queenstown College, he faced the dilemma of balancing his business and education, ultimately dropping out of college for the second time to focus on his business due to time constraints. Becoming a father prompted him to prioritize building his business to provide for his family's future, so he chose to invest his time and energy in making his business successful.

James and his college friends have maintained their bond by attending various events together post-reunion, including parties, sports games, and comedy shows. Their recent gathering was Slim's baby shower, a year after their reunion at College Town. In July, B Money, LV, Slim, Smokey, and Ray visited James at his new business, where they caught up and spent time together, creating a hopeful and enjoyable atmosphere as they conversed in front of his establishment.

"Look at you, man, just a year ago you were fresh out of jail with no job, and now here you are, a self-made businessman," Ray commented.

"Look at you, man, just a year ago you were fresh out of jail with no job, and now here you are, a self-made businessman," Ray commented, before James shared his tactics with his friends as they listened carefully, soaking in the knowledge.

"Look, guys. So far, I earned money legitimately, and learned from my past errors. I took control of a family business and made investments. I'm actively promoting and advertising my business. I launched a website, and I'm looking to expand further by opening additional stores."

While at the location, Rich and Charles joined James. Since Smokey wanted to smoke, James took a break to smoke with his friends, asking his workers to cover for him.

James spent the next few months networking regularly and building connections with various carriers. His connections helped him identify which professions to pursue and which to avoid. Through networking, he learned about industries such as construction, carpentry, nursing, teaching, investing, engineering, policing, transportation, marketing, publishing, and writing. James chose to diversify his business ventures instead of continuing to focus solely on his risky small businesses.

A year after James and Rose reunited at College Town, Rose and her child moved to New Amsterdam to live with James, who had his own apartment by then. James realized Rose had been by his side through thick and thin, cared for him, and even supported him financially when he was struggling after his release. He cherished her support, motivation, and their child, leading him to believe she was the one. Thus, they decided to get married within the first couple of months after moving in together. They invited family and friends, including their whole crew from Spirits University, for the wedding. Rose's family, who were from College Town in Hamdallah state, also attended the wedding.

CHAPTER NINE

BIA TIME

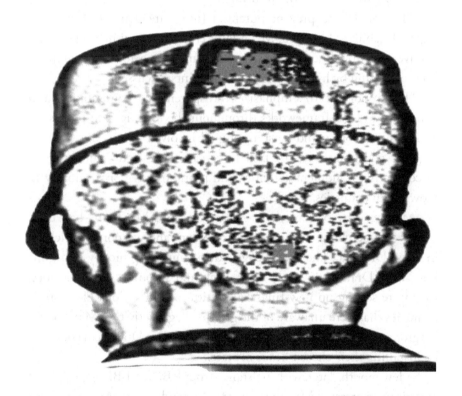

It had been a year and a half since James was released from the DMCE prison. Christopher and Gabriel were now Deputy Directors for the BIA. Steve had become a Director of the National Intelligence Spirits Agency five years prior to that. He organized a meeting with officials from various Fabrican organizations to address Manuel and his associates' fraudulent activities impacting Flowropia and West Drakillia's economies. On that morning, they were all present at the meeting as Steve addressed the attendees.

"We need to establish a joint task force to investigate FARN, gather evidence, identify culprits, and ensure justice is served. The collaboration is aimed at fostering regional cooperation and unity among all the countries around Ginnia," he explained.

After Steve finished explaining, Mr. Adams spoke.

"Mr. Peters and Mr. DeVos have been tasked with motivating Flowropian officials to collaborate on trade, security, and sustainable development," Mr. Adams paused to ensure he had their attention before proceeding to provide more information.

"The goal is to prevent potential future incidents and enhance regional stability," he added. Mr. Adams emphasized his message. Then, Mr. Iverson also acknowledged the communication before Steve wrapped up the meeting by highlighting the key points discussed.

"It's important to emphasize transparency, accountability, and adherence to legal frameworks throughout the investigation process to maintain credibility and trust among all involved parties. By working together collaboratively, the task force can make significant progress in combating fraudulent activities and promoting regional stability in Flowropian countries."

Manuel, Mr. Boucher, Mr. Alexandre, and Mr. Louis had been involved in activities such as theft, terrorism, and weapons trafficking in West Drakilla. They were engaged in smuggling money and guns into West Drakilla in exchange for natural resources. Furthermore, they were setting up new financial institutions in various Flowropian countries that were unaware of the group's illegal activities. Manuel and his group now planned to gain control of some West Drakillian countries by installing their chosen heads of state.

A few months later, with assistance from RBI and BBI agents, James and his team arrested Mr. Boucher, Mr. Alexandre, and Mr. Louis. This led to the closure of most FARN companies and the seizure of associated assets. Manuel lost a significant fortune and turned to exploiting countries outside of Rancenia and Bellivia, engaging in worldwide money laundering and collaborating with leaders of undeveloped nations. He followed in the footsteps of his predecessor Samuel by working with the

WDU leader at the time, providing money and weapons in exchange for resources from West Drakillia.

Fabrica and Freeland had been allies for decades, thus Jack Obama, the new leader of West Drakillia, sought to uncover how Manuel gained control of the natural resources in Freeland and two other West Drakillian nations. The region under scrutiny produced a significant amount of aluminum, gold, and diamonds globally. Manuel held sway over ninety percent of the natural resources in these countries, which concerned Mr. Obama. In response, Mr. Obama informed Fabrican President Kennedy Lincoln, who had recently succeeded Mamadou R. Diallo as the one-hundredth president of Fabrica, about the theft of West Drakillian natural resources by the FARN organization.

Mr. Obama contacted Lincoln and explained how Manuel had attempted to bribe and blackmail him to comply with his demands. Saying he denied Manuel's offer even after promising considerable compensation like securing him another term in office by eliminating his competitors. He confided in the president that due to his refusal, Manuel was now targeting him, which prompted his request for assistance. He also told the president that the FARN was terrorizing and attempting to take over the entire West Drakillian region. Mr. Obama asked President Lincoln to help him remove Manuel and his associates from his country because they were stealing their resources and terrorizing the population. He described how Manuel and his group had been oppressing his country for many years, often evading detection through the countries' presidential leadership transitions.

Afterwards, President Lincoln considered Mr. Obama's request and reached out to Steve and ordered him to start examining the FARN organization again. Steve was excited to hear that President Lincoln was determined to pursue Manuel, even if it meant violating existing agreements with the UNG. Steve decided to cease the ongoing investigation and focus on capturing Manuel.

After Mr. Obama returned to Drakilla, President Lincoln assured Mr. Obama of sending reinforcements to West Drakilla. Lincoln planned to have the BIA investigate the FARN occupation in Freeland and neighboring countries, with Steve and BIA directors choosing the team. Therefore, BIA directors were summoned to strategize a new plan for the mission. Steve, Gabriel, and others attended the conference in Sékoubaria at the Diamond House in the capitol building. The discussion began after all guests were seated. The Fabrican president discussed Mr. Obama's proposal to assist Freeland and neighboring countries in regaining control of their resources.

"I have gathered you all here regarding the FARN organization's activities in West Drakilla. I am weary of their actions and require your top agents for the task. This is classified information known only to the meeting attendees. Our strategy involves sending an initial team to surveil and neutralize their security, followed by aiding west Drakillia in its resurgence. Make sure you handle this operation efficiently and prevent any harm to the Freeland citizens, their president, Telly Diallo, and his administration," President Lincoln explained the situation. Afterwards he sought perspectives from Steve and the rest of the attendees. The meeting concluded after discussions and input from Steve and others.

Since James was distracted when he went out of state for college, it prompted Holly to choose an in-state college for Jeremy. Jeremy is now interning at the BIA agency under the Science and Technology department. At that time, Sam was working for the Weapons Intelligence, Nonproliferation, and Arms Control Center under the Intelligence department, so Jeremy bumped into Sam at the agency and later informed James about their encounter. The moment Jeremy told James that Sam worked in the same department, causing James to become suspicious of Sam. Thus, James contacted Gabriel to express interest in joining the agency.

It had been two years since James was released, and he was now off probation and parole. The BIA needed five skilled agents to train and prepare for the upcoming mission against Manuel and his group. James had recently discovered his flying abilities and began using them to rescue people and jinns in the city. A few days early morning he woke up to the smell of fire, quickly flew to the burning building, and saved a couple of families from the flames. After the rescue, he flew back to his home, which was located around twenty thousand miles away from the city. Gabriel was there waiting, as he had popped up unexpectedly to visit his daughter, Rose. During dinner, James mentioned his interest in working for the BIA. Coincidentally, Steve wanted to offer him a job as a BIA coder since he was no longer on probation or parole. After Gabriel broke this news to James, he was eager to join the agency and was very pleased with the offer. Therefore, Gabriel mentioned he would inform Steve about James's interest in joining the BIA. Finally, he instructed James to get ready to use his talent for the agency before leaving.

Antoine and Sam had reappeared after vanishing eight years prior during the BIA's investigation of Alex's death. When Antoine returned to New Amsterdam he chose to work for Mr. Jackson since he knew he had lost the trust of the BIA director. He had now advanced to the position of executive assistant director for the national security branch at NISA when he encountered Steve again.

Weeks later, Gabriel organized a dinner to introduce James to his colleagues. It was a fine evening, and traffic was heavy as Gabriel and James were heading to meet Mr. Iverson in the city. However, Gabriel was unaware they had met before when James interned at Christopher's company. As the sun was setting, causing the sky to transition from bright to dark, James and Gabriel entered a restaurant. Mr. Iverson and Christopher were already inside, waiting for them upon their arrival. After Christopher shook James's hand, turned, winked at Mr. Iverson, and gave a hand gesture to him, then said, "I believe you two know each other."

"Hey, Mr. Jordan, It's good to see you again. How are you?" Mr. Iverson acknowledged.

"Hello, sir, I'm great! It's a pleasure to see you again too," James replied.

Christopher gave a speech to James during dinner.

"The Bureau of Intelligent Agents operates through various offices and fronts like the State Transportation company you interned for when you were in college to hide their identity. Special agents recruited are carefully observed from an early age to determine their suitability for the job. The agency, initiated by Jinns and monitored by angels, aims to control leadership positions globally through secret societies. Organizations like the Bureau have existed since ancient times, adapting to change by altering their identities," Christopher explained.

James was intrigued as he found a connection between the

information shared by Christopher and details from a dream where his father mentioned similar concepts.

Soon after James departed, leaving Gabriel and colleagues to discuss his potential squad leadership in a mission against the FARN, they later contacted Steve to share their insights on James.

"OK, I'll assign him to the FARN mission. However, beforehand, he will have to work in the Intelligence, Weapons Intelligence, Nonproliferation, and Arms Control Center for at least six months," Steve declared.

Steve's decision was supported by his team, who also see James as the best option for the mission. Christopher and Gabriel particularly feel that James is suitable due to his father being the lead agent on the same mission previously before his death.

As Steve was preparing to recruit James, Ben called Steve to share Rich's ability to help the BIA. He also mentioned the necessity of keeping an eye on Antoine because he suspected that Antoine was involved in Alex's ambush and his son's imprisonment. Steve reassured Ben that Antoine had been under surveillance since resigning. Following this conversation, Steve instructed Gabriel to ask James to visit his office the next day. Shortly after Gabriel notified James. Subsequently, James visited Steve in the afternoon as instructed. Upon arriving at the office, James noticed a young lady who was invisible at first. Despite her appearance, James's keen senses allowed him to perceive her presence.

"Hello," he greeted her.

"Hello," she replied and suddenly became visible.

"How did you know someone was here?" she added.

"I just felt your presence, so I took a lucky guess," James replied and smiled.

"Hmm, impressive," she said as she gazed at him as if she was trying to figure out how he was able to sense her when most couldn't.

"How may I help you?" she asked.

"My name is James," James was impressed by her skills so he wanted to ask more questions, however he introduced himself before he mentioned that Mr. Beaumont was expecting him.

She smiled and nodded, still showing her admiration for his talent.

"*What a peculiar being,*" she thought.

Moments later, James greeted the other agents in the office as he made his way to Steve's office. Afterwards, James was ushered towards Steve's office, where they had a lengthy conversation. Steve revealed he was hired and explained details about the agency. He also briefed James on the ongoing events related to the extraordinary forces in the world of Ginnia where they resided.

"There are corrupted beings from larger nations targeting smaller countries to control and exploit resources. Organizations like BIA collaborate with other federal organizations to counter the wicked forces and maintain balance in Ginnia. Both sides work quickly to eliminate threats before they escalate. Here at BIA, we deploy agents globally to ensure order and fairness among nations. With your invincible speed, power, and genuine heart, you indeed have the potential to make a significant impact in protecting the world from malevolent forces, therefore we are offering you a position in the Intelligence department. It's important for you to embrace your role with courage and dedication to fulfill your destiny as a guardian against these dark forces," Steve explained.

"Wow, I'm honored, sir. Hearing this coming from you, means so much to me. Thank you very much; I always wanted to be part of something significant. I aspire to follow in his father's footsteps by using my abilities for a noble cause," James replied with enthusiasm as he was excited for the opportunity.

"Just remember one thing: if you accept our offer, be prepared for some serious battles ahead. We were all impressed by your track record, including the remarkable performance in college and the heroic act of saving Gabriel's daughter. We are confident in your exceptional ability and believe you are destined for greatness. Despite encountering many talented agents, your potential for greatness stands out due to your unmatched talent at a young age," said Steve.

"Thank you again, sir. I promise I will not disappoint you," James responded.

Steve was not surprised when Antoine returned to New Amsterdam, as he was unaware of the allegations against him. He was certain that no one from the agency knew what he had done to Alex. James had been initially recruited by the Science and Technology Department under the Global Access center. Since Steve didn't trust Sam or his father, he saw this as the perfect opportunity for James to be transferred to their department before embarking on the FARN mission. He reassigned James to the same department as Sam to observe his true intentions. Steve had planned the entire strategy before proposing it to James. He instructed James to pretend he was unaware of their betrayal and encouraged him to work with Sam, an offer which James accepted. Steve believed it was a good idea and assigned James to the same unit as Sam. He thought this would allow James to anticipate any potential moves by Sam or his associates. Steve and James agreed to let them continue working with the BIA until Manuel was captured, to lure them both.

After six months at the BIA and investigating his father's death, James discovered that, in addition to Manuel, Victor, and Antoine, there were other Fabrican officials implicated in his father's demise and the attack on his family. He discovered that Peter, Mr. Johnson, the secretary of DE, Mr. Jackson from ISA, and Mr. Palmer from DMCE, were all complicit. He also realized that they were connected to FARN and several Fabrican agents. This realization led him to uncover that these same Fabrican officials were part of organizing the hit on his dad in Sékoubaria GD, and on many other attacks during the same period. The incident resulted in Alex, other agents, and their family members losing their lives. While he suspected Manuel and Victor, he was unaware of the broader scope of their organization, including Antoine, Peter, Mr. Johnson, Mr. Jackson, and Mr. Palmer.

James visited his family in Freeland and discussed the FARN situation. Vincent also shared a message from James's late father. James was engrossed in a voice memo as the audio recording of Alex's voice played:

"Dear son, I recorded this message to inform you about the FARN and the sacrifices I made trying to bring down this organization. I believe I was betrayed by some colleagues of mine, starting with Peter, my initial partner at the agency. When Peter discovered my marriage to a human and the implications for our children, he attempted to influence the BIA and NISA directors against me. After failing to turn the directors against me, he then joined this hazardous FARN organization, led by Samuel, a Rancenian minister with a history of anti-West Drakillian conspiracies.

Samuel's son Manuel took over FARN's leadership following his death. My team and I almost succeeded in shutting down the company, leading to severed connections with many Flowropian countries and West Drakillan countries. Consequently, Manuel and his group had to go into hiding as numerous top global agencies were actively pursuing them. Remember that the focus of Manuel and his network is solely on you, with no knowledge of your brother and sister. Otherwise, they would have been targeted by them as well. Manuel maintains extensive connections and surveillance, including within Fabrica, and must be stopped at all costs. Hujinns, like you, are deemed the only ones capable of halting Manuel's actions, making individuals of your kind a prime target for their pursuit. Their objective is to gain control of West Drakilla, which includes their intended target of overtaking Freeland, the homeland. By successfully acquiring control over West Drakilla, they could potentially become the wealthiest and most influential organization globally. Which brings me to my next point - the BIA is actively recruiting talent, and I am certain that you could be their top agent by far. Therefore, I urge you to contact Steve, fulfill the mission to defeat Manuel's network, and save our world, Ginnia, from these tyrants. It's very important for you to complete what my team and I have set out to do. Use your unique abilities to make a difference for the future of Ginnia as it is at stake."

James had a better understanding of the FARN situation after listening to Alex's message. He thanked his uncle and decided to return the following day. Meanwhile, it had been a year since James had joined the BIA, so President Lincoln reached out to Steve to discuss appointing a new First Option for the FARN mission. Steve believed James was the ideal candidate for the role, despite the president considering other potential agents. As they talked that day, Steve was working on convincing President Lincoln of his choice.

"Oh, I have the perfect guy for the task, his name is James," said Steve.

"As you wish, just make sure he has at least five years of experience and is willing to stay overseas until the job is complete," Lincoln specified before Steve continued.

"The candidate I am recommending is like us and was raised by a respected top agent within our organization," he said, then prompted President Lincoln.

"Guess what?"

"What?" asked the president.

"I believe James is even more skilled than his father!" Steve revealed then the president double checked by saying, "Is that right?"

"Yes, I promise you!" Steve replied calmly then Lincoln approved.

"No problem then, based on your recommendation, we can go with your candidate."

After Steve's conversation with the Fabrican president, he shared his decision about choosing James as the new primary option with Gabriel and Christopher. He discussed the mission with them and revealed his intention of targeting Victor before Manuel. Steve also believed that eliminating Victor would make Manuel vulnerable, so he intended to have James start with domestic targets like Victor before pursuing any international targets like Manuel. Victor, residing in Fabrica, was considered a crucial first step. Finally, Steve mentioned that he was angry that Victor, who was responsible for killing Alex, remained in the same country they were in.

Meanwhile, Antoine visited the BIA agency to persuade Gabriel because he wanted Gabriel to consider naming Sam the new First Option.

"I have a great agent in mind!" said Antoine.

"I spoke to Steve earlier; he said that he has it under control. He believed James is the best choice to lead this mission," said Gabriel.

"Is Steve sure about this James guy because I heard rumors of his arrest back in his college days. I'd say that is not the type of agent you choose to lead a mission. Trust me, Sam would be a better fit for this position," Antoine asked.

"You know what, we'll have them work together!" Gabriel responded.

"Yeah, great point, just in case James gets sidetracked or decides to disregard our orders," said Antoine.

"Remember Jordan?" Gabriel asked.

"Oh yeah, Alex, the First Option who got ambushed in Sékoubaria, G.D.?" Antoine responded.

"Yeah, him!" Gabriel confirmed.

Steve walked in on Gabriel and Antoine's conversation. Gabriel paused, looked back, then continued, "He was our First Option too. I heard his son might be better. At this rate, it seems like he'll protect Jordan's legacy."

As soon as Antoine realized Steve was there, he changed his approach from trying to slander James' name, to praising him.

"Enough said! He is right because Mr. Jordan was our best agent by far. If he's anything like Alex, I'm fine with that because the mission will be in great hands," Antoine acknowledged before leaving.

A week later, Steve received a call from Christopher, who told him Victor was in the city. Immediately after talking to Christopher, Steve called James. James answered the phone after a few rings.

"Hello," he said simply.

"PEACE AND BLESSINGS BE UPON YOU, Mr. Jordan!" Steve greeted James. James replied to Steve's greeting by saying, "MAY EVERLASTING PEACE AND BLESSINGS BE UPON YOU TOO, sir!"

"Christopher just confirmed Victor is in New Amsterdam. I'll explain everything when I see you. Just hurry up and meet me at the office as soon as possible," said Steve.

"Ok, on my way boss. I should be there in less than thirty minutes!" James responded.

"Ok, I'll see you at the office," Steve acknowledged him and was about to hang up when he heard James inquire enthusiastically.

"Should I bring anything with me?"

"No, you are not going anywhere yet, I just wanted to simply lay out a plan with you," replied Steve.

"Understood!" James voiced and quickly ended the call, then walked out of the bathroom. He walked to the bedroom and informed Rose about Steve's urgent request.

"Rose, I'm sorry I can't come with you to the museum today. My boss just requested that I report to the office as soon as possible, so I must leave for work immediately," he explained.

Rose appeared disappointed as she watched James explain the situation while getting ready.

"Ok, babe, I was really looking forward to spending the day with you today, but I understand," Rose voiced, then walked to the bathroom.

About half an hour later, James was at the Office of the Director of National Intelligence. As they were talking, Steve told James about Victor's betrayal of Alex in Bellivia before discussing the larger problem at hand.

"Listen to me, James. It's time for you to know this. There is a war happening out there between good and evil spirits. However, only a small portion of the population is aware of this conflict. Manuel is our target as he is the leader of the evil spirits. He is considered one of the most dangerous beings due to being a hujinn like yourself. He is extremely dangerous because he possesses incredible power that can only be matched by a few hujinns." Steve briefly paused in his explanation to check a text message on his phone before resuming.

"His organization has taken control of several nations in West Drakilla with the help of the West Drakillian Union leader. Manuel and his group have been controlling and exploiting resources for years, and they have recently hypnotized many spirits in Ginnia through social media to manipulate their minds."

He paused again and checked to see if James had understood the given directions. However, James remained silent and expressed his desire for Steve to continue with a nod, indicating that he did not wish to interrupt.

"For now, I would like for you to focus on Victor since he's here, while leaving the outsiders like Manuel for later. When the time comes you and your team are to monitor Manuel and await our authorization to eliminate Manuel" Steve continued.

"The priority now is to locate Victor and prevent him from leaving again before capturing him."

"No problem, I understand. Focus on Victor first, then go after his master," James acknowledged the instructions then voiced concern for his loved ones.

"Don't you think our families will be in danger after I stir up the situation by killing Victor?" he asked,

"I understand you, your team, and your families will be in great danger. However, I promise that the BIA will provide support and protection for you and your loved ones."

Steve reassured James as he felt a mix of excitement and apprehension because his family would also be at risk.

"Don't worry, James. My team and I believe in you, which is why we have chosen you for a very important and powerful role called the First Option. It will be crucial for you to work closely with your team and stay focused on the mission to handle the challenges posed by the adversaries," Steve assured him.

James was extremely excited about the mission against Victor due to his involvement in his father's murder, expressing gratitude for the opportunity.

"Don't forget this task will serve as an individual test for you under the president's observation." Steve reminded him before ending the call.

James and his wife were discussing his upcoming mission while driving home the following day.

"My team and I have an upcoming overseas mission, but first, our stop will be in Sékoubaria GD. Following that, we'll travel to Rancenia and Freeland before returning home," said James.

"What? No, babe, no. I can't be without you for that long!" she said.

"I know babe but this is bigger than us, it's for an important and significant cause. This will decide the future of our world, the well-being of their children and all inhabitants of Ginnia. Not to mention that this was the same group responsible for my father's death, so I feel the need to act against them." James explained.

"This is what I'm talking about. You know they'll easily recognize that you are his son and kill you too."

She expressed as tears ran down her face. Then he slowed down the car, comforted her by wiping the tears from her face with his hand, and said, "Rose, I was destined for this mission and have desired to carry it out since my father's passing. Don't worry babe, I'll be fine."

"I know but do you have to go so soon?" asked Rose.

"Honey, you, and I've discussed this before. My job comes with an inconvenience. I was hired because they saw that I was reliable. I've never let them down since they signed me, even when I drove for them or worked at the support center or the Science and Technology department. When a situation like this comes up, I have no choice but to represent the bureau. I mean, the guys really count on me, you know!" James emphasized.

"Ok, ok, I got it. The world needs more people like you, babe. I'm really going to miss you, babe. Lately, you've been working a lot. Promise me we'll spend more time together when you get back," Rose had finally accepted the fact that his mind had been made up no matter what she said.

"Wait, I believe we are being followed. Strap your seat belt; I'm about to fly us out of here." James voiced calmly then drove aggressively through traffic. He weaved in and out of lanes, passed many cars, and performed a couple of donuts, showcasing his impressive driving skills. Suddenly, the car was blown up from underneath, causing it to flip in a 360-degree motion, and eventually land in a river. Victor's bandits rushed to assist them after the accident. They rescued him and his wife from the car but brought them to a warehouse instead. James was injected and rendered unconscious by the bandits after being taken to the warehouse. He regained consciousness after some time when water was thrown at his face and discovered that his wife had been taken by the assassins to a different location. He had cuts on his forehead from the accident and various bruises and bumps from the beating he received while unconscious. He successfully subdued his captors who were in front of him and subsequently defeated the two bandits behind him.

Shortly after, James learned his wife's location from Victor. He flew to FARN's main office in Longville, New Amsterdam, and quickly arrived at the location where Victor was keeping his wife. He covertly took out lookouts and guards before they could alert the other security personnel or Victor. Then, he encountered more security who tried to stop him, prompting him to use his power to disarm and control their guns by dismantling them, along with their walkie-talkies, to prevent them from notifying Victor, who was on the penthouse floor. Afterward, he flew to the top floor after incapacitating the guards and found Victor conversing with Peter at a desk. Upon entering, James saw his wife being held captive by five guards on screens in a room adjacent to where he confronted Victor. Victor recognized James because he greatly resembled his father. Initially, he thought he was seeing Alex's ghost due to their striking resemblance. Victor shot continuously at James with his gun as James made his way towards him.

James, resembling his father greatly, was recognized by Victor who mistook him for Alex's ghost. Victor shot at James as he approached. During the confrontation, Victor ordered the guards to shoot his wife, but James broke Victor's hand and choked him while using his power to control the guards' guns to protect his wife in the adjacent room. The guards attempted to use their weapons, but the triggers were rendered unusable because James was able to manipulate them with his mind, preventing them from being fired.

"Hello, who is this? Hello, hello!" Peter repeatedly asked until the call got disconnected after James hung up. Peter called back multiple times without success as James used mind control to make the weapons float away from the guards. Victor, realizing he was defeated, pleaded for his life, and revealed that James should focus on his father's right-hand man, as he was the one who set him up.

James could have already killed Victor but wanted to see what information he could get out of him first. While squeezing Victor's neck, James demanded to know more about the man he was claiming to be his father's right-hand man.

Victor confessed that Antoine was the one who orchestrated the setup.

"I know about him already, call your boss," said James before instructing Victor to call his boss, Manuel, and put the call on speaker. Manuel eventually answered the call.

"Hello," he voiced.

Hello," Victor responded simply.

"What's going on, are you ok?" Manuel inquired.

During the conversation, James unexpectedly joined in and threatened Victor by saying, "I'm coming for you next," while tightening his grip on Victor's neck. Victor continued to make choking sounds and displayed signs of distress, while James increased the pressure on his neck.

"You shouldn't have worked with them, then!" said James before realizing Victor had stopped breathing, throwing him to the floor. James went through the wall quickly and found his wife tied up with a blindfold. He removed the blindfold, picked up his weakened wife who had endured some torture.

After killing Victor, James considered targeting Antoine, along with any disloyal Fabrican administrators. However, he decided to adhere to the agreement with Steve and focused on gathering more evidence of Antoine's betrayal. James was very disappointed to discover that Antoine was working with Manuel's men to harm his family; therefore, he sought guidance from Ben to understand the betrayal better. As James consulted with Ben to assess Antoine's involvement, Ben confirmed that Antoine orchestrated the hit on Alex. Ben also revealed that there were other Fabrican officials collaborating with FARN. James revealed to Ben that he killed Victor and planned to target Manuel and his entourage next. He also asked if Ben would allow Rich to join him on his missions.

As James was rescuing his wife Antoine met up with Sam to discuss the BIA decision on the new First Option position and James being selected for the job. Afterwards, they planned for Sam to arrange a job with James, only to then betray James by abandoning him in a remote place. During their planning, Antoine received a call from Manuel who could not reach his associate Victor and suspected an attack. He also requested Antoine to investigate the source of the attack and gather more details.

Later that day, James informed Gabriel about killing Victor and expressed his certainty about Antoine's involvement in his father's murder. He asked for permission to eliminate Antoine before his mission to Rancenia. Gabriel advised James to wait until after completing his mission before going after Antoine. The next day, James asked Gabriel and Christopher if he could go on the mission earlier to prevent Manuel from seeking vengeance for Victor. They accepted James' proposal and informed the squad that it was time to proceed with the mission. James, along with his team consisting of Kevin, Rich, Sam, and Alpha, met at the agency and they were introduced to each other. The squad met a few times that week before being deployed to Rancenia at the end of the week. Prior to deployment, Christopher gave the team a motivational speech.

Later, President Lincoln received a call from Mr. Obama, who informed him about the disappearance of two West Drakillian Ministers.

He said that he suspected that FARN was responsible for their abduction. As a result of this apprehension, President Lincoln instructed Steve to have the BIA initiate the FARN mission and instructed Steve to instruct James and his squad to remain in Rancenia until they located Manuel. James and his team left that night to go to Rancenia. When they arrived, they were welcomed by Mr. Peters, director of the RBI, and were offered a place to stay not too far from their agency.

In the following weeks, James and his team investigated the FARN and their activities. The team proceeded to explore key locations in Rancenia in greater detail. Manuel initially believed his company was being scrutinized by an internal enemy in Rancenia, assuming his immunity from UNG still protected him from foreign agencies. However, he later realized it was the BIA investigating his businesses.

Manuel had been living in Freeland for a couple of years. When he returned to Rancenia, he initially planned to ship more weapons to Freeland and stay in Rancenia for a short period; however, he got caught up in dealing with his associate's death. Now he also had to address an investigation into his businesses. Antoine had reached out to Manuel upon his return to Rancenia to discuss his thoughts on the cause of Victor's death with Manuel. Antoine told Manuel that James was responsible for Victor's death and mentioned that James was also leading the BIA against him just like his father had been. He cautioned Manuel that the BIA was coming after him with full force. He mentioned that a team led by James, with his son Sam included, was already established for this purpose. Manuel then revealed to Antoine that he had been residing in Freeland for the past two years, a secret not even known to his own organization. Manuel suggested setting up a trap for James and his team, involving Sam, considering Sam was a member of James' team. Antoine revealed he was already planning to set up this trap and gave Manuel Sam's contact information.

Manuel's paranoia had increased after losing Victor and many of his Rancenian operations. He decided he would go back to Freeland to seek cover and protection. However, before leaving, Manuel contacted Sam to confirm the information he got from Antoine. Manuel called Sam and introduced himself as a friend of Sam's father Antoine, saying he got Sam's number from him.

"I need your assistance, but first I have some information that I want to share with you relating to BIA," said Manuel.

"No problem. If I could help, I'd be more than happy to assist you!" replied Sam.

"Ok then, did you know that the name "First Option" is used by the Fabrican government to identify the chief agent. The First Option has the authority to change the mission as needed, unlike the other agents."

Manuel continued, "During your father's time in the BIA, James's father Alex was their First Option. Your father was always second to him. Sam, I want you to make your First Option pay for overlooking you and your father by helping me eliminate your First Option, who also was chosen ahead of you and killed my partner. Just so you know, I'm the leader of FARN. If you can prevent the exposure and destruction of our positions by eliminating the First Option and successfully hacking into the National Intelligence Spirits Agency's security database, I will offer you a prominent position within my organization.

"Ok, give me some time, and I'll try my best to access the NISA database and eliminate him," Sam responded.

Afterwards, Antoine also called Sam, to clarify what Manuel had explained to his son. Antoine instructed Sam to betray his squad and told him to focus on James instead. He also advised Sam to ignore other team members and the FARN organization and highlighted James as a priority target due to his potential as a superhujinn. Emphasizing James's power and the need to neutralize him before it was too late to prevent any potential threats.

For the next few weeks, Sam collaborated with James and their squad, providing updates to his father, Manuel, on their progress in the mission. James eventually divided the group into three teams, with James opting to take on a task alone as the First Option because there were five members in total. Sam was paired up with Alpha, and Kevin with Rich.

The previous week, James and his team had detected a weapons trafficking operation into Freeland, and they discovered that the operation was conducted by Manuel's networks. Weapons were traded for aluminum, gold, and diamonds. Shortly after, Sam and Alpha were sent by James to inspect one of Manuel's properties related to weapons trafficking. As they were on their way, Sam shot Alpha three times in the head, causing harm worse than what Antoine had done to Alex when Antoine was with Alex in Sékoubaria GD.

After twenty-four hours, James had still not heard from Alpha. James asked Sam to join him in finding Alpha; however, Sam also betrayed James, leaving him to face fifty or more of Manuel's agents alone. Despite the odds, James defeated the agents and contacted Gabriel to update him on the situation.

Gabriel was sitting in his office when the phone rang. He picked up, and James updated him on the progress of their mission up to that point, as well as notifying him about Alpha's absence. "I believe that Sam is double-crossing the team and was responsible for my ambush. I also believe that Sam is linked to Alpha's disappearance, as they were meant to be together when Alpha went missing. I discovered that Manuel no longer resides in Rancenia; he was only here for business but has returned to Freeland. I'm going after him, but first, I must take out Sam before I leave," James declared.

"Great work. That's why I would rather have you on my team any day than someone who doesn't know how to make executive decisions. Don't worry about anything. If you believe that is the best move, I trust your judgment and decision-making abilities, so you have the freedom to make changes to the mission as needed," Gabriel responded.

Meanwhile, as James was speaking to Gabriel, Sam was talking to Manuel and disclosing his latest developments. "Hello, sir, I'm calling to inform you that James had me trapped; however, he prevailed and decapitated all your men. Nevertheless, I just killed his cousin, Alpha, who was paired up with me. Due to this, the BIA would likely suspect me. As a result, I have decided to leave the agency," Sam explained.

"Then we should go after his family," Manuel replied.

"No problem, I am very acquainted with James and his family. We grew up together, so they will not see it coming from me. I know where his wife and kid stay in New Amsterdam City," Sam replied.

Manuel praised Sam for his work and likened him to his father, showing enthusiasm and a sign of appreciation for his service. He then asked Sam for a moment to gather his thoughts. *James must be a superhuman. The way he easily defeated my men in New Amsterdam and in Rancenia, only a superhuman was capable of that. How did I miss it?*

James was the one I have been looking for all this time, yet he is right in front of my eyes. My ego led me to overlook warnings from Peter and ignore James' development. Now, he could be the threat I've been searching for. James could lead to my downfall. He must be eliminated quickly to prevent interference in my west Drakillian takeover," he thought.

Manuel resumed his conversation with Sam after taking some time to think.

"Sam, since you are still in Rancenia, stay there and continue gathering information about James' activities, while I arrange for Peter to detain his family."

Manuel ended his conversation with Sam and instructed Peter to collaborate with Antoine in kidnapping James' wife and child, as James was becoming a significant threat as the new BIA's First Option. Peter agreed to Manuel's instruction and then called Antoine to request that Sam locate the whereabouts of Rose and her son. Peter video-called James a few days after commending his investigation. He advised James to leave Rancenia as soon as possible and come home. He mentioned being a friend of James's father and said that the two of them had unfinished business. Peter switched the camera to Manuel in Freeland. James recognized Peter but did not know he was Steve's brother. This was James's first-time seeing Manuel.

James questioned Peter's authority and asked why he should listen to him. Peter switched the camera feed to show James that he had his wife and kid hostage, then laughed menacingly, making it clear that they now had control of the situation. He told James that he could come to get his family within seventy-two hours to ensure their safety, but first, he had to hack the NISA database and download then delete all the information that they had on FARN. Manuel threatened to harm his family if he told anyone about the situation. James agreed to fulfill their request and asked for guidance on how to communicate with them. Peter told James that he would arrange the meeting time and place, then emphasized the importance of keeping the situation confidential.

James left Rancenia promptly after speaking to Peter and Manuel. He flew from Rancenia to New Amsterdam in under two hours due to his jet-like flying ability. The flight from Rancenia to New Amsterdam usually took eleven hours, giving James ample time to spare before Peter and Manuel would expect him. He assumed Peter and Manuel wouldn't expect him to arrive in New Amsterdam so quickly because they were unaware of his flying capabilities. James believed that since they expected him to be home the following day, they wouldn't find out about him defying their order. Therefore, James stopped by Steve's house because it was late at night and told Steve that he had to temporarily abandon the mission. He informed Steve that Peter and Manuel had his wife and child, so they couldn't take immediate action against them. James didn't mention to Steve that it was Peter who threatened him because he was unaware that Peter was Steve's brother. James informed Steve that they requested him to hack the NISA database to download and delete files related to FARN in exchange for something related to Steve's family. James was threatened to comply with Peter and Manuel's demands and keep silent, however despite the threats, he chose to inform Steve assuming they believed he was in Rancenia and unable to communicate.

Steve reassured James that they would retrieve his captured family soon. He stated that he would accompany James and direct his men to stand down from their usual operations. James insisted that he must go alone initially and requested Steve to follow him shortly after he left. James explained that he couldn't bring someone along because he was instructed to meet with the attackers and take some of the men to Sékoubaria G.D. to hack the BIA headquarters' database while leaving some of them to stay with his family. Steve then asked James if he had a plan, and James said that he would lure them away from his family by pretending to lead them to the BIA's database while Steve and his men tried to rescue his family. Steve agreed and waited until the morning and informed Gabriel and Christopher about the plan.

Afterwards James went home and waited for a call from one of the attackers. It was now the next day, and he had not heard from anyone, so he was impatiently waiting for instructions. Suddenly, Peter called him. James flew straight to the meeting place as instructed. Peter and Antoine saw James on their surveillance cameras and allowed him in by opening the gate. He was immediately surrounded by their men, chained with steel chains, and taken to where Peter and Antoine were.

Peter told Antoine to remain with James's family and to be prepared to kill them if needed, emphasizing the significance of eliminating

James's family if the situation took a turn for the worse. James was then locked up in a steel chamber and taken to the Gold House by Peter and his men. Soon after Peter left, Antoine informed him that BIA agents had attacked the building, suspecting James of tipping them off. Antoine suspected that James had informed the BIA about their situation, so he informed Peter. Peter suggested to Antoine that he should keep James's family nearby in case he needed to take drastic measures, such as killing them or using them as leverage. However, the situation turned dire, leading Peter to suggest to Antoine that he should kill James's family and make an escape. James, locked in a chamber, overheard Peter's instructions on harming his family and transformed into a superhujinn. Afterwards, James emitted intense heat from his body and melted the steel chains restraining him. He then decapitated Peter's men. Witnessing James transform and easily decapitate his men, Peter realized he was outmatched and teleported himself away from the location. With Peter gone, James ignored the remaining men and focused on his goal—flying towards his family's location.

James was flying towards the location when FARN hujinn agents suddenly appeared and possessed other beings near him. These mercenaries were nearly indestructible, with the ability to change forms instantly, including humans, jinns, or other creatures. They had immense strength, bullets passed through them, and they caused destruction around James by controlling the spirits of those they transformed into. The agents created chaos as they continued to transform and spread mayhem along the way. During the battle, the FARN agents chased him in various forms. James used his abilities to dodge attacks and control objects with his mind to fight back, successfully escaping.

As James was defending himself from FARN assassins, Steve and his men arrived at the location James was heading to. Steve and his men also engaged in a fight against the assassins at that location. Antoine saw Steve on surveillance and witnessed Steve easily decapitating his men, causing him to fear confronting Steve. After witnessing Steve's superior skills, Antoine felt inferior to him, so he ordered his men to take Rose and Joseph, and they fled to meet Peter and handed James's family over to him. Soon after, Steve disabled most of their security, prompting the rest to surrender and disclose Rose and Joseph's location to him. By the time Steve was done combating the FARN agents, James showed up. However, James discovered his family was still captive when he arrived at the location.

Since Steve had discovered the Fabrican members involved in Manuel's secret circle, he informed the Fabrican president that Mr. Palmer, Mr. Jackson, and Mr. Johnson were compromised by the FARN. However, Steve did not mention Antoine and Peter to the president as he had plans to handle them personally. He then asked President Lincoln for permission to arrest the compromised agents. Upon receiving approval from the president, he dispatched some agents to their offices and apprehended them.

Meanwhile, a couple of hours later, with no leads on his family's whereabouts, James remained determined and camped outside the location given by the cooperative agent earlier in the hope of eventually locating his family. James managed to capture Antoine upon reaching the destination and tried to pressure him into disclosing his family's whereabouts, but Antoine remained steadfast in not revealing the location. Ultimately, James suffocated Antoine by stepping on his head and pressing it against the floor until it splashed open, crushing his skull and causing his brains to spill out.

Steve, after coming up with a new plan, contacted President Lincoln to inform him about the tragic events that had befallen James's family. Steve assisted President Lincoln in comprehending the rationale behind James's decision to deviate from the initial plan. Following their discussion, Steve informed the president that he had instructed James to revert to the original mission and pursue capturing Manuel. Steve proposed that this course of action was strategic as James could potentially use Manuel as leverage for the safe return of his own family.

James, apprehensive of losing more team members after Alpha's death in the prior mission, contacted Steve at the thirteenth hour to persuade him to allow him to undertake the mission solo, expressing concern about endangering additional colleagues. Steve questioned if James didn't want to go with backup. James declined backup, believing he performed best when alone. Steve explained that agency protocol required agents to have a team for support. Despite acknowledging James' skills, he assigned Rich and Kevin to accompany James to provide additional coverage and prevent potential surprise attacks. James, expressing his deep familiarity with the city due to his roots and time spent with his grandparents, believed he could handle the mission alone. He emphasized his confidence in being able to confront potential threats without jeopardizing any additional agents, referencing the recent loss of Alpha. Steve acknowledged James' ability to complete the mission solo but emphasized the benefits of working together and suggested that having others accompany James could provide a learning opportunity for them. Then he acknowledged James' personal losses and the emotional weight that influenced his desire to go solo on the mission nevertheless, he emphasized the gravity of the situation, highlighting that the mission's significance went beyond individual capabilities. James agreed to go on the mission as instructed by Steve. Steve informed him that he would depart the following morning to arrive at the destination around midnight. James reminded Steve to go after the other attacker who was with Antoine and escaped. Steve assured James he would apprehend the fleeing assailant and cautioned him that Manuel was a hujinn who possessed substantial powers. Lastly, James reminded Steve not to overlook Sam in the situation and suggested stopping by Rancenia to deal with Sam before going to Freeland. Steve advised against dealing with Sam immediately and suggested focusing on a bigger target first.

Peter had relocated Rose and Joseph to an undisclosed location known only to Manuel, ensuring their safety. Meanwhile, Sam had returned to Fabrica upon learning about his father's passing in Rancenia. Peter called Manuel the next day and shared details about the BIA investigation and Antoine's death. Manuel told Peter to ensure James's family safety in case they were needed again in the future. Due to Manuel's trust in Sam, Manuel asked him to go back to Fabrica and work with Peter to retrieve his files from the NISA database. Manuel instructed his men to carry out a coup d'état in Freeland during this period. Steve, upon learning of Manuel's takeover of the Freeland administration and the kidnapping of President Barry, felt a sense of urgency to act and decided not to delay any further.

Steve reached out to President Lincoln for help after being informed about the hacking attempt. Despite Steve's efforts in contacting President Lincoln, Sam successfully hacked into the NISA's security system.

Manuel's records being stolen and the security system passcodes being altered in the NISA database led to concerns that Fabrica might be his next target. Therefore, the Fabrican administration allied with multiple large administrations in Ginnia and convened to strategize on recovering the access codes for the National Security database and apprehending Manuel. President Lincoln, UNG directors, Steve, and many other top officials were present. During the meeting, UNG approved the global pursuit of Manuel, assured of handling any repercussions, and informed Fabrican allies. UNG also secured support to dismantle the FARN organization. President Lincoln directed military forces to prepare for possible engagements with factions supporting Manuel.

By this time Manuel and his army had carried out three coups d'état in west Drakilla and took control of the countries. Despite these countries having been independent for over sixty years, Manuel compelled them to surrender their natural resources. He manipulated the west Drakillian administrations by supplying weapons to the leaders and persuading them to seize the presidents.

James, Rich, and Kevin were scheduled to board an army plane the next morning to be airdropped into Freeland for a mission to locate and confront Manuel and his army. However, they encountered a large explosion at the airport in the terminal they were departing from when they arrived. James saw the incident as a signal to go solo despite his agreement with Steve. He possessed the ability to fly independently without an aircraft. He knew he could travel faster on his own than with a traditional plane so he chose to proceed with the mission solo after the airport explosion. He managed to complete the trip to Freeland in less than an hour. His early arrival meant it was still evening when he reached Freeland. Shortly after James reached Freeland, he met with Mr. Obama, the WDU director at the time, and discussed the origin of the FARN mission.

Mr. Obama explained as James nodded and listened carefully, "Your father was very close to completing this mission against the FARN. However, due to their ties to powerful Flowropia and Fabrican officials, he was set up. Our agency discovered this corruption with the help of Alex during his time executing the mission. Now, you are a crucial part of this mission due to the exceptional abilities you possess. I advise you to work alongside our agents and help us regain control of the region and restore leadership."

"Wow, thank you for the history lesson. Can you please tell me how they conquered the region?" James asked.

"The FARN have been stealing natural resources from Drakillian countries for decades, which has led to poverty and negative impacts on this region. influenced West Drakillian officials by compromising administrators through bribery or elimination if their offers were refused. They supplied weapons, cheap medicines, poor energy, and poorly designed water systems to maintain control. They used leaders as scapegoats to conceal their actions and maintain control over the region," Mr. Obama replied.

It was now the following morning, Rich and Kevin had just reached Freeland and were detained by airport security, who were also FARN agents. Rich and Kevin were detained by Freeland airport security for questioning, where they were asked to provide additional information about their travels. Manuel had agents placed in various transportation departments such as railroads, bus terminals, airports, and seaports. These agents were tasked with helping to identify potential spying activities by external groups.

After Kevin and Rich presented their documents, it was confirmed that they were Fabrican agents. Thus, the FARN agents notified Manuel, who requested his agents to detain Kevin and Rich to gather more information about their visit. Further interrogation revealed that their mission was ordered by the Fabrican BIA. Realizing that they were not alone prompted the authorities to assign agents to locate their partners.

After searching for Manuel all night and being unsuccessful, James reached out to Gabriel and Christopher for assistance as he had run out of options on how to continue pursuing the matter. They informed him that Rich and Kevin had just reached Freeland and were detained by airport security. James was advised by his directors to cause a scene to force airport security to arrest him to locate Manuel. He confirmed with his directors by asking if he should make a scene to prompt security to arrest him.

After speaking with his director, James realized that they were right; it would be easier to locate Manuel if the FARN agents guided him to him. James realized that he was running out of time to find his family, so he went to the airport, provoked the airport authorities, before he could reunite with his fellow team members. He willingly allowed airport security to capture him and deliver him to the FARN agents. He deliberately provided his true identification when checked by the FARN agents, revealing that he was a BIA agent like his detained team members. He told the FARN agents he had a message for their leader Manuel, insisting he would only disclose it to Manuel himself. He managed to convince the FARN agents to let him speak to Manuel by promising them that he would recommend them for a promotion for their assistance. It was a short distance between their positions. The proximity of the FARN agents to Manuel was due to the compact and easily navigable layout of the city, allowing James to reach Manuel quite easily. A half an hour later, James entered the room to meet Manuel with heavy security and kept his hands behind his back as he walked. James remembered Manuel's face from a picture in his father's West Drakillian Mission folder which used to be in his father's office. Therefore, he recognized Manuel upon seeing him and became exasperated. His agitation led him to break out of his cuffs and chains. He swiftly incapacitated all the guards one by one and managed to be alone with Manuel. James made a fast approach towards Manuel, throwing multiple punches, all of which were blocked by Manuel. However, Manuel was caught off guard by a surprise Superhujinn blast. The impact of the Superhujinn blast made Manuel flip three times and crash against a few walls before hitting the ground. James continued his attack, causing them to go through multiple buildings. Manuel was unable to stand up before James closed in on him. James delivered another Superhujinn combo that finally incapacitated Manuel and injected him with a large dose of Midazolam to keep him asleep until they reached Bellivia. Then James requested Steve to send a military chopper to transport him to Bellivia. He whisked Manuel away to a nearby safe area and waited for Steve to dispatch a chopper for transportation.

An hour later, James carried Manuel's sleeping body and boarded the helicopter when it arrived.

"I have to find my family," James said to himself. Then, he prioritized rescuing his family before the exchange. Steve promised James that he would personally take charge of ensuring the safe retrieval of his family.

Upon reaching Bellivia, Manuel woke up and provided James with Peter's contact information. James made the call and put the phone on speaker so Manuel could communicate with Peter.

"Hello, Peter. This is Manuel. I've been apprehended by James, and he has proposed an exchange involving myself and his family," said Manuel.

"Ok, boss. I'm going to make it happen right away," said Peter.

"Listen to me, keep the backup strategy ready and activate it if you stop hearing from me," Manuel added before James spoke out.

"Peter, Steve will provide you with an address. You are to go to the specified address and hand over my family to your brother Steve while I bring Manuel back to his men," James instructed Manuel.

Peter informed Sam that Manuel had been caught after their conversation, and Manuel requested them to keep the backup strategy ready and activate it if they lost contact with him. Manuel had put a backup plan in place for Sam and Peter to activate if needed. He had hired advanced FARN scientists to develop the contagious virus and placed it in bombshells a few years ago. He intended to unleash a deadly virus, created by his scientists, upon the New Amsterdam City residents.

James was posted in Bellivia, awaiting Steve's approval to either release or eliminate Manuel. During the trade, Peter decided it was time to release the infectious disease. He instructed Sam to release the infectious gas to prevent James from chasing them after the exchange. James required Steve to confirm that he had successfully retrieved Rose and Joseph before he agreed to release Manuel. Peter handed Rose and Joseph to Steve and his agents and left immediately, as he was aware that Sam was about to release an infectious gas. Steve confirmed to James that Rose and Joseph were safe and with him, and James released Manuel right before the virus attack occurred.

James and others were taken by surprise by the sudden explosion of the virus, especially since Steve had just confirmed the safety of Rose and Joseph before informing James about the virus attack in New Amsterdam City. James discovered that sSam and Peter were the ones behind the selfish act. At that moment, James decided that he would abandon the mission and go back to Fabrica instead. James left immediately after deciding to abandon the mission and flew back to Fabrica to assist in rescuing his family and other victims. He arrived at Fabrica promptly and discovered his family was not dead from pollution but were severely affected by it. However, Steve was fine as the virus didn't affect Hujinns.

Steve found it challenging to come to terms with the reality that his own brother was associated with the group responsible for the outbreak of the disease and kidnapping of James's family, so he pursued Peter. After Peter picked up the call, Steve decisively said, "Enough is enough!"

Meanwhile, James's wife, son, and many other individuals who were exposed to the virus spread by Sam and Peter fell ill. James was furious upon discovering his family's illnesses. Therefore, he went to the FARN center to demolish their facility and possibly confront Peter. When he arrived at the FARN center, he found the area blocked off due to a police investigation by the New Amsterdam police. Ambulances and police cars were present in front of the building, and Steve confirmed the situation to James with a look as they spotted each other. James realized that Steve had reached Peter before he did, as the reality of the situation sank in. Afterwards, Steve revealed to James that the assailant was his own brother. Earlier that day, Steve had pursued Peter without informing anyone in his organization. He met with Peter with the intention of arresting him. However, it turned out to be a tragic turn of events. Steve confronted Peter alone, unaware of Peter's plan to have a hitman shoot him with poison bullets upon entry. Peter was shot and killed during the encounter when Steve dodged the shot, causing Peter to be hit instead.

James thought to himself, "Holy moly Steve killed his own brother."

Steve called James and expressed disbelief to James that Peter, his own brother, had tried to eliminate him. Then he informed him that he had killed Peter and explained that he didn't arrest him because he believed Peter was extremely wicked and wanted to prevent future troubles. James agreed and expressed that Peter, Antoine, and Victor got what they deserved. James inquired of Steve if he could believe that Sam was still alive and mentioned that the next course of action was to go after him and Manuel. Steve agreed with James about the situation and expressed being shocked as well, then informed James that he was going to Sékoubaria the next day to see the president and mentioned that they would come up with a solution. Lastly, Steve mentioned that he needed to leave.

"Steve took care of Peter, and now I must take care of Sam and Manuel," James thought as he was determined to punish Sam for killing his cousin Alpha, his role in getting his family sick, and affecting many lives before going after Manuel. Therefore, he went to the club where Sam frequented on a Friday night. Instead of confronting Sam in front of a crowd, James decided to use a charming young lady to lure Sam outside of the club. He interrupted Sam, who was kissing the lady, by appearing suddenly. The lady ran away when James showed up, and Sam shot at James' face with a gun. Despite being shot at, James managed to dodge the bullets and flew towards Sam. He immediately attacked Sam with a powerful punch, causing him to fall to the ground. Taking decisive action, knowing Sam was going to die, he struck Sam again, causing destruction around them, and ultimately buried Sam underground.

Steve contacted James to inform him that Manuel had organized a private funeral for his deceased colleagues in Larycia. Upon receiving this information, James immediately flew to the funeral site as advised by Steve. After attending Manuel's funeral in Larycia, James hurried back to the RBI center. Upon his return, he discovered that Manuel had not attended the funeral himself but had sent a doppelganger to stand in for him. Steve informed James that Manuel was back in Freeland a few hours after James arrived. James quickly flew from Larycia, the capital of Rancenia, to Connaby, the capital of Freeland in half an hour after confirming Manuel's location, a journey that typically took six hours by plane. James once again acted independently. He flew through the facility floor by floor upon arrival using a swift attack that proved successful as he eliminated all defenses with that.

After Manuel and James finally confronted each other. Manuel revealed he was also a superhujinn like James then he transformed into his superhujinn form to battle James. Manuel anticipated the fight based on their previous encounter. In this intense rematch, unlike the initial encounter where Manuel underestimated James, the battle reached new levels of fury. They caused heavy objects to fly around and astonished the onlookers with the extraordinary display of power. They engaged in a fierce battle, as Manuel proved to be nearly as powerful as James with matching abilities. The battle was unlike any they had experienced before, as they were facing opponents who matched their own unique abilities and strengths, presenting them with a formidable challenge. Despite Manuel's agents attempting to assist him in the fight against James, they proved to be no match for James's immense strength, so he easily fended off their attacks as he continued fighting Manuel. However, James realized he needed to reach the ultimate level to defeat Manuel. Ultimately, James experienced a transformation where his body became engulfed in flames, and this transformation granted him a substantial power increase over Manuel signaling the ultimate level a superhujinn could attain.

As James prepared his next attack, even Manuel was terrified because no superhujinn had reached that level before; James was the first. Manuel was a superhujinn as well. Nonetheless, James had gained the advantage; he was at the highest level known to them. Manuel used his final trick up his sleeve: he entered James's body and tried to control it, but James's power was too much for him to handle. As a result, Manuel detached himself from James. When James finally unleashed another blast, the power and heatwave were stronger and larger than Manuel's. Manuel and the entire area he floated on burned down; even the ground was destroyed by the strike. Nothing could stop the wave; fortunately, he aimed the strike high towards space, ultimately preventing further destruction on their planet, Ginnia.

After defeating the FARN mastermind, Manuel, James returned to New Amsterdam City. Upon his arrival, he heard that his little brother Jeremy and his lab mates had invented a cure for the infectious virus that had devastated their community. The gas had caused harm and isolated many in the city. The remaining FARN members were arrested by WDU.

A week later, a ceremony was held to celebrate James and the BIA's victory. Many of James's colleagues and his father's colleagues attended the ceremony. James's surviving friends, along with their families, attended the gathering. Many of James's friends were now parents and held significant professional roles. Some of them had become CEOs of their own companies. Jeremy, Holly, Rose, Steve, UNG directors, Gabriel, Christopher, President Diallo, President Lincoln, Mr. Obama,

WDU members, Mr. Iverson, Mrs. Washington, Kevin, Vincent, Mr. Peters, and James' college friends all attended the ceremony. Steve expressed pride in James before the ceremony and revealed they both were hujinns.

During the ceremony, President Lincoln spoke first and awarded James with a Medal of Honor for his achievements in Rancenia. Steve then took the stage and shared James's heroic story.

"James is seen as a superhero and a role model for guiding the younger generation. He started as a street kid but developed skills in various trades, including the medical field, mechanical work, technical expertise, cooking, service, sports, acting, and more. He is an inspiration for others to follow. I praise him today and highlight his journey to give you an idea of the type of individual he is."

Steve acknowledged James and invited him to accept an award in front of the crowd, where he delivered an acceptance speech about facing obstacles and discovering his purpose on his journey.

"Hello everyone, first and foremost, I'm grateful to God for giving me a great gift and guiding me through my journey thus far. I will continue to use my gift to help the world. I want to thank my mother Holly Jordan, my siblings Jeremy and Jolie. Additionally, I want to thank Mr. Beaumont, Mr. Houston, and Mr. Smith for their guidance and support. I wouldn't have gotten this success without their support over the years. Special thanks to my beautiful wife, Rose, whom I truly appreciate. Even a superhero needs love and support, and she provided that for me!" James expressed himself, paused to let the applause subside, and then continued.

"A few years ago, I was disappointed in myself because I went away to pursue a promising education, yet I failed to complete the degree I had set out to achieve. Nevertheless, I valued the experience I gained from the journey out of state because I acquired valuable lessons through my experiences. Despite my initial setback, I decided to try again to complete my bachelor's degree after feeling let down. However, I ultimately quit once more due to my desire for financial gain. I understood the importance of education, and I regret prioritizing the pursuit of money and fame over education in the past. Following this difficult period in my life, I discovered a newfound passion for reading and writing, which

I found fulfilling without any external pressure. Soon after, I recognized the significance of education and decided that pursuing continuous learning would be beneficial for my future. Initially, I thought it was too late to attain a solid education; however, I later understood that I could continue to educate myself independently. I drew on the knowledge I had acquired in school and expanded upon it. I developed a habit of studying and learning independently and turned it into an enjoyable pastime. Despite facing failures, I embraced them as learning opportunities. Now, when I reflect on my journey, I see the benefit of having that perspective because my education guided me through my journey. I am grateful for my teachers, advisors, counselors, sponsors, and role models' support and influence. After this setback, I believed nothing else could bring me down. Then I unexpectedly lost my best friend and cousin, Alpha. I was greatly affected by his death; we were closer than anyone. We'd known each other our whole lives and were close in age. We were not only close family members but also friends who shared everything with each other, including secrets and bad habits. We were each other's ultimate competitor and biggest fan, inseparable, and did everything together. Even though Alpha lived far from the jail where I was incarcerated, he visited me frequently. We had a strong bond of trust, love, respect, and we supported each other through good and bad times. I want to take the moment to honor him."

James paused, sniffled, and held back tears before continuing.

"As a result of my enlightenment, I realized the lack of control I have over my life. I didn't have control of my past, don't have control of my present, and will not have control of my future. Many of us strive for a satisfying and fulfilling life but fail to recognize that we lack control over it. I believe that the future is uncertain and unpredictable and we learn and adapt as events unfold. All living entities are under the providence of a higher power, with no say in our origins. Similarly, we lack control over our end because we lack agency in the cycle of life. The desire for control over our life and future is driven by a constant awareness of the unknown and a feeling of powerlessness. We fantasize about gaining control as a means of finding fulfillment in our existence. The truth of the matter is that each one of us is simply one of many living organisms in the universe, advocating for patience and emphasizing the importance of time in gaining wisdom. Once again, I'm grateful for my experiences and consider myself to be very blessed. This is why I'm committed to giving back to the world and determined to stand up and pray for all souls in the world of Ginnia. After initially wasting time on insignificant matters, I learned the value of time through the consequences. I discovered patience, humility, forgiveness, responsibility, and the importance of utilizing time wisely. By educating yourself and understanding your purpose, you could avoid legal troubles and be prepared when your dream opportunity arises. Learning the importance of time will help you acknowledge your lack of control yet find purpose and faith."

After James's speech concluded, he received applause.

James expressed his gratitude by saying "thank you" repeatedly. He then proceeded to sit down.

Following the award ceremony, everyone attended a dinner at the God House. President Lincoln congratulated James on his victory over the FARN during the dinner. Lastly, Angel G appeared before James to commend him for fulfilling his mission and emphasized that it was his inherent purpose.

EPILOGUE

We learned that James believed that counting blessings and cherishing existence were crucial to happiness. He found peace and understood life's importance after struggle, valuing time and using setbacks for self-improvement. Despite incarceration, James unexpectedly became the new BIA First Option through perseverance. He never gave up on his dreams, utilized challenges for growth, and maintained gratitude during tough times. James acknowledged the value of his life post-maturity and viewed his time in prison as pivotal. Finally, and most importantly, submission to the highest power was regarded as the key to James's happiness.

Work cited page:
1. https://irp.fas.org/cia/orgchart.pdf

Printed in the United States
by Baker & Taylor Publisher Services